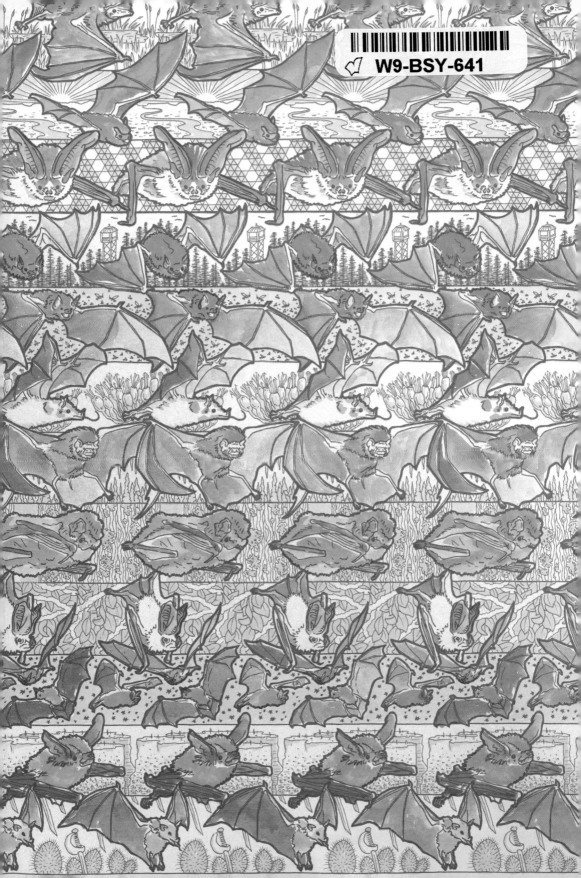

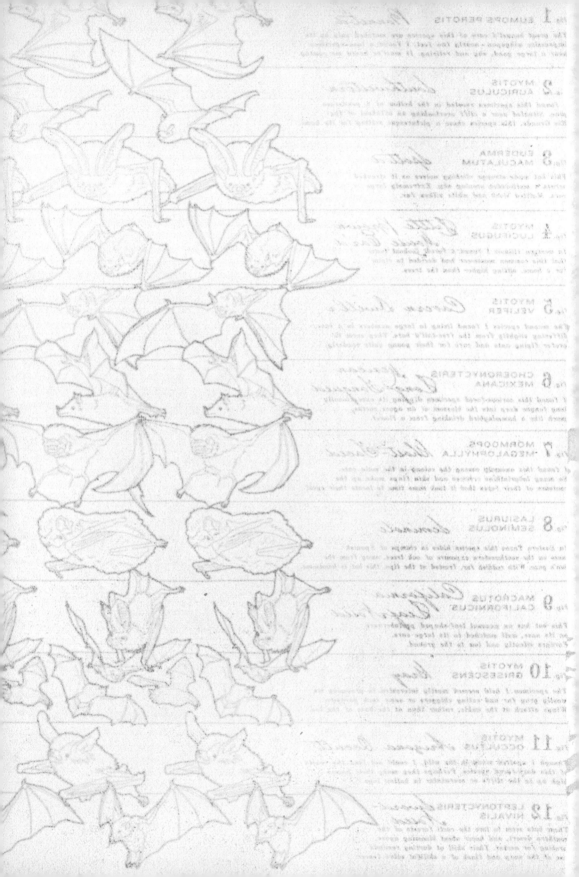

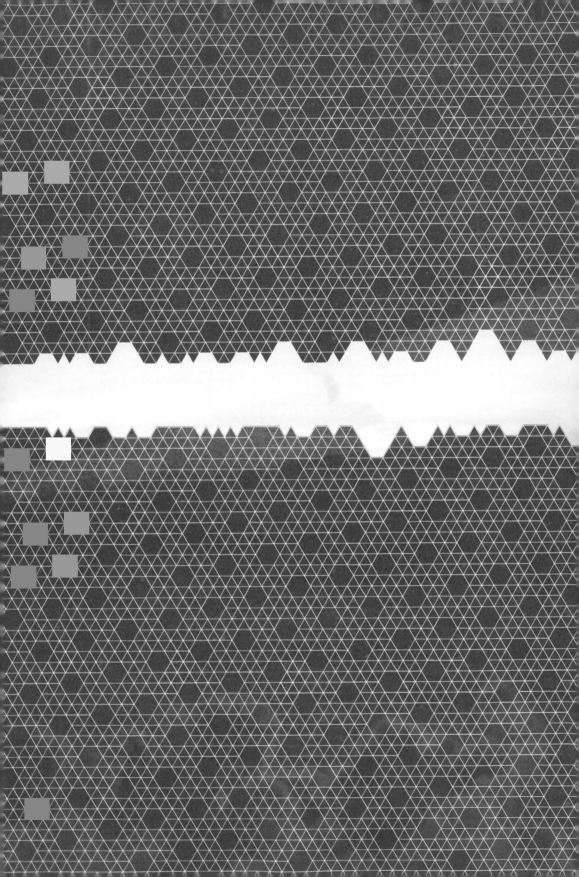

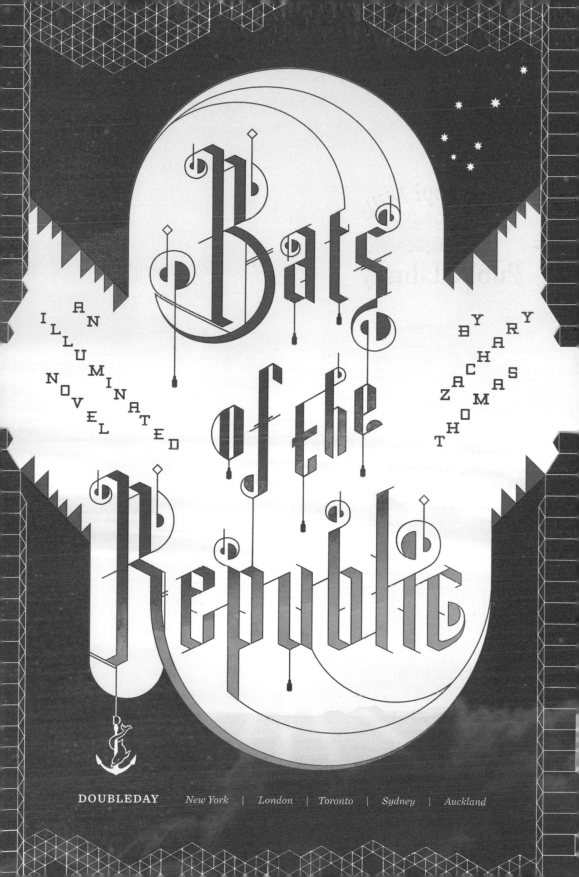

Bats of the Republic

An Illuminated Novel

by Zachary Thomas Dodson

DOUBLEDAY   New York | London | Toronto | Sydney | Auckland www.doubleday.com

COPYRIGHT © 2015

BY ZACHARY THOMAS DODSON

All rights reserved. Published in the United States by Doubleday, a division of Penguin Random House LLC, New York, and distributed in Canada by Random House of Canada, a division of Penguin Random House Ltd, Toronto.

TX

BOOK DESIGN BY ZACH DODSON

Library of Congress Cataloging-in-Publication Data

Dodson, Zachary Thomas.
  Bats of the republic : an illuminated novel / Zachary Thomas Dodson. —
First edition.
      pages   cm
  ISBN 978-0-385-53983-8 (hardcover) — ISBN 978-0-385-53984-5 (eBook)
  I. Title.
  PS3604.O333B38 2015
  813'.6—dc23
  Manufactured in China

2015007636

11 10 9 8 7 6 5 4 3 2 1

BATS
OF THE
REPUBLIC

I can do nothing but fly in the wake of my kin.
I will soar onward undaunted and die on the wing.
   —Alasdair Roberts

And everything with wings is restless, aimless, drunk and dour ...
   —Joanna Newsom

I'm not happy.
   —Favorite saying of my grandfather's

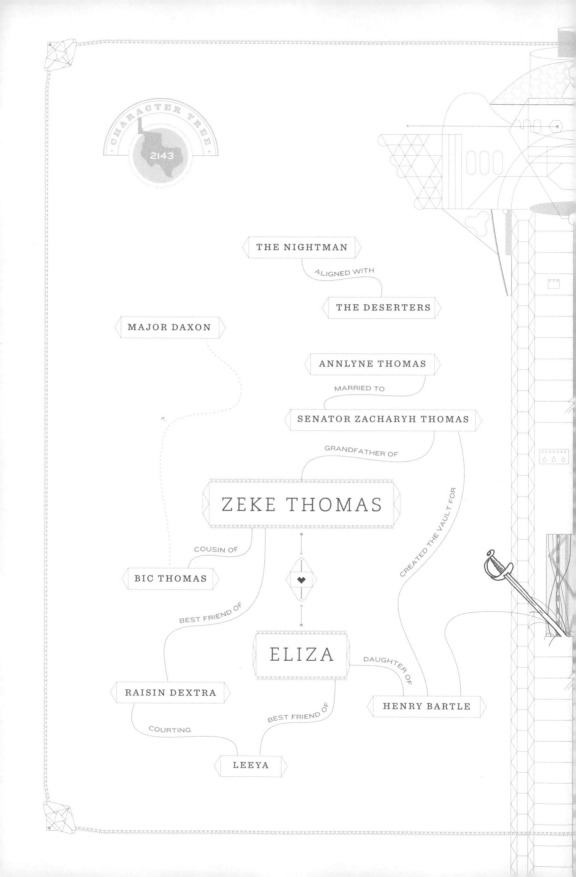

CHARACTER TREE
2143

THE NIGHTMAN

ALIGNED WITH

THE DESERTERS

MAJOR DAXON

ANNLYNE THOMAS

MARRIED TO

SENATOR ZACHARYH THOMAS

GRANDFATHER OF

ZEKE THOMAS

COUSIN OF

BIC THOMAS

CREATED THE VAULT FOR

BEST FRIEND OF

ELIZA

DAUGHTER OF

RAISIN DEXTRA

HENRY BARTLE

COURTING

BEST FRIEND OF

LEEYA

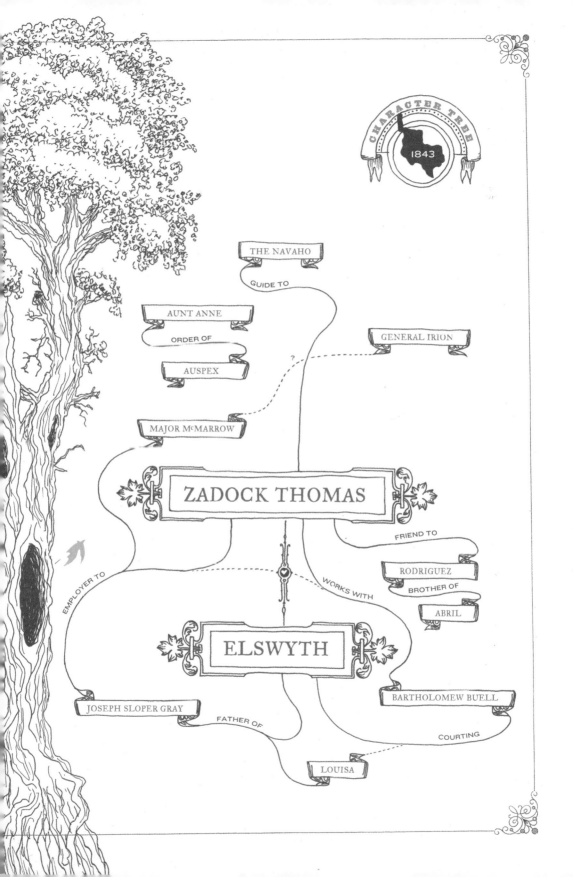

CHARACTER TREE

1843

THE NAVAHO

GUIDE TO

AUNT ANNE

ORDER OF

AUSPEX

GENERAL IRION

?

MAJOR McMARROW

ZADOCK THOMAS

FRIEND TO

RODRIGUEZ

BROTHER OF

ABRIL

EMPLOYER TO

WORKS WITH

ELSWYTH

JOSEPH SLOPER GRAY

FATHER OF

BARTHOLOMEW BUELL

COURTING

LOUISA

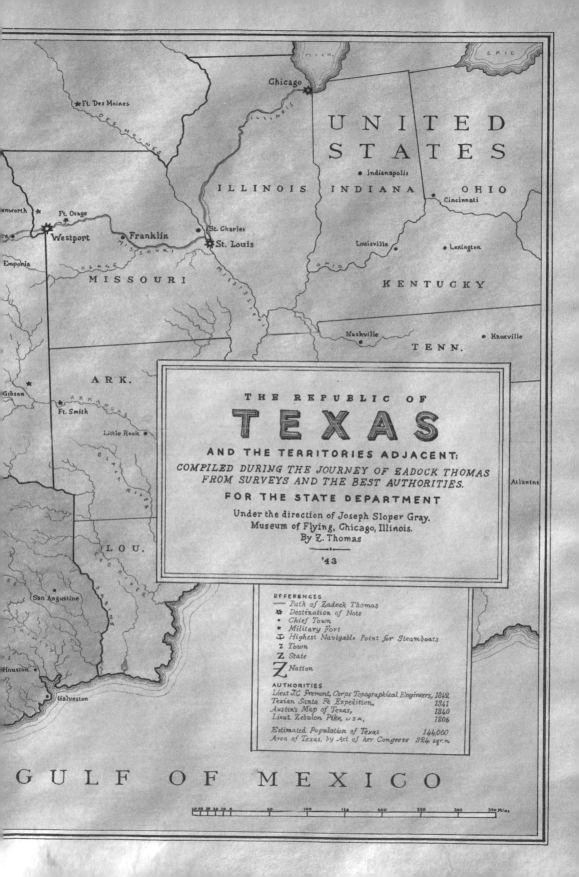

Chicago

UNITED
STATES

ILLINOIS   INDIANA   OHIO

• Indianapolis

• Cincinnati

Ft. Des Moines

DES MOINES

mworth

Ft. Osage

Westport   • Franklin   St. Charles

St. Louis

Louisville •   • Lexington

Emporia

MISSOURI

MISSOURI

OSAGE

MISSISSIPPI

KENTUCKY

OHIO

ARK.

Gibson

ARKANSAS

Ft. Smith

Little Rock •

BLACK RIVER

Nashville •   • Knoxville

TENN.

Atlantas

LOU.

RED RIVER

San Augustine

SABINE

TRINITY

Houston •

Galveston

THE REPUBLIC OF

TEXAS

AND THE TERRITORIES ADJACENT:
COMPILED DURING THE JOURNEY OF ZADOCK THOMAS
FROM SURVEYS AND THE BEST AUTHORITIES.

FOR THE STATE DEPARTMENT

Under the direction of Joseph Sloper Gray.
Museum of Flying, Chicago, Illinois.
By Z. Thomas

'43

REFERENCES
— Path of Zadock Thomas
✳ Destination of Note
• Chief Town
★ Military Fort
⊥ Highest Navigable Point for Steamboats
z Town
Z State
Ƶ Nation

AUTHORITIES
Lieut. J.C. Fremont, Corps Topographical Engineers, 1842
Texian Santa Fe Expedition,   1841
Austin's Map of Texas,   1840
Lieut. Zebulon Pike, USA,   1806

Estimated Population of Texas   144,000
Area of Texas, by Act of her Congress 324 sqr.m.

GULF OF MEXICO

10 40 30 20 10 0   50   100   150   200   250   300   350 Miles

witnessed. It was by far the worst.

Those men who had met with death were strewn about me, in grotesque geometries, inky blood leaking from bent limbs. I scratched my way through the desert scrub, the smoke breaking on a clearing.

I could see the streaming bats in the sky again. Tumbling toward a certain death, panicked. As was I. I watched my life's work, all the species I had discovered, escape over my head. The sharp clap of musket fire, though I could not see its source. Slow and beautiful, the bats fell from the sky. The burnt husks of extinguished stars.

Texas, the last outpost on my beastly errand, so big and strong, was collapsing around me.

The Republic would fail.

Even if it meant my death, I was determined not to likewise fail.

I had no one left. Nothing. I had no weapon. Only the letter to deliver into his hands.

It was then, in that fresh graveyard, that I saw him, and the veil fell from my eyes.

It was then that I saw the future.

It was the third massacre I'd witnessed.
It was by far the worst.

Those men who had met with death were strewn about
me, in grotesque geometries, inky blood leaking from
bent limbs. I scratched my way through the desert
scrub, the smoke breaking on a clearing.

I could see the streaming bats in the sky again.
Tumbling toward a certain death, panicked. As was I.
I watched my life's work, all the species I had discovered,
escape over my head. The sharp clap of musket fire, though
I could not see its source. Slow and beautiful, the bats fell
from the sky. The burnt husks of extinguished stars.

Texas, the last outpost on my beastly errand,
so big and strong, was collapsing around me.
The Republic would fail.

Even if it meant my death, I was determined not to likewise
fail. I had no one left. Nothing. I had no weapon.
Only the letter to deliver into his hands.

It was then, in that fresh graveyard, that I saw him, and
the veil fell from my eyes. It was then that I saw the future.

The City-State

NOVELTY OF FUTURE TIMES

E. ANDERSON

To those who brewed my blood,
in particular

MY GRANDFATHER

◇◇ ⌁ When Zeke received news of his grandfather's death, he retrieved the sabre that hung on his mantel and used it to sever the power lines to his house. ⌁ ⌁ ⌁ The sabre was heavy, with a silver handle. It was very old. The power lines were shiny copper tubes, full of pressurized steam. They ran up the side of a watchpost that towered over his home like a tree. ⌁ ⌁ ⌁ It took three good swings. The first severed the casing and dented the door. The second broke the semaphore and phosphor lines clustered inside. The third severed the main power tube and a blast of steam fissed into the still evening. ⌁ The force of the expulsion hit him square in the chest, right over his heart. He took two backward steps. His white dress shirt was soaked. The taste of phosphor filled his mouth. ⌁ The pressure meter spun backward and the watchpost slowly exhaled the last of its steam. The phosphor lamps lining his block flickered and their green light faded to dull dark. Quiet took the street, as all the pressurized steam vacated the block's power lines. ⌁ ⌁ ⌁ It took little physical energy, but Zeke was exhausted. His arm went limp and the sabre clattered to the street. He wiped his brow with his shirtsleeve. ⌁ His cousin Bic had told him the news. ⌁ ⌁ ⌁ ⌁ ⌁ ⌁ ⌁ ⌁ ⌁ ⌁ ⌁ ⌁ ⌁ ⌁ Dust blew through the city-state around him. A flat dread overtook him. ⌁ ⌁ ⌁ ⌁ ⌁ ⌁ ⌁ ⌁ ⌁ ⌁ ⌁ ⌁ ⌁ ⌁ ⌁ ⌁ ⌁ I could not feel. I was bright blank inside. ⌁ ⌁ ⌁ ⌁ ⌁ ⌁ ⌁ ⌁ ⌁ ⌁ ⌁ ⌁ ⌁ ⌁ ⌁ ⌁ ⌁ Zeke shuffled indoors, leaving the sabre in the street. ⌁ His body collapsed onto the floor mat. The clockwork clicked to a halt inside the timepiece on his mantel. The hour was frozen. He removed his boots and his dress shirt, which was ruined. ⌁ ⌁ He sat, waiting in his perfect dark. ⌁ ⌁ ⌁ ⌁ ⌁

He waited for a knock at the door. He waited for the whistling alert of the Law. He waited for someone watching to notice what he had done. He thought he could hear the blood pulsing heavy in his veins. He scanned his apartment. It seemed foreign. There were the rounded white walls and simple furniture, identical to every unit on his block. There was the kitchen, with neat little cabinets. A porcelain sink and a single dirty teacup. Eliza had rolled the mats and lined them up along the baseboards. He loved her, even at her most fastidious. There was the mantel with the stopped timepiece. And pegs to hold the sabre, now missing. The weapon had belonged to his grandfather. And his grandfather before him. He did not know how many generations it had been passed down through his family. He wondered which of his ancestors was the last to use it. He wished his grandfather were still alive so he could ask him. He sat for a long time.

Eliza came home. Her brown work uniform was buttoned up tight. Her face was flush, her dark eyebrows twisted. "What's going on? How long has the power been out?" Zeke stared at the timepiece. "About an hour." "Did you check the box on the watchpost outside?" Zeke didn't answer. Eliza dropped her satchel and went outside. Copper tubes clattered in the street. He heard her drag the heavy sabre back up their walk. She locked the door and pulled the shades. "You'd better hope no one was in that watchpost. You'll go to jail." She stood in the darkened livingroom, peering out through the shades. The air fluttered. "Zeke, what is wrong? You are not acting like yourself." He slowly uncurled his back, lying down flat on the floor. He closed his eyes and waited. "We need to get out of Texas." She put the sabre back in its place above the mantel and ran her finger along the dull edge.

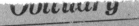

Zacharyh Ross Thomas
Beloved Senator

Senator Zacharyh Ross Thomas died Wednesday morning at the age of 84. He was a beloved husband, father, and leader, a lifelong defender of our civilization, and a 24-year-member of the National Senate.

He was born in Emporia, Kansas, on June 18, 2059, the son of Sakari Thomas, a Finnish oil importer, and Gertrude Gundy, an American homesteader. Shortly after the Collapse he was relocated to Salt-Lake. There he met his wife, Ann-Lyne, in one of the first city-states to be walled off.

His life bore witness to the great revival of our civilization, and emergence from the Collapse. He plaid an active role in rebuilding, as a civil servant

he saw the great geothermal springs tapped for their steam power, and aided the efforts to lay the foundations and piping. But he is best remembered for setting up the Vault of Records in Texas. It was a great service to our collective knowledge and the preservation of our culture. Though he disliked arms, he conceded the need to defend what was left of folks' collected knowledge, and installed security forces around the Vault, ensuring access to them for future generations.

This success led to a Senate run in 2119. The McCrea bloodline had abdicated their seat, and the Thomas family endeavored to take it. Though there were some bloodline challenges, in

up to scrutiny, and Th— icies and winning nat— landslide victory.

In the Senate he over— civil works, and char— inclusive, nonviolent — argued against the W— Contraptions Measur— ed the Ban on Elec— Fire, and was the s— er in the Abolishmen— Thomas also institu— troversial repopulat— Aiming to increase— rate, cities were di— generation, and pro— came a matter of d— progressed from o— to the next accordi— en Lifephase Syste— revolt against th— System led to the —

s's pol- | the sole dissenter, arguing for
led to a | integration. The Senate voted to
build a separate city for them,
many | and Atlantas was created.
ned an | The Thomas seat remains open
ety. He | in the Senate as a Khrysalis has
ons and | not yet been named.
upport- | Zacharyh is survived by his
ity and | wife, AnnLyne Thomas; one
dissent- | of their children, Chesbart
f Paper. | Thomas; and two grandchil-
a con- | dren, Ezekial Thomas, son of
scheme. | Ely Thomas, and Bic Thomas,
e birth- | son of Chesbart Thomas, both
d up by | of Texas. Memorial ceremo-
ting be- | nies will be held in all seven
Citizens | city-states, including a special
city-state | statue dedication in the Repub-
his sev- | lic of Texas. Citizens wishing
he Queer | to attend should contact their
Lifephase | local law office with ID papers
er Com- | and blood samples at the read
was | for admittance into Natio

Eliza changed out of her work uniform in the bedroom. "I have to go back to Chicago-Land for the funeral," Zeke said. "Of course," Eliza said. "I'm sure your grandmother can get clearance for you to travel." Zeke stuffed clothes into his bag robotically. His hand-kerchiefs were limp and drab. Eliza stood up behind him, and cautiously touched his shoulder. "It's late. You can do that tomorrow." She made the hand signal for *morning*. "I'm going to make a cup of tea. Let's drink it on the roof." Zeke nodded, almost imperceptibly. He could easily imagine his grandfather in Chicago-Land, at home,

MORNING

reading the paper. He let himself be led into the kitchen and then up onto the roof of their unit. Zeke and Eliza sat in their familiar chairs, placed on the roof for this purpose. It was unusually dark with the power out. Beyond their street, the dull green phosphorescent lamps slowly blinked all the way to the edge of the barrier. The city-state, and all the lights with it, stopped there. Settling in beside Eliza, Zeke instinctively reached out for her hand. She put her hand in his, moving it around like a burrowing animal until it found a comfortable place. Eliza's hands were small and delicate. Hand signals were a way to avoid the listening ears of the government, but Zeke sometimes preferred the way Eliza spoke with her hands. They had a precise grace that was hypnotizing. It was something Zeke loved about her. "They must be inspecting the watchpost," Eliza said. Muddled voices rose up from the street. "You worry me, Zeke. You're lucky there wasn't a Recorder in the top of it." **"There hardly ever is,"** Zeke said. The sun had already sunk below the barrier's false horizon. The evening was a relief from the long sharp afternoons when the blistering light bounced off the white walls of all the buildings, creating a dry, hot haze. Dust coated everything. "There isn't enough funding," Eliza said. The Law couldn't afford to keep Recorders in every watchpost, listening and transcribing conversations. "But it isn't worth the risk of getting caught." ∧∧ ∧∧ ∧∧ **"No one is listening. They just want folks to think they are. There are dead zones all over, where nothing gets recorded,"** Zeke said. ∧∧ ∧∧ ∧∧ "You don't know where those are. The Vault gets hundreds of transcripts a day. You can bet there'll be a thread on this tomorrow." Eliza worked in the Vault, where they kept carbon'd copies of everything that happened in the city-state. ∧∧ ∧∧ ∧∧ **"We'll see,"** Zeke said. ∧∧ ∧∧ "I'll check your ID tomorrow," Eliza said. ∧∧ ∧∧ **"At least something would be added to my record. I'm tired of this city-state. Nothing happens. We're trapped inside these walls until they transfer us out."** Eliza sighed. He leaned his head on her shoulder as though he were the one in need of comforting. ∧∧ ∧∧ ∧∧ "You could end that now, you know. Now that your grandfather's seat is empty." ∧∧ ∧∧ ∧∧ Zeke stood up and peered cautiously over the edge of the roof. The watchpost was lit by Law flashers. A handful of uniformed Lawmen stood watching a lone workman try to extract the broken pipes and power lines. ∧∧ ∧∧ Zeke didn't know how he'd be able to enter his grandparents' house in Chicago-Land. He had many good memories there. His grandfather's oft repeated stories, his black humor. They'd had a bond that no one else in his family shared. He waited for the flood of emotions to come, but there was nothing. The city-state blinked below him, unreal. ∧∧ ∧∧ ∧∧ "We could move to Chicago-Land and be done with the Republic of Texas. You'd be named to the Senate before your cousin." ∧∧ ∧∧ ∧∧ Zeke pulled a small phial of laudanum out of his pocket and droppered a dram into his tea. He could feel Eliza watching him. She didn't know how often he took the sedative now. ∧∧ ∧∧ ∧∧ "Zeke, we need to stay alert. There was another murder today." ∧∧ **"It wasn't an isolated incident?"** ∧∧ "No, the thread at the Vault now has three cases. That's not a

THE CITY-STATE

Republic of Texas
NATIONAL IDENTIFICATION PAPERS

NATIONAL ALLIANCE OF CITYSTATES

42.770

NAME: Ezekial Thomas
GENDER: Male
BTH DAY: 24-10-19
LF PHASE: Yng Adult
CLASS: Ind
BLD TYPE: A-B positive
ECHELON: Khrysalis

BLOODLINE   Thomas Family   7th Generation

FOUNT RATION

(TX) (TX) (TX) (TX) (TX) (TX)

TRAVEL AUTHORIZATIONS

Rep of Texas
Chicago land

ID RECORD: 4277
CITY-STATE: 3 SIL
QUADRANT: NORT

HEIGHT: 6 ft 1 in
WEIGHT: 174
HAIR CL: Red
EYE CL: Hazel
SCARS: None

THE SILVER CITY-STATE
NATIONAL LIFEPHASE PARTICIPANT

ECHE

1: Khrysali
2:
3:
4:
5:
6:
7:

NAMESTAMP: Z. T

coincidence. It's getting dangerous here." ⌃⌃ "What are Lawmen good for if they can't catch a murderer?" ⌃⌃ "They don't have the men." ⌃⌃ ⌃⌃ "That's just it. I don't want to spend my life trying to solve problems like that. Playing politics." Zeke took a slow sip, allowing the familiar bitterness of the laudanum to sting his tongue. ⌃⌃ ⌃⌃ "You could be the Khrysalis." Eliza had never pressed him much on their future. "It's your duty to take the empty Senate seat." ⌃⌃ ⌃⌃ "It should pass to Bic. He wants it." ⌃⌃ ⌃⌃ "Your grandmother loves you the best. She wouldn't choose your cousin," Eliza said. ⌃⌃ ⌃⌃ The seven seats of the Senate were passed down by bloodline. Only Zeke and Bic were eligible to take the Thomas seat. The decision lay with their grandmother, the Senator's widow. ⌃⌃ ⌃⌃ "She'd be disappointed if I declined," Zeke said. Eliza reached over to hold both of his hands. Her forehead wrinkled, her eyes searched his. ⌃⌃ ⌃⌃ "But I don't want it. I just want to have our life. Start our family. Our own bloodline." Eliza nodded assent. She had been left by her father as a child. She didn't know her ancestry. ⌃⌃ Zeke slipped his fingers into the hair at the nape of her neck. He kissed her, lightly. Zeke felt his mustache brush her lips, and she pulled away. ⌃⌃ ⌃⌃ "Sorry," he said. ⌃⌃ "A kiss without a mustache is like tea without the spice." She smiled. ⌃⌃ "I love you," he said. ⌃⌃ "You are my blood," she responded. ⌃⌃ ⌃⌃ It was dark enough on the roof to see a few bright stars shimmering in the sky above them. The Lawmen below made their reports, clacking loudly on the typowriters they had hooked into the communication line of the watchpost. Eliza hummed a melancholic song under her breath in time. ⌃⌃ "These murders scare you," Zeke said. She nodded, just barely. ⌃⌃ "I don't want anything to pull us apart. We need to be careful." ⌃⌃ ⌃⌃ "A moment's impulse. It's passed," Zeke said. ⌃⌃ "Drink up. The tea will relax you. Or would you like me to sing?" ⌃⌃ "Please." Zeke closed his eyes. It was his favorite thing. ⌃

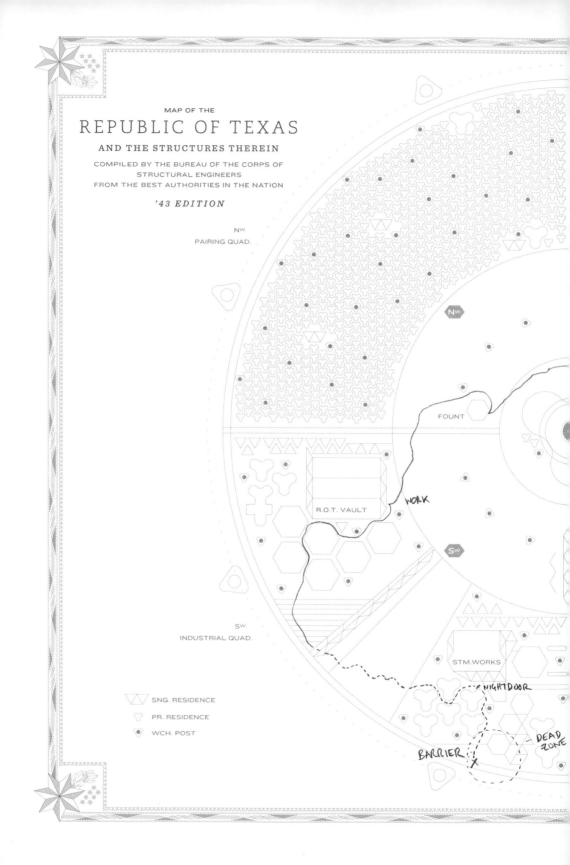

MAP OF THE

REPUBLIC OF TEXAS

AND THE STRUCTURES THEREIN

COMPILED BY THE BUREAU OF THE CORPS OF
STRUCTURAL ENGINEERS
FROM THE BEST AUTHORITIES IN THE NATION

'43 EDITION

Nᵂ·
PAIRING QUAD.

Nᵂ

FOUNT

WORK

R.O.T. VAULT

Sᵂ

Sᵂ·
INDUSTRIAL QUAD.

STM.WORKS

NIGHTDOOR

DEAD
ZONE

BARRIER

SNG. RESIDENCE

PR. RESIDENCE

WCH. POST

Eliza, I feel as though every letter I write you is an apology. It was an impossible decision, for a father to leave his daughter, his blood. It has caused me nothing but heartache since. You were a child. But it was out of my hands. Nothing else could be done.

To write to you is the only way I can be in your life now. It makes me feel as though we're together. I'll put these letters in a file for you to read when I'm gone. Perhaps you'll know me then.

It was lucky I was given the job of Historian. I have kept the records. Tended them, pruning extraneous information, debugging biases, and training the long straight branches so that plain truth emerged, simple and strong. It is a gentle art, and one requiring patience. Once I knew how to do it well.

I thought there were principles. Rules to govern which facts should endure and which should dissolve into dust. But now I see my criteria were arbitrary. I chose objects or moments, and they became real. I draw worlds from crumbling stacks of paper, and they are given meaning through my careful attention. The designs of the Historian become history's lessons.

If there was one advantage to the job, it was that I had easy access to your files. I've read about you, all these years. Since I abandoned you, you are missing a history. I owe you one now.

You have followed me, in a way, in my line of work. I am so proud of you for achieving the rank of Threader. You don't know it, but the Vault in Texas was largely my design. It gives me great pleasure to think of you skillfully threading documents in the great halls of drawers and cabinets, according to the system that I engineered. I remember you as a precocious and clever child, and it does not surprise me that you would be promoted.

What has surprised me was last week's society column in the Texas broadsheet. I read that Zeke Thomas has been courting you. My heart leapt at the thought of you with the next Khrysalis. Your life will be comfortable, and easy. Zeke is good blood. I met his grandfather, the Senator, when we were constructing the Vault of Records. He was a hard man, but he was infinitely wise, with a good heart. He was a champion of the Vault in the Senate, and I'll never forget that.

Now that he's gone, I imagine young Zeke will take his seat. It is unusual to skip a generation and he will have to learn the ways of politics quickly, and you with him. I often think of the future now. Yours is the generation I have hope for. The Vault is what I leave behind, because now that the Recorders document every single thing, my work no longer seems valuable.

The past is like a tree in the darkest night, filled with black birds barely seen. Truths that flutter, escaping the edges of peripheral vision. First they are birds lost against a dark sky, then they are simply leaves, blown about by an animating wind. The longer I looked, the more difficult it was to see. So I retired.

I have decided to reconstruct one final history, to make up for the one I left you without. Since you will make a pair with Zeke Thomas, your children, my grandchildren, will carry his blood. You should know his bloodline lineage in detail. Looking through the Thomas family files, I have found a storied past.

It is fitting to start with a courtship. Zadock Thomas, a distant relative of the Senator, left rare firsthand records: letters, sketches, maps. I am threading together his history.

Zadock wasn't famous. He was poor, painfully sincere, and sickly. A failed naturalist, too weak for his journey across the untamed Southwest of 1843. Even so, the facts surrounding him form an unusual constellation, and his story has the dimensions of destiny beyond the Historian's control.

It began when he asked for the hand of Elswyth Gray, a Chicago socialite and the daughter of his employer.

Mr. Joseph Sloper Gray,

I write to ask your formal permission for your daughter Elswyth's graceful hand in marriage. I believe she would be amenable to the idea. The fruition of this bright arrangement could not yet pass for, as you are aware, I lack the funds for a wedding befitting your daughter's noble standing. Though your employ has kept me in health these many years, I'm not certain it provides enough salary on which to raise a family. This letter contains a solution.

Though I have more interest in studying the bird collections of your Museum of Flying, plants also hold some appeal. I have been on small excursions with groups from the Zoological Garden to the western part of the state to collect specimens for their holdings. Using my skills as a specimen collector, illustrator, and typesetter, I could perhaps produce a publishable volume about the plants of this fine state.

Mr. Joseph Sloper Gray,

I write to ask your formal permission for your daughter Elswyth's graceful hand in marriage. I believe she would be amenable to the idea. The fruition of this bright arrangement could not yet pass for, as you are aware, I lack the funds for a wedding befitting your daughter's noble standing. Though your employ has kept me in health these many years, I'm not certain it provides enough salary on which to raise a family. Allow me to propose a solution.

Though I have more interest in studying the bird collections of your Museum of Flying, plants also hold some appeal. I have been on small excursions with groups from the Zoological Garden to the western part of the state to collect specimens for their holdings. Using my skills as a specimen collector, illustrator, and typesetter, I could perhaps produce a publishable volume about the plants of this fine state.

Between the universities of Europe and the American societies, there might be enough customers for a text on the natural sciences. By proving my worth with this volume I hope to make a profession of observing the natural world. If the fates allow, the income would provide for your daughter and any children that we may have.

Our interest in books is one of the many things Elswyth and I share. Her writing is lyrical and mine is practical, and that makes a fitting match. I do not wish to be improper, sir, but my feelings for her are quite overwhelming, on an order of magnitude that I could not myself have imagined, expansive as the great western sky.

I also believe marriage could improve Elswyth's health. As you know, I've attended her bedside during her recent illness, and helped the doctor extract the black humors from her blood. Though she sleeps a great deal, my presence at her bleedings has brought us closer. She requires a husband to care for her and to lift her up in spirits.

With the most sincere respect & esteem,

Zadock Thomas

Zadock,

I am quite familiar with your character, and duly appreciative of the services you have provided me during your years at the Museum of Flying. However, your lack of propriety in this request is disconcerting. To speak of my daughter in such language chafes my ear. I hesitate, in good conscience, to give you Elswyth's hand in marriage. This letter contains the reasons.

To start, I am not entirely convinced that her courtesy toward you constitutes an exceptional affection. I know you have come calling many times, but my daughter is more woman than girl, with emotions more complicated than even she may understand. As you are well aware, she has other suitors. Some possess the lineage to make an

Zadock,

I am quite familiar with your character, and duly appreciative of the services you have provided me during your years at the Museum of Flying. However, your lack of propriety in this request is disconcerting. To speak of my daughter in such language chafes my ear. I hesitate, in good conscience, to give you Elswyth's hand in marriage for the following reasons.

To start, I am not entirely convinced that her courtesy toward you constitutes an exceptional affection. I know you have come calling many times, but my daughter is more woman than girl, with emotions more complicated than even she may understand. As you are well aware, she has other suitors. Some possess the lineage to make an impression on society and improve her standing in Chicago.

However, she has long been introduced to society and her twenty-six years are overripe when it comes to marriage. But she is a particular sort, as am I. Both my daughters are given to fantasies, I fear, Louisa with her dollhouses, which she will not give up. But Elswyth as well, buried deep in the worlds of her books. It has been difficult for my eldest to match in reality the notions such novels have given her.

This concern aside, your financial and professional situation remain. You are correct in guessing it is insufficient to marry into the Gray family. I know of the Zoological Garden, and I find it dubious at best. Flora simply cannot capture the imagination of the public like the animals, chief among them those who rule the air. Without an audience any such society or museum, or even a well-prepared publication, is doomed to failure.

Fortuitously I have a pressing task that requires an employee willing to travel. Far beyond your normal duties here, this is a matter of great urgency. I not only would be able to increase your salary for the duration but would also, albeit with some reservation, consent to your marriage to my daughter. It is that important.

family here. I would send Mr. Buell
were he not instrumental in the running
of the Museum. I trust you would
attend to the errand with haste and
solemn duty.

The Republic of Texas, where
General Irion is encamped, is 900
miles from Chicago. My daughter does
not know I have set this task as a
condition of her marriage, and I think
it would serve your interests not to
make a point of it. Simply state that
you are under my employ for a special
task. If you agree, please make your
preparations. I require my courier to
depart with the letter this week.

Sincerely,
Joseph Fray

Elswyth's consent to marriage is a further condition, and an undertaking I leave to you. A nursemaid does not a husband make.

The task I require of you is to act as courier by delivering a letter to a colleague, General Edwin 'Speed' Irion. He is the commander of a rogue troop in the nascent country of Texas. The letter is of great import. It cannot be delivered in the normal way. He is an intelligent man in a sensitive position, but his time in the wilderness has made him a bit mad. He has broken from the new republic and hopes for annexation to the United States. This has only aggravated Texas's war with Mexico, who will not recognize her status as a sovereign nation.

It is a dangerous land. I would provide for your transportation with an army unit under the command of Major McMarrow, an equal man to the general, who should serve as adequate protection.

One thing is paramount. The letter must be delivered directly into the hands of General Irion. Whatever happens, you must not open this letter yourself nor allow anyone else to do so. It is of a sensitive political nature. The government's postal service will not do. I need someone whom I can trust. One who will deliver the letter at any cost.

Time is of the essence. I would travel myself, but for my age and my family here. I would send Mr. Buell were he not instrumental in the running of the museum. I trust you would attend to the errand with haste and solemn duty.

The Republic of Texas, where General Irion is encamped, is 900 miles from Chicago. My daughter does not know I have set this task as a condition of her marriage, and I think it would serve your interests not to make a point of it. Simply state that you are under my employ for a special task. If you agree, please make your preparations. I require my courier to depart with the letter this week.

Sincerely,

Joseph Gray

◇◇ ∿ At city-center, Zeke ran to catch the tram out of Texas. The main watchpost read 07:02, OCTOBER 4. Zeke bought a ticket to Chicago-Land. It was hard to leave Eliza behind. Since her father had left her, she didn't like to be parted from anyone. ∿ ∿ ∿ ∿ ∿ ∿ He rode the rotovator up the tether in the center of the city-state. It docked with the tram, which floated in near-earth orbit to the dock above Chicago-Land. He wished he had more laudanum. His palms began to sweat the moment he boarded. He could only think of the worst. The statite car might drift into space. The steam thrusters might misfire. The car was attached to nothing. Zeke imagined it falling. ∿ ∿ He looked nervously at the landscape painted below. It felt strange to be outside the protective wall of the barrier. The other passengers didn't seem to mind. In their minds, they had not left the bounds of civilization. ∿ ∿ ∿ Outside the barrier there were few trees, few lakes, and no buildings. Lots of rot: brown, barren, burning. The storm country was huge. Each trip, Zeke would scan for signs of life. The car was too far from the ground to see anything. Ghost rivers of smoke drifted along the earth's floor. Some said the land was burning. That there were folks outside, in the rot, setting fires. But nothing could be seen. Not even the flocks of birds Zeke had read about in old books. It was as dead and flat as a page of text. ∿ At the house he found his grandmother cutting the lawn, despite her bony hands, nearly crippled with arthritis. He watched her for a long moment, her back bowed under the weight of a long life. Sensing his presence, she looked up and gasped, clutching her hands to her breast like two bony wings. ∿ "Gram, it's Zeke." This unfroze her. ∿ ∿ ∿ "You gave me a start. I thought I was looking at the ghost of your grandfather." She exhaled. "You look smart. I'm glad you're here." Zeke nodded. "There will be many folks here tomorrow. We must prepare." ∿ ∿ ∿ Senator Zacharyh Thomas had had a long and eventful life. But he was old. He'd had a bad knee, trouble breathing, and a touch of dementia. He'd been tired. The winter before he'd looked Zeke in the eye and said, "You don't want to get as old as this." ⌒ ⌒ ⌒ The funeral was well attended. It was a national day of mourning. Chicago-Land was the seat of the government and where the oldest generation lived. Everyone wore fineries: uniforms, dress boots, and brimhats. His grandmother sat with the wives of the other Senators, all in black robes. Womenfolk cried behind their fans. The mood was deeply mournful, even though he'd had a long, full life. ⌒ Zeke sat in the front row with Bic, his cousin. Bic wore too much wax in his hair. He was usually smug about his military training but cried unabashedly during the funeral. Zeke was surprised to find himself feeling sorry for someone he often tried to avoid. The feeling dissipated after the funeral, when Bic started talking about the Senate seat and his own ideas for it. ⌒ ⌒ At the end of the day another Senator presented Zeke with his grandfather's inheritance bundle and a special armband for his uniform. Newspaper clippings of successes, photos of ancestors — it contained many documents pertaining to the long history of the Thomas family bloodline. But most important, it meant he'd been chosen as Khrysalis. He could feel Bic's green eyes from across the room. ⌒ ⌒ Having a seat in the Senate was a difficult job, with many problems. His grandfather had done much in his time. Only a fraction of the population was left alive after the Collapse. Folks banded together in a few remaining cities. They put up the barriers, for protection. A few folks remained outside, to their peril. His grandfather was a leader in the Senate, instituting many of the systems that ensured the culture's survival. ⌒ Zeke tried to imagine life before the Collapse. Open cities, no restriction on travel, no barrier to the outside world. Civilization and chaos commingled. What was won, was earned. Now jobs were assigned by the government, based on heredity.

Like his new job. ︿ ︿ Zeke stayed with his grandmother for almost a week. Age hadn't slowed her down, though she was often confused. Wisps of white hair escaped her bobby pins. He had to tell her where he lived now, how old he was. ︿ ︿ ︿ They talked as she prepared a tea service with nourishing fount-water. Never having been taught, Eliza had struggled to learn its intricacies from Zeke's grandmother, who could perform the ritual without thinking. ︿ ︿ ︿ "I don't think I want to join the Senate." Zeke spoke openly with his grandmother. "I just want my private life. With Eliza. I don't have that kind of energy." ︿ "You can claim a period of mourning before you take the seat. Your grandfather always said you were the brightest of the bloodline. We've both looked forward to what fate would deliver you." ︿ ︿ "So far, my fate has been pretty forgettable." ︿ ︿ "There are some of your grandfather's shirts and hand-kerchiefs that I thought you might want. I put them in the downstairs closet." She took his cup into the kitchen. "Only if you want them. You look plenty handsome already." ︿ ︿ ︿ Zeke walked through the large empty house. Everything was made of polished wood and glass. The fixtures were porcelain, adorned with silver. He walked down the staircase. It coughed dust clouds with each step. ︿ ︿ ︿ The house felt strange without his grandfather's presence. His grandmother had not changed anything. It was all meticulously organized. The cupboards opened to food and glasses in neat little rows, labels facing out. Photographs of past generations lined the walls. The few books left were categorized, dusted. It was a museum of their life and their great love affair. Without his grandfather the possessions meant nothing. Zeke thought, ︿ The truth of nothingness, that is despair. ︿ ︿ ︿ His grandfather's shirts were arranged by color in the storage closet. The fabrics created a rainbow of pattern. He thumbed through the shirts. One was misplaced, a white shirt in the middle of the greens.

He held it up to his front. Lifting the sleeve out to match his arm, he dropped the shirt. As he picked it up, a letter fell from the front pocket. It was old, still sealed. "DO NOT OPEN" was handwritten on the front. He wanted to open it. ⌁ ⌁ ⌁ ⌁ Instead, Zeke brought the shirt and the letter into the breakfast room. ⌁ ⌁ ⌁ "What's this, Gram?" ⌁ She glanced at it. "Looks like an old letter of your grandfather's." ⌁ "It's sealed. It's never been carbon'd." ⌁ ⌁ "Your grandfather would have had it carbon copied when they did all that. He took all the paper and books to the tents set up downtown, just like regular folks. He was so proud of the new Vault. I remember—" ⌁ "But this one can't have been carbon'd if it wasn't opened. The point was to have a copy of everything in the Vault of Records. Gram, we need to turn this in. We'll explain it was always sealed so we don't get in trouble." ⌁ "Well"—she turned it over in her hand "it's probably one of those silly love letters your grandfather used to write me. Before the phonotubes and all that." ⌁ ⌁ "He wrote you love letters?" ⌁ "There used to be a mail service." ⌁ "Hh, well, I'm going to take it to the Vault in Texas." He slid the letter into his inheritance bundle, with the other family documents. ⌁ ⌁ ⌁ ⌁ ⌁ "We could open it if you like, dear. I'm too old to be embarrassed anymore." ⌁ ⌁ "The minute we open it we've got an uncarbon'd document on our hands. Possessing papers the government doesn't have copies of… Besides jail, it could cost this family the Senate seat." ⌁ ⌁ ⌁ "Whatever you like, dear. Did you want a tea service?" ⌁ ⌁ "Gram, you just made me one." ⌁ ⌁ ⌁ ⌁ "Hh, I did, didn't I. Well, I put some of your grandfather's shirts in the downstairs closet for you to try on." ⌁ ⌁ ⌁ ⌁ ⌁ ⌁ ⌁ ⌁ ⌁ He held up the white one for her. It was too big. His grandmother tilted her head and gave him a strange look, as though she were seeing through him, far into the past. He agreed to take the shirt home. ⌁

➤ Eliza, it is my fault that you can't know our own family's history. These letters will be in your inheritance bundle. When I die, you will finally know everything. Your bloodline, and Zeke's as well.

At Joseph Gray's request, Zadock Thomas indeed made his journey west. A member of his progeny would return that way to take his seat in the Senate generations later. Your Zeke is next. This migration is part of history's pattern.

After the Collapse, the country, the whole world, was in chaos. Civilization was decimated. The records have described those horrors and there is little point in repeating them here. Suffice to say, hanging on to some semblance of order was not easy. The folks in the remaining seven cities were scared. Walls were built to keep marauders out and to protect scarce natural resources. Seven Senators were chosen to preside over the nation. Each would pass their seat to a blood relative. In this way blood became political currency. Senator Thomas was a man possessed of a particular vision. He knew that knowledge was power. He knew that passing it along to the next generation was the thread that held a civilization together.

I was tasked with helping to set up a permanent Vault of Records, so that the history we had left might be preserved. It was a momentous assignment. It also served to distract me from thoughts of you. I had a new purpose. I devised a system for the classification and categorization of records and documents. We inherited few, most had been destroyed in the Collapse. To aid future Historians, it was decided more ought to be recorded. The Senate assigned men to document the daily life, speech, and movements of influential people. At the time I did not imagine how this idea might become corrupted. We were naïve.

Outside the barriers, the world continued to burn. It is a barren wasteland. They say that the folks who were shut out of

HENRY BARTLE

the city-states are all dead now. That animals can't even survive in the rot. This, I feel, discounts the resilience of life.

At first frost, the wanderer butterfly (*Danaus plexippus*, of the family Nymphalidae) used to make the great journey from northern climes southward to Mexico. However, no individual made the entire journey. The migration spanned three to four generations of butterflies. The great-grandchildren of the overwinter generation returned to the exact same conifer their ancestors departed from a year prior.

They had no guide back. Their history was within them.

I have found more from Zadock Thomas. In the year of his letters, 1843, America was caught up in the task of fulfilling its Manifest Destiny. Nothing could stand in the way of the westward expansion. It was, in a way, the opposite of the Collapse. A fever dream had taken the nation. Train tracks were laid, buffalo were cleared. Smallpox claimed the lives of great numbers of American Indians in the plains. Before their minds could assimilate the white man coming over the hills firing "shouting sticks," their bodies were defeated by his diseases.

The Great Migration of 1843 saw settlers flood the Oregon Trail. Even prior to the gold rush, the overland trails were busy highways, fueled by the promise of paradise in the west. Telegraph systems were built, the typewriter invented.

John Tyler became the U.S. president by succession and grappled with issues of expansion. He called for the annexation of the vast Texan territory (which included New Mexico and much of Colorado), a land grab rivaled only by the Louisiana Purchase and accompanied by a good deal more bloodshed.

At the invitation of Mexico, Stephen Austin's "Old Three Hundred" families had settled Texas seven years earlier, the first white men to do so. Refusing to give up a cannon at

Gonzales, they organized a determined new nation, and the Texas Revolution began. After massacres at Goliad and the Alamo, Sam Houston forced Mexican General Santa Anna's surrender at San Jacinto. Their treaty was never recognized and Texas continued to battle a disorganized Mexico.

The great wagon trains rumbled westward looking for Eden on earth. A terrestrial land of milk and honey had been promised by Lewis and Clark and all who returned to tell tall tales of the west. But the promises of romantic nationalism were false. There was no earthly paradise. America was a failed utopia. Resources dried up. Wars ensued. The Collapse was perhaps inevitable, written into the story from the beginning.

While reading this, you must remain aware that Zadock Thomas and his contemporaries had no idea what would befall their offspring. Despite his failures, he is a more fascinating character than many men who accomplished much more.

Zadock Thomas was the son of Zebediah Thomas, a druggist and the owner of an apothecary. Zadock was introduced to the natural world through a sympathetic aunt who noticed he had begun to collect beetles, butterflies, and other winged insects in the back of the shop where he worked with his father. Joseph Gray, of the then-nascent Museum of Flying, accepted him as an apprentice when the apothecary went bankrupt.

He worked outdoors, collecting specimens from the Midwestern fields. There he learned surveying techniques and methods of astronomical positioning. However, his health proved too fragile to continue outdoors. He suffered from nearsightedness, shortness of breath, and heart palpitations. These symptoms, given that he was unusually tall and slender, with stooped shoulders, flat feet, and an uneven mustache, have led me to suspect Marfan syndrome, an inherited disease.

Owing to Thomas's poor health and unemployment, Joseph Gray offered him residence and a small stipend from the Museum of Flying to continue working there as a plate setter. He slept in the same room as the insect collection, on a cot underneath a ceiling hung with the skeleton specimens of many bird species. Gray wrote in his letters that

> ...the boy was birdlike in and of himself, being disposed to eat in small quantities, and no more than milk and bread, and the occasional egg. He might subsist on 24 cents a day.

Gray established a journal that mirrored his museum in being a compendium solely for animals that could fly, like insects and birds. The publication of *The American Journal of Flight* was uninterrupted for many decades. Gray acquired a typowriting machine to produce the editions himself. Originally Zadock's job was to set type, but he was a poor typist, and the task was given instead to Bartholomew Buell, his fellow employee. Zadock was relegated to drawing and preparing the specimen plates. His illustrations were passable for the time.

I include some in this thread, as well as Zadock's letters to Elswyth. He was eager to begin a questionable journey. He didn't compose much beyond these starry-eyed musings, written during his southwest expedition on Mr. Gray's errand. I have discovered one letter missing from the Vault, which is highly unusual. Namestamps show that the Thomas family had checked it out many times, but its file folder is empty. I have reported it as a missing document to the authorities. Does anyone except me care what these old drawers contain?

We must know where we have been. If we cannot see our own patterns, then we are nothing but a mindless flock of birds flapping blindly in the night, scraping and pecking in the dust.

Dearest Elswyth,

Last night I called on you to make a proper goodbye. I should not have left my visit till the final hour, for when your Aunt Anne showed me to your chambers you were asleep, having endured another bleeding. I tried to rouse you a little and you waved me away with a limp and delicate hand. I could not very well deliver my news for you in your weakened state I care for your constitution above all else.

I am going away, to Texas, on a special errand of your father's

I look to the future.
The payment for this errand shall afford a wedding that befits you. I cannot deny you the finery you are accustomed to. Your beauty will be ~~only~~ augmented by beautiful things. You must remain brave, and steel yourself, as though I were going off to war. Hardly had the truth of our separation set in, when a desperate longing was born in my heart.

I must confess, I took a keepsake....

Dearest Elswyth,

Last night I called on you to make a proper goodbye. I should not have left my visit till the final hour, for when your Aunt Anne showed me to your chambers you were asleep, having endured another bleeding. I tried to rouse you a little and you waved me away with a limp and delicate hand. I could not very well deliver my news for you in your weakened state. I care for your constitution above all else.

I am going away, to Texas, on a special errand of your father's.

The payment for this errand shall afford a wedding that befits you. I cannot deny you the finery you are accustomed to. Your beauty will be augmented by beautiful things. You must remain brave, and steel yourself, as though I were going off to war. Hardly had the truth of our separation set in, when a desperate longing was born in my heart.

I must confess, I took a keepsake. Something of you to bring with me on my journey. The blood pan was at your bedside, and I had some of my specimen kit, so I captured a single heartbeat's worth of your lifeblood in a small phial. I hope you will forgive me, I cannot bear the thought of being wholly without you.

Afterward, lying in bed and listening to the call of the whip-poor-will outside, something moved in me. The idea formed to compose to you a series of letters as I go on my adventure. Though I will not send this one till I am gone, preparation is an auspicious beginning.

Perhaps it would have been too difficult to say goodbye. I leave many things unfinished. I have not prepared the study skins of all the birds I wanted to this season (only thirty-four). And I have not repaired the museum's insect cabinet, as I ought to have done, as I've recently discovered live moths inside, eating the specimens.

Instead I busy myself packing. I intend to act as official naturalist of this expedition. I imagine myself returning with fantastic specimens, and great things in store for my future as a respected collector and adventurer. I might make a real profession of this study, rather than simply assisting your father with his cabinets of winged curiosities. I mentioned to him that there might be some as yet undiscovered birds in the wild territory, but he would not loan me the necessary instruments for documentation. No matter, there is nothing that prevents me from bringing my own jars and drawing pad.

I have also packed my mapmaking apparatus. My skills at reading the stars should save me from being lost, and I have the idea that a map, made of the fresh territory I inhabit, would be of great value to some surveying company or government office.

Finally, on the very top of my pack rests my mission's cause. Your father's letter for General Irion. Written upon the front is the phrase "DO NOT OPEN," which does not exactly strike a tone of trust. But I would never pry. This delivery is of the utmost importance to your father, and I shall prove myself true.

Buell found me assembling my kit, and heard tell of my new task with not a little jealousy. He has always been the favored employee. So I was surprised, then, that he gifted me one of his sabres. Even though he has many, it was a kind gesture. You may find some comfort in the fact that I have such a weapon, though you should know I intend for it to remained sheathed for the duration of my trip.

This morning I was paid a farewell visit by Aunt Anne. Your mother's sister knew much about the journey already. She took the phial of your blood and added to it some elixir meant to strengthen its liquid properties and keep it from hardening. She is quite the alchemist.

I must admit Aunt Anne has become not only my confidante but also adviser in love. I told her that I am loath to leave you, but we both know my courting has run its course. To be a new man is my best hope.

She was insistent on reading my tea leaves one last time. She produced her grandmother's Lowestoft tea set, a beautiful porcelain with flitting birds. She pricked my finger and made the tea in the customary way. We both drank, and in the wet leaves at the bottom of my cup I discerned a mountain, upside down. Aunt Anne sat in a long silence, watching the birds trace life lines in the sky above. Her ability to sit while allowing her soul to travel and commune with other such souls is miraculous indeed. She and all her Sisters share the oracular gifts of the Auspex, for better or worse it is hard to say.

When the prognostications were all told I rather wished I had refused the oracle. Aunt Anne was convinced I faced a journey full of hindrance and spiritual danger. But it is already known that Texas is no land of milk and honey. A single bat fluttered from her doorway as I departed. I cannot put much stock in the tea leaves, though. All my thoughts have the pain of being away from you at their center.

We are born and live the full thread the fates have trimmed for us and then we are gone, absorbed into the great darkened sky of the past and forgotten completely. Some men have legacies. Stars that remain bright. But how to become such a man? I know little of my great-grandfather, and if we marry and have children of our own, what will their offspring know of me? I would be content to be even a small star in the vast and churning night, an asterisk in the history of man.

Darwin and Audubon will be known as long as the heavens spin above. Think on the generations unborn who will say their names, while ordinary men like myself will be subsumed in the great sand dunes of generations that have lived and died. Though my body will turn to dust, I might turn my thoughts into paper, and keep hope.

All the more reason to write my adventures to you, now that it seems as though the fates have something in store for me. I am your servant in this, as in all things.

Per your father's orders, I am to join the troop of Major McMarrow. The steamboat for St. Louis is already being prepared. It feels as though to-morrow morning will never come, yet could not come soon enough.

Regretfully Departing, Zadock

<u>Packing list</u>

Letter for General Speed Irion
Clothing bag, Boots
Roborant
Letter of introduction to McMarrow
Specimen case
Tubes for collection
Nets, dredges, killing jars
Cyanide, blow drill, glass plates
Field glasses
Compass, Telescope, Sextant, Vernier
Sabre from Buell
Blanket roll
Phial of Elswyth's blood

<u>Ink Formula</u>

Copperas &
Tannic Acid — A Teaspoon of each

Gum Arabic — a Pinch

Rainwater — a Pint

Packing list

Letter for General Irion

Clothing bag, Boots

Roborant

Letter of introduction to McMarrow

Specimen case

Tubes for collection

Nets, dredges, killing jars

Cyanide, blow drill, glass plates

Field glasses

Compass, Telescope, Sextant, Vernier

Sabre from Buell

Blanket roll

Phial of Elswyth's blood

Ink Formula

Copperas & Tannic Acid - A Teaspoon of each

Gum Arabic - a Pinch

Rainwater - a Pint

FAM. EMBERIZIDAE

GEN. MELOSPIZA

the little last birds sing the prettiest songs

FAM. EMBERIZIDAE
GEN. POOECETES

Dearest Elswyth,

I am on my way now, and this is the first chance I've had to write. I think of you constantly. I am so far from home. Five days hence we traveled to Joliet, observing the construction of the Illinois and Michigan Canal. If it had been opened, we could have reached the Missouri by way of Lake Michigan. As it was, we had to travel by land for many days before we could join the river. There are great flocks of passenger pigeons here, so many to a flock that they blot out the sky.

Once we arrived we met the steamboat. It is a beautiful machine. The bow lifts up out of the water like the neck of a great white goose with his head held high, the deck carried between the wings on his back. A gush of white churning water issues from behind the stern, trailing violently. Just as the goose's great paddle feet churn underneath the surface of a calm lake, so too is the machinery of the boat concealed underneath. The effect is perfect. We began the descent of the Illinois River on Tuesday, and made for St. Louis.

The first night, I presented myself and my letter of introduction. I was invited to the captain's table for supper that very afternoon. I quickly changed in my quarters, though my attire was still not entirely suitable. Nervous that I might prove inadequate, I wore my sword. I felt flash with the silver sabre cracking my shins.

The guests around the table were distinguished indeed. The first I met was an enterprising Mexican trader by the name of Rodriguez. He had a slight accent and a formal manner, but I liked him immediately. There was a garrulous historian who bragged to us of his Socialist cause and magazine. Rodriguez deftly put him in his place.

Also present is Major McMarrow, with whom your father has arranged for me to travel all the way to Texas. He seems a serious man, perhaps fifty years of age, with thin lips and darkly ringed eyes. He first asked after my occupation and health. He looked upon me as a general would an unfit soldier. Glancing at my sabre, he grumpily suggested I might put away my appetite for blood during a civilized dinner. I was ashamed and had to leave the table quickly to secure the sabre back in my quarters. He must concern himself with appearances as he changed his entire uniform during the course of the evening.

Yesterday Rodriguez told me of a legend that accompanies Major McMarrow. Some years back, he led his troops into a battle In the unorganized territory. Though outnumbered, he was so confident his men would win that he sat reading a book in the saddle, while the battlefield steamed with violence all about him. It was nearly over when some opposing soldier fired at him, dead straight. The musket ball pierced all the pages of his book, coming through the very sentence he was reading, but at such a reduced speed that it bounced harmlessly off his chest. The book is credited with saving his life.

This would all seem fantastical if McMarrow's cargo wasn't also strange: a large cage covered in cloth, which bleats plaintively. Rodriguez thinks it contains a sacred goat. McMarrow will say nothing on the matter. Others on the boat have taken notice, and not kindly.

We are traveling to meet a small unit of soldiers at Fort Osage whose colonel was killed by sickness. McMarrow says protecting me is incidental, as his orders are to escort Mexican and American traders such as Rodriguez along the Santa Fe Trail. I took his statement to mean I should not reveal his arrangement with your father.

Each night, as always, I kiss the phial of your lifeblood. It is worn against my chest, always next to my beating heart. I hope that the doctor has not had to let any more of your precious blood, and that the summer's fever has not returned to anguish you further.

The steamer will remain here at Franklin two or three days to have repairs done, and then we are meant to take back up the river. McMarrow has expressed dissatisfaction with the delay and the captaining of the steamer. This river is not the broad Illinois. We have been pressed by the currents upon numerous planters, sandbars, and snags. It requires considerable effort to extricate ourselves once grounded. The trials attendant upon the piloting of a steamboat on the Missouri are numerous, and I do not envy the captain his position.

This evening I stood silently and looked south, with the setting sun on my right hand. The eventide star, Venus, was sole representative of the wandering stars on this night. She was accompanied by Cygnus, a pet asterism, the tail of Deneb dipping toward the water as though he were diving for a catch. I thought of you in the yard with your father's geese. The tips of houses, buttressed by spruces and bare spots of hill, were silhouetted neatly against the sky.

Did you know I thought of marrying you the first day I met you? Aunt Anne had answered the door and told me Mr. Gray might be found in his office, for my interview. Searching for your father's office, I wandered from finely appointed room to room, entering each with held breath. I was dampening my finest with anxious sweat when I stumbled upon you reading in a drawing room. A winking sun through the window draped dappled light about your shoulders. The moment I saw you, it was as though the sunlight had framed for me my fate.

Do you remember? You marked my presence and held up a delicate hand, fixing me in the doorway. You finished a paragraph in your book and, deftly marking your place with a ribbon, rose with a sigh. You bade me follow and led me down the polished wooden halls to your father's office. You disappeared from sight after that, but never again from my mind. I long for a letter from you, but have had none.

In St. Louis, McMarrow surprised me by asking to see the letter your father gave me. I did not know how to refuse. He took it to his quarters for an hour and then returned with it unopened. I was much relieved to see that it remained sealed, but the anxiety that hour gave me has led me to vow that I will never again part with it for any cause.

He spoke openly of my errand to seek General Edwin 'Speed' Irion. I had thought my mission secret. McMarrow said that the unit he is to command was ordered by the secretary of war to attend to Irion's encampment on the remote Texian-Mexican border. This is his primary objective, my goals matter little. Your father knew of his orders and paid him a handsome sum to allow for my passage with them.

McMarrow now proposes to leave the steamboat behind and perform a pedestrian tour to Fort Osage. I will make a map for you. Given the considerable bend that the boat must navigate, he believes we can arrive before her. This he told myself and Rodriguez tonight in the hall, after we had all dined and partaken of the rough grain alcohol that is all that can be got here. Rodriguez thought it foolish to leave the boat, swift as it is, but agreed to McMarrow's plan. The Major was red in the face, and it seemed unwise to resist him.

Only tell your father that I am well and progressing. The journey's difficulties are between you and me. Also give my fondest to your sister. Read her any parts of my letter appropriate for her amusement. I would guess her introduction to society draws nearer and soon I expect the Gray household will receive a long line of young men with silver pinned to their chests or else lining their pockets. I hope she has the good sense to wait for true love. She is young for fourteen.

Aunt Anne will be a good guide in that, as in all things. Please give my love to her, and tell her that much of what she had seen has already come to be. The fates keep few secrets from her. Also: scratches for the belly of your fine hound. I miss him more than I would have imagined.

Tonight I will lie out on the deck of the steamer for one last look at the stars reflected in the black water. The Dog Star and its attendant heat burn brightly these summer nights. As he trails after Orion's footsteps, so do I, with the aim of following that far lone star all the way back home before snaking Scorpius begins his wintry nipping at the hero's heels. Home, where my heart lies in wait.

With eternal and undying Love, yours,

Zadock Thomas

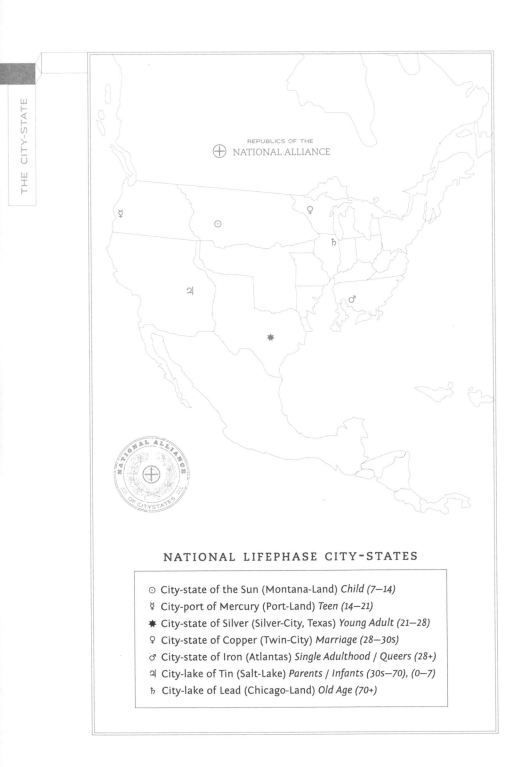

REPUBLICS OF THE
NATIONAL ALLIANCE

NATIONAL LIFEPHASE CITY-STATES

- ☉ City-state of the Sun (Montana-Land) *Child (7–14)*
- ☿ City-port of Mercury (Port-Land) *Teen (14–21)*
- ✳ City-state of Silver (Silver-City, Texas) *Young Adult (21–28)*
- ♀ City-state of Copper (Twin-City) *Marriage (28–30s)*
- ♂ City-state of Iron (Atlantas) *Single Adulthood / Queers (28+)*
- ♃ City-lake of Tin (Salt-Lake) *Parents / Infants (30s–70), (0–7)*
- ♄ City-lake of Lead (Chicago-Land) *Old Age (70+)*

◇◇ ⌇⌇ Zeke rolled over on his floor mat. The room was empty white. Eliza had drawn the shade up to let in the morning half-light. ⌇⌇ "I'm so glad you're Khrysalis," she said. ⌇⌇ **"I haven't accepted yet. But why fight the fates, I guess."** ⌇⌇ She kissed him and said, "Bye forever." He signaled *Bye*. ⌇⌇ He had brought the letter home to Texas. It was in the pocket of his grandfather's shirt, in the closet. He could have asked Eliza to take it down to the Vault to be carbon'd. They'd gladly accept it still sealed. But something stopped him from telling her about it. He reached out from under the covers and pulled the shade all the way down. ⌇⌇

GOODBYE

⌇⌇ Eliza had been a sickly child. Doctors often came and took her to the infirmary. When she was pulled away from her father, she'd turn and tell him "Bye forever." She was only seven. She loved to watch her father's eyes go wide, to trigger that fear. As the doctors wheeled her sickbed from the visitation rooms she'd say "Bye forever" and laugh. ⌇⌇ ⌇⌇ But then her father was suddenly gone, before the lifephase was over. He never came back. Eliza didn't know why. ⌇⌇ ⌇⌇ Her mother had died just a few years before. The lifephase system was not made for anomalies. The seven cities were modified for specific stages of life: childhood, courting, marriage, parenting, and old age. Eliza was prematurely moved from the City of Tin, where she and her parents had lived, to the childhood city, Montana-Land. She was given the last name "Gray," that of orphans. There were more doctors and supervisors there. She clung to her sickbed and cried. But it made no difference. She had to grow up quickly. She learned to follow the rules, to stay in control. ⌇⌇ ⌇⌇

⌇⌇ Now Eliza said "Bye forever" all the time. She needed to believe the phrase held no real power. ⌇⌇ ⌇⌇ It made Zeke's heart leap, just a little, every time. The room was still without her. Zeke's eyes fixed on a seam in the metal wall, perfectly machined. Two unmovable panels of silver-plated iron curved under and met each other with tectonic pressure. He put his finger on the seam and stared. The walls were thick enough for someone to stand inside. ∧∧ ∧∧ Zeke traced the seam up past his head. He let his body follow his finger, and stood to trace the seam all the way around the wall of the bedroom. He kicked through a pile of neatly folded shirts in the corner. He'd have to pick them up later. The small units were hard to keep neat. He angled into his boots while keeping his finger on the line. He followed it around the corner, through the door, out into the livingroom. ∧∧ ∧∧ The seam ringed the entire inside wall. Zeke couldn't imagine how it was made. The plates were fastened from the inside, so there had to be another seam somewhere. A door, a screw to turn, something that would allow one plate to be affixed to another. It was too perfect. ∧∧ ∧∧ He kept his finger on the seam as he climbed over the sofa, around the small end table. The sun lit whorls of lazy dust in his wake. In the kitchen, he saw that Eliza had made his usual breakfast tea. It was mixed with fount-water, which provided all the sustenance and nutrients necessary for survival in the city-state. ∧∧ ∧∧ He reached the front door and pushed against its solid wood with his shoulder. The seam didn't stop at the door frame. He stepped out into the static morning, blinking, in his nightclothes and boots. ∧∧ ∧∧ It was quiet. The air was the same temperature as Zeke's skin. It felt like nothing. The Washers had come last night to scrub all the dust from the buildings. The units lined his block like squat molars, struck sharp white in the sun. They would soon be dirtied again. The weather pylons just outside of the barrier kept out the storms and rain, but they couldn't keep out the dust. ∧∧ ∧∧ ∧∧ He continued around the outside of the unit. The morning light was blinding. He closed his eyes and let his finger guide him along the gently curved wall. He knew the building well. The whole block, even. The seam was the same on the exterior. The metal plate arched up to meet a glimmering cluster of porcelain pressure valves on the roof. They topped each unit like a metal crown on a bone-colored tooth. The streets zagged around him in a honeycomb grid. ⋀⋀ ⋀⋀ Zeke's wall blended into his neighbors' and his seam became theirs. He followed it. A lone steamcarrier clanked down the street. He looked at the splintered wooden plankways under his feet, new and already crumbling. The buildings in this quadrant had three units, which each housed a pair like him and Eliza. The singles lived in another neighborhood. Most left in the morning to work in the industrial quadrant: the great steamworks or laundry facilities. As a Khrysalis, Zeke's life was privileged. He stayed home and read. Even though he no longer wanted the Senate seat. He didn't know what it meant. ⋀⋀ My uses for meaning have somehow died, he wrote with his finger, over the seam. ⋀⋀ ⋀⋀ Recently he had checked out a large illustrated birding book from the Vault. It was old, with hand colored illustrations that seemed almost alive. His favorite part was a section on migration. Birds of all sorts — geese, storks, black-necked grebes — all flew huge distances over mountain ranges and open prairies. Flocks big enough to black out the sky. It sounded impossible to Zeke. Fighting to stay aloft over such great distances. The effort of it sapping the lives of the weaker birds. He imagined the moment of failure, mid-flight, a finished bird falling from the sky like a small white stone. Zeke wanted to know what it looked like. Birds didn't fly over the city-states. The weather pylons kept them out. ⋀⋀ ⋀⋀ ⋀⋀ He traced the seam to his neighbors' front door. It ended there. His mission was pointless. He walked back to his door, glancing up at the city clock clicking in the slanting light. It was late morning and he was outside, dressed in nightclothes, walking in circles around his unit. It was hard to tell if there were Recorders in the watchposts, but if there were his behavior would definitely be noted. ⋀⋀ ⋀⋀ He considered following the seam back to bed. Coming around the curve, he stopped short. ∿ There was a Lawman at his door. His thin red mouth frowned above a brown uniform. The dark rings of a laudanum user hung beneath his pebble eyes. ∿ "Zeke Thomas?" ∿ **"Yeah?"** ∿ "This is a recorded conversation." The Lawman pointed his thumb at the watchpost over his shoulder. It was the one Zeke had smashed with his sabre. ∿ They had found out he cut the power lines, Zeke thought. This conversation would be typed out by a Recorder sitting up in the watchpost, hooked by semaphore lines to a carbon copier in the Vault of Records, printing out every word of his confession in triplicate. ∿ ∿ ∿ **"Understood."** Zeke wondered if the jail was built with the same metal walls as his unit. ∿ ∿ "Identification papers?" ∿ **"They're inside."** The Lawman frowned at Zeke's nightclothes. **"I'll get them for you."** ∿ "Murderer on the loose, can't be too careful." The Lawman pushed past Zeke into his unit. He began lifting cushions and opening drawers. ∿ ∿ Clenching his jaw, Zeke retrieved his identification papers from the desk drawer. The Lawman glanced at them. They disappeared into his uniform pocket, decorated with high-rank insignias. ∿ "Major Daxon, Republic of Texas." He flashed a silver badge. "We received a report of an uncarbon'd document in the files of Zacharyh Thomas. You've got the inheritance bundle. We're opening a thread." ∿ The Major slammed the cupboards, each echoing loudly. Zeke thought of the letter, resting unopened in his grandfather's shirt pocket. The Law knew about it after all. If he turned it over, the Major would probably rip it open on the spot. ∿ ∿ **"My bundle had lots of his letters. But they've all been carbon'd,"** Zeke said. ∿ The Major searched the unit in a lazy, disdainful way. Zeke couldn't tell if he thought the task beneath his standing or if he knew Zeke was lying. He looked up Zeke's ventilation pipe, above the steam heater. ∿ ∿ "You got a license for that thing?" Major Daxon pointed to the sabre on the mantel. ⌇ "You're the record keeper." ⌇ The Major picked up the phonotube and peered down it. The watchposts had hollow tubes into all the units. The Recorders could hear everything, indoors or out. ⌇ ⌇ ⌇ ⌇ "What's this?" The Major pulled a small dropper of laudanum out of Zeke's bottom desk drawer. ⌇ ⌇ Zeke stared. ⌇ The Major slipped it into the front pocket of his vest. "That might go in your thread." He was careful not to say aloud what he had found. The Recorders would hear and he'd have to report it. ⌇ "I have no letter. The file needs to be corrected. As Khrysalis, I order it." ⌇ ⌇ "Hh. That's not official. And no one is above the Law as long as I'm the Major of Texas." He grunted. "I don't have time for this. I've got a loose animal on my hands." ⌇ "An animal?" ⌇ ⌇ ⌇ "A monster ... I mean, a man. An evil bloody killer. Unless you want to implicate someone else, you must produce the letter. You've got a fortnight." His face twitching, he pulled a paper receipt from his vest. "Turn it in by October 24 or you're looking at the cell." Major Daxon dropped the receipt. It fluttered to the floor. He walked out of Zeke's unit, leaving the door open, the cupboards open, the drawers open. ⌇ Zeke closed the door and started to pick things up. Then he remembered the letter and rushed back into the bedroom. It was still there. ⌇ He took Eliza's sewing kit from her bureau. He cut the front pocket off the shirt. He threaded a needle with green thread. Then, turning the shirt inside out, he sewed the pocket to the inside of the shirt. He slipped the letter inside and sewed the top of the pocket closed. The green thread made a little zigzag pattern on the outside of his shirt, but he'd be wearing a jacket this time of year anyway. He carefully reassembled Eliza's sewing kit. ⌇ A Khrysalis wasn't told the secrets of the nation until he entered the Senate. Zeke had never had a secret of his own. It was hard to know how to hold it. ⌇ ⌇ ⌇ ⌇ ⌇ ⌇ ⌇ When the phonotube rang, he jumped. ⌇

RECORD: 1740214

SCRPT DATE: 0010.0010.2143

SUBJECT:
                       ZEKE THOMAS & RAISIN DEXTRA

BEGIN UNIT TRANSCRIPT:

R. DEXTRA » I hate the sun.

Z. THOMAS » Well, there's no escaping it here.

» Unless you can escape the city-state.

» Stop reading that Deserter propaganda.
  As your closest friend: It's fantasy.

» Shhh, man. We're on the phonotube.

» I'd say that's your usual paranoia, but I
  was just visited by a Lawman. So, maybe.

» They have no respect for the Khrysalis?

» They aren't listening. They're short on
  men. They have another murder, besides.

» This animal loose in the city-state?

» That's just a rumor. Though he did say
  something strange...

FLAG ▶ » Plenty of animals in the rot. Plenty of
  folks too. The Deserters are organizing. ‹ DESERTER

» You shouldn't worry about anything
  that's not inside the walls. Remember
  when we were kids in Salt-Lake, they'd
  let those animals in for the fair?

» No. My parents never took me.

» There was a mine game I wasn't allowed
  to play. And the animal show, you could
  see the animals, maybe pet a few.

» I've never seen one.

» It was sort of scary. They had these little
  wooden cabinets with glass doors. I
  remember a rabbit, and a wolf cub that
  kept nudging the door with his nose. I
  was sure he was going to get out, and —

» And do what?

» I don't know, I thought he could possess
me or something.   ‹LAUGHTER

» Don't laugh. I was a kid. I had never seen
animals either. Anyway, we spent the most
time at the goose house. There were six or
seven, in constant motion. Like a... unified
chaos. When one gander looked up, they
all did. Crossing the small pen, they would
all turn at the same time. That weirded me
out, them all moving as one like that.

» Looking for a way out.

» I think it must have taken some nudging
from my mom to get me to approach the
wire mesh. When I was close enough,
the geese slowly circled around to meet
me. They were these spotted brown ones
with golden beaks. They would step, and
peck the ground, and turn their little
black eyes on me, searching for food. I
didn't have any and they would wander
away again, pecking at pebbles, stepping
in time, huddling themselves into a pile
against the side of the goose house.

» They still do this?

» I don't know. Maybe only in Salt-Lake. Or
they banned them completely.

» Too bad. I'd like to see that.

» Probably suits the animals fine. I wanted
to free them that day. There was this one,
a white one, with a tuft of neck feathers

that looked like a scarf or fur collar. He stayed near the mesh, twisting his head, and doing little dances. For my benefit, I was sure. When I moved down the fence, the white goose followed. I wanted so badly to take him home and keep him as a pet. I named him Schmoe.

» Schmoe?

» Hh, yeah. I couldn't take Schmoe home, of course. I was heartbroken. My mother had to drag me out of the fair, inconsolable. I was in love with that goose. Some other fate awaited him.

» I'm sure he found his pair and had some baby geese.

» Goslings. What if he began life as a wild goose? He probably didn't have a choice.

» I don't think I'll ever be paired. I'm going to end up in Atlantas, with the Queers. Which actually sounds like more fun than having kids, to me.

» Leeya still won't talk to you?

» Have you seen her?

» Eliza has. It was better when the four of us could hang out together. You've got to lay off the Deserter stuff, Raisin. That's no way to court someone. If Leeya thinks you're going to flee over the barrier or, more likely, get yourself thrown in jail, why would she want to pair up with you? Or have kids?

» They've got some ideas, the Deserters.
I mean, pretty good ideas. I've been
reading lots of pamphlets. They're going
to build a whole new kind of place,
outside the city-states. If I can get
Leeya out, we can be together and live
free. They say it's beautiful out there. A
natural paradise. All the land you could
want. A real place. None of this being
transferred every lifephase.

5 SECONDS DEAD AIR

» No one knows what it's like out there now.

» The government does. Why aren't
we allowed out? The Collapse was
supposed to have destroyed everything.
Either things are happening out there,
or we're not where we think we are.
They control all the information. Why
did a Lawman just show up at your
place? That's a bad sign, Zeke.

» My grandfather had enemies. This is
just routine harassment.

» So you're not worried about it?

» I'm telling you, Raisin, the best thing to
do in this city-state is to lie low. Wait it
out. Get transferred. The less people pay
attention to you, the better off you are.

FLAG▶ » Well, then we shouldn't be on the   ‹WHISPER
phonotube. They must listen sometimes.

» Let's get a drink at the square soon.

» Yessir, Senator.

END UNIT TRANSCRIPT

LEEYA,

IT FEELS GOOD - THRILLING EVEN - TO HAVE THIS
PENCIL IN MY HAND. IT IS SUCH A SHAME THAT
THE ART OF HANDWRITING HAS BEEN DONE AWAY WITH.
THE YEAR I ENTERED SCHOOL WAS THE YEAR THEY
STOPPED TEACHING IT. MY FATHER DIDN'T THINK
THAT WAS RIGHT, SO HE TAUGHT ME HOW TO MAKE THE
LETTERS AT HOME, S L O W L Y , PATIENTLY. AT
FIRST I WAS FRUSTRATED THAT MY LETTERS WEREN'T
PERFECT. I WANTED MY CORNERS SHARP. I THOUGHT IT
SHOULD LOOK LIKE TYPE.

NOW I LOVE THE IDIOSYNCRASIES OF HANDWRITING.
I'VE EVEN MADE IMPROVEMENTS OVER WHAT I WAS
TAUGHT. LIKE "G" I USED TO WRITE THEM LIKE
THIS: "G" BUT DON'T YOU THINK THIS IS MUCH MORE
CIVILIZED: "G"? I'VE FORGOTTEN ALL THE CURSIVE,
ALL THE LOWER CASE. ALL I HAVE LEFT ARE THE
CAPITALS. BUT I LOVE MAKING THE MARKS. IT
REMINDS ME OF BEING A CHILD, OF SALT-LAKE.

MY FATHER WAS ALSO THE ONE WHO TAUGHT ME
ALL ABOUT DOCUMENTS, OF COURSE. AFTER HE LEFT,
IT DIDN'T HELP ME FIND HIM AGAIN. I LOOKED
UP DEATH RECORDS, BUT NONE MATCHED THE DATE HE
DISAPPEARED. EITHER HE ABANDONED ME, OR HE WAS
THROWN OVER THE BARRIER. I DON'T EVEN KNOW WHICH
I WISH IT WAS. IF HE'S ALIVE IT MEANS HE'S
CHOSEN NOT TO COMMUNICATE WITH ME EVER AGAIN.
EVEN AFTER ALL THESE YEARS, I STILL CAN'T BRING
MYSELF TO UNDERSTAND THAT...

I ONLY EVER KNEW HIM AS "DAD". NO LAST NAME.
THE RECORDS ARE FULL OF GRAYS, w/o A BLOODLINE.

IT'S BAD ENOUGH THAT HE LEFT, BUT HE TOOK MY PAST
WITH HIM. I WAS LUCKY THAT ZEKE DIDN'T CARE.

THE DOCUMENT SKILLS STILL COME IN HANDY.
GOOD THING -DAXON- DOESN'T RUN A TIGHT SHIP AT
THE VAULT. IT SEEMS EASY ENOUGH TO GET THE
CONTRABAND MATERIALS FOR WRITING AND DRAWING.
USING THEM IS ANOTHER MATTER. AS LONG AS WE
DON'T GET CAUGHT. !!!

IT'S THE ONLY WAY I CAN TELL YOU SOMETHING I
DON'T WANT THE RECORDERS TO HEAR: <u>I PULLED ZEKE'S FILE</u>

I TOLD HIM I WAS JUST GOING TO CHECK IF
THEY HAD THREADED HIM TO THE POWER LINES HE CUT
IN FRONT OF OUR UNIT, BUT THEN I ENDED UP READING
MORE THAN I SHOULD HAVE. I FELT SICK WHILE I DID IT.
● A ROCK-HARD PIT IN MY STOMACH ● BUT IT WAS
A COMPULSION THAT I COULD NOT RESIST. IT SEEMS
BEYOND BETRAYAL TO INTRUDE ON HIS PRIVACY WHEN
THE CITY-STATE GIVES US SO LITTLE TO BEGIN WITH
BUT I HAD TO KNOW WHAT IS GOING ON WITH HIM.
EVER SINCE HE RETURNED FROM HIS GRANDFATHER'S
FUNERAL HE HAS BEEN IN A STRANGE STATE. HE
IS WITHDRAWN. IT'S LIKE HE BARELY HEARS MY
QUESTIONS. NOT EVEN MY SINGING CALMS HIM IN
THE WAY THAT IT USED TO.

THEY'VE GOT AN OPEN THREAD ON THE WATCHPOST, BUT
HE HASN'T BEEN LINKED TO IT. WE WERE IN A DEAD
ZONE AT THE TIME. IT FREAKED ME OUT, WHAT HE
DID W/ THAT SABRE. OF COURSE I REALIZE HE IS
GRIEVING THE LOSS OF HIS GRANDFATHER BUT STILL;
IT FEELS OUT OF CHARACTER - AND BEYOND HIS USUAL
MOODS. THOSE I KNOW HOW TO NAVIGATE, BUT THIS...

(TURN OVER FOR TRANSCRIPT →

IS DIFFERENT - AND IT IS SCARING ME. I WAS BEGINNING TO WORRY - PRETTY FOOLISHLY - THAT HE WAS INTERESTED IN BEING A SINGLE AGAIN — THAT OUR PAIRING WAS NO LONGER WHAT HE WANTED. I JUST FEEL LIKE THERE IS **SOMETHING** HE WON'T TELL ME.

I FOUND THIS TRANSCRIPT OF A PHONOTUBE CALL W/ RAISIN. IT'S CLEAR THEY ARE RECORDING OUR UNIT NOW. WE'RE NO LONGER IN A DEAD ZONE. IT IS BIZARRE TO HEAR ABOUT ZEKE'S CHILDHOOD - HE SO RARELY TALKS ABOUT IT WITH ME. IT MADE ME FEEL EVEN MORE DISTANT FROM HIM. LAST NIGHT, AFTER THE WATCHPOST INCIDENT, ZEKE EXPRESSED DOUBTS ABOUT TAKING THE SENATE SEAT. HE'S BEEN NAMED KHRYSALIS, BUT HASN'T ACCEPTED. I KNOW THAT FULFILLING HIS GRANDFATHER'S LEGACY IS IMPORTANT TO HIM. BUT I HAVE MY OWN DOUBTS ABOUT WHAT THE SENATE WOULD MEAN FOR OUR LIFE — AND FOR OUR CHILDREN. WE'RE SO YOUNG, AND WE'D BE TRANSFERRED EARLY, OUT OF THE LIFEPHASE SYSTEM. INSTEAD OF MOVING CITY-STATE TO CITY-STATE WITH YOU, I'D BE STUCK IN CHICAGO-LAND WITH GOVERNMENT WORKERS AND OLD PEOPLE FOR THE REST OF MY LIFE. WE'D MISS THE OPPORTUNITY TO HAVE A REAL FAMILY, TO BE AMONG OUR PEERS. I DON'T EVEN KNOW HOW LONG WE'D BE ALLOWED TO KEEP ANY CHILDREN WE HAD.

~ ZEKE MUST BE WORRIED ABOUT THAT TOO, RIGHT? ~

I AM ALSO FULLY AWARE OF THE ADVANTAGES AND RELATIVE FREEDOM IT COULD AFFORD US. IT FEELS LIKE ZEKE'S DUTY TO HIS GRANDFATHER AND TO THEIR ENTIRE BLOODLINE. WE'D BE IMPORTANT PEOPLE TO THE NATION OF CITY-STATES.

ANOTHER THING FROM THE CALL: RAISIN STILL
WANTS YOU. I WANTED YOU TO SEE THIS. I KNOW
THE PUSH AND PULL WITH HIM IS HARD. HE IS
STILL STUCK ON DESERTING. BUT I DO KNOW HOW MUCH
YOU FEEL FOR HIM. I DON'T THINK HE'S A BAD
FELLOW. WHY ELSE WOULD I ALTER YOUR RECORDS?
REMEMBER, I ALSO WANTED YOU TO TRANSFER EARLY
SO YOU COULD BE WITH HIM. I JUST WORRY THAT
ULTIMATELY RAISIN IS A WASTE OF YOUR TIME
— AND POTENTIALLY DANGEROUS.
   I JUST WANT US TO SURVIVE TEXAS AND BE ON
OUR WAY TO ANOTHER CITY-STATE. I ASKED TO BE
ASSIGNED TO THE THREAD FOR THE MURDER CASES.
THE RECORDS ARE BIZARRE AND DIFFICULT TO DECIPHER
THERE IS A CLEAR THREAT — PARTICULARLY FOR YOUNG
WOMEN. I KNOW YOU'VE DONE SOME OF THE FILING FOR
THAT THREAD. PLEASE TAKE EXTRA CARE.
   SOMEONE IS WATCHING MY WORK, I KNOW. WHOEVER IT
IS USED MY NAMESTAMP TO FLAG A BOOK, SO IT MUST
BE SOMEONE INSIDE THE VAULT. I LOOKED UP THE
BOOK IN THE STACKS — JUST A DUSTY OLD VICTORIAN
NOVELLA. IT'S CALLED The Sisters Gray SO I KNOW
IT'S MEANT FOR ME. BUT IT SEEMS STRANGE.
   - IT HAS A HOLE IN IT.
   I MADE A DRAWING FOR YOU — I HAVE
BEEN WORKING ON SEVERAL OF THESE NOW THAT I HAVE
THIS PENCIL. IT IS SUCH A RELIEF TO DRAW. IT HAS
BEEN A LONG TIME. ANYTHING TO TAKE ME OUT OF
MYSELF, EVEN FOR A MINUTE
   LOVE YOU LIKE A SISTER,
      ELIZA ✳

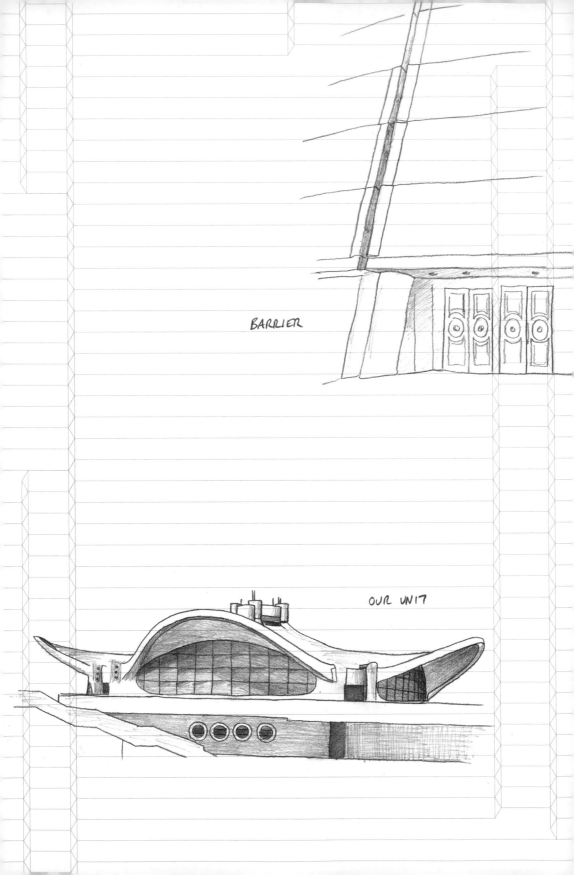

BARRIER

OUR UNIT

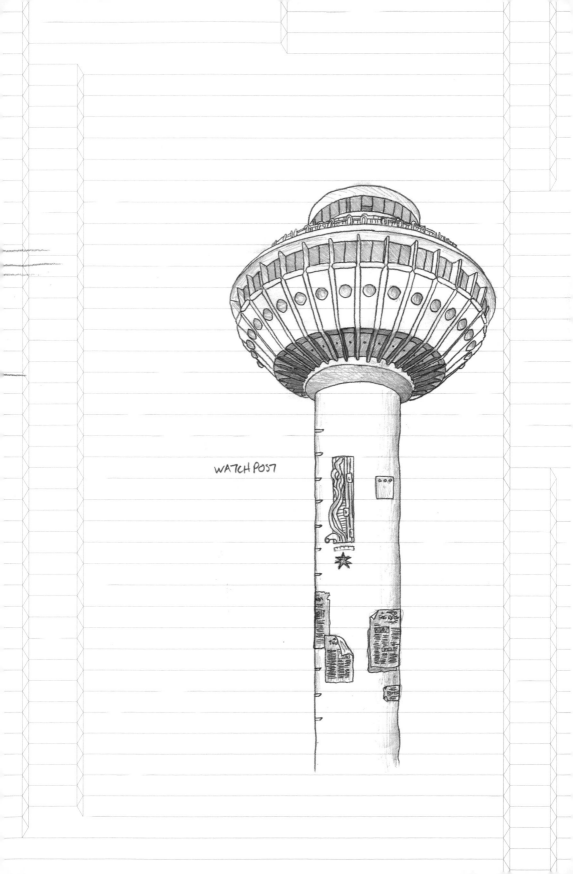

WATCH POST

➤ Eliza, I flagged a book at the Vault, with your namestamp. It is a risk, but I thought you should see it right away. I'm worried there may be a problem. I think the uncarbon'd letter is important.

If the Law wants it, there's a chance it calls Zeke's bloodline into question. I'm building this case for him, for you both, as a precaution. I have the creeping feeling, which only visits old Historians, that there is some key, some small bit of text that would unlock the pattern. Something that would soar beyond a simple summation of fact and yield the bird's-eye view.

Zadock's letters are filled with wide-eyed descriptions and breathless recounting of the excitements of his first journey. Though by the standards of the day, the party's trip down the Illinois was fairly uneventful.

It is difficult to verify historical figures such as the Mexican trader Rodriguez. I have even been unable to find records about McMarrow, though he was a major in the army and seemingly commanded some important battles. It does not help that Zadock muddles his accounts with the prognostications of his spiritual aunt and odes to Elswyth, his love.

I feel I am sifting through useless details. There are gaps. I cannot profess that any artifact is more important than any other. Contradictions are inevitable. The more research available, the clearer the landscape of the past becomes. But detail begets complexity. And the truth becomes obscured.

I hope you will check out *The Sisters Gray* from the Vault and peruse it. I namestamped it for you to find. It looks to be from the turn of the twentieth century. It is, without a doubt, a work of fiction. A flimsy and melodramatic one at that. Nonetheless, pertinent facts may be hidden in the story.

Though you share a last name now, these aren't your forebears, as I'm sure you know. I only wish I could give you the

Bartle family tree. The first I reconstructed, it contains its fair share of characters. This book was authored by "L. W. Gray." This must be a pen name — someone anonymous determined to set down the family stories. It would be better if he or she had stuck to nonfiction. It is overwrought, gossipy, preoccupied with social norms, and dripping with overelaborate illustrations.

The only interesting part is the third, beginning on page 86. The plot concerns the daughters of Joseph Gray. Beyond his initial letter to Zadock, I had not investigated him thoroughly. He now seems worthy of a closer look. I have cobbled together a brief biography from society publications. Business was his main sphere of influence, and though his ventures are well documented, little can be gleaned from numbers and ledgers. He kept no diary and wrote few letters. Here's what I know:

Joseph Sloper Gray arrived in Chicago in 1835 with two daughters, a wife, and her six sisters. He heard of the opening of the Illinois-Michigan Canal and, believing it an opportunity to expand his powder-mill business, he moved to the Midwest. This decision proved wise. Due to the canal, his business boomed. He quickly realized the potential of the new city.

Gray diversified by investing in Chicago-area land. He organized the city's first waterworks and built a pine reservoir in south Chicago. Under his able management, the business grew, riding the crest of the Chicago boom. He opened branches of Gray's Powder Mill in St. Louis and Milwaukee.

He also became a member of Chicago's urban elite. A group of men like Gray, who had come from New England and made their fortunes in the west, dominated city politics and business as well as intellectual and philanthropic endeavors. Gray lent support to a wide array of civic projects, among them the Chicago Historical Society, the Chicago Academy of

Sciences, and the Chicago Relief and Aid Society. The "Prairie Aristocracy," which he was demonstrably part of, was entirely self-selected. The only bar to entry was wealth. Blood counted for little, since most well-connected families remained in the social systems that had been established back east, in New England. In Chicago, anyone who managed to push his way to the top could become a community leader, no polish necessary. This was certainly the case with Joseph Gray, who scaled the ladder with some aplomb. Given that he didn't have a prestigious bloodline, he was certainly looking for upward mobility for his two daughters.

His tours of Chicago for the newly arrived became infamous. Secured in his open carriage, he would regale his guests with lectures about the future of Chicago as he drove his animals wildly through the streets, kicking up dust and disorder.

The north side of Chicago was essentially a forest when he constructed his large home there. He thought the tall elms and cottonwoods gave his estate a rural feel despite its close proximity to the center of the city. The plot of land was soon surrounded on all sides by a rapidly growing Chicago.

The year 1837 brought setbacks. The settlers of Texas had just declared their independence from Mexico. Gray took a marked interest in this revolution. Perhaps he viewed the coming war for the southern territory as a boon for his gunpowder mill. He was distracted by Texas when the national panic of 1837 hit.

Most of his capital was tied up in his flagging businesses. Investors across the world pulled back rapidly and banks went under. Joseph Gray was one of a group of community stewards who were forced to use their own fortunes to prop up the Illinois Bank and issue scrip, a paper money that kept business moving until the economy recuperated. This further depleted his fortune, which had seemed so solid just a few years before. The scrip worked and in the early '40s, when the homesteaders returned to Chicago in droves, the boom resumed. Unfortunately, Gray did not see a return on his investment and his mills continued to struggle.

It was during this time that Joseph Gray turned much of his attention to what would be his obsession for the rest of his life: the Museum of Flying. The first location was the ground floor of his large estate in Lincoln Park.

The Museum of Flying was born of a fascination with the Ark, a natural history museum in Cleveland, Ohio. A visit sometime in the late 1830s to that small wooden building filled with animal specimens ignited an interest in Gray that never subsided. The Museum of Flying was founded in an attempt to establish scientific credibility. Gray was enamored of the adventuring naturalists who went on exploratory missions across the western United States, discovering and documenting new species. He wanted to be included in their circles. He met, and was very taken with, John James Audubon, the famed illustrator, naturalist, and publisher of *Birds of America*.

Gray organized many small specimen-gathering trips around the Midwest, but was never able to leave for long. He had two daughters who were in his sole care.

Joseph Gray married Elizabeth Anderson in 1816, before coming to Chicago. The girls were born after they arrived. Elizabeth died in childbirth along with a third daughter. Gray never remarried, though he looked after his wife's sisters.

Before she died, Gray's wife imparted to their daughters a love of literature. She penned a novel about a fantastical city set far in the future, entitled *The City-State*. It was uncommon for women of her time to write, and even less common for them to be published. Unfortunately, her work was not. The records state that the only copy in existence is housed in the collections of Texas. But I do not think I can travel to your city-state. Running into you would be too dangerous. I won't risk it. It's better that you just read. You'll see what I see in this book.

Gray had trouble attracting as much investment as he would have liked to the odd museum, and finding funding proved difficult. He persisted past the point of reason. He could not seem to apply his business acumen to this particular project. Coupled with his mills' dire straits, the Museum of Flying stretched the family's finances to the limit.

Even so, he spared no expense on the things he built, commissioning custom display cases and tables for his growing collection of specimens. Most of the records that I could find concerning Gray were debtor's notes.

The Sisters Gray paints a less than rosy picture of the great patriarch and his museum. However, the novel provides details that are tempting to incorporate in the historic record, and certainly form my conception of what the man was like.

Be cognizant that its origins are hidden to us. Caution must be exercised in taking what is clearly a novel of manners for a piece of the historical record. Nonetheless, it mentions a Mr. Thomas as a suitor for Elswyth's hand in marriage, and for this reason it is pertinent to Zeke's bloodline. Joseph Gray was the reason for Zadock's journey westward. If only we could separate the facts from the fiction.

I long to talk to you about this book and bloodline in person. But if I speak to you, or even flash a hand signal, they will arrest me. They would if they knew I was writing this. The reasons I had to leave are difficult to explain. Please know it was not because I don't love you. It was never that.

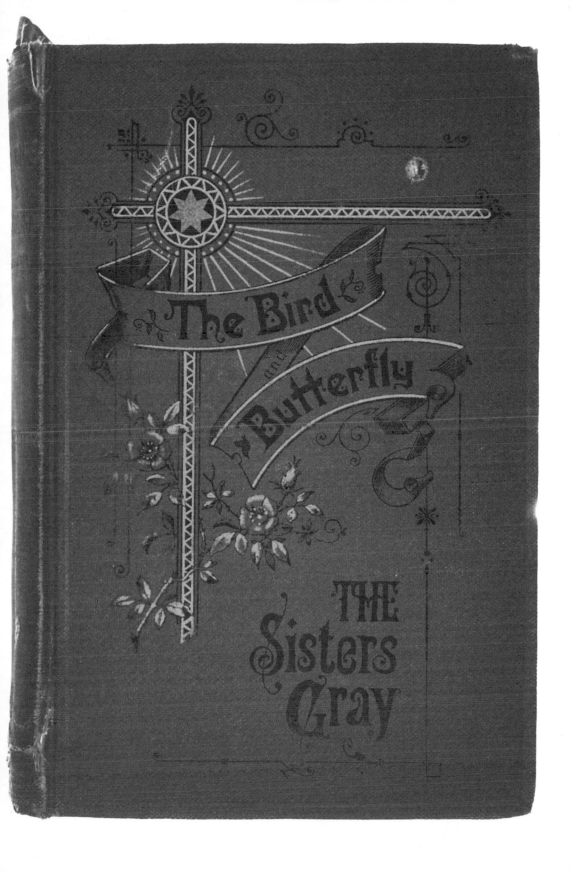

The Bird and Butterfly

THE Sisters Gray

E. GRA̤

H . BARTLE

THE
SISTERS GRAY

* Feebly Fabricated.

L. W. Gray

FAMILUS
DRAMATIS

THE SISTERS GRAY STUDY A BOOK OF BIRDS.
ELSWYTH ADVISES HER SISTER AGAINST
A CERTAIN SORT OF SUITOR.

s daylight waned, the sisters Gray sat on the antique carpet of their father's large library. Elswyth, the elder, held an enormous book open on her lap, and was patiently turning the pages for her younger sister, Louisa.

Verily they both loved the book, nearly as much as their father, Mr. Gray, did. He kept Audubon's *Birds of America* on a large table in the middle of the library room. The table had been specially constructed by the best furniture maker in Chicago for the sole purpose of displaying the enormous volume. Its leaves unfolded like the wings of a majestic bird. Mr. Gray had purchased the new octavo edition with sixty-five additional plates of wondrously illustrated fauna. It was his stated desire to build the museum into a living version of what was depicted upon those pages. Indeed, it had been the museum's first investment, and its most costly. Mr. Gray purchased the book from Mr. Audubon himself, whilst he was in Chicago to secure subscriptions, his daughters anxiously huddled behind him. Every new plate was a thrill.

Before she died, their mother used to read the descriptions to them. She was a writer, and would embellish the beautiful watercolors with finely spoken words. Now older, the sisters had looked through the book many times, often without their father's permission. That morning they had driven to City Cemetery on North Avenue to visit the site of their mother's grave.

'Will you read from Mother's book?' Louisa asked upon their return. She never tired of listening to someone read from the stack of pages that made up their mother's novel.

'*The City-State* is tiresome to read, Louisa, it has too many devices and made-up words.' Elswyth was unsettled after the graveside visit, and besides, she hadn't been able to bring herself to read the novel since her mother's death. It was simply too painful to hear her voice. 'What about *Birds of America* instead?'

Louisa eagerly agreed—she was easy to please—and Elswyth began turning the large pages of the open book.

'Why did you skip the hawk?' Louisa asked.

'His beak is too much like a dagger. And his eyes are stupidly far apart. He rather reminds me of ugly Mr. Buell.'

Louisa frowned. Mr. Buell had been one of Elswyth's suitors. Louisa was fascinated by the idea of suitors, being only fourteen and not yet introduced to society.

'Tell me of courting. I can't wait to play at it.'

'It is no game. I went to a lovely party the other night. There was music and it was quite gay, but I had to remain guarded. There were many men there, but none I would accept as a suitor.'

'Like who?' Louisa clung to every detail when Elswyth told her stories of courtship, and carefully remembered all the names.

'Well, there's Mr. Marback, who goes to all the matinees, but rather than dancing, spends all his time staring at me. I don't speak to him. Mr. Newberry is a midshipman whom I met for the first time. I thought he was twenty-two, but he told me he was twenty-eight, though he still seems like a boy to me. Mr. Clybourn is very refined and fastidious, not to mention exceedingly handsome. He gave me his photograph and the seventh button off the left side of his coat, and a fine green ribbon. And then, a stunning bouquet of white camellias. You can see how he is rather too much.'

'Did you flirt with him?'

'Oh no, I won't flirt, it is a contemptible thing. Some gentlemen run after girls as soon as they are in petticoats and seem to know all the things to say to them. Others are quite indifferent until a certain girl rouses them. That's the kind I prefer. You shouldn't accept too many callers.'

'Just the ones you want to marry. Like Mr. Thomas.'

'Well, Mr. Thomas is a puzzle. He's not a very good caller. To make a suitable husband, he should have either fame or fortune. Or good blood. There is something to him though. Perhaps the only thing to recommend Mr. Thomas is his fine mustache.'

'You like him!' Louisa protested. Elswyth smiled slightly. Her sister continued, 'I'd prefer Mr. Buell.' Mr. Buell had been in their father's employ for many years and often loitered about the house.

'Mr. Buell's persistence is a bit disturbing. He is always looking for an excuse to show off his skill at fencing.'

'I like fencing.'

'Then from your lessons you should know that it's not something to be practiced carelessly. He is too flash about it. Especially when he has been carousing. His cheeks become flush with drink, and he begins to imagine others insult him, dressed in all his fineries. Or perhaps he enjoys the fighting. He is certainly inclined to seek pleasure. He is not the sort to marry. But he would never dare to cross Father. And he keeps some of the other less desirables away.' She turned the page of the oversize book and they looked upon some small snipes attended by reeds.

'He doesn't keep Mr. Thomas away.'

'He is simply employed here as well, not necessarily courting. Courting is only for discovering if someone is suitable. Mr. Buell is more like this snipe here. You see, you must never marry a snipe-legged man. That is not the best sign for a marriage.' Here she channeled her mother and embellished a bit. 'A snipe-legged man is delicate, born of spring's uncertain dew. He is a man who flits about, picks at his food, stares, or is nervous with smiles. These are bad signs. They mean a man is mocked by insecurity, trying to flee himself, driven by distraction.'

'What's a better bird?' Louisa asked, pulling at the corners of the large pages. 'This one? Is he like Mr. Thomas?'

Elswyth read the page aloud to her sister:

The flight of this species is strong, rapid, and greatly protracted. Its movements on wing are similar to those of the oystercatcher and, unless during breeding season, are performed low over the waters. They seldom rise without emitting their usual notes, which resemble the syllables will-wilet, or will, will, willet, and are different from the softer and more prolonged whistling notes which they emit during the pairing season…

'Well, not much, though Mr. Thomas does compose mournful love notes. Maybe no bird at all is better.' Elswyth pulled the book away. 'A bird-man is only happy left to his own devices, building a dirty nest, sharpening his beak on a frozen branch, or picking dark earthworms from the dirt. He can't take notice of the change in season, save to stop singing and pine for warmer climes. He looks always to leave you. Even beside you, he is often gone, called by the morning sunlight dancing on the stream. At

night his heart beats too fast, and he fidgets terribly, anxious for
the pink light dawn.'

'Mr. Thomas is sweet. Why don't you marry him?'

'There might be another with a family to speak of. Louisa,
if you have suitors, then you must be patient. Be particular
about who may ask for your hand. If you marry a bird-man, the
hatchlings he fathers for you will have heads shaped like eggs.'

Louisa giggled at the thought. 'Are there men who are like
moths? Moth-men?' Moths were Louisa's favorite creature of all
the winged denizens of the Museum of Flying.

'I'm afraid not.' Elswyth closed the book. 'Let's read something
else.' She fitted it back into the open drawer, sized to hold the
volume in the custom-made table, closing it carefully away. Their
father was an enemy of shoddy workmanship. He preferred only
the finest, best-made things. If a book was crafted unconvincingly
he would refuse to read it on grounds of aesthetics. Elswyth perused
the rest of the library. Louisa watched her sister count down the
rows of labels. 'Will you teach me how to file the books?'

'One day I'll set down the instructions on paper. As well as
some of my advice on courting. We don't have the bloodline that
other girls do, so we must be perfect in all other ways.'

Elswyth had begun, indeed, to compose bits of advice to
Louisa. She planned to bundle them together and give them to
her sister upon her introduction. Neither of them had a mother
to navigate them through the perplexing wilderness of society.
Their Aunt Anne was reclusive and little help in this regard.
Elswyth thought to compose a set of instructions. She had been
courting a long time, after all. She had a secret hope that her
insights might be astute enough to comprise a book of manners,
could a publisher be found. And if one couldn't, perhaps Mr.
Thomas would do the printing for her. He might learn a thing or

two about how to approach her by proximity to the advice.

'Father's grand donor gala might be your first opening out. Of course, I have to help with the preparations, Father needs it more than ever this year. I hope that the winter plague lets me alone.'

'What should I wear?'

'An excellent question for a lady!' Elswyth knew that Louisa wanted to see the fine things she wore to parties. 'And I am ever the one to ask. Do not let Aunt Anne dress you for a party, ever. You shall be as a twig of wallflower, growing along the cracks, attracting no one but dust. You don't want to be stuck living with Father as long as I have.' They hooked arms and promenaded to Elswyth's large closet, almost a separate room off her bedroom.

Elswyth plucked each individual garment from within and presented them to Louisa, who stood at rapt attention.

'You could wear any to your introduction. This linen dress, over silk petticoats. Or this white nainsook overdress, see the green ribbon under the puffings?'

'Is there one with a mottled pattern?'

Elswyth fetched another. 'Braided hussar? Maybe not a jacket for your first outing. What about this gray silk with black Valenciennes? I wear it with Mother's seed-pearl brooch as a corsage, and you could too, if you promised to be mindful of it.'

'Yes, that one!'

'Or my favorite, green faille silk of the most delicate springtime color, trimmed with white lace. To be worn with a tall whitechip hat, very high, with two large feathers and a little green parrot wing to match. As stunning as can be.'

Louisa ran her hand over the silk.

'What is this?' Elswyth pulled at a loose thread on Louisa's smock-frock. The entire hem had come undone. 'Don't tell me you need playclothes?' Louisa's face dropped. 'You must start acting more like a lady if you ever expect to be one. No more play time. Come along, we'll get some thread and put things

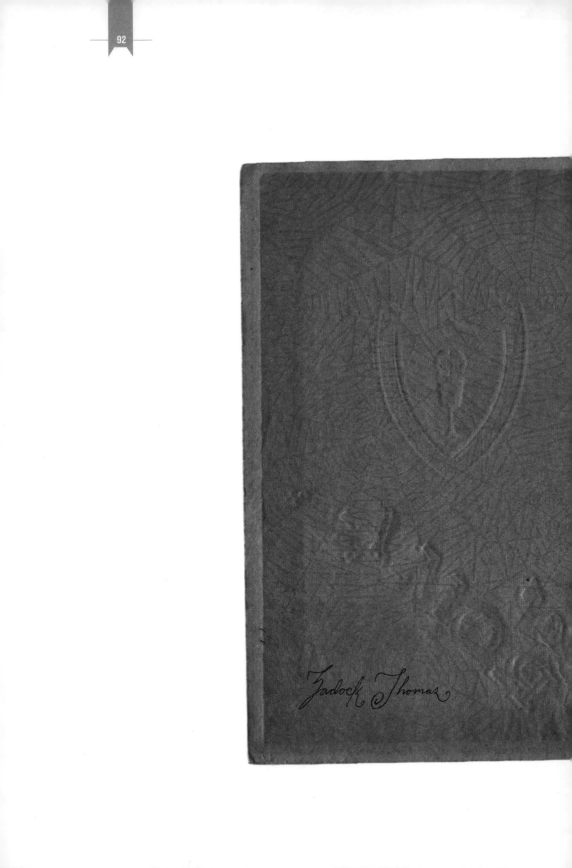

Zadock Thomas

MR. GRAY INSTALLS A BISON. ELSWYTH QUARRELS WITH

HER FATHER. LOUISA BREAKS A CASE OF MOTHS.

MR. BUELL'S CHARACTER IS DEBATED.

ull arms around it, Joseph Gray wrestled the giant bison until they were both standing. It frowned in ingratitude, its fur mangy and terrible. Stuffing overflowed from the seams. I should put him behind glass, Mr. Gray thought.

Louisa was startled when she saw her father that way, holding a furry monster as though they were dancing.

'Father, I can't find Grapes.'

'Grapes?' He wiped his brow with one hand while the other steadied the great behemoth.

'My grayhound. My favorite.'

'Oh, that old thing,' he said. 'You've too many hounds. I'm certain he'll return. That is the nature of a well-fed dog. If his heart does not, his stomach will surely lead him back.'

'He was scared by the thunderstorm. He's been gone a week. I miss him.'

'He's probably out running with other dogs.'

'Will you look for him?'

'Little kid-doe, I have plenty to look after in this buffalo at the moment.'

Louisa stared at the bison dejectedly, keeping her distance. 'Where did that ghastly thing come from?'

'A wealthy historian provided a great deal of money for my museum,' he said. 'Unfortunately he also gave me this buffalo. I'm afraid we have to display it before he arrives for the gala.'

'That's silly in a museum for birds.' The bison's glass eyes were covered in dust and looked quite unconvincing.

'Aunt Anne said he must be installed and we don't question her, do we? Your mother had five more sisters than you, all in league. Can you imagine arguing against six sisters? Mr. Buell helped me haul him up here and promptly disappeared. I'm not quite sure what to do with a buffalo.'

They stood, contemplating the enormous problem in the museum's dedicated display hall. About them were a great many cabinets, cases, and boxes, containing all manner of birds. Mr. Gray himself had selected the matching wood and had overseen the construction of the displays. Some were large enough for ibises, other small drawers were the proper dimensions for rows of ruby-throated hummingbirds.

'He certainly draws attention to himself, doesn't he?' Louisa said. 'Why don't you decorate him?' she proposed. 'If I am unhappy with a room in my dollhouse, I've found simply changing the furniture can do a world of good. Or I just add more people till the room is full, like a wedding party. Maybe he needs a bride?'

'I'm afraid one buffalo is quite enough for my Museum of Flying. We shall have to put up with him. No money arrives without strings attached. I dread what will be foisted upon us at this year's gala.' Mr. Gray sighed. 'Maybe you should run along and look after your missing hound.'

'What if we pin butterflies and moths about him, as though he is just lolling about in a field somewhere?' Louisa asked. She pointed to the moth case, her favorite.

'He looks as though he'd devour all the butterflies of the field,' Elswyth said. She lifted her skirts to step through the small doorway. She hardly glanced at her younger sister. 'Father, may I have a word with you?'

'You should be in bed…' he began.

She cut him off, her voice immediately at a querulous pitch. 'Why ever would you send Mr. Thomas away?'

Mr. Gray smoothed his hair back with one hand, propping up the bison with his other. 'I had a very important errand. He was the one to do it. He is in my employ after all. He is to collect specimens from the western territories. There are many examples this museum is currently lacking. I asked him to…'

'Father, he was my suitor!' Elswyth said. Her face was flush with indignation. Louisa pulled nervously at a ribbon in her hair.

'My dear, calm your voice. He should not be courting you. You've always spurned him. And you certainly didn't fuss when he left.'

'I was ill. How was I to know?'

'Didn't we agree Mr. Thomas was a bit below your stature? I know I have not gifted you girls noble blood, but we have made great inroads in Chicago society. You certainly have a chance at a husband with a good fortune and pedigree. Think of your sister. Think of the Gray name.'

'What should that name mean if I'm only to replace it with another's?'

'Mr. Thomas is not your only suitor. What of Mr. Buell?'

'I refuse to receive him any longer. He is piggish, Father, a leering peccary.' Elswyth's voice was snippish.

'When it comes to the museum, he is to the manner born.'

'To the manor, more to the point. Mr. Thomas is intrepid. He will make his own fortune. You know how he arrived?' She turned to Louisa. 'He made his way quite independently to Chicago by railcar and steamer, walking the last leg himself. When he arrived he had only his muddy boots hung from a stick on his shoulder and a flask of whiskey, to bathe his blistering feet, not to drink. He was carrying his boots so he could look for work the day he arrived. He came straight to the museum.'

'And that is why I chose him for my errand. He is possessed of a dogged determination. But should his character fail in the end, I won't have you made a pauper.'

'I have never spied a silver spoon in Mr. Buell's mouth, though it is often hung open. If he does have money, he certainly doesn't spend it on his clothing. As to noble lineage, he tells stories that are quite fantastical, and that is least amongst the reasons I no longer receive him.'

'If you must marry one of my employees, why wouldn't you choose him? Mr. Buell at least comes from good blood. A much more appropriate choice given his stature here. He understands my endeavor more keenly than any.'

'Then why not choose him to be the honorable errand boy?'

'Because he is of greater use to me here.' Mr. Gray shifted the bison's awkward weight to his other arm. 'About all Mr. Thomas is good for is tinting the pattern plates. He possesses no imagination. Mr. Buell must be the one to draw them, as his skill in that is far superior. Not to mention he can taxidermy, catalog, and set type. If this museum is ever to produce a guide of repute, then he should be the one to oversee it.'

'Mr. Thomas can catalog. He is flighty but entirely loyal to you, Father. He works hard at whatever he sets his mind to. It isn't his fault if he doesn't know how to court me properly. Shall I be courted instead by his portrait?'

'He doesn't know the proper way to do most things. True, Mr. Thomas can catalog, but in the way any common bird watcher might. You, my dear, are a better filer. He has not paid sufficient attention to his studies. He has no great talent for species identification. Mr. Buell is a gentleman and a scholar.'

'A good employee is different from a good husband. And he most certainly is not a gentleman, Father. My fencing lessons are an ordeal. He talks about my form in the most improper way.'

'I like my fencing lessons,' said Louisa. She was fiddling with the latch on the moth cabinet, locking and unlocking it. 'The lightning bug is missing.'

'Don't play with that, dear,' Mr. Gray said. 'Elswyth, you gave me no indication that you were serious about Mr. Thomas as a suitor, and besides, the thing is done. So you'll have to become accustomed to the fact. The task that I need him for is no small matter. In fact, it is essential. To our museum and livelihood both. If he does not…' Suddenly there was a great crash. Elswyth reeled, and the bison nearly slipped from Mr. Gray's grasp. Louisa had pulled one of the moth drawers out too far, and it came loose from the cabinet and crashed to the ground, shattering the glass.

She stood helplessly, tears pooling in her eyes. Her feet were surrounded by shards of glass and bent moth wings.

'Elswyth, come hold this blasted buffalo,' Mr. Gray shouted. She hurried over to replace him as the specimen's prop. Mr. Gray took three loping steps toward Louisa, then lifted her free of the glass with some effort. 'You are trouble, kid-doe. You help your sister hold the buffalo and I'll run and fetch the broom.' Louisa put one hand on the bison's knee and wiped her cheeks with the other. Mr. Gray hurried off.

Louisa mournfully peered out of the great display windows onto the boulevard outside. Her sister huffed. She loved summer in Chicago, especially the tree-lined street on which the museum was located. The branches moved placidly in the breeze, and she wondered to herself why her father should want to spend all his time indoors stuffing musty birds when the ones outside were bursting forth with songs of life. He said Chicago was being built too hastily. He found the whole business shoddy. Elswyth would often echo this complaint, if he passed through a room where she lay, draperies drawn. Hay fever was her excuse for never venturing out-of-doors.

'You should try and grow up a bit,' Elswyth said to her sister. 'Have some grace. You are always destroying things.'

'No I'm not.' Louisa stopped sniffling to scowl at her sister and the bison both.

'You are so. Just this morning I found a fingertip cut from my gardening gloves. Who do you suppose did that? We treat things properly in this house. You heard Father. His fortune isn't endless.'

'My doll needed a bathing cap.'

'A doll's bathing cap? Simply absurd.'

'What am I supposed to do until Father finishes building my room? I'm bored.'

'You might come downstairs and spend time with the living versions of us, rather than manipulating dolls in your little dramas. You can't go on playing at that. You're too old to waste all the hours of the day moving pretend people about.'

'I like my dolls. Maryposa was going on an adventure, and needed to look modest in case they had to ford a river.'

'You don't bathe in a river.' Elswyth straightened Louisa's plaits, one of which had started to come undone. 'Father put the museum right near Lake Michigan so we could go and bathe when it pleased us. You should do that instead of making up stories about rivers.'

'I'm sorry I cut your gloves.' Louisa looked as if she might cry again.

Elswyth sighed. 'It's fine, don't be a tittymouse. Put both your hands on the buffalo. It's heavy.'

Louisa did as she was told. 'It's just making up stories. Like Mother did. Soon Maryposa is adventuring to the west with Wild Zed Blackfoot.'

'And who, pray tell, might that be?' Elswyth's arm ached terribly from holding up the bison. She leaned her back against it instead, pressing her feet into the floor.

'Wild Zed lives in Texas Territory and he's twice as tall as any man, but skinny enough to sleep in a log, and he can talk to all the animals, and knows their language, and birds make nests in his hair…'

'Where on Earth did you hear this nonsense?'

'Mr. Buell told me all about him and his deeds.'

'You shouldn't listen to that man's foul stories. I'm quitting my fencing lessons as of this minute. I certainly don't have to see that boar, much less entertain the idea of marrying him. Don't tell Father.'

'Mr. Buell says we don't always have to fence at fencing time. And instead sometimes he tells me about Wild Zed and how he met him and went on trips too, and how Maryposa and I could go too because every gentleman needs a companion, even Wild Zed Blackfoot.'

'At least Mr. Thomas can be believed.'

'We talk about our adventures together, and sleeping under the stars, and meeting all of the animals of the world and speaking to them in their language…'

'Stop all this nonsense. Louisa, you mustn't indulge in fantasies. Life is about making do. All we have is the blood we are born with. Father is trying to be practical. He is just too stubborn to see. We don't have to marry whom he chooses. We simply must tolerate his interference. There are other ways we might change our circumstances.'

'Mr. Buell is nice. Besides, you don't like any men. You said Mr. Thomas was a bird-man.'

'That's entirely different. You and Mr. Buell ought to stick to fencing. Quiet. I hear Father.'

Mr. Gray returned with a broom and began to clear away the mess. 'That buffalo shall have to go to the workroom until I can stabilize him. I've got to get him prepared and behind glass before the gala, or I shan't receive donations of any kind anymore.' He coughed into a cloud of dust. 'I don't think young women will be allowed in the museum display room anymore, either, until it is complete,' he said. His voice was not unkind.

The sisters looked down with shame.

'This buffalope smells horrid,' said Louisa.

ELSWYTH VISITS HER AUNT. A DARK PROPHECY IS
FORETOLD. ELSWYTH REFUSES THE LIFE OF A SISTER.

 Elswyth knocked repeatedly on the door to her aunt's cottage. It had been converted from a coach house when Aunt Anne had come to stay with them. Elswyth's father needed help after his wife died. Her sister had been kind enough to volunteer for the duties, which seemed temporary at first but became more fixed by the day. It was as though Mr. Gray took orders from his wife's weird Sisters, doing only their bidding.

The converted coach house was a perfect example. The carriage was in the street, and Elswyth didn't know where it would be kept come winter. Aunt Anne had made herself quite at home in the coach house. Being an Auspex and a vestal woman, she had resolved to live separately from any house in which a man also resided.

Elswyth did not like disturbing the cottage. Her aunt did not care to be bothered. Besides, she had filled the little room with a menagerie of the strange and vile.

After much shuffling about inside, the door creaked open, a strange smile stretched on her aunt's face. It quickly dropped away when she saw the state Elswyth was in.

'Why dear, please come in. Whatever is the matter?'

Elswyth hurried into the darkened room and perched at the rough wooden table. Stale air hung low in the cottage. She took small whistling breaths to keep from bursting into tears.

'Do you think Mr. Thomas will write?' She twisted her hands around one another. 'Am I to die an old maid?'

'I'm surprised he hasn't already. I'll make some tea. Let's see what can be done.' Aunt Anne removed her withered hand from her niece's back and reached up into her shelves of ranged jars and canisters. They contained the most curious preparations. Some were labeled: ginger, holly, tar, castor oil, horn of toad, spirits of wine, even goose feathers, all preserved in glass jars.

Aunt Anne had seemingly carved two round holes in either side of the coach house for ventilation. She removed one of the wooden slides now, which let in a modicum of light. It allowed her to find the jar of tea. She set some to steep in a pot of water.

'Would you like a bit of batty-cake with your tea?'

'I could stand never to eat again.'

'For dinner tonight I have rabbit, fried potatoes, and strawberries. Surely you can't refuse such a meal as that?' Aunt Anne set two tin cups down at the table and adjusted her spidery shawl around her shoulders. 'My child, I desire to be a comfort to you in this, but I must speak plainly: I share your anxiety for his return.'

Elswyth sat up at this pronouncement, tugging at her sleeve. 'Can you augur news of him?'

'It's true he came to see me before he left, and I sent my soul out walking ahead to learn what I could from the fates.'

'And what did you see?' Elswyth had little patience.

'I met a soul, a strange girl of the wild lands to the west, and she foretold grave dangers for our poor Mr. Thomas. War, injury, snake-storms, all manner of calamity, the half of which I could not bring myself to tell him. It all blended together, as in a nightmare, and my own clairvoyance was clouded by the ways of this girl.'

'A girl existing in your head?'

'In my alchemy.' Aunt Anne's voice diminished to a serious rasp. 'When I finally wrested my own thoughts back, in a flash I saw one of the bristling Beasts of Revelation, his black jaws round Mr. Thomas's throat.'

'Religion is not what I need at the moment, I do believe.'

'You have the blood of my Sisters, Elsie. The vision runs through our family. It only requires cultivation. Now is the time, when change is afoot. I think you ought to return to your mother's book and read what is written there.'

'I have. Many hundreds of times.'

'Sometimes it matters most when you read a thing. *The City-State* concerns the future of this family's bloodline. Before you are wed you need to read it more deeply. Your mother wrote it for you. Your path is contained in those pages. I've seen it.'

Elswyth frowned. 'I'm envious of those who believe in dreams, presentiments, and ghosts. How much meaning is afforded them.' She had become haughty. 'I should attend to my writing.'

Her aunt held up a bony hand, 'You should not refuse signs just because they don't agree with your whims. Perhaps you need to be bled again.'

'I'm quite sure I'll be fine.' Elswyth gathered up her skirts and made for the door. A sliver of sunlight cut through dust and lit her aunt, crouched blinking at the table. 'I must practice my speech for the patrons at the gala. I think my topic should be marriageable daughters and the price they might fetch by standing upon a stage finely dressed.'

'Elswyth, your father has designs for all things. You can turn your nose up at my tea leaves, but Mr. Thomas may not return.'

This proclamation halted Elswyth. She returned and alighted again at the table, now worried by the thought of her father's uneven scheming. His best-laid plans often went wrong.

'How can you be sure he will not?' she finally asked.

'We could send a blackbird as a messenger, and perhaps learn that way. If you are disinclined toward ghosts, I trust you would not want one as a husband. I imagine we share an opinion about the desirability of the suitor your father suggests?'

'He thinks Mr. Buell has some manner of charm.'

'Only that which a man employs against a woman. He implies that she is the single person in society in whom he is supremely interested, only to twist her heart out upon marriage.'

'I don't believe any of his stories about his bloodline.'

'It seems your father is quite taken with them.'

Elswyth sat silently. A chill shook her. Aunt Anne fetched another one of her ancient shawls to put round Elswyth's shoulders and, picking at the corners, sat beside her.

'All my Sisters were your age once, and your mother was the only one to find a man suitable for marriage. She was lost in the fancy of writing books till Mr. Gray captured her imagination. And her heart.' She gave a little pat on Elswyth's arm to encourage her to drink more tea. 'The rest of us had to find another way. That's how the order was formed. We became Auspices.'

Elswyth had been to the Auspicium many times as a little girl, and it always gave her an ominous dreadful feeling. It was like a convent but with a pall cast over it. Her mother would take her and Louisa to see all their aunts, but Elswyth knew, even as a child, that she did not care to visit those dark halls for very long.

'Leave these endless tracasseries with your father behind. You are no longer a child, and should think on the future of your own blood. Devote yourself to your soul, that it will remain ever pure, and the profanities of this mortal coil will be as dust to you.'

Elswyth clenched her toes in her day slippers. Talk of eternity churned her insides in a most unsettling way.

'We are preparing an elixir at the Auspicium, a holy water that changes the soul and preserves for the end of days. The end prophecies cannot touch those whose blood flows with the waters of the true way. For them there is no end, only change. We have guarded the Auspicium for those like you...'

Elswyth had heard the conversion speech for nearly the entirety of her life. She hastily threw off the shawl and took up again her indignant mantle.

'Shall I allow everyone to tell me what to do? If only I were in need of a master rather than a suitor, a saved soul I would be.'

'You ought to braid that anger into your hair. The task would remedy your idle hands as well.'

'I won't idle in this place much longer.' Elswyth spat out her words bitterly and left them hanging in the cottage. She skittered back up the stone path to her father's great house, a jay noisily mocking her as she went.

Alone in her room she felt sorry for her rudeness to her aunt, who had only been trying to show her a kindness. But she would not read her mother's book again. It held no answers. Aunt Anne's words set fire to a fear within Elswyth. She *had* waited too long.

Most marriages seemed uncomfortable arrangements for the convenience or benefit of others. That she should be an exception to the general rule seemed exceedingly improbable as her count of years increased. She loved Mr. Thomas, but he satisfied none of the other conditions for marriage.

There were few people with the ability to feel love, and fewer still who did indeed feel it, and fewer than that who found their great love returned in equal measure. Could it be that all this had

PLATE 7. WILD ZED BLACKFOOT, OF THE REPUBLIC OF TEXAS

and the profanities of this mortal coil will be as dust to you."

Elsyth dug her toes in her dry slippers. Talk of eternity churned her insides in a most unsettling way.

"We are preparing an elixir at the Auspicium, a finer water that changes the soul and preserves for all eternal days. The end prophecies cannot touch those who bless their way with the waters of the true way. For them there is no such change. We have guarded the Auspicium for these …

Elsyth had heard the sanctimonious speech for nearly the entirety of this lifephase. She twisted … off the stand and took up again her indignant mantle.

"Shall I allow everyone to whisper me to do? If only I were in need of a master rather than a … would I be."

"You ought to tend this … ere long. The task would remedy your idle hands to …

"I won't idle in this … longer." Elsyth spat out her words bitterly and … to … tarrying in the cottage. She skittered back up the … to her father's great house, a joy nearly mocking her …

Along in her prayers … her tenderness to her aunt, who had only been nothing but a kindness. But she would not read her beloved … 's doleful answers. Aunt Anne's words set too tangled a … Elsyth. She had waited too long.

Most parents secure considerable arrangements for the convenience of … positioning. That she should be an exception in the … she seemed exceedingly improbable as her chance of … she loved Mr. Thomas, but he lacked some of the … tenderness for pairing.

There were few people with the ability to feel love, and fewer still who dedicated … to it, and fewer than that who found their great love in magnified equal measure. Could it be that all this had

PLATE 7. WILD ZED BLACKFOOT, OF THE REPUBLIC OF TEXAS

◇◇ ⌢⌢ Zeke paced inside the unit. Every few minutes he found himself back at the closet, checking to see if the shirt with the false pocket was still there. A circular, looping migration. His grandfather lived for eighty-four years without opening the letter. Zeke had only had it a few days. Perhaps he didn't have the strength of his ancestors. He wanted laudanum. The Major had taken his last dram. All day he had thought of calling Eliza at work. He pictured her at her desk outside the long hall with giant sliding doors that led to row after row of metal filing cabinets. Transcripts of conversations arriving constantly from the Recorders in the watchposts. Namestamped and put away by tired Filers. The history of the city-state. Artifacts from the Collapse. The smell of ink and paper. The sounds of clacking typowriters. ⌢⌢ Eliza did well there. She was a diligent, clever Threader. Leeya was still only a Filer. Finally, he heard the soft latch of the front door. ⌢⌢ ⌢⌢ ⌢⌢ ⌢⌢ ⌢⌢ ⌢⌢ Eliza found Zeke in the bedroom and kissed his mustache hello. ⌢⌢ "I have a date with Leeya at the square. I've got to rush so we can get home before nightfall." ⌢⌢ She turned a freckled shoulder to him, to slip off her workclothes. ⌢⌢ **"Don't leave me."** He dropped to his knees in mock protest. ⌢⌢ Eliza stroked his hair. Her fingertips were rough, scabbed over from where they pricked her each day. A blood ID was required to enter the Vault. Zeke hated how it marred her otherwise perfect hands. ⌢⌢ "Leeya needs me." ⌢⌢ **"Leeya needs another boyfriend."** ⌢⌢ "Be nice. Raisin hurt her." ⌢⌢ He watched her put on a white linen frock and brown boots. Her movements were delicate, precise. She picked out a fan to match her fashionclothes. It would be dusty at the square. ⌢⌢ "I've got to call her." ⌢⌢ ⌢⌢ In the livingroom she uncapped the speaking end of the phonotube and stopped. "What's this?" She handed Zeke the tube. A damp paper note was rolled inside. It had been steam-blasted through the tube. The note was typowritten. An original, not a carbon.

```
Z,
You don't know me, but I am
anxious to talk to you after
grandfather's death.
A note for me could be
slipped into file#2477044
at the Vault of Records.

Utmost discretion required.
```

He rolled the note back up and Eliza took it from him. "What is this, Zeke?" ⌃⌃ "Paper. We've got to destroy it. I wish fire wasn't banned here." Eliza cautiously picked up his hand. "I'll soak it instead. The waterroom." He started in that direction, but Eliza didn't let go of his hand. ⌃⌃ "What is this about, Zeke?" ⌃⌃ He sighed. "A letter. Uncarbon'd." ⌃⌃ ⌃⌃ "What's in it?" ⌃⌃ ⌃⌃ ⌃⌃ ⌃⌃ ⌃⌃ ⌃⌃ ⌃⌃ ⌃⌃ ⌃⌃ ⌃⌃ "I don't know. It was part of my grandfather's bundle." Zeke looked out the window. The phosphor lamp at the top of his sabotaged watchpost flickered green. It hadn't been repaired. ⌃⌃ ⌃⌃ "When are you going to accept the Khrysalis?" ⌃⌃ "I have to decide what to do about the letter first. My grandfather may have been trying to tell me something about the Senate. Or it could be a test." ⌃⌃ "There's already an open thread on the power lines you cut. And now you've got an uncarbon'd document? Zeke, I'll lose my job. You'll lose any chance of carrying on your bloodline." She was upset, sputtering. "I'll help you. We'll take it to the Vault. You didn't know it was uncarbon'd, right?" ⌃⌃ "I want to keep it." ⌃⌃ ⌃⌃ ⌃⌃ At this Eliza stopped her questions. Zeke sucked in a breath. He felt surprised at the strength of his own statement. ⌃⌃ ⌃⌃ ⌃⌃ "The murders make everything dangerous, Zeke. You don't know how Major Daxon operates. If he can't find someone to arrest soon, he'll just go through the open threads and pick someone as a scapegoat.

I've heard stories about him. He'll lose his job if he doesn't produce a culprit. The victims have all been young girls, newly arrived to the city-state." ∿∿ **"How do you know that?"** ∿∿ ∿∿ ∿∿ "I ... I asked to be assigned to the murder thread." ∿∿ **"What! Why?"** ∿∿ ∿∿ "Whoever is really doing this needs to be caught." ∿∿ **"And you're telling *me* to keep a low profile?"** Eliza sat down and folded up her fan. Zeke could see her thinking. ∿∿ ∿∿ ∿∿ ∿∿ "Why don't you turn in something else?" Eliza said. "I can steal some paper and a pen from the Vault. An envelope." ∿∿ ∿∿ **"They might already know what's in it. The Major was looking for it. He issued me a deadline."** ∿∿ "Daxon was here? In our unit?" There was a violent knock at the door. Zeke and Eliza looked at each other in panic. ∿∿ ∿∿ Eliza moved slowly to open the door. Zeke shoved the note deep into his pocket. ∿∿ ∿∿ ∿∿ ∿∿ It was Bic. He wore full Republic regalia and a pouting sneer. ∿∿ ∿∿ "Congratulations, cousin." Bic's tone was snide. He wouldn't look Zeke in the eye. "Ready for the ceremony?" ∿∿ ∿∿ Zeke looked blankly from Bic to Eliza and back. ∿∿ ∿∿ ∿∿ "They're unveiling the statue tonight," Bic said. ∿∿ Eliza turned to Zeke. "Now I have to cancel with Leeya?" ∿∿ ∿∿ Zeke's shoulders dropped. ∿∿ **"I completely forgot. I'll be ready in ten."** He flashed Eliza a hand signal to follow him, but she ignored it. He walked into the waterroom to splash some water on his face. ∿∿ ∿∿ "Don't you ever read the broadsheets?" Bic called after him. "You would think a Khrysalis would pay attention." ∿∿ From the waterroom Zeke could hear Eliza trying to make polite conversation with Bic. Her voice was edged with anxiety. "Bic, have you been courting anyone sweet lately?" ∿∿ "I meet a lot of girls. They're all eager to be paired when they meet me. Attractive girls. But I have to think about more than just that, you know? I have to be certain that my pair has good blood in her veins." ∿∿ ∿∿ ∿∿ Zeke hurried so Eliza wouldn't have to listen to

FOLLOW

the blustering. Bic's talk would hurt her feelings. In the bedroom, he opened his closet. The letter was still safely sewn in its pocket. ⌃⌃ ⌃⌃ He pulled out his Republic fineries. When he was younger he was made to attend functions of the city-state with his grandparents. His disdain for the events extended to the stiff brown uniform with its overwrought piping and silver detailing. He attached the armband signifying the rank of Khrysalis to his sleeve. ⌃⌃ ⌃⌃ He reemerged in the livingroom in the wrinkled uniform, smelling of mothballs. He removed his grandfather's sabre from the mantel and slid it into its scabbard. ⌃⌃ ⌃⌃ "I'm sorry," he said, touching the hilt absentmindedly. ⌃⌃ "You look kitted to slay the beast of the Republic," Bic jeered. Zeke and Eliza didn't laugh. ⌃⌃ "The murders are being committed by a man," Eliza said. ⌃⌃ "How would you know?" Bic scoffed. "Man or beast, the second they get their hands on the murderer they'll throw him over the barrier. There's no room in jail. I for one can't wait to watch the brute run from the city-state and get cooked alive by the steammoat." ⌃⌃ "I guess I've got to change again." Eliza stood. She walked past Zeke into the bedroom without meeting his eye. ⌃⌃ "I want to wear the sabre for today's ceremony." Bic pointed. "You always get to wear it." ⌃⌃ "It's mine." ⌃⌃ "The birthright belongs to both of us, Zeke. You already got Khrysalis." ⌃⌃ "Not officially. And the sabre belongs to me." ⌃⌃ "Just let me wear it." Bic's tone sharpened. "Just this once." ⌃⌃ ⌃⌃ Zeke didn't want to have this argument with his cousin. ⌃⌃ "Blood/ Air/Water for it?" It was a simple game to decide on things. They had used it often as boys. Zeke wouldn't have suggested it without knowing he would win. Blood was always Bic's first shot. They tapped their palms three times, and then flashed the hand signals. The results were just as Zeke thought. He would wear the sabre. ⌃⌃ ⌃⌃ Eliza emerged in her fineries. She pulled all the windows closed, and they left the unit. Bic stayed a few steps behind, glowering.

THE CITY-STATE

BLOOD / AIR / WATER
OR HOW TO DECIDE THINGS

Each player shall tap their fist three times on the flat of their open palm, and then on the fourth strike reveal their gestures simultaneously with their opponent. The winner is decided according to the following system:

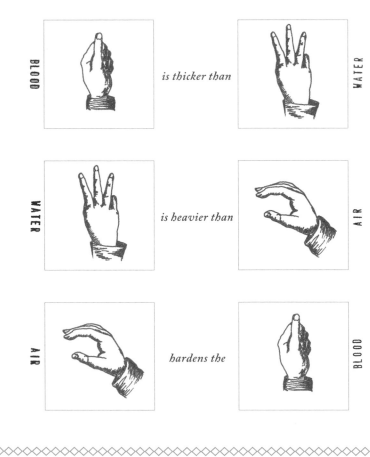

⌃⌃ ⌃⌃ ⌃⌃ ⌃⌃ ⌃⌃ ⌃⌃ ⌃⌃ ⌃⌃ ⌃⌃ Senator Zacharyh Thomas was having a statue dedicated in his honor after his death. ⌃⌃ ⌃⌃ The ceremony was in the industrial quadrant next to the steam-distributor building. It was a dusty, uninhabited part of town. The only people who ventured into the southwest quadrant were those assigned to the steamworks, the clocklike machines that kept the phosphor lights glowing and provided power to the city-state. ⌃⌃

⌃⌃ ⌃⌃ The Thomas statue was being erected in the city-state of Texas because it housed Zeke's grandfather's pet project, the Vault of Records. Zeke suspected Major Daxon decided the statue would be erected in the industrial quadrant. Not exactly the location of highest honor. Zeke would have preferred it in front of the Vault, but that was Daxon's seat of power. ⌃⌃ ⌃⌃ ⌃⌃ Three times the height of a man, the statue was covered in an expanse of white cloth, which twisted impatiently in the wind. It looked like a giant ghost trying to flee even though its feet were melted to the floor. ⌃⌃

⌃⌃ ⌃⌃ The participants slowly filed in, filling the rows of chairs that had been set up for the ceremony. There weren't many folks there. The city-state had been on edge and night was about to fall. Normally Zeke would stand at the front left of such ceremonies, with the other Khrysalises. But tonight he stood on the right, for family. Presently Bic filed down the line as well, blatantly eyeing the ladies. One snapped up her fan to shield her face. Bic stopped in a spot next to Zeke. ⌃⌃ ⌃⌃ "Some fine specimens here tonight." Bic smoothed down the front of his uniform. Sunset light sliced off of the silver medals on his chest. ⌃⌃ ⌃⌃ Zeke glanced at Eliza. She was standing with the other women in the row behind them, beautiful in fine dress. Formal events made her uncertainty about her social status more acute. She had been silent on the way over. He couldn't catch her eye. ⌃⌃ ⌃⌃ ⌃⌃ The light seemed anxious to disappear. Dust snaked through the air, coating everything. ⌃⌃

Zeke squinted, both from the glare of the low sun and to keep the dust from stinging his eyes. ∧∧ ∧∧ The master of ceremonies hobbled up to the podium on the hastily constructed stage. He began droning through a loudspeaker in front of the statue. ∧∧ ∧∧ ∧∧ The remaining six Senators shuffled onstage. Then one by one, like stars appearing in the night sky, the Auspices began to gather around the statue's feet. They took their places so subtly that Zeke hadn't seen any single one arrive. Their long black robes and shrouded faces were ominous. The Sisters shunned the stage and Zeke felt their strange energy ripple through the crowd. ∧∧ ∧∧ ∧∧ Bic leaned over and whispered hotly in Zeke's ear, "Just promise me one thing. If you take the seat, get rid of those creepy witches." Zeke shifted uncomfortably in his uniform. His Republic-issued boots still weren't broken in. "Now that Gramp is gone, you should refuse Khrysalis. If you gave it up, you wouldn't have to do this stuff." Zeke just watched the stage. ∧∧ ∧∧ ∧∧ "We both know you don't even want it," Bic said. Finally Major Daxon took the stage. He had cleaned himself up for the event. He gave curt nods to each of the Senators as he passed them. He did not acknowledge the Auspices. ∧∧ ∧∧ ∧∧ "You receive any ... strange notes lately? Through your phonotube?" Zeke asked Bic. ∧∧ "You mean on paper?" Bic snorted. ∧∧ "Yeah." ∧∧ "That's illegal." ∧∧ "I know, just —" ∧∧ The note was strange. Eliza could look up the file number at the Vault, but it could be a trap. ∧∧ "You ought to be paying attention. The Law is about to speak. These weak old Senators should listen as well." ∧∧ ∧∧ ∧∧ Just as Daxon reached the podium, he met Zeke's eye in the front row. Looking away he then launched into a gravelly harangue. ∧∧ ∧∧ "The nation now enters a new era. We are thankful for all of the founding Senators' efforts and intentions but the coming generation will be the ones to realize their grand plans. We must repopulate. This requires strict adherence to the lifephase system, and an increase in security to make sure the fruits of our labors are not taken from us or left to rot. Atlantas has been plated in iron, the strongest barrier yet. But we must not give over its control to Queers and degenerates. All of our resources must go to perpetuating the generations." 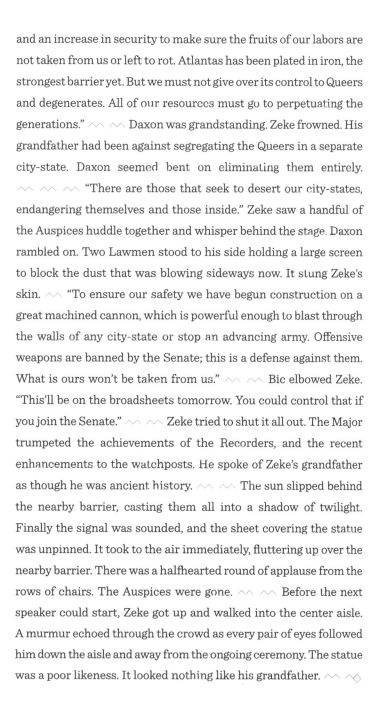 Daxon was grandstanding. Zeke frowned. His grandfather had been against segregating the Queers in a separate city-state. Daxon seemed bent on eliminating them entirely. "There are those that seek to desert our city-states, endangering themselves and those inside." Zeke saw a handful of the Auspices huddle together and whisper behind the stage. Daxon rambled on. Two Lawmen stood to his side holding a large screen to block the dust that was blowing sideways now. It stung Zeke's skin. "To ensure our safety we have begun construction on a great machined cannon, which is powerful enough to blast through the walls of any city-state or stop an advancing army. Offensive weapons are banned by the Senate; this is a defense against them. What is ours won't be taken from us." Bic elbowed Zeke. "This'll be on the broadsheets tomorrow. You could control that if you join the Senate." Zeke tried to shut it all out. The Major trumpeted the achievements of the Recorders, and the recent enhancements to the watchposts. He spoke of Zeke's grandfather as though he was ancient history. The sun slipped behind the nearby barrier, casting them all into a shadow of twilight. Finally the signal was sounded, and the sheet covering the statue was unpinned. It took to the air immediately, fluttering up over the nearby barrier. There was a halfhearted round of applause from the rows of chairs. The Auspices were gone. Before the next speaker could start, Zeke got up and walked into the center aisle. A murmur echoed through the crowd as every pair of eyes followed him down the aisle and away from the ongoing ceremony. The statue was a poor likeness. It looked nothing like his grandfather.

➤ Eliza, these letters will come to you when I'm dead. They can't arrest me then. Before that happens, I'm determined to read all of Zadock's letters. I hope you will too.

As his western journey continues Zadock's letters become more fascinating. The traveling party was well received in an Indian village, and remained there for three days. Zadock made notes on the tribesmen. There were no women among them. Based on their location, and his description of them, I believe they were the Konza tribe. He tried to ask questions about the animals used for their skins and feathered dress. He attempted drawings of the warriors and their garb. Strangely, McMarrow seemed to prefer the Indians' company.

McMarrow clearly had an interest in the fight for Texan independence and sympathy for the Indians. In 1843, the U.S. secretary of war was eager for negotiation with Texas and Mexico. McMarrow was rightly worried that U.S. annexation of Texas would bring war with Mexico, who still claimed the state.

But McMarrow was opposed to the preceding president of Texas, Mirabeau B. Lamar, and his followers, who were separatists. Lamar was against annexation, and took steps to establish Texas's legitimacy as a nation. He also attempted to drive all American Indians from Texas lands.

Violence in Texas was inevitable.

Though Zadock's letters provide a somewhat continuous narrative, much is left out, and I remain desperate for supplementary sources. Too many holes remain. Even if I am barred from telling you of your ancestry, I can make up for it by building a case for Zeke's. He is your family bloodline now.

I decided to come to Texas. Only for the letter. And to ensure that Zeke's claim to the Senate seat is legitimized. I will not give in to my desire to see you. It is too risky.

So far, I can't say I find Texas to my liking. It seems that after its commissioning, this city-state was allowed to grow according to its own perverse idea of justice. It troubles me.

Chicago-Land is beautifully constructed. Many buildings there survived the test of time. After the Collapse, it was the most intact of any city-state. This new republic is flimsy and poorly designed. Dust coats everything, and your neighbors can readily be heard through thin sheet-metal walls.

I had hoped that my spirits would be lifted by the Vault. I had never seen it before yesterday. I'm sorry to say my careful plans were poorly realized. The architecture is not what I pictured. It is massive. But the materials used are cheap. It feels clinical and stale. Much more like a laboratory than a library.

They have kept one essential part of my design: The roof of the Vault is a sanctuary for bats. At night they emerge and eat moths and bookworms that would otherwise destroy the Vault's paper contents. They are the only creatures here, and it is forbidden to kill them. The only price is a thin layer of guano.

I purposefully visited the Vault on your day off. My blood ID as a Corrector still allowed me entry. It is amazing what the Auspices do with their blood alchemy. Their work sustains the entirety of the city-state, yet they are ostracized for it. It still seems like magic to me. With a drop of my blood, the guard ID'd me and let me into the Vault. There was a palpable energy to the place, Threaders bustling through rows of files and folders, but it is far from what I had dreamed of.

Though I was allowed entry, I felt nervous there. I'm poking around where I shouldn't, advancing dangerously into foreign territory. I should fade into the dark and give my mind some respite from troubling thoughts about missing books and letters, the contents of which I can't guess at.

How do you live with watchposts at every intersection? It is a forest of echoes. I wholeheartedly believe in documenting our lives, and in the protection of that accumulated knowledge as the sacred seed of culture. However, Texas is a gross perversion of the founding principles of the Vault system. I'm worried that I'll be seen near you, even accidentally. Especially as much time as I'm spending at the Vault.

The Lawmen want it to seem as though they are always recording everything. Every single anomaly is flagged, and offenders are outed and ostracized. The dead zones, created by the short-staffing, make the system arbitrary and unfair. It's fear-mongering. This was never the purpose of recording, and I know Senator Thomas would object to the surveillance here.

The most egregious offense is the targeting of Queers. I had not realized Texas had backslid so far. Many said the lifephase system would threaten the hard-won rights of Queers. Texas makes me think that this is now coming to pass. Once someone here is identified as Queer they are immediately shipped off to Atlantas. I know that many choose to live there, free of the pressure to procreate. But forced segregation is another matter entirely. There is the sense that the authorities in Texas would rather just throw the Queers into the rot.

I have been told of the steammoat that rings this city. It seems like a mechanical torture device. Zeke's grandfather would not have condoned the banishment of citizens outside the walls of society, even for the punishment of murder, a crime which is unthinkable in Chicago-Land.

I hope it is nothing more than a fear tactic. The hand of the Law is weak here, yet they would have you believe it is made of iron. Perhaps they think a totalitarian performance will ensure order. I would say the opposite is true. The city-state is on edge.

Zeke, your pair, should be warned.

I thought I might gain information through his cousin Bic, and bypass the need to disturb Zeke and interfere in the life of your pair. I went to Bic's unit in the singles' quarter. Escaping the notice of the watchposts was easy. I simply waited for the rotation of Recorders to cycle away from his unit.

Bic lives in a slovenly fashion. Dust is tracked inside and his things are scattered everywhere, sabres and savage paraphernalia. It was dark and smelled of sweat. As a person, he is also repulsive. He refused to answer questions about his grandfather, and was suspicious and arrogant toward me.

Slowly, I realized that Bic was jealous of Zeke. He said Zeke had all the family documents. He had been left with nothing.

So I went back to the Vault of Records to investigate. Bic is a Lawman himself, or was. His record is without a blemish.

What I've found in Zeke's file is disturbing. He had a flag: a deadline for an uncarbon'd document. The file had been doctored so that no one would know it was an open case. Daxon has taken the thread on personally, highly unusual given his rank. His namestamps were all over it. I instantly knew it was the letter. By reporting it I only meant to discover it. I never thought that it might be something the Thomas family was hiding from the Law. Being here, I can see why they would.

Somehow, by trying to help, I have endangered you. I must set things right. It is imperative that I talk to Zeke. I have left a note for him at your unit. I must convince him to let me see the letter. If he destroys it or gives it to Daxon, it will be lost to the historical records forever.

We will have to meet without your knowledge. I'm sorry all this has happened, and that you will find out about it through these letters. Zeke may be able to explain when the time comes.

FAM. LEPORIDAE

GEN. LEPUS

8.7.43, 19:30, 55 deg., 5 knots, 7/10ths cloud coverage

Marching through the Missouri Territory

Jackrabbit, long straight ears. White markings along stomach and feet. Seen in a field by the river, late this eve. Out looking for something to eat, or maybe a bit of adventure, he froze when I approached. In contrast to the smaller hares commonly seen in Illinois, he was content to sit patiently while I drew him. I would have expected him to flee.

Dearest Elswyth,

We have traveled the Illinois and the mighty Missouri, a good deal overland. There has been much marching, and my feet ache in ruined shoes. I doubt your sympathy for my condition would preclude a sly smile at my uncouth presentation, outfitted in roughs for the forest and all my provisions and field instruments slung there on my back. There was a good bit of adventure in it all, and I have collected many specimens already, some I know will interest your father a great deal. The land became marshy, and our forward progress, especially that of the animals, was impeded with regularity. I tried to sketch a rather boisterous river beaver, and my page was grabbed and ripped up by McMarrow. He called it a waste of time. He then berated Rodriguez for bringing so many pack animals, which have caused the delays.

Finally we arrived and met McMarrow's newly commandeered troops at Fort Osage. There is a soldier among them, who suffered a severe snakebite to his lower lip, and so had it removed to spare his life. He now looks as though his teeth are always bared. I don't like him.

Rodriguez told me that late on that same night he spotted three figures emerging from the Major's quarters. They wore gray robes hung with silver jewels, and he thought at first they were "ladies of the evening." But when they left they took the goat cage with them. It was conspicuously silent and looked heavier to carry. Rodriguez was suspicious, but he has been sore since McMarrow's fit by the river.

Rodriguez has twelve wagons waiting for him in Westport. He is anxious to make that outpost to-morrow. His brothers travel east and buy goods from contacts there to ship by steamboat to Westport. Then he drives them over the Santa Fe Trail and sells them in Nuevo Mexico or to other traders in the territories. At quite a handsome return in silver bars, I might add. He made this trip last year and said strong troops with a trustworthy leader, unlike McMarrow, are needed. Otherwise, he fears we will be attacked by freebooters or Indians.

Rodriguez was doubly consternated by what happened today. This morning, after his visit from the robed women, McMarrow moved us all away from Fort Osage, and set up camp near an Indian village.

McMarrow seemed much more comfortable with the Indians than with the men he is now supposed to lead. Friendly, even. He finds the Missouri troops wanting, and barks orders and insults ceaselessly.

I wish you could meet these native men. They are a fascinating tribe, gayly adorned in feathers and paint. They are called "red men," but to me they simply look like white men who have been burned by staying out in the sun too long. They do not seem foreign at all, save their faint southern accents. I made to depict one in full regalia, but my skill failed me. It is a poor rendering. I shall stick to the animal kingdom from here on out, in service to the museum.

At this camp the mosquitoes are especially troublesome. At supper, a swarm came upon us so ferociously that even our considerable hunger had to give way to the discomfort they caused, and our meal was left unfinished. It is very late now, and I have just seen McMarrow to his tent. As though the day were not enough trial, this dark night has proved particularly agitating.

I was already awake, due to mosquitoes inside my tent, when I heard a commotion outside. I emerged in time to see the Major's shape collapse into the remains of the evening's fire. It took Rodriguez and me both to extract his large frame from the fire pit. McMarrow escaped with only a few personal papers turned to ash and a small bit of his boot melted at the toe. I do not know how no greater injury was caused him. He was greatly intoxicated. After we rescued him from the fire, Rodriguez returned to his tent in a huff. He was not amused by the drunken antics. I was left alone with McMarrow in the moonless night, only the silver river of the Milky Way strung above our heads.

He then began to tell me disturbing things. It was hard to make sense of it, his speech was slurred and his breathing labored. He told

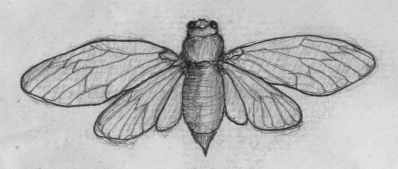

FAM. NOCTUIDAE

GEN. PHOTURIS

10.7.43, 21:00, 45 deg., interior

In my tent, a few miles from Westport, Missouri

Moth, gray. No antennae, elongated thorax. Very large, nearly two inches. Has been trapped inside my tent for the better part of an hour, softly bumping against the sides. I'm not sure that I can sleep, in any case. Certainly one of the largest moths I've seen, and not a species I recognize. So I decided I might draw her. Perhaps by a trick of the moonlight, she was strangely devoid of color, and unsettled about returning to the out-of-doors, despite that being her natural environment. Her thorax glows like that of a firefly, and for this I name her Lightning Moth.

Louisa would love this bug

me General Irion was a true Texian who wants annexation for the territory to the U.S. He thinks that Texas would best be a state, and draw on the strength of the Union for peace. But many men in the Republic of Texas wish to remain separate. McMarrow describes Irion as a peaceful man driven to violence by circumstance. He would prefer to negotiate somewhere other than the fields of battle.

He claims Irion has rescued many prisoners, and his camps give a home and a life to loose, wayward men. Finding a place for these outliers is his true work. He said that your father has been friends with him for many years, and the man is civilized at heart.

Yet he also extols the general's skills at warfare. McMarrow described a cunning victory at the Battle of the Secret Tunnel. Irion wanted to take a seemingly impenetrable citadel. After a long siege, he finally ordered his men to burrow underneath its walls, so that they might emerge in the heart of the city and attack. The story was garbled and I would not vouch for the veracity of it.

McMarrow said the separatists only look to take advantage of a lawless place. They care not for the war over Texas but arm themselves as an excuse to search for the Indians' hidden cities of rare precious metals that they may plunder them. He said that Irion would be the future of Texas, if only she would accept him. He was disconsolate, and his words became squawks. I was able to stand him up and help him to his tent, where I listened until his sobbing turned to snoring.

For my part, sleep is even further off now. The news of the Texian's internal conflict has disturbed me greatly. Despite this, I constantly find myself wishing that you were with me. The journey to come does not suit a lady, surely, but if you had a traveling soul like your Aunt Anne's, perhaps you could visit my dreams at night and we could speak of the particulars and peculiarities of all that I am experiencing.

Anxious, Alone, I remain respectfully Your Obd Servant,

Zadock Thomas

RECORD: 1740682

SCRPT DATE: 0012.0010.2143

SUBJECT: ZEKE THOMAS & ANNLYNE THOMAS

BEGIN PHONO TRANSCRIPT:

Z. THOMAS » Gram, that letter that I found? The unopened one? Did Gramp want me to have it?

A. THOMAS » Oh, certainly dear. Any of his things that you want, you can feel free to take...

» No, I mean ... yes, thank you. But I was asking if he left it to me. Specifically. You know, for me to keep.

» Well, I wouldn't know anything about that, dear.

» I ask because apparently it was supposed to be in my bundle. The Law knows about it.

» That letter you took to be copied? Are you in trouble?

» No, I won't be, I'm going to have it carbon'd. I'm getting around to doing that. I just wanted to know if it was, you know, special or something.

» Oh, I'm sure it was, dear.

» But that one in particular? Would he not have wanted it carbon'd?

» Which one?

» It says "DO NOT OPEN."

» Then maybe you better hadn't open it. There might be a reason someone wrote that on there.

» Gram, that's the feeling I had. Which is why I'm asking you. Is it important?

ELIZA GRAY/ID.42984

0012.0010.2143

:ACCESS

:DATE

129 P.

E. GRAY

» Your grandfather began to regret that carbon copy law. That and lots of things. Recording of everyone all the time. That was never his purpose.

» I wish he had lived long enough to see me do ... something. Besides waiting.

3 SECONDS DEAD AIR

» So, no reason for that particular letter?

» Oh, I wouldn't know anything about that, dear. You can have it if you like.

» OK, Gram. Well, thanks for talking with me. I've got to run now.

» And how is...

» Eliza. Well. She remembers the tea service.

» Oh good. That's the key to civilization. A good tea served properly.

» Yes, it is. I miss yours. Gram, I have to go now. I'll try to come see you soon.

» Please do, dear. In fact, you've got clearance. As the Khrysalis, you can travel to any city-state. You're cleared to come to Chicago-Land anytime. Some of the Senators are anxious to meet you. We're all awaiting your decision.

» I know. I'm thinking about it.

» Goodbye now. You just do what you think is best.

2 SECONDS DEAD AIR

FLAG►   » With the letter.   <WHISPER

» What? Gram, are you there? Hello?

END PHONO TRANSCRIPT

◇◇ ∿ After hanging up the phonotube Zeke somehow felt more restless. Eliza had gone to pick up the laundry from the central washatorium. She wouldn't be home for a while. Zeke called Raisin and arranged to meet him down at the square. He put on his jacket and hand-kerchief, and pulled his brimhat low. ∿ ∿ ∿ He closed the front door behind him, checking the lock twice. The evening air shimmered. ∿ ∿ ∿ Zeke walked down his street, away from the north quadrant, hands folded in his jacket pockets. He had walked every quadrant of the city-state at least a hundred times. He needed to think. Should he take the seat, or open the letter first? The phosphor lamps on the watchposts flickered above him. ∿ ∿ ∿

∿ A flutter of bright flashes above. Bats. They were the only animal that came within the boundaries of the city-state. Birds got caught in the weather pylons, domestic animals were banned, but the bats left their home in the Vault every evening and flew over the barriers in search of food. The phosphor lamps lit the underside of their bellies and tinted their translucent wings greenish white. ∿ ∿ ∿ ∿

∿ ∿ ∿ ∿ ∿ They flashed across the sky like shooting stars. Swooping after the insects drawn to the lamps. ∿ ∿ ∿ ∿ ∿

∿ Zeke stopped to watch them for a long moment. ∿ ∿ ∿ ∿

∿ ∿ ∿ ∿ ∿ ∿ ∿ ∿ ∿ ∿ ∿ ∿ The city-blocks were identical. Steam valves releasing excess pressure, hissing blindly. Zeke walked past the grocery, a large, brightly lit tent carved into the night sky. Signs advertised the goods inside. Flavors to add to fount-water. Expensive, naturally grown fruits and vegetables. He pulled his jacket tightly against a dry chill. ∿ ∿ ∿ Zeke walked past more watchposts; most were empty, with pasted-on broadsheets struggling in the wind. He counted the wooden planks disappearing under his feet. Then they stopped. ∿ ∿ ∿ ∿ Zeke looked up. The barrier towered over him. The rim was empty. Lawmen weren't on patrol tonight. He had come to the barrier.

P. 132

THE BARRIER

T NOW

⌃⌃ ⌃⌃ The curving slope of the barrier leaned above him. The gleaming metal façade seemed unscalable. ⌃⌃ ⌃⌃ ⌃⌃ He followed it, walking east. The quadrant was empty. No one ever wanted to be seen near the barrier, lest they be accused of trying to flee. He could see the hatches that led to the outward-facing loopholes, windows for the cannon or scorpio weapons. And the toeholds that allowed Lawmen to climb up and patrol the ledge. ⌃⌃ ⌃⌃ ⌃⌃ He tipped back his brimhat and stared up at it. Thick ropes of dust swirled across it, caught in the vortex the walls created. His eye caught a shadow on the perfect face of the wall. He walked closer. ⌃⌃ ⌃⌃ ⌃⌃ Someone had dipped a mop in a bucket of ink and written giant letters: "OPEN IT NOW." Zeke's first thought was of the letter. But the message was not for him. It was about the barrier. The Deserters wanted the wall to come down. They spread their propaganda through painted slogans, written in the night. The Washers hadn't gotten to this one yet. ⌃⌃ ⌃⌃ Zeke looked around cautiously. There were no watchposts nearby. He stepped closer. The handwriting was messy, human. He touched one of the dripping letters and brought his black finger to his nose. The ink was fresh. It smelled earthy and intoxicating. Zeke thought of the letter. Eliza's reaction had scared him a little. She hadn't always been afraid of authority. ⌃⌃ ⌃⌃ ⌃⌃ ⌃⌃ ⌃⌃ ⌃⌃ They had met at a fountain saloon in Port-Land. There was no alcohol, just flavored fount-water. They were giddy, surrounded by the young generation in an uninhibited city-state. Laughter rolled off their tongues like mercury. Eliza had never tried pomegranate water. She wasn't used to luxuries. Zeke bought her one. They moved to a booth, away from their friends. ⌃⌃ ⌃⌃ ⌃⌃ They weren't supposed to court. That was reserved for Texas, the city-state of pairing. Zeke bought her more pomegranate water until he ran out of money. The sugar gave them both stomachaches. She told him about her father and her status as a Gray. He didn't care, despite his own bloodline. The system didn't account for how he felt. Eliza had begun to train with the records, but couldn't find her father. ∧∧ ∧∧ She was clever with the files. Zeke was a year older and was transferred to Texas first. He avoided the square and the courting that his friends did, and waited for Eliza. They talked on the phonotube constantly. Later she would doctor the records to make it seem as though they had met in Texas. ∧∧ ∧∧ ∧∧ It was such a relief when she finally transferred. Raisin was paired with Leeya, and the four of them were inseparable. He missed those days. ∧∧ ∧∧ ∧∧ ∧∧ Zeke suddenly remembered he was supposed to meet Raisin at the square. He hurried away from the barrier, pulling up his hand-kerchief against the dust. ∧∧ ∧∧ ∧∧ ∧∧ ∧∧ ∧∧ He neared the center of the city-state. It was lit by many flickering phosphor lamps, a swarm of green fireflies in the dusty air. ∧∧ ∧∧ ∧∧ The square was filled with folks. Flash silver jewelry refracted green flecks of light. White flowing fashionclothes and sharp brimhats were on display. Singles stood outside on the plankways in front of saloons flashing hand signals across the square. The signals had started as a way to evade the constant surveillance of the watchposts but had evolved into a sly form of courting. The ladies used elaborate fans to hide their flirtatious gestures. Drunken laughter crackled through the air cut by the occasional Law whistle. Zeke scanned the crowd for Raisin. ∧∧ ∧∧ ∧∧ "Thirsty?" a voice whispered beside him. ∧∧ ∧∧ Zeke turned. A young fellow dressed like a Deserter. Hand-kerchief pulled up, shirt torn, and boots stained. He was making the hand signal for *laudanum*. ∧∧

LAUDANUM

Zeke gave a slight nod. He dug in his jacket pocket and palmed a wad of greenbacks to the fellow. ∧∧ ∧∧ He glanced up at the watchposts around them. None had an angle. The fellow had picked a good dead zone to ply his trade. Inside his handshake was a full phial. ∧∧ ∧∧ ∧∧ Zeke tensed, listening for a Law whistle, but none sounded. The transaction had been successful. The fellow slunk back toward the square. ∧∧ ∧∧ Zeke slowly sucked half the phial into his glass dropper and shook it for good measure. He dropped seven beads of laudanum on the back of his tongue. The familiar warmth spread through him. He slipped the paraphernalia inside his jacket. He closed his eyes. Thick, syrupy air entered his lungs. His thoughts slowed down. He retreated into them. ∧∧ ∧∧ Zeke had considered spending his remaining days in the warm comfort of the drug. On it, he was an observer, composed only of thoughts. He was no longer the force that contracted muscles, that blinked eyes, that ate and drank, that talked and worked, that was a pair or a grandson or a Khrysalis. He no longer had to decide what to do about the letter. ∧∧ ∧∧ It was nothing to press his hands against the plankway, nothing to lift himself to standing. ∧∧ It was nothing to straighten his legs, nothing to walk back into the square. ∧∧ It was nothing to push open the wooden doors, nothing to walk into the saloon. ∧∧ ∧∧ ∧∧ ∧∧ ∧∧ ∧∧ ∧∧ ∧∧ ∧∧ ∧∧ ∧∧ ∧∧ ∧∧ ∧∧ ∧∧ ∧∧ ∧∧ ∧∧ ∧∧

Zeke elbowed his way up to the polished bar. Low phosphor lights made the bottles twinkle menacingly. A long-dead chandelier hung from the ceiling like a cluster of stalactites. Dust blew in each time someone walked through the door. Entrances were watched by everyone. Young folks gossiped behind fans and hand-kerchiefs. He ordered a drink and paid for it with the last crumpled greenback in his pocket. ∧∧ ∧∧ ∧∧ Outside he sat on the wooden planks a distance from the saloon crowd. He sucked on ice cubes and spat them back into his glass. The crowd started to murmur excitedly, and Zeke could see Law flashers just beyond the square's edge. An arrest. Whispers and hand signals sparked through the crowd. ∧∧

〰 〰 〰 〰 〰 A loud conversation at the table nearest to him surged. The Law was here for a body. A young girl. She had been tossed off a roof. He spotted Raisin. He was standing, shouting at a table of folks. He advocated opening the barrier. His rant sounded like a Deserter pamphlet. Zeke didn't move. 〰 〰 〰 〰 "Down with the claustrotopia," Raisin shouted at another fellow. 〰 〰 〰 "You'd be dead without the barrier." His opponent maintained the cadence of civilized speech. "If the Queers want to live without it, let them." 〰 "Total integration. Now." Raisin slammed his fist on the table. Zeke cringed. "Or the folks in the storm country are going to destroy us." 〰 "How, by killing all the young girls?" 〰 〰 "That's not the Deserters. That girl is probably a suicide. When you've been here long enough, you'll see." Raisin was twitching. They had the attention of the saloon. Fans had stopped fluttering. The crowd tensed for a fight. 〰 〰 〰 Two Lawmen slid down on handwheels from the nearest watchpost and advanced toward them. They looked young in their pressed brown uniforms, weapons holstered across their backs. 〰 〰 〰 The laudanum held Zeke hypnotized. He wanted to call out but could only watch what was happening. The other fellow stood up. Raisin had made him mad. 〰 "You've been here too long. There's clearly no pair for you. Tram over to Atlantas. Go join all the other lonely wolves." 〰 Raisin pushed the fellow's chest with both hands, hard. "I'll show you a wolf," he shouted. 〰 One of the Lawmen blew his whistle. Raisin's opponent made a break for it. The Lawman shot a bolo-catch at his ankles. The whizzing rope caught his feet up, binding them together. He fell face-first into the dirt. The Lawmen ran over and wrestled his wrists into a bolo-tie. Then he tied Raisin's. Zeke stood up, without thinking. 〰 〰 The Lawman pointed at him. 〰 "You, come here. We need a witness." 〰 〰 〰 〰 〰 〰 Zeke gave Raisin a look of exasperation. His friend was tied, still panting. 〰

"Come here." The Lawman unlatched his holster. He reached over his shoulder and pulled his steamsabre out by its hilt. Zeke walked over. The laudanum sloshed in his head. "What did this Deserter say? You were listening." The Lawman pointed the weapon at Zeke. The steam was switched off. ∧∧ ∧∧ "I wasn't really." Zeke remembered that he needed to stay away from the Law. ∧∧ "You were sitting right there. You are a witness." ∧∧ **"He said he's got a dustbomb strapped to him, and that the barrier is coming down."** Zeke thought a joke might lighten the mood. The Lawman frowned. ∧∧ ∧∧ "What?" He jabbed his dead steamsabre into Zeke's side. The Law wasn't going to give them a break. ∧∧ ∧∧ **"Why don't you just throw us all over the barrier?"** Zeke mumbled. It was loud enough. He was surprised at the forcefulness of his words. ∧∧ Muscles along the Lawman's jawline tightened. "I'm arresting this one too," he called to his partner. ∧∧ The Lawman grabbed his shoulder. Zeke's glass shattered on the wooden plankway. The Lawman twisted Zeke's arm behind his back. He fastened a bolo-tie around his wrists. The rope twisted into a configuration that made it impossible to escape. It burned. ∧∧ ∧∧ ∧∧ The three of them were brought out to the main street. The Law had called their movable jail cell, a glass cabinet mounted on a steamcarrier with blinding Law flashers on top. The Lawman punched their names into the typowriter mounted on the side. The door hissed closed, sealed by the carrier's supply of steam. ∧∧ ∧∧ ∧∧ The prisoners sat in the back on rough benches. The Lawman called up a watchpost to have their files pulled. The Recorder reported back down that Zeke was a Khrysalis. This made the Lawman nervous. He put in a call for the Major. The other fellow sneered at Raisin. His chest puffed up and down. Raisin sat still and looked at the floor of the cell. Zeke could hear the Lawmen talking about him. He knew it would be best if he and Raisin pretended not to know each other.

Eliza was asleep at home. A call from jail would wake her up. ⌃⌃ ⌃⌃ Finally Daxon arrived. ⌃⌃ "Two days in a row?" His eyes swam as he tried to focus on Zeke. His face was sallow, with dark bags. He pretended to flip through their files. ⌃⌃ ⌃⌃ ⌃⌃ The Major produced a pointed blood dropper and pressed it against Zeke's forearm. The sharp pinch left a red mark. Zeke wondered what the Republic did with all the blood they collected. The Major stumbled toward the junior Lawman with the evidence. He seemed drunk. ⌃⌃ ⌃⌃ "I'm not a Deserter. I don't want outside the barrier," the other fellow mumbled. "I want other folks to be able to get back inside." ⌃⌃ A deafening whistle sounded. Everyone jumped up. It blared through the streets. ⌃⌃ "Who pulled an all-quad alert?" Daxon shouted above the whine of the whistle. ⌃⌃ ⌃⌃ ⌃⌃ One of the Lawmen approached quickly. "Sir, seems the cannon has gone missing." ⌃⌃ "Missing?" He lowered his voice into a menacing hiss. "Don't say a thing to anyone. And turn that bloody alert off! Now!" ⌃⌃ ⌃⌃ They were left alone in the cell while the Lawman went scrambling up a watchpost to phone in the order. ⌃⌃ ⌃⌃ "The jails are full." The fellow with them was despondent. "We'll all be thrown over the barrier. The whole city-state will watch as we're blasted by the steammoat." ⌃⌃ Zeke kept silent. ⌃⌃ "I'd rather that," said Raisin. "You can outrun the steammoats. That's how Speed earned his nickname. He taught other Deserters how to do it. They've got an army out there. Of men and hounds both." The fellow looked terrified. ⌃⌃ ⌃⌃ The Major pulled a valve on the jail cell, releasing pressurized steam. The door swung open. "Get out," he shouted. ⌃⌃ They clamored out of the cell, wrists still tied. Zeke felt unbalanced. "Not you." The Major shoved the other fellow back in the cell. ⌃⌃ ⌃⌃ Abruptly, the whistle sounded again. The Major sighed heavily. "Will nothing in this tinpot city-state function properly? Now everyone knows we've got a murder." He removed his brimhat and mopped at his brow. "That cell," he said to the Lawman, "goes back to the jail." He took the bolo-ties off Raisin's wrists with difficulty. He grabbed him by the hand-kerchief around his neck. "Don't show up on record with those folks again." Raisin shot Zeke a look, and scurried off into the dark. The Major pointed at Zeke's wrists. The Lawman untied them. "The girl's got no blood, sir," he said to the Major. "Completely drained. How are we going to ID her?" The Major grunted. "Another one." He waved Zeke's file in his face, like he was tired of all the paperwork. "Just trying to keep the peace. How can I get anything else done around here while this is going on?" The Major heaved an exaggerated sigh. "Somebody opens the neck of every girl he can get his claws on, and I'm up all night. I should be looking for a knife, not a letter." The steamcarrier let loose a hiss. It chugged down the street toward the city-center. The fellow sat inside like a captured animal. The carrier would slide right into the jail building, and he'd be surrounded by other prisoners in glass cells. The Major turned to the Lawman. "If that fool hadn't been sitting in a mob of witnesses, we could pin the whole thing on him. Get me a drink from that saloon. Before I strip you of your uniform." He ran off to fulfill the order. The Major continued, "My Threaders are all looking for loose animals. My suspect doesn't exist. Tricks of the light." "Look," the Major said. His speech was muddy. "I just want the uncarbon'd document. To close the thread. So here's the deal. I'm going to let you go, and you go back to your filthy little nest and get me that letter. Understood?" **"I don't have it."** Zeke could still feel the laudanum in his system. "Hh, yours is a generation of liars. I can play that game too. I'll pin a note with your name on it to the next girl we find. Our handwriting always holds up in court." **"I have my deadline."** The Major shuffled away, his neck cranked back at Zeke. "We're recording every move," he said.

MR. BUELL MAKES LOUISA A DIORAMA. SHE RECEIVES
A NEW DOLL. TALES ARE TOLD OF ZED BLACKFOOT
AND THE BLACK-EYED SHUCK. MR. BUELL
BADLY FRIGHTENS LOUISA.

Arranging various branches, Mr. Buell knelt on the polished wood floor of the large salle. He poured little piles of sand and fixed pebbles at their edges. He felt foolish, playing dolls with a girl half his age, but when Louisa entered for her fencing lesson, her face lit up. She saw the sand and leaves, lit by the morning sun streaming through the windows, and knew immediately it was a miniature landscape, set for her.

Louisa skittered across the floor, clasping her hands together. She smiled at him. 'It's a truly marvelous setting.'

Mr. Buell hunched over his landscape, stiffly arranging a last twig. He stood laboriously, dusting off his large black coat. It was old but of a fine make, and carried the heavy scent of cologne.

'I thought we might tell stories,' Mr. Buell said. He studied his pupil closely. 'Or would your rather drill your riposte?'

Louisa gave him her most crestfallen look, her green eyes batting back crocodile tears. Mr. Buell had large set features and a thick complexion, but his face softened at this.

'As I thought. Fencing is a pastime for men, anyhow. I'm not sure why your father insists on lessons for girls who are clearly more suited to the feminine arts.'

The upstairs floor had been arranged by the girls' mother as a ballroom meant for entertaining any number of guests who might care to dance. Mr. Gray had argued that the space could be put to better use, and had managed to install a fencing cabinet and some drilling targets. After his wife's death, he could not bring himself to change the room at all. He decided to build new rooms instead. Dancing lessons had ceased but the fencing lessons continued.

'Well, then. Did you bring Maryposa?'

Louisa fished the doll from its usual home in her dress pocket. 'I shall go get her house, and furniture, and her babies...'

'I don't know if she needs all that. What if she had another adventure in the western wilderness?'

'I did fashion a new bathing cap.'

'Ah, we shall need a river then.' He took his blue silken scarf and snaked it around little hills of dirt and between branches. 'There we are. A *Rio Grande*. Maryposa might have a place to bathe. And perhaps a partner.'

'Zed Blackfoot?'

'If he appears.'

Louisa flung herself down onto her front and stood Maryposa at the edge of the river, tugging the pink bathing cap, made from the tip of the gardening glove, over her blonde hair.

'My sister says I am too old for dolls.'

'These are merely props. For a more elaborate form of story-telling. Hasn't your sister always fancied fiction? And your mother?'

'Will you read me *The City-State?*'

'I don't have your mother's book. But I remember the story well. It was set in Texas, not far from the *Rio Grande*. The name means "big river" in Spanish.' Mr. Buell sat down beside her and arranged the blue silk, pinching its folds into little waves. 'Do you know how thi*s* *Rio Grande* came to be so big?'

Louisa wrestled Maryposa's fragile limbs through the holes of a pink bathing costume that had also appeared from her pocket.

'It was Zed Blackfoot himself who made it,' said Mr. Buell.

'A whole river?' Louisa looked at him in anticipation.

'Really truly. He wrote of it to Maryposa in his letters when he first made his way to the wilds of Texas. He came by steamboat, but found that the land was much too dry, and the river became smaller and smaller as he traveled south. The boat was getting stuck because the river was too small. So what did he do?'

Louisa raised an inquisitive eyebrow.

'Well, he pulled up the anchor of that steamship, and used it like a pickax. It was so big and heavy that every stroke made the riverbed that much wider and deeper. So deep that it became the biggest river in Texas, and they named it the *Rio Grande*. It could only have been accomplished by way of him being so tall. His limbs were long, sinewy, and tough, like the branches of a pecan tree.'

'How tall was he?'

'Let's see.' From behind his back Mr. Buell produced a figure carved of wood. He was dressed in a brown city overcoat, not unlike Buell's, but he had the chaps of an Indian scout, and his feet had been blackened with ash. Mr. Buell stood him up next to Louisa's doll. 'About that tall, I suppose.'

Louisa gasped. 'He's beautiful! Where did you get him?'

'I fashioned him this very morning. He is yours to keep, my dear.' She took the carved man and turned him round and round in her fingers, admiring the workmanship.

'After all that effort he was so thirsty he took a mighty gulp out of the *Rio Grande*, but the water was so muddy and full of swimming numrats that he spat it back out. And when he did, everyone saw that the water had been changed and cleaned by the white teeth of Zed. Giant drops of the purest mineral water were splashed all about Texas, landing in small groves of brush and tree. They say if you find one and drink from it, immortal life will be yours. From that day forth numrats never plagued the land again. The filthy cities are overrun by their cousins, but Texas waters are free of such creatures.'

'Maryposa can bathe in it!' Louisa dipped her swimmer in and out of the imagined river. Mr. Buell retrieved a chair from the other side of the salle and set it next to the western landscape. He sat in silence for a long moment and watched Louisa crawl along the floor, her skirts in disarray.

Presently she stopped and looked back at him. 'Are you going to court my sister? Mr. Thomas is gone.'

'I'm not sure she'll have me.' Mr. Buell paused. 'Sadly. I courted her for a long while, and she spurned me. I don't think she cares for me. I don't know who will have me now...'

'She doesn't care for any men. Only sewing. And books.'

'So she says. I'd venture she cared for Mr. Thomas, though she spurned him as well. Quite surprising.'

'She didn't care for him until he was gone.' Mr. Buell seemed very far away. 'Another story,' Louisa demanded.

'Very well.' Mr. Buell crossed his legs. 'What will it be? How Zed Blackfoot defeated the rolling hoopsnake? Or how he wrote on the sky with lightning? Or painted all the giant moths, and thus invented butterflies?'

'Yes! I love butterflies!'

'Or how his feet became black, and he earned his name?'

'Oh yes! That one!' Louisa was rapturous.

'Very well, come here then, sit on my lap, and I shall tell you the story.' Louisa stood, but looked back at the play set. 'Come dear, it's a long story and I need your close company. You may bring Maryposa.'

Louisa hesitated, then sat cautiously on his lap. He shifted about a great deal, and she picked at her doll's hair.

'There, that's better, isn't it,' he said. 'Now then, the Story of How Zed Blackfoot Came to be Called Blackfoot.'

'The Indians called him that.'

'That's true, they gave him the name, but not for just any reason. There is logic yet in the savage mind. I'll tell you how he came to have those black feet. It all started with the sun.'

'I'm rather too warm myself.'

'Just listen.' He patted her knee. 'The sun in Texas is so hot, a terrible giant sun, unlike the one above Illinois. Zed had been under it for many days, because he was out in the great white desert where the trees are few, and he had no hollow log to sleep in, as was his custom.

'He had chased the evil hoopsnakes to the very edge of the desert, but as you know, the hoopsnake rolls very quickly, and he had mounted Dexter, his grayhound, in pursuit.'

'A grayhound like Grapes?'

'Yes, except much larger than any hound before or after, and only Zed could ride him. But they were both thirsty and tired from being out in the desert so long, and the heat was oppressive, and Zed could not find his way back. But Zed was clever. He was a naturalist, like I am, a friend to animals.'

'Like me.' Louisa twirled her doll's bathing cap on her finger.

'That is how I first met him, and heard his tales. Like any good naturalist, he had his specimen kit with him. So he took his glass slides one night, when he was almost spent, and he captured a scrap of the night sky between them. He held fast all night to a tiny bit of the black sky pressed between two pieces of glass. And then, when he saw the dawn approaching over the horizon, he buried it in the ground. The sun would not be able to erase his captured bit of nighttime with its bright rays.

'As specimens sometimes do, that little bit of night sky took hold in the ground. Just like the burrowing shrews there, it grew and grew, so quickly that Dexter almost fell in, for it was becoming a great black hole. Presently, it was large enough for Zed to go inside, and he walked into the great hole under the Earth and realized that he had created the world's first cavern. It was a perfect hiding place from the wicked desert sun. It was dark and quiet inside, and pools of clear water could be readily found.

'However, his problems were not through. He couldn't see to drink the water or to make a bed. He had carved out a little piece of night, it was true, but a night without stars was akin to blindness. So, being the clever naturalist he was, and deeply in touch with the creatures of the world, he took the shrews with their glinting eyes and hung them from the roof of the cave, intending to use their bright eyes for his stars. They were as pets to him and did his bidding, clinging to the roof of the cave in a cluster, as to paint the nighttime sky with starry eyes. However, once the shrews' eyes were used for lights they could no longer see, and they became blind. They couldn't find their way down from the roof again, and so had to grow wings that they might travel through the darkness. With this, the lot of them turned into bats. And that is where the bat comes from.'

'Bats are icky.' Louisa fidgeted. Mr. Buell was damp and sweaty, and his odor mixed with the cologne on his coat was almost as overwhelming as the smell of her father's bison. It felt as though he were trying to stand. 'Are you going away?' Louisa asked.

'Would you come with me, Louisa, if I were to go away?'

'I'm to have a new room soon, with a skylight.'

'Farther th‸ ‸our room. I mean away from Chicago.'

'To the western wilderness?'

'If your heart desired.'

'I'm scared of the bats. Did Zed kill them?'

'No, no, he didn't.' Mr. Buell took up his storytelling voice once again. 'Zed Blackfoot liked the bats very much, only now he could not keep them, for, being blind, they could no longer tell the day from the night, and all flew from the great cave in the middle of the night, leaving Zed again in the darkness. So he ran out after them, and it was only then that he looked down and discovered that his feet had become gray.'

'How?' Louisa asked, anxious for the conclusion of the tale.

'Well, bats produce droppings. But Zed had not known this, having just created them. The bats had covered the floor of the cave in their droppings, and he had been stepping in it all, graying his feet entirely.'

'Ew.' Louisa wrinkled her nose.

'The smell was quite strong, and it was unfortunate that Zed had brought it outside. To remedy the stench and to guard against the night he decided to build a campfire. Texas is no safe place once darkness has fallen. It was to prove a fateful night indeed. The smoke of his campfire attracted a Black-eyed Shuck.'

'What's a Black-eye Shuck?' Louisa peeped up at Mr. Buell's unshaven face.

'Have you never heard of the Black-eyed Shuck? Oh, he is a terrible beast to behold. His hair is made of the thorns of cacti, and his tail is a tumbleweed. His front paws are that of a wicked monkey and the rest of him looks like a beast that came of a fox eaten by a wolf eaten by a buffalo. One of the worst ever seen. Or barely seen, because he only comes out at night, and walks backward with his head between his legs. Few men even glimpse that terrible sight, because before they know the creature is upon them, the Shuck has drunk all their blood from their shadows.'

Louisa was held rapt.

'He will suck the life from goats, though he most prefers children. He kills them for their hearts, which he uses to line his dirty nest and keep it warm and wet with blood. He hunts alone in the dead of the night and his eyes are bright black like the unlit disc of the moon.'

'What happened to Zed?' Louisa blurted out, greatly distressed.

'They had a great wrestling match, all around the edge of the campfire. Dexter the grayhound was frightened off completely. The Black-eyed Shuck was big and a mighty wrestler. His jaws were powerful, and he had long fingers with claws on the end, like those of a witch. He had Zed pinned down and was sipping blood from his moon-shadow, nearly draining the life from him, when Zed took a chance. Owing to the great stench of the bat droppings, he suspected that they might be flammable, and on this clever thought, he stuck his feet into the roaring campfire. Immediately they flared to life, and he had two great torches at the end of his legs. Though he did not know it, a torch is the best weapon against a Shuck. They are allergic to flames. So Zed kicked the great beast back into the night using his feet of flame. He was in a great deal of pain, but managed to run the Black-eyed Shuck off. He buried his feet in the sand just in time to keep them from becoming consumed by flames entirely. However, they were plenty cooked, and their appearance remained as such ever after. Thus when the great chief of the seven tribes saw his fire-blackened feet, he named Zed…'

'Enough.' Louisa stood. Mr. Buell saw that her cheeks were wet with tears.

"Did I scare you? I'm sorry, I...' Mr. Buell began but Louisa walked quickly cross the salle and pressed her face against the wooden fencing cabinet where all the sabres were kept.

Mr. Buell got up and hobbled over. He cautiously put a hand on her back.

'Come now. What's wrong?'

'Grapes is gone.'

'Grapes is gone?' Mr. Buell thought for a moment. 'Louisa, he'll come back. That dog always does. He's just off on an adventure.'

'I can't find him.' Her voice was barely audible against the thick wooden doors.

'I'll help you look. We can go on a hound hunt. That's what a naturalist does. He looks for animals. Zed can help us.'

'He is hurt. Or dead.' Louisa began to sob, softly.

'We'll find him. Don't let a story upset you. There are no such creatures in Chicago.' She only sniffled. 'Remember the story of when Zed ventured forth from Chicago? He had a lady love who had been false with him. He was supposed to be married to her, but she broke their engagement, and he learned that a man might not be wed to the simple girl that he thought was fated him. He was heartbroken and had to leave Chicago for the west, but what did he tell people?'

Mr. Buell waited for her answer, hovering behind her.

'What did he say to explain away that ungrateful girl?'

Between breaths, Louisa managed to squeak out, 'I need more elbow room.'

'That's right.' Mr. Buell turned her around slowly. He smiled widely at Louisa. 'And that's how Zed met Maryposa, isn't that right, out in the woods? Now come away from the cabinet, we've no need of sharp things.' He offered his hand and she took it. He wrapped his arms tightly around her though she still shook.

'We all need stories to tell ourselves. Just like Zed needed Maryposa to keep him warm. They were always together. They sent the Black-eyed Shuck back to Chicago, right to a Zoological Garden, where he might be poked and prodded at for the entertainment of passersby. They were never troubled by him anymore. They found Dexter the grayhound, and he was the best of their friends and a faithful companion from then on.'

Louisa sniffled and rubbed her nose on his shoulder. He kept his arms around her. She slid her hands into the pockets of his black coat. To her surprise, the left pocket contained a letter. Without quite knowing why, she slid it out of his pocket and into hers. Slowly, so that Mr. Buell wouldn't notice.

He continued to comfort her. 'The three of them always slept outside afterward, under the stars, or pressed together in one of Zed's hollow logs, always together, always touching.'

FAM. **VIPERIDAE**

GEN. **CROTALUS**

4.8.43, 15:00, 75 deg., 35 knots, heavy rains

Muddy fields, Unorganized Territory approaching Black Pool

Mud Snake, adult. Near the Texas border the rain chased up many snakes. They were coated in mud and difficult to identify. It is strange that life should emerge from the Earth and when this snake meets his end, that his bones return to the same mud he basks in now. I had a moment's horror at the thought that all the muddied earth around us might be a nest of writhing snakes. I could not see where heads began and tails ended. The processes of nature are cyclical, eternal, and for what end I do not know.

Dearest Elswyth,

My apologies for the delay in writing. We are now camping near the waters of the Cimarron River. Much has happened since Westport.

That town was a hive of activity. It felt as though it were being built around us as we slept. The air was full of dust kicked up on the busy streets. The Indians, still following us, would not enter. We were given army quarters: cool log houses, amply long, with capacious fireplaces and plenty of kindling. I thought I longed for these civilized comforts, but I quickly became eager to return to the road and the camp life. Though it could never be said it is without difficulty, I feel quite accustomed to it now and can sit on the ground in "tailor fashion" with my tin plate or drawing board before me. I can partake of fried middling and bread and feel as though I've enjoyed a proper dinner.

The Santa Fe Trail has proved a mud slide. The first day we did not get but four miles from town, the wagons becoming mired in devilish mud holes. Rodriguez and McMarrow argued at length about how best to extract a wheel stuck in mud. Then eventide overtook us and with it a thunderstorm the likes of which I've never seen. Violent dark clouds approached from a long way off. We prepared for it by tying the wagons and beasts down and wrapping ourselves, but there were no embankments to shelter us. We were caught on the naked prairie and there was nothing to break the rage of the skies.

The clouds flew in from all quarters. They wouldn't have seemed as black, save for the vivid flashes of lightning that clove them and revealed their density to us, great mountains inverted in the sky. With a sky-splitting crack, lightning struck the ground right behind us. One of Rodriguez's beasts reared and pulled out his picket. When he bolted, the rest of the pack were driven to stampede. The pickets must have been nearly washed out, because the animals broke away easily, with only the weakest staying tethered.

A roundup was too dangerous to attempt in the nighttime storm.

McMarrow was furious and cursed Rodriguez for his stupidity, the rain sopping from his hair. Rodriguez said that it was McMarrow's soldiers who had tethered the animals. This hardly tempered his anger.

That morning, the watch gave an alarm cry to the camp. I went out of the wagon, and silhouetted against the horizon's crack of light were the Indians, all mounted in the mist of morning and deadly still. The troops came to formation frantically, gripping their arms with frozen knuckles. McMarrow was roused, and all anticipated a fight with the Indians.

But McMarrow, in his long underwear and boots, simply strode out to meet them on the ridge. Without saying anything he grabbed the reins of two of the horses and walked them back across the line of wide-eyed soldiers. He handed the reins to one of the traders and went back for another beast. It was then that I realized there were two steeds for every Indian. They had somehow managed to round up all our animals in the night. Even more remarkable, they were returning them, handing them over to McMarrow one by one. They stood motionless, barely seeming to notice us or what was happening at all. McMarrow squished noisily through the mud, bringing the beasts home, glowering at the huddle of his dumbstruck soldiers. The man with the bared teeth looked angry. Drool ran down his chin.

Starting with the beast-masters, McMarrow ordered all the soldiers to strip out of their uniforms, which they did. The men cowered, covering themselves. With a motion of his hand, McMarrow brought the Indians forward. Each picked up a discarded uniform and began to dress themselves. Turning to the traders he declared the Indians our new escort, deeming them more worthy than the men stripped before us. He told the surprised soldiers to follow the river to Fort Gibson in a company of cowardice. They slunk off, heads low.

This development has made Rodriguez livid. The traders whisper rumors of Texian raids on the train—many of them are Mexican nationals and at war with Texas. Rodriguez told me the tale of a fellow countryman who had set out upon this very trail in the spring of this year, at the wrong time with too small a party, and had been captured by a band of Texians. They shot him through the heart. They apparently have no love for the Mexicans and will kill traders or soldiers indiscriminately to interrupt trade on this route.

McMarrow assured the traders that the roads are safer after General Irion disbanded a bloodthirsty group of freebooters from Texas. He says the chief danger along the trail is snakebite. It is strange to me that instead of the danger of attack from Indians (who are now our silent guards), we must worry about being robbed by men who were so recently citizens of the United States. But such is the state of war. We will soon enter the "disputed territory," though few call it that, having definite opinions about who Texas should belong to: the U.S., Mexico, or herself. The lawlessness does make me nervous.

Otherwise, we make progress. We feast each day upon buffalo hump ribs and sausages, fish, marrowbones, and beans. At camp, the traders build great frameworks of willow brush and hang the meat to dry upon them. The hunters in the group consider it sporting to ride up alongside galloping buffaloes. This is unnecessary, as the creatures have very poor eyesight. I was able to draw one sitting but a few yards away and indeed I have seen them killed from a rifled musket at point-blank range. It seems unfair. The nightly camps can become boisterous, with the Indians taking their soldier's ration of whiskey straight to heart and spinning yarns or singing into the night. They speak perfect English. A few are surprisingly affectionate with one another, kissing vigorously and wrestling. You would like them, I think.

Since his assigned soldiers were dismissed, McMarrow seems a good deal less angry, though none could claim he is more controlled in his behaviors. He continues his reveries through the day and has on more than one occasion gone off leaning in his saddle to hunt.

After camp is made he usually wrangles as many of the traders as possible (and sometimes me) into his tricky card games. He has made paupers of half of them. Rodriguez won't play. While losing their shirts, his opponents must tolerate his grandstanding stories of war.

The stars that inform my map tell me that we are still far from Santa Fe. At the Cimarron canyon the low desert has given way to high piney forests through which the river winds, shadowed by towering sills of sheer rock. The Texians claim this tract of northward land as part of their new nation but can't control it, so the north and west of Texas are still held by Mexico. Rodriguez thinks it wise to reduce the number of Indians in our company, as not to appear a raiding party entering foreign territory. He speaks endlessly about Nuevo Mexico.

He longs to find the miraculous waters of the Buenaventura, which none have seen. He told me of his grand family hacienda south of Albuquerque, where his sister, of whom he is quite fond, lives. She is learning the ways of the Navaho there, and he ascribes them great powers. Truly, Rodriguez just seems anxious for familiar lands. He is eager to be away from McMarrow, whom he openly despises.

Today the Major took my sabre without asking, and used it to carve up some buffalo steaks. He said it was his as I had lost so badly at cards. After he fell asleep I retrieved it. He will not remember.

It is dark now. The Milky Way, Hera's river of Ambrosia, cleaves the southern sky. I wish that I could bottle that restorative elixir and bring it home to you, to heal your sickness. I am anxious to make Santa Fe as there is a post there. Though you've long delayed, I know in my heart some missive will be waiting for me. I have humbly included a sonnet in mine, dedicated to you. Please accept for yourself the bottomless, unchangeable feeling that resides in my heart and courses through every vein in my body: an affection of the man who justly adores all your virtues and who loves you as men have rarely loved.

Your Destiny made Manifest, Zadock

FAM. BOVIDAE
GEN. BISON

12.8.43, 13:45, 75 deg., 25 knots, 6/10ths cloud coverage

Open grassy fields, Texian Territory

Bison, adult male. Very dark brown coat, almost black about the face and legs. At least 6 foot to the shoulder. Have seen these grand behemoths for days now, but today we lunched long enough for me to complete a sketch. They are far more imposing than I had imagined, but in temper gentle and cow-like. They stand as shaggy masters of these open fields. Curiously, both sexes have the horns, but the male's are much larger. Their young move about them much as calves do cattle, and sport a rusty reddish brown coat as opposed to the darker adults. It is magnificent to see them run, and the many times we've ridden up alongside the herds it is as though their speed adds to ours. When the men shoot them, it seems a great shame to me.

➤ Eliza, there is some pleasure in assembling this thread on the Thomas bloodline for you. For instance, can you imagine Zadock's excitement upon his arrival in Westport in 1843? This juncture of the Missouri and the Konzas River was the main outfitting point for the Santa Fe Trail. The great migration had begun, and settlers high on Manifest Destiny flocked to the Oregon Trail.

I cannot help but to compare it to my journey to Texas. At moments I find myself haunted by a similar sense of fate.

The idea of the West was always aspirational. In the 1840s exaggerated advertisements for a newly discovered Garden of Eden appeared. The expeditions of John Frémont and Kit Carson produced quixotic tales of the western lands, as well as maps allowing settlers to seek their private utopias.

Falsities abounded. The Buenaventura River that Zadock speaks of here is a ghost river. It appeared on many maps of the era, yet no such waterway ever existed. It was a myth.

Stories aside, I find the desire of these early settlers to venture past the bounds of their civilization compelling. Homesteaders would be beyond the reach of any government, in unexplored and dangerous land. Farther, perhaps, than any colonizing enterprise had attempted to go, with the notable exception of the long journeys across the Atlantic. To maintain a belief that the wilderness could be subdued and the brambles turned to civilization required an astonishing faith.

Just when I think I am done with the Historian's duties, some new moment or person piques my interest. The Santa Fe Trail had been opened by Missouri traders carrying wholesale goods to Santa Fe to be sold in Mexico. Eventually, wealthy New Mexican families wanted a share of the booming economic trade. By 1843 Mexican traders, like Rodriguez, from New Mexico and Chihuahua comprised the vast majority of the overland traffic. These departing caravans needed considerable supplies and services, and could pay. This fueled Westport and the frenzy of commerce that Zadock accurately notes.

Unlike the Oregon Trail, the Santa Fe Trail had to be guarded from unfriendly American Indian tribes and, later, detachments from the Republic of Texas. Comanche and Apache were not keen on trespassers. Both conducted raids on caravans, often stealing goods and livestock, more rarely killing.

Conventional wisdom held that there was safety in numbers, especially if those numbers included soldiers. In Zadock's caravan they were replaced by Indians, which seems nearly unbelievable to me. That Mexican and Missourian merchants would accept such an escort speaks to either McMarrow's charm or his belligerence, I'm not sure which.

Zadock's anxiety to deliver the letter and complete the task it represented is palpable. Another parallel. Funny that I came to Texas in search of perhaps the very same letter. But the tram makes my journey much easier.

For Zadock, the Santa Fe Trail was a difficult undertaking: more than nine hundred miles of desolate landscape composed chiefly of arid plains and desert. Despite the great rains of 1843, water would prove a challenge, especially because the party took the lower branch of the trail, the Cimarron Crossing. The Cimarron River, though full, would have been the only source of water in what increasingly became a desert landscape as they moved west. This terrain was new and strange to Zadock, and his excitement is evident in the many drawings of desert creatures he produced while on the trail.

Despite my difficulties, if my mission here had some semblance of progress I would be far less anxious.

Zeke has not answered my note. I resolved to go and see

him, and knock on your door, as risky as that seemed. As I approached your unit, you came out, dressed for work. I ducked behind a watchpost, afraid you'd spotted me. To see you made my heart ache. You have grown into a beautiful woman. You look self-assured and graceful like your mother, and at the same time entirely like your seven-year-old self. I was overwhelmed.

I will have to think of another way. These letters, this thread I am preparing — I have begun to think you need to see it sooner than I had planned. I cannot simply leave it in your inheritance bundle. There is not time to wait until after I'm gone.

Defying the ban on our communication is very dangerous. The punishment would be harsh if either of us were caught with a thread like this one. I had sometimes thought of myself as a harmless historical symbiont riding the back of the government's stored knowledge, taking what I need. Now I have begun to leech away that lifeblood and adopt the attitude of a malignant parasite. My relationship with this government has always been strained. On the one hand they ruined my life, and on the other saved it.

Your mother was beautiful. Sometimes I'm glad her sickness took her before the rest occurred. I cared for her, but we weren't in love. How could I be? I am Queer.

It was something I had long known, but it had been impossible for me to tell anyone. After the Collapse, the lifephase system was initiated out of the dire necessity to reproduce. The population had dwindled to a range we had previously used for animals on the verge of extinction. A key part of reestablishing civilization was procreation.

The Queers were left out, then ostracized, then persecuted. One of the first watchposts in Salt-Lake recorded an illicit affair I was having with a man. The punishment at that time was to be thrown out into the rot. After the Collapse, there was very little patience or tolerance for diversity. Folks were scared.

Many Queers that were my friends had been thrown over. I suspected they were out there, banding together. I wonder if I'd have taken the risk to join them if it weren't for you.

You made me a special case. Being Queer, I didn't fit the lifephase system and therefore neither did you. The Lawmen would have thrown me over and declared you an orphan. Instead one Senator struck a compromise. You would take the Gray name and leave my bad bloodline behind. The Law agreed it would give you a fresh start. I was allowed to live but forbidden to ever contact you again. I was given a post in the new government, under the Master of Records, by the Senator who had advocated for my life, Zacharyh Thomas.

I've thought about you every day since. I've celebrated every birthday of yours. I wonder if you even know when that is.

When I think of our reunion, it always looks like the day we were torn apart. The judgment had come down quickly, and I was sent to Chicago-Land immediately. I brought you with me to the tram terminal to say goodbye.

I can picture that afternoon perfectly. Long lashes of sunlight coming through the tall windows, the terminal empty with charged air. The oiled gears of the tram, the newness of the white upholstery coloring the air with a clean bright smell.

I said goodbye, that I didn't know when I'd see you again. What else could I say? You were seven.

To you, my explanations were flimsy. What was true was the pain. Your chin trembled, confusion flickered in your eyes. You didn't know what was happening, but you knew it was bad.

It's been so long. I can only imagine that your hurt and anger have compounded over the years. How could you ever forgive me, when I can't explain why it had to be this way? I have lived in secrecy and shame all these years. I reject this society's bigotry, but I am still afraid. Senator Thomas later campaigned for acceptance. And my sexuality is no longer a crime. But neither is it equal. Most of my fellows have been relegated to Atlantas.

I sympathize with the Deserters in this city-state. The Republic has bred mistrust. I wish our societies were governed according to human nature. The lines drawn between nations and states exist only in the imaginations of men. Our government has forgotten that. I would have them study America's nascent stage, to discover the valuable lessons contained in history's tragedies. The American Indians, for example, had no boundaries. Their minds, previously free, were circumscribed by foreign conceptions of flags and maps and then decimated by foreign disease and violence.

The foreigners visited violence upon themselves as well. The land grab for unclaimed territory in the middle part of the century is unmatched in world history. As the U.S. took on more territories and ratified them as states, some of them tried to break away, nearly resulting in a split of the whole country. The American Civil War was fought against the Southern states a few short decades later. Bigotry again, in its worst form.

During those years, the Texas territory held by a thread. It rightfully belonged to Mexico, but the Texans, in their long, open rebellion, were having some success forming a republic. Mexico was not organized enough to control the territory.

Texas wrote a constitution, set up a government, and began printing currency. The war, however, dragged on, and caused disruption in the trade routes and political relations with the neighboring countries. The U.S. worried from the sidelines. Some wanted to annex Texas and be done with it. This might cause a war with Mexico, but they weren't opposed to a fight. Some even advocated for the occupation and acquisition of the entirety of Mexico, but the U.S. government did not want responsibility for that many non-Anglo citizens. The issue of whether Texas would be admitted as a free state or a slave state hung over the question of annexation.

The nation hesitated. Major social upheaval caused by wars and shifting boundaries inevitably leads to death and the ripping apart of families. A stable civilization is necessary for the maintenance of family ties and bloodlines. So they say.

As much as I want to, I can't speak to you. I'm afraid you'll hate me. In order to avoid another run-in, I looked at your file and learned your daily routines. It was here I discovered that your namestamps are all over the murder thread that has plagued this city-state.

I wish you had not taken the thread on. One Corrector can always tell the work of another, and every file that relates to the murders has been heavily corrected. Someone is manipulating the thread. Major Daxon keeps tight reins on the Vault, and I don't think he can be trusted. I don't know how to warn you of all of this without revealing myself.

I am determined to fix what I have made wrong in your lives. I regret that I reported the letter missing. I will go to Zeke. *The Sisters Gray* makes it clear that this letter is an important family record. I will warn him of the danger you both are in.

Take care. You were always a clever girl. And a funny one. I remember your tricks well, your teasing "Bye forever" that would stop my heart every time. A dark prophecy, that was.

I'm keeping an eye on Daxon's files. And, of course, yours, but only out of love and fear for your safety. There is no worry like that of a father for his daughter.

taken to sleeping on the leather sofa in the museum room ever since Mrs. Gra___d died. Aunt Anne often found him here, and roused him to make him retire to his proper bed.

Mr. Gray woke slowly, sitting with great effort and trying to smooth his hair back in place. 'I was dreaming of my daughters.'

'Is that so?' Aunt Anne always listened to others' dreams with curiosity. Mr. Gray took it for politeness.

'A mad general had come to me to tell me that both their suitors had been killed in battle and that they should never marry. They were up in the trees, the tops of them were all tied together with rope, the forest was a giant net. Elswyth was sick again and I could not break the news to her as she was being bled quite horribly. She lay in a giant nest, as a wounded bird, whilst Louisa flittered all about her on the wings of a moth. It was maddening. I tried to catch her hem but could not bring her out of the air.'

'My premonitions about the girls have also been dark of late. Unless they lie with the men they are fated to, it bodes ill.'

'As I told you, Mr. Thomas was needed for my task. He is the only one who can deliver the letter.'

'And the one who can marry the Thomas and Gray blood.'

'I don't believe in all your blood alchemy. I told Elswyth she should find another. Mr. Thomas belongs in Texas. If the war does not end, what will future generations matter?'

'It is the future generations that will bring it to a stop.'

'Zadock cannot be the only man in the Thomas bloodline. Couldn't you find someone for Louisa when her time comes to marry? Doesn't Mr. Thomas have a brother?'

'Yes, and Seth is queer.'

Mr. Gray stood, and wobbled. The last few years, the financial strain of the museum added to the trouble at the mill had exacted a toll. 'I don't understand why this Thomas bloodline is so desired.

He behaves like a twit half of the time. You and your weird Sisters are too concerned with the marriages of other▓Was my wife so prescriptive about her daughters' fate?'

'She wrote the book on it. You have read *The City-State*. The future demands the bloodlines meet. She foresaw it. Unless this happens, nothing can be true. Stop fretting over your little errand or your little war. Your concern should be for what happens here, with your daughters.' Aunt Anne took his arm with her crippled hand and they walked slowly from the darkened room. 'Louisa needs discipline, if she is the one to be married. She is in danger, even now. I sense a change within her. If Elswyth does not find a suitable husband, there is always the Auspicium. Our walls are meant for protection from the outside world, to keep in what is sacred. Our texts, our rituals, everything about our way of life must be secured. The world is full of murderers and beasts.'

'I understand, but I'm afraid my elder daughter shares her mother's aversion to structured life and the direction of others.'

Aunt Anne sat him on the kitchen stool and busied herself with the kettle. 'I'll brew you something to aid your sleep.' She pulled a carmine feather from the pocket of her sleeve, ground it into a fine dust, and sprinkled it into an empty teacup.

'Elsie would balk at being confined to the company of women-folk. Especially if it seemed I simply couldn't afford a wedding.'

'Her speech, along with your new specimens, will be more than enough to sway the gala patrons to open their pocketbooks.'

'Subscribing to Mr. Audubon's entire series was too costly. To finish the *Birds of America* folio, the girls will have to be wedded to wealth. The fates have resolved to keep me penniless.'

'You are their father. I'm sure your solution will be considered,' Aunt Anne said. She patted his arm. He flinched at the touch of her withered claw. 'Take your tea upstairs. I've already turned

FAM. **LEPORIDAE**

GEN. **TEMPERAMENTALUS**

24.8.43, 16:15, 100 deg., 5 knots, no clouds

Raton Pass, Texas. Rocky desert country. Small dry brush

Jack-a-lope. Large hare quite similar to the Jackrabbit, but featuring small antlers, like that of a young antelope. Fearsome personality. I imagine resources are scant in these climes, and the necessity of preserving territorial boundaries has made for fierce fighting headwear on an otherwise peaceful animal. Nature is a most thoughtful giver of gifts!

Elsworth — this drawing is for Louisa, meant to match her imagination. I feel sure it will make the most wonderful stuffing. I hope it delights her, however much the proportions are distorted.

Lucky!

ELSWYTH RECEIVES A SONNET. LOUISA IS ILL.
HER SECRET IS REVEALED.

Keeping a holy silence, Elswyth had risen early that day and opened all the windows to reveal a dark gathering of rain clouds. She had spent the better part of the morning working on her novel of manners. She had been composing it for months, mostly in her head, and it was high time to get a few things down on paper. Louisa would need the advice—Elswyth had struggled mightily in society without a name to recommend her.

She should instead be writing her speech for the Museum of Flying's annual gala. It was imperative to the survival of her father's venture and thus happiness, but she was too cross with him at the moment to feel like he deserved an act of kindness.

Her next task was mending the pockets of Louisa's dresses. Elswyth didn't quite trust her sister's ability with needles.

When she turned out the first pocket, a letter fell out. Elswyth picked it up. It was addressed to her, and in Mr. Thomas's hand. It was torn in the middle as though someone had run it through with a dagger. She hardly had time to register her surprise before she opened it and unfolded the single page. It had broken sentences at the top and bottom, so most of the letter was clearly missing. The only thing left in the envelope was a sonnet.

The stars that light the desert blank burn bright,
Yet the seer's globe is a darkened moon
Casting not the hour dawn should here alight,
Or if I will again know song of loon;
The lost heavens in-exhausted and cursed,
Weary the soul and drain its well of strength,
I cannot draw from it to sate this thirst,
For my fear knows not its own journey's length.
So bright beacon of hope's face remembered,
At once lift dark dust and lighten my stride.
Above, thine visage fine stars have rendered,
Thy horizon's arms enfold me inside.
Thus an empty land now begets home,
With a turn toward thee, a far star alone.

It was insipid, almost unreadable drivel. Yet it moved her. It was the only thing she had seen in Mr. Thomas's hand since he went away. How ever did Louisa come to have it? She read the sonnet over a few times, considering its sentiment.

She couldn't write anymore, her head filled with thoughts of Mr. Thomas. It was her father's fault for sending him away. As she walked down the hall past his room, she resolved to remain upset. She needed to ask Louisa about the letter's provenance.

She was surprised to find her sister, usually quite sprightly in the morning, still tucked tight in her small bed. 'Louisa, you ought to be up. You know Aunt Anne despises late breakfasting.' Her small body remained motionless. 'Have you been stealing my post? I've just found my letter in your pocket, half destroyed.'

'It was by the fencing cabinet, speared on a sabre.' Louisa's voice sounded weak and far away. Elswyth came and laid a hand upon her forehead. It was warm. The health and freshness that characterized her sister's looks were alarmingly absent.

'Are you ill? D̶ your stomach pain you?'

Louisa nodded cautiously.

'You lie there. I'll fetch a remedy.' Shortly Elswyth returned with a cold compress. She pulled back the covers and brushed the hair from Louisa's forehead to apply it. 'This is the blood that I said would visit you each new moon. But you must simply bear it. And my post is to be given directly to me. I'm expecting it.'

Louisa was as a shadow. 'Tell me a story from Mother's book.'

'I don't know any by heart, kid-doe.' She arranged the pillows to sit herself up next to Louisa. 'When I was a little girl, Mother would simply speak to me of the future.'

'The future?'

'Yes, my future. It was only when I was ill enough that I had to be bled, but she would tell me all the wonderful things that my future held in store for me: society tea, many handsome suitors. I had an entire library of dresses that I could choose from for any occasion. The closet was a great hall, with row upon row of beautiful gowns and dainties and fine things rare. I was the keeper and could comb through them to see what I might wear. In the future, there are enough material goods for all, and an abundance of food and drink unknown to us now. Chemical lights, and skies full of bats. All rain will cease to fall and…'

Louisa vomited all over the front of her nightgown. Elswyth jumped up, startled. Louisa began to cry.

'Oh dear, you really are ill, aren't you?' Elswyth unfastened her own skirt, to keep it from the mess, and helped Louisa clean up. She pulled the nightgown over her sister's head gingerly, turning her nose away. She collected the dress and the bedclothes in a basket meant for flowers. They would require thorough washing.

'Do you need some new undergarments as well?' Louisa nodded, shivering in her white knickers. Elswyth caught sight of a dried spot of crimson on the nape of her sister's neck. A rather nasty scratch. 'Tell me you haven't been riding the hounds again? You know very well how they bite.'

'I want Mother.'

'Shh.' Elswyth fetched an old star-patterned quilt from a trunk and spread it out on the bed.

'Elsie, I didn't... I'm not bleeding.' Louisa's voice was small.

'You're not?' Elswyth didn't believe her. 'Well you certainly seem to be cramping, and your little stomach is quite swollen.' She pulled a clean nightgown over Louisa's head. When her head emerged the sisters' eyes met and at once Elswyth knew.

'You're with child!'

Louisa crawled back in bed and pulled the covers up over her head. Elswyth pulled them down. 'Is it true?' Louisa looked sullen. 'You haven't even debuted! The gala... Did someone hurt you?'

'No one. Zed Blackfoot.'

'You mean Mr. Buell.' Elswyth reared up and a fierce light came into her eyes. She opened the sash and pulled up the window despite the dark sky outside. Panicked birds traced escape routes through the humid air. The clouds flashed, telegraphing a storm. Her eyes searched the grounds.

'Father will be furious...' She couldn't turn to look at her sister. She felt as though she might cry herself.

'You mustn't tell,' Louisa pleaded.

'Furious at him...' Elswyth sat on the bed and began to smooth Louisa's hair. Her sister trembled in her lap. 'Like I am. Like you...'

'I have to find Grapes.'

'You stay right here in bed,' she said, trying to make her voice sound grown-up. The way it quavered revealed to them both how very scared Elswyth was.

PLATE 15. MARYPOSA, A GRAYLING OF THE FAMILY NYMPHALIDAE

ELSWYTH DELIVERS UNWELCOME NEWS TO HER FATHER.

SHE SUGGESTS A DESPERATE PLAN.

MR. GRAY RELUCTANTLY AGREES.

lswyth found her father in his office, sitting behind his great desk stacked high with an enormous pile of bills, ledgers, files, and documents.

'Come in, my dove. I would that you were an accountant, but a daughter will do.'

His affectionate teasing stopped the words on her lips. How could she put such an awful thing into the air?

'Mr. Buell has yet to go to the post today. How it all piles up. The building of an institution is no easy task. Between a display case for that stupendously worthless buffalo and the scheduling of carpenters to work on the additional rooms, I'm not sure we'll ever know what it means to have finished something. And I won't have anything done in substandard fashion. I've always held that if you are to embark on some endeavor, everything must be done in the most carefully considered way.'

Elswyth sat down across from the stacks of paper. 'That is because you love it, Father. You love the museum above all else.'

Mr. Gray frowned. 'I suppose you're old enough now to know. Things are a bit more dire than I have let on. I fear this year's gala could be the last, and before the museum has truly had a chance to get off the ground. The banks hurt us all a great deal. Unless we find a patron willing to give some nest egg to see our efforts sustained, I shall have to declare bankruptcy. But I would sell all this before leaving my daughters wanting. You'll both require a dowry. And *you* are what I love above all else.'

'Father, there's something I have to tell you.'

'With the crash, everyone was broke because of land, and I sold my interest in powder, you see. My land holdings are not insubstantial, but I wasn't diversified. This is why you need to marry someone with a head for business. Even after the crash, the canal needed powder, so we would have been provided for...'

'Louisa is pregnant.' At this her father stopped and stared at her, his head arrested at a strange angle.

'That can't be.'

'I've just seen, and she is. She knows it too.'

'Impossible. She's not even been introduced yet. She's meant to debut at the gala. She doesn't have any suitors...'

'She has had Mr. Buell.' Elswyth braced herself, thinking that if anything could break her father's spirit, this news would be the instrument. He did not easily lose his composure. A much more frightening thing happened to his face now. Rather than go red, it turned a pale white, and he slumped back in his chair as though he had been struck a great blow. Elswyth remained still.

'I'll run him through,' her father said. His tone was entirely unnerving. 'He will not father my kin. I'll have him flogged in the public square, I'll amass a mob to cast stones at him.' Mr. Gray had become very businesslike.

'And what will that mob think of Louisa afterward? They will know who has sired her child.'

Her father softened and was quiet. 'Your aunt foresaw this.'

'It wasn't hard to see, if you observe anything about that man.'

'My kid-doe. A child out of wedlock.' Her father's complexion was still ghostly. He sat, and folded his hands in his lap. 'Aunt Anne will not forgive us this. Buell is a monster to hurt her.'

'He has taken advantage. Of us all. But you can't kill him. Louisa does not understand. She cares for him.'

He father closed his eyes. He seemed very far away.

'I have a plan,' Elswyth said. She sat up straight. 'We should first consider Louisa's health and happiness. She can't debut at the gala. We must keep her inside until the child is born. Aunt Anne will be the midwife. We can claim Louisa is sickly, which should be passable given my long history of ill health.'

'And when the child is born?'

Elswyth smoothed her skirts. 'I shall also remain indoors. When the child is born, it will be mine. If anyone is to bear a child out of wedlock, it should be me. I am older, and have no suitor.'

'Elswyth.' Her father sighed. 'No. This will ruin you socially. If I cannot stand for one of my daughters to fall from respectable society, why should the other be any better?'

'Louisa would have a chance at marriage yet.'

This gave her father pause. 'There is still the trouble of a dowry.' He began to arrange the things on his desk, straightening the papers into neat rows with great care. 'The money is gone, my dear. Do you know what that means for us? We have no name. You'll have no chance at happiness. Unless you marry.'

'Then I must be married to the father of my new child.' Elswyth's voice took on a rapid, desperate cadence, her chin at a cavalier angle. 'I will take Mr. Buell, and no one will be the wiser.' Her father turned a shade whiter. She looked down, her stomach churning with hatred and disgust. 'I can see no other way.'

He closed his desk drawer slowly, and it emitted a lonesome

creak. 'You haven't even allowed him to court you for ages.'

'This shall be a short engagement then.'

'But think how long the marriage. I should send you both to your aunt's Auspicium instead. I should have done it long ago.'

'You know babies are not allowed there. And I do not care to abandon the world entirely. I've had enough of being alone. My last suitor is lost to the wilderness. Sent away by you. This is the only way to undo the family's shame.'

Her father just shook his head in disbelief or disagreement, it was impossible to tell. 'Father...' Elswyth's voice was heavy with sentiment. She could see he was overcome. 'You can do one thing for me now. Mr. Buell must propose to me. I don't know how to make him do this. I spurned his advances for so long.'

'I know you have offered this out of love for your sister. I doubt it will satisfy your aunt's wishes for you, but if this is how you would have things...' He stood from his desk, and Elswyth knew the conversation had reached its end. 'I'll speak to Mr. Buell myself, and he will agree.'

Elswyth kissed her father on the cheek and left the room hurriedly, her jaw set. Could it be that this is what would come of her life? She knew of no other way to help her sister.

She went outside, to the laundry. Louisa's bedclothes had been soaking in a ten-gallon tub of rainwater since that morning. She violently shaved a pound of soap into the tub, the curls dissolving off the end of her knife. She picked up the stirring stick, but then, thinking better of it, ran back to her room.

She fetched her barely begun manuscript of manners. Tumbling back outside, she flung it into the tub, splashing water everywhere. She then set to stirring vigorously. The dark tendrils of ink snaked out and stained the white bedclothes, thereby ruining both.

Leeya,

I AM SO TOTALLY FRUSTRATED — AND TERRIFIED. THINGS ARE NOT GOING AS PLANNED. MY HEART IS RACING. I WISH I COULD PICK UP THE PHONOTUBE BUT GIVEN EVERYTHING THAT IS HAPPENING THAT WOULD BE FOOLISH. BESIDES, IT IS SO LATE NOW.

I RETURNED HOME FROM WORK AT THE USUAL TIME BUT FOUND OUR UNIT EMPTY. ZEKE HAS BEEN SO ANTISOCIAL SINCE RETURNING FROM CHICAGO-LAND THAT I WAS SURPRISED TO FIND HIM GONE. I WAS A LITTLE ON EDGE, SO I DECIDED TO DRAW WHILE I WAITED. IT IS TWO IN THE MORNING AND ZEKE HAS YET TO RETURN HOME. I AM <u>SICK</u> WITH ANXIETY.

I WOULD NOT BE SO WORRIED IF THINGS WERE NOT SO STRANGE LATELY. ZEKE RECEIVED A CRYPTIC NOTE IN THE PHONOTUBE — WITH A FILE NUMBER. IT WAS SUSPICIOUS AND I ASKED ZEKE WHAT WAS GOING ON. HE EXPLAINED THAT HE HAS AN OLD LETTER FROM HIS GRANDFATHER THAT HAS NOT BEEN CARBONED. I INSISTED AS STRONGLY AS POSSIBLE THAT HE HAS TO DEAL W/ THIS IMMEDIATELY. IN TYPICAL FASHION, HE SQUIRMED AROUND THIS. HE WANTS TO KEEP THE LETTER. I DON'T KNOW WHY HE WOULDN'T JUST ACCEPT THE SENATE SEAT. WHAT WILL HAPPEN TO US IF HE DOESN'T?

I LOOKED UP THE NUMBER THAT WAS ON THE NOTE — AN OLD FILE ASSIGNED TO SOMEONE NAMED BARTLE. HIS RANK IS CORRECTOR, BUT I COULDN'T FIND ANYTHING ELSE ON HIM. CORRECTORS TEND TO ERASE THEMSELVES OUT OF THE RECORDS, THOUGH. SOMEONE IN THE VAULT IS CLEARLY TRYING TO

MESS WITH MY HEAD. ALL OF THIS MAKES ZEKE'S
ABSENCE TONIGHT FEEL MORE FRIGHTENING.

I HATE TO SAY IT BUT THIS REMINDS ME OF
WHEN RAISIN WAS REALLY UNDER THE BLANKET OF
LAUDANUM. I REMEMBER THOSE NIGHTS WHEN YOU
WOULD CALL CRYING AND AT LOOSE ENDS. I KNOW
HOW HARD THAT TIME WAS FOR YOU AND I HOPE YOU
REMEMBER THAT IS THE ONLY REASON I QUESTION
YOUR PAIRING. I KNOW IT IS HARD TO FIGURE OUT
WHAT TO DO. JUST REMEMBER I AM HERE FOR YOU.

I SHOULD STOP WRITING. IT'S NOT MAKING ME
FEEL LESS NERVOUS. THERE ARE MORE RECORDS OF
MISSING GIRLS THAN MURDERS. THAT THE TWO FILES
HAVEN'T BEEN COMPARED SPEAKS TO THE MAJOR'S
INCOMPETENCE. HE'S PASSED-OUT DRUNK ON HIS DESK
HALF THE TIME. I'VE MADE SOME PROGRESS ON
THE THREAD, AFTER PULLING TOGETHER THE DEATH
RECORDS OF ALL THE GIRLS, THE EARLY INJURIES
WERE ALL INFLICTED W/ KNIVES : SHARP AND
PRECISE. IT'S ONLY LATER THAT THEY BEGIN TO
SHOW CLAW MARKS AND BITES. AND THOSE ARE
INCONSISTENT. THEY STARTED AT THE SAME TIME
AS THE 'ANIMAL IN THE CITY-STATE' RUMOR. AND THEN
PEOPLE BEGAN TO CLAIM ALL THE SIGHTINGS AND
WORRY ABOUT DEAD ZONES. I THINK THE MURDERER IS
TRYING TO FAN THE FLAMES OF THAT PANIC. THE
ONLY ANIMAL ON THE LOOSE IS A **SCAPEGOAT.**

KEEP SAFE. WRITE YOUR NAME IN THE DUST UNDER
MY WORK DRAWER, SO I'LL KNOW YOU SAW THIS NOTE.

I LOVE YOU LIKE A SISTER,

ELIZA ✳

FOUNT

THE SQUARE

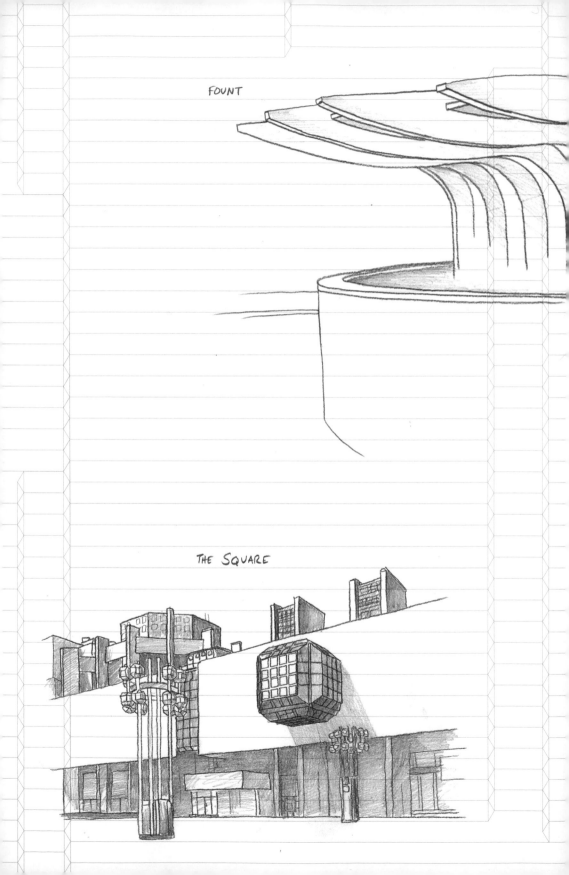

VAULT OF RECORDS

⊗ ∧∧ "I was up all night, worried sick. I got back from the washatorium and you were gone." Eliza stood over Zeke. He was lying on the floor mat in the livingroom, wearing last night's clothes. ∧∧ ∧∧ ∧∧ Zeke kept his eyes closed. He could feel grains of sand between his teeth. ∧∧ ∧∧ ∧∧ ∧∧ ∧∧ The night before returned in flashes: the Major's sweaty brow, the jail cell shunting down the street, the fellow Raisin argued with pressed against the glass, staring back at him. ∧∧ ∧∧ ∧∧ ∧∧ ∧∧ ∧∧ ∧∧ ∧∧ ∧∧ "Are you hungover?" Eliza asked. "If you go to the square alone folks will think you're out courting." She went into the waterroom, slamming the door. He could hear the pipes groan to life. ∧∧ ∧∧ ∧∧ ∧∧ Zeke stumbled into the kitchen for a glass of water. He collapsed into a chair at the kitchen table. A pair of pomegranates rested in a bowl on the table. ∧∧ ∧∧ ∧∧ ∧∧ ∧∧ Eliza reemerged in her work uniform. Her damp hair was tightly braided. "What happened last night?" ∧∧ ∧∧ "I wanted another drink. I went to the square. I got drunk." ∧∧ "And arrested?" The accusation came out in a funny voice. She must have called the Vault during the night. "I thought you were keeping a low profile. I know a girl who lost her suitor that way. They were right about to be transferred." ∧∧ ∧∧ ∧∧ ∧∧ ∧∧ "They let me go. They just wanted me as a witness to someone else's fight." ∧∧ ∧∧ ∧∧ Eliza pressed her lips together in a tight seam. ∧∧ ∧∧ ∧∧ ∧∧ ∧∧ ∧∧ "The Major doesn't like me is all." ∧∧ ∧∧ ∧∧ Eliza pulled mixes out of the cupboards and put them on the counter. ∧∧ ∧∧ He picked up one of the pomegranates. It was hard. He didn't know how to properly open it. Its skin was the color of blood. ∧∧ ∧∧ ∧∧ ∧∧ ∧∧ ∧∧ ∧∧ ∧∧ They had bought the pair of pomegranates for dessert on their anniversary. They had purchased an elaborate fount-water tea service, natural foods, and wine. It was expensive, the pomegranates especially. ∧∧ ∧∧ ∧∧ The mood had been off that night. He had been sluggish. She'd made conversation, reminisced about the past year, held his hands. He hadn't wanted to converse. The bottle of wine had been emptied. He'd been too tired to eat the pomegranates. They had been sitting in the bowl on the kitchen table for weeks. ∧∧ ∧∧ ∧∧ ∧∧ "You're not anonymous, Zeke. You're about to be Khrysalis. You exist in the world," Eliza said. ∧∧ And I exist, with the world, without care. ∧∧ Zeke thought to himself. ∧∧ ∧∧ ∧∧ "I'm a Gray girl, I don't care about bloodlines. But if you don't accept the seat, what will we do instead? The Senate is waiting." Zeke was silent. He watched her fill two shallow porcelain bowls. ∧∧ "I don't even know what you want anymore." Eliza whisked fount-water in furious little movements. ∧∧ **"How do you think we should open these pomegranates?"** ∧∧ ∧∧ "How many days do I find you here, still in your nightclothes, with laudanum on your breath?" ∧∧ "I quit laudanum." ∧∧ "It's just another thing that puts us both at risk." ∧∧ ∧∧ ∧∧ ∧∧ ∧∧ ∧∧ **"They probably would have showed us how to crack them."** ∧∧ ∧∧ "You can't wait anymore, Zeke. You have to act. They're listening to you. They'll find something. You'll end up in jail, and I'll end up alone." ∧∧ ∧∧ ∧∧ Zeke got up and went to the waterroom. He needed a moment alone. He stared at his face in the silver-backed glass. There were dark circles beneath his eyes. He took a few deep breaths. He opened and closed his mouth. It was strange to think that his ancestors had looked roughly like him, for tens of thousands of years. He wondered what their lives had been like. If their experiences had left some mark on his soul. He contorted his face, trying to look like a different person. ∧∧ ∧∧ ∧∧ ∧∧ He went back into the kitchen. Eliza was staring into her bowl of fount-water, now emptied. She was blinking rapidly, which was what she always did right before she started to cry. She muttered, "I would go out to the square if you ever wanted to go out with me." ∧∧ **"You know I don't really like it there."** ∧∧ "When was the last time we went out? To do anything at all?" The blinking held back her tears. ∧∧ ∧∧ ∧∧ ∧∧ He dipped a finger in his bowl. "Your single friends don't like me around. A pair is bad luck in a group of singles." ∧∧ ∧∧ ∧∧ "Then just the two of us," Eliza said. ∧∧ ∧∧ "You never want to hang out with my friends either." ∧∧ "You mean Raisin? He is not that easy to be around." It seemed she didn't know Raisin had been arrested last night as well. "You saw how he was with Leeya. He drove her half crazy with the Deserter talk, those rot conspiracies. He probably would have signed her up had it gone any further." ∧∧ ∧∧ "Leeya's immature. She lives in a fantasy world." ∧∧ ∧∧ "And Raisin doesn't? He left her. Courted her forever and then insisted on some harebrained escape plan." ∧∧ "It upsets him, you know. That you hang out with Leeya." ∧∧ "We're best friends. And she's in bad shape. I've got to find her someone else. That's why I go out. She can't stay single. She has to be transferred too. Who will come with me to the nature replicas? Raisin is never going to make it to Twin-City." ∧∧ ∧∧ "Raisin is your friend too. You shouldn't just assume where everyone will end up. That would hurt his feelings." ∧∧ "I can't imagine why. If he's single, it's his fault. He'll end up in jail. Maybe you need some other friends." ∧∧ ∧∧ "You're supposed to be my friend." ∧∧ ∧∧ "I'm your pair. That's different." ∧∧ ∧∧ "I could use the help of a pair, too." ∧∧ "Well, that's difficult when everything is a secret and I need the Vault of bloody Records to tell me you've been arrested, you're going crazy, trying to chop down watchposts with a sabre, drunk or on laudanum, or whichever it is today." Eliza's voice began to swell. Zeke stood still. ∧∧ ∧∧ ∧∧ "My grandfather died." ∧∧ "Yeah." Eliza slammed her empty bowl down on the counter. "Everyone knows that, Zeke." ∧∧ ∧∧ He picked the bowl back up and slammed it down harder in the sink. It cracked neatly into four pieces. They both stopped and stared at what Zeke had done. The identical quarters of the broken porcelain looked staged in the empty sink. The air hung motionless. Eliza began to cry. Zeke reached out for her hand and she pulled away. ∿ ∿ ∿ ∿ ∿ ∿ ∿ "Welcome to the lousy day you've created for yourself." She teetered out of the room, heavy boots on a thin wood floor. ∿ ∿ ∿ Zeke heard the door slam. "Bye forever," he whispered. ∿ ∿ ∿ ∿ He lay down on the couch. If he didn't move, maybe the ache would subside. He might regain sleep. He slid into a dream about his grandfather. ∿ ∿ ∿ ∿ ∿ ∿ ∿ ∿ ∿ In the dream, the Senator was holding court at the family breakfast table. He was carving up a snake that had been wound around a pig's skull and cooked. Everyone at the table was writing down his words. Quill pens scribbled in furious unison. A door whistle interrupted his grandfather's lecture. ∿ ∿ ∿ ∿ ∿ ∿ ∿ ∿ ∿ ∿ ∿ ∿ ∿ ∿ ∿ Zeke woke up. The door whistle sounded again. Eliza must have forgotten her satchel. He couldn't bring himself to get up. The knob turned on its own and the door opened. ∿ ∿ ∿ ∿ ∿ "Zeke Thomas?" Another voice in the room. Zeke squinted. The brown blur of Eliza's uniform was replaced by another. Zeke wanted to stand. His body was filled with sand, his muscles too heavy. ∿ "I've got a fortnight." ∿ "Excuse me?" ∿ "I've got... eleven days. You can't arrest me. I don't have it." Zeke imagined jumping up, running, getting tackled, trying to wrestle the man off. He lay still. ∿ ∿ ∿ ∿ ∿ "I'm not here to... I'm not the Law." ∿ ∿ Zeke opened his eyes a little more. The man wore the uniform of a Vault worker. He was bearded and balding, too old for the city-state of Texas. His thick square glasses were the wrong shape for his face. ∿ ∿ ∿ "You're not the Law?" ∿ "Officially, I'm a Corrector. But I hope you'll think of me more as a friend... of the family. My name is Henry Bartle." This might all be recorded, a trap. ∿ "Hh. What do you want?" ∿ "I sent you a note, you never answered it. I was trying to reach out to you. There's something

QUIET

urgent that I had hoped we could speak about. I'm worried about you and... your pair. This unit maybe isn't the most suitable place for talking." ⌃⌃ ⌃⌃ ⌃⌃ ⌃⌃ Bartle made a small hand signal and drew his thin lips into a smile. Wrinkles radiated from the corners of his eyes. He was nervous, twitchy. He was off. ⌃⌃ ⌃⌃ **"I'm suffering from Law brutality. I need sleep."** Zeke rolled over. ⌃⌃ "Bic and I talked about the Senator's..." He squeezed one of his hands in the other. "About your grandfather's passing, and I wanted to offer my condolences." ⌃⌃ ⌃⌃ ⌃⌃ **"My cousin isn't the best representative of the bloodline."** ⌃⌃ "I introduced myself last week when I arrived here. He wasn't as helpful as I'd hoped." ⌃⌃ **"Can't stand him."** ⌃⌃ ⌃⌃ ⌃⌃ ⌃⌃ "I noticed your sabre there." Bartle pointed to it, motionless above the mantel. Zeke tensed. "Looks like a gift from Bic's collection. He showed me some very old sabres." ⌃⌃ **"It was my grandfather's. Listen, I've got things to do today."** ⌃⌃ "That's actually the very thing I hoped to ask you about. About your grandfather." ⌃⌃ ⌃⌃ ⌃⌃ Zeke searched the strange man's face. For a moment he wanted to trust him, open up, tell him about the letter, ask for help. ⌃⌃ ⌃⌃ **"He's dead, so I'm sure it can wait."** ⌃⌃ ⌃⌃ ⌃⌃ ⌃⌃ Bartle pulled off his glasses. He cleaned them with threadbare shirtsleeves. ⌃⌃ ⌃⌃ ⌃⌃ ⌃⌃ ⌃⌃ **"The sun is barely up,"** Zeke said. ⌃⌃ ⌃⌃ "Look at this, please." Zeke took a file stuffed with paper and carbons from Bartle's thick hand. He leafed through it silently. When he looked up he caught Bartle staring at a picture of him and Eliza on the mantel. "I couldn't, maybe, use your waterroom? If it's not too much trouble," Bartle asked. ⌃⌃ **"It's in the back,"** Zeke said. ⌃⌃ ⌃⌃ ⌃⌃ ⌃⌃ ⌃⌃ ⌃⌃ ⌃⌃ ⌃⌃ ⌃⌃ ⌃⌃ ⌃⌃ ⌃⌃ ⌃⌃ ⌃⌃ Zeke inspected the file Bartle had handed him. It was full of classified documents: stoic black-and-white photos of relatives, newspaper clippings, birth and death records, all dated back hundreds of years. ⌃⌃ ⌃⌃ ⌃⌃ Someone had done a lot of additional research on his bloodline. He stopped at an elaborate rendering of the Thomas family tree. ∧∧ ∧∧ Zeke read over the old names slowly. Had his ancestors ever felt this restless, this uneasy? Was it the barrier, or was it in his blood? ∧∧ ∧∧ ∧∧ ∧∧ ∧∧ ∧∧ When his grandfather ran for the Senate, his bloodline was thoroughly vetted. The Correctors employed by his opponents pried all the files open. They were looking for dirt, disinheritance, disgrace. ∧∧ ∧∧ Some stories had become exaggerated over time. But the reputation of the bloodline held. His thread was clean and he ascended to the Senate seat. ∧∧ ∧∧ Why would someone reopen his file? ∧∧ ∧∧ ∧∧ ∧∧ Zeke heard a drawer close. It was not near the waterroom. He leapt up and ran into the bedroom. Bartle was crouched in front of his desk. Half of the drawers were open. He spun around. ∧∧ "What are you doing?" Zeke's voice surprised him. Bartle's hands trembled. Worry lines banded on his high forehead. ∧∧ "I ... You don't understand what's at stake —" ∧∧ "Get out before I call a Lawman." ∧∧ "Zeke, I'm sorry, if you'll just —" ∧∧ "I'm calling a Lawman." Zeke ran back into the livingroom. He popped the cap off the phonotube and punched in three zeros. ∧∧ ∧∧ ∧∧ "Republic Dispatch." A woman's officious voice reverberated through the unit. "What's the situation?" ∧∧ ∧∧ ∧∧ Bartle scuttled to the door. He glanced back at Zeke and ran out. Light flooded the open doorway. ∧∧ "Identify yourself. Is that Zeke Thomas?" ∧∧ "Hh, yes, sorry. Zeke Thomas." He picked up the end of the phonotube. He could report Henry Bartle to the Law. Even if he was a Corrector. "It's nothing. Bad punch. Never mind." ∧∧ "Your thread shows an uncarbon'd document. Did you wish to —" ∧∧ Zeke capped the tube. He pressed his face into his hands. The house was silent. ∧∧ ∧∧ ∧∧ ∧∧ ∧∧ ∧∧ ∧∧ ∧∧ ∧∧ ∧∧ ∧∧ ∧∧ He thought of the letter. He hadn't checked it since yesterday morning. He ran back into the bedroom. When he opened his closet door, the shirt was gone. Bartle hadn't been near the closet and he hadn't had a shirt with him when he ran out. Zeke flipped through the hangers. It wasn't between any other shirts. He searched the floor of the closet. He plowed through a pile of dirty clothes on his desk chair. He tossed handfuls of fashionclothes out of Eliza's hamper. He pulled out all of his desk drawers, thumbing through stacks of paper. He looked through Eliza's things. He searched each drawer of the bureau. Neither shirt nor letter could be found in the bedroom. Had he moved it in a laudanum haze? ∧∧ ∧∧ ∧∧ ∧∧ ∧∧ He closed all the windows in the livingroom. They didn't seem to latch tightly enough. A violent wind was kicking up dust outside. It hissed against the walls. He would have to search the entire unit. He looked everywhere. All the cupboards, the drawers, the closets. Under the sparse wooden furniture. Every corner. Inside the end of the phonotube. Everywhere the Major would have looked. The letter was not inside the unit. ∧∧ ∧∧ ∧∧ He went back into the bedroom and kicked clothes around the floor of the room, still searching. He picked up every item of clothing and put his hand in every pocket. The touch of paper in one made his heart jump, but it was just an old wrinkled greenback. ∧∧ ∧∧ ∧∧ The letter was gone. The shirt was gone. Bartle had to have taken it. Even though he had nothing with him when he left. Zeke looked through the file left behind on his desk. It started with the Thomas family tree. Bartle was clearly obsessed with his bloodline. Zeke realized he had no idea how to find him again. ∧∧ Zeke put the stack down and quickly climbed to the roof, in case Bartle could still be seen. Up top, a whipping duststorm stung his face. There was no one out on the plankways. On the barrier's horizon he could see a churning thundercloud, slowly being destroyed by the weather pylons before it could reach the city-state. Lightning flashed and thunder reverberated inside the city-state like a musket ball rattling around in a tin can. ∧◇

24   I COULD NOT FEEL. I WAS BRIGHT BLANK INSIDE.

44

65

185

207

200

269

280

298

386

397

404

434

∞

Z.THOMAS

HENRY BARTLE

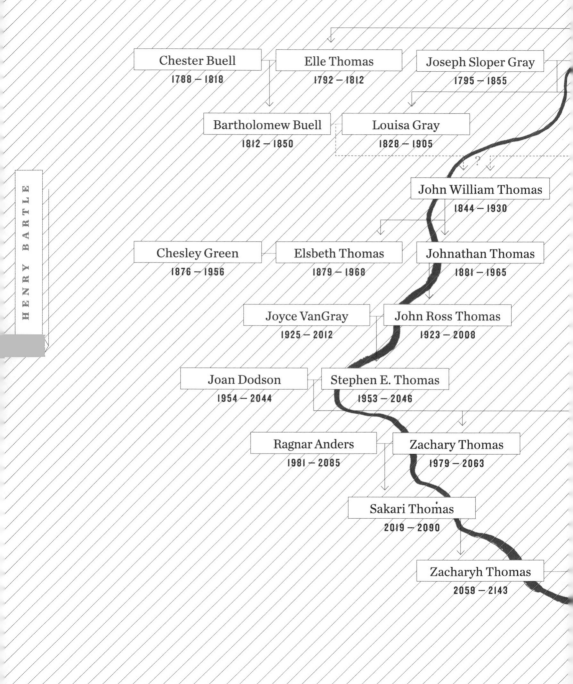

Chester Buell
1788 — 1818

Elle Thomas
1792 — 1812

Joseph Sloper Gray
1795 — 1855

Bartholomew Buell
1812 — 1850

Louisa Gray
1828 — 1905

?

John William Thomas
1844 — 1930

Chesley Green
1876 — 1956

Elsbeth Thomas
1879 — 1968

Johnathan Thomas
1881 — 1965

Joyce VanGray
1925 — 2012

John Ross Thomas
1923 — 2008

Joan Dodson
1954 — 2044

Stephen E. Thomas
1953 — 2046

Ragnar Anders
1981 — 2085

Zachary Thomas
1979 — 2063

Sakari Thomas
2019 — 2090

Zacharyh Thomas
2059 — 2143

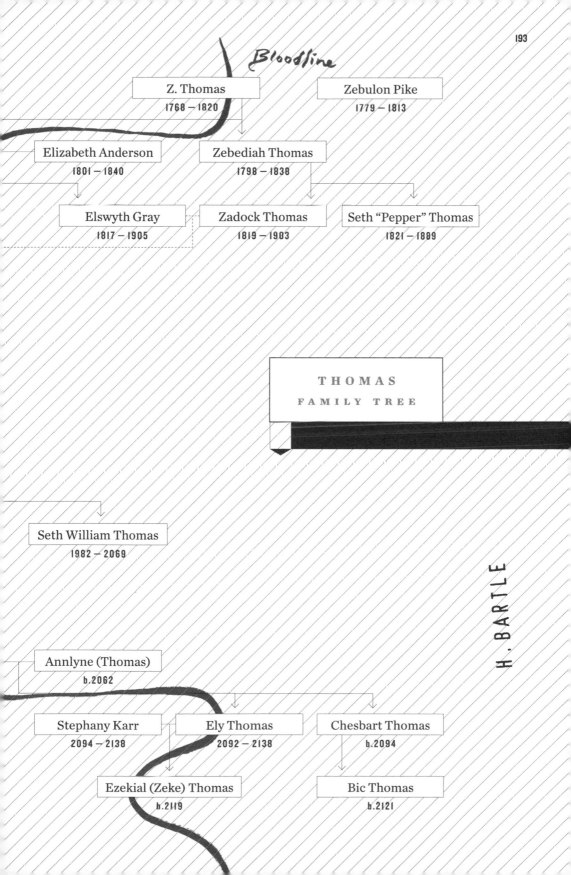

Bloodline

Z. Thomas
1768 — 1820

Zebulon Pike
1779 — 1813

Elizabeth Anderson
1801 — 1840

Zebediah Thomas
1798 — 1838

Elswyth Gray
1817 — 1905

Zadock Thomas
1819 — 1903

Seth "Pepper" Thomas
1821 — 1889

THOMAS
FAMILY TREE

Seth William Thomas
1982 — 2069

Annlyne (Thomas)
b. 2062

Stephany Karr
2094 — 2138

Ely Thomas
2092 — 2138

Chesbart Thomas
b. 2094

Ezekial (Zeke) Thomas
b. 2119

Bic Thomas
b. 2121

H. BARTLE

FAM. **ANTILOCAPRIDAE**

GEN. **ANTILOCAPRA**

7.9.43, 13:45, 95 deg., no wind, no clouds

Mountainous desert country. Blazing hot

Antelope. Skinny, light brown coat. White and gray markings. Diminutive twisted horns. I have seen many thin herds of these desert antelope, which are quite small and have the character of a goat crossed with a grayhound. They cling tightly to their peer groups and shun the rest of the animal kingdom, though this lady I caught sleeping. They do not make for much of a meal.

Dearest Elswyth,

The hour is late now, but all along the last few miles we heard the rattling cry of the prairie woodcock. I have found it quite common here, but tonight its peculiar song seems an echo of my loneliness. Our separation is wearing, I have slept little, and my heart is heavy.

We made an open camp. Rodriguez says McMarrow receives telegrams from his command, which he shares with no one. Rodriguez thinks they concern this fantastical gun that General Irion possesses, which I thought at first must just be a ship's cannon. The further he described its size and firepower the more it seemed another instance of Rodriguez's paranoia. Though McMarrow has his vices — lying and gambling — I remain thankful for his rough-and-ready leadership.

Last night we passed through the ruins of an ancient pueblo. When we first crested the hill, a figure in rags ran off, leaving a cart behind. In it we found a cage containing a motley coyote. There was little debate that the animal should be left in its prison, though it pained me to see its distress. It did give me ample time to draw it, however.

Our Indian escort would not come near the pueblo, claiming it was haunted. Among the crumbling walls, occasional geysers of steam hissed straight up into the air. Rodriguez wanted to investigate, if for nothing else than to separate from McMarrow for a spell.

The long-deserted village was indeed impressive. How did they procure enough water to sustain themselves in this desert? The structure in best repair was the church. I dismounted and Rodriguez and I went inside to look about. It was large, but built of the same sunburnt bricks common in this territory. The ceiling was quite high and doleful in appearance. There were many glyphs carved in and about the dwellings, including on the wood of the great door. An indication of a literate civilization aware of the grandeur of myths.

On this door was found a curious creature devouring its own tail. Rodriguez said it is the Indians' principal deity, a bird-snake. This benevolent god was the morning star, and created a new race from the bones of the old by adding a drop of his blood to make them live. Rodriguez seems well-versed in Indian lore.

In a room with a fire pit he began to tell me that the pueblo was inhabited until recently by one family, the remnant of a once very large population. Rodriguez also spoke of the temple on the other side of the village which housed old bones. The temple was supposed to have been in use five hundred years before the Spanish arrived. Legend holds it was built by a race of giants fifteen feet in height that preceded even the Aztecs. The ladder in the center of town was made to allow giants to reach to the heavens, or appears that way. It is broken now.

The Navaho fear these ancient people and their ghosts, Rodriguez told me. Only the sorcerers of the Navaho visited this place now. The primary ingredient in their witches' brew is the bones of the deceased, and I expect they find them here in no short supply.

The ghosts are called skinwalkers for their souls' ability to take the form of any animal. I thought of Aunt Anne, and wondered if her traveling soul could visit this place.

All around the church and temple there were ruins as high as three stories. These rooms were entered by ladders up against the buildings that could then be drawn up in case of an attack. The inhabitants were secure to throw stones or any other missiles at enemies below.

The sky has turned muddy and dark. We are again in flat desert. At supper, I gave a small bit of my ration to the caged coyote, who hungrily devoured it. Don't fret. I'm sure once we are gone, its owner will return for it. We camped not far from the edge of the ruins and I admit feeling strange next to the ruins of such a city. Rodriguez's tale has spooked me, which was perhaps his intent. The sky is moonless. The dust blowing strangely through the bones of the old town whispers in the night, and mixes eerily with the coyote's plaintive cries.

May These Bones Return to You, Zadock

LEEYA,

I FOUND ZEKE'S LETTER. I WAS GATHERING OUR CLOTHES TO TAKE THEM TO THE WASHATORIUM AND I FELT IT CRINKLE IN ONE OF ZEKE'S SHIRTS.

I PUT THE LETTER IN MY BAG AND BROUGHT IT TO WORK. IT WAS LIKE I DIDN'T EVEN DECIDE TO DO IT.

I HAVEN'T BEEN ABLE TO CATCH MY BREATH ALL DAY. WAS IT A REALLY STUPID THING TO DO?

BUT I HAVE A PLAN. I'M GOING TO DUPLICATE THE LETTER. I CAN STEAL SOME CORRECTOR'S GLUE, AND RESEAL IT. THEN I'LL PUT IT BACK IN ZEKE'S SHIRT AT HOME. IF HE NOTICES IT'S GONE, I'LL JUST SAY IT'S AT THE LAUNDRY, AND I'LL RUN DOWN HERE AND GET IT. EITHER WAY, I'LL BRING IT BACK AND HE'LL NEVER KNOW THE DIFFERENCE.

THAT WAY IF HE DOESN'T TURN IT IN BY THE DEADLINE, I CAN TURN IT IN FOR HIM, AND KEEP THE FAMILY NAME CLEAR, AND THE SENATE SEAT AVAILABLE. IT'S A SAFEGUARD, SO THAT ZEKE DOESN'T GO TO JAIL FOR AN UNCARBON'D DOCUMENT.

HE ALMOST GOT ARRESTED THE OTHER NIGHT. !!! A SALOON BRAWL, OF ALL THINGS. I HAVE NO IDEA WHAT IS MAKING HIM ACT OUT THIS WAY. IF IT'S THE LETTER, THEN I INTEND TO TAKE CARE OF IT.

BUT I CAN'T TELL HIM ABOUT IT. WE ARE REALLY FIGHTING NOW. OUR FIGHTS ARE SO STUPID. THEY'RE NOT EVEN ABOUT ANYTHING. WE FIGHT OVER... POMEGRANATES OR SOMETHING. I DON'T UNDERSTAND WHY HE PUTS US AT RISK. WE HAVE TO GET OUT OF TEXAS SOON. YOU TOO.

I HOPE I DON'T HAVE TO LIE TO ZEKE. I THINK I CAN RETURN IT BEFORE HE NOTICES. SOMETHING HAD

TO BE DONE — DAXON KNOWS HE HAS IT. DAXON MIGHT ALSO KNOW THAT I KNOW. I CAN FEEL HIM WATCHING ME AT WORK. I USED TO BE INVISIBLE TO HIM AND NOW HIS EYES LINGER ON ME WHENEVER WE ARE IN THE SAME HALL. IT IS TOTALLY CREEPY.

THE MORE I THINK ABOUT IT, THE MORE I'M CONVINCED IT'S DAXON WHO'S MESSING W/ MY WORK AT THE VAULT. HE USED MY NAMESTAMP ON THAT BOOK. HE'S TRYING TO USE ME TO GET AT ZEKE AND THE LETTER.

HE PAYS NO ATTENTION TO MY REPORTS ON THE MURDER THREAD. HE IS ENTIRELY DISMISSIVE OF MY WORK THERE, BUT VERY INTERESTED IN WHAT I'M DOING OTHERWISE. MY NERVES ARE FRAYED.

NOW MORE THAN EVER, I AM DETERMINED TO GET US TO CHICAGO-LAND. I AM CONFIDENT IF WE CAN GET THERE THEN WE CAN START AGAIN AND HAVE A FAMILY. I HAVE BEEN WAITING FOR THAT SINCE THE DAY MY FATHER LEFT. FOR YEARS, I RESENTED THE PRESCRIBED PATH OF THE LIFEPHASES, LIKE ZEKE DOES. NOW IT'S ALL I WANT.

IF ZEKE AND I START A FAMILY TOGETHER WE WILL BE ABLE TO RECONNECT — HE WILL HAVE SOMETHING OTHER THAN THIS SENATE SEAT — SOMETHING OTHER THAN HIMSELF — THAT FEELS MEANINGFUL AND REAL. MAYBE THIS IS A MISDIRECTED IDEA BUT I HAVE NOTHING BUT MY INSTINCT LEFT TO RELY ON.

I LOVE YOU LIKE A SISTER,

ELIZA

◇◇ ⌒ In the morning the air was hung with dust. Zeke wondered if their filter was broken. ⌒ He wanted to tell Eliza about Bartle and the missing letter, but couldn't breach the silence between them. She would be upset that he lost the letter. He wondered if he could get books in jail. Or laudanum. ⌒ ⌒ ⌒ Jail might be unpleasant, but maybe there he could fully retreat into himself. He might train his mind to travel by itself, in the night, across distant lands, to commune with all sorts of other minds. ⌒ No shadow of thought would be left behind. ⌒ ⌒ ⌒ ⌒ ⌒ Eliza pulled on her brown Vault uniform. ⌒ "Did my clothes go to the laundry?" ⌒ Eliza slid the door closed without answering. She left without looking at him. ⌒ ⌒ He went to the waterroom. The mechanical pump hissed and clanged as steam filled the copper pipes. Clean water ran down his back. He breathed the steam in deeply. ⌒ ⌒ He traced out the words "It will be OK" on the steamed glass of the waterroom door. Droplets rolled off the bottom of the letters. ⌒ ⌒ When they first moved from Port-Land they left each other notes. Eliza snuck a pencil out of her job at the Vault. The small theft excited her nerves. They used it to write on scraps of paper until Eliza got paranoid and took it back to the Vault. It was illegal to keep writing instruments. So Zeke began to write the notes anywhere he could: on fogged mirrors, in the dust that coated their walls, in the steam from their power lines. ⌒ It was easier than speaking, sometimes. No one else could listen in. He enjoyed tracing out the shapes of the letters with his fingers. ⌒ ⌒ ⌒ He watched his message disappear as the condensation evaporated. He wondered if it would reappear when Eliza took a shower. ⌒ ⌒ Back in the bedroom he opened the closet. He stared at the spot where his shirt had been. It was really gone. What if it had been a warning? He couldn't take the seat unless he knew. ⌒ He needed to think, so he decided to go to the fountry. ⌒ ⌒ ⌒ The city-state was

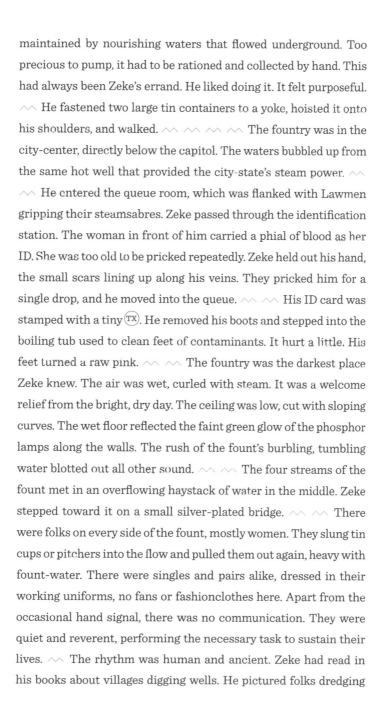

maintained by nourishing waters that flowed underground. Too precious to pump, it had to be rationed and collected by hand. This had always been Zeke's errand. He liked doing it. It felt purposeful. He fastened two large tin containers to a yoke, hoisted it onto his shoulders, and walked. The fountry was in the city-center, directly below the capitol. The waters bubbled up from the same hot well that provided the city-state's steam power.

He entered the queue room, which was flanked with Lawmen gripping their steamsabres. Zeke passed through the identification station. The woman in front of him carried a phial of blood as her ID. She was too old to be pricked repeatedly. Zeke held out his hand, the small scars lining up along his veins. They pricked him for a single drop, and he moved into the queue. His ID card was stamped with a tiny ⓣ. He removed his boots and stepped into the boiling tub used to clean feet of contaminants. It hurt a little. His feet turned a raw pink. The fountry was the darkest place Zeke knew. The air was wet, curled with steam. It was a welcome relief from the bright, dry day. The ceiling was low, cut with sloping curves. The wet floor reflected the faint green glow of the phosphor lamps along the walls. The rush of the fount's burbling, tumbling water blotted out all other sound. The four streams of the fount met in an overflowing haystack of water in the middle. Zeke stepped toward it on a small silver-plated bridge. There were folks on every side of the fount, mostly women. They slung tin cups or pitchers into the flow and pulled them out again, heavy with fount-water. There were singles and pairs alike, dressed in their working uniforms, no fans or fashionclothes here. Apart from the occasional hand signal, there was no communication. They were quiet and reverent, performing the necessary task to sustain their lives. The rhythm was human and ancient. Zeke had read in his books about villages digging wells. He pictured folks dredging up wet mud with bare hands, laying stone walls, carrying water daily. ∿ ∿ ∿ ∿ Zeke found a place at the edge of the fount and waited for a surge that would fill his container entirely. The fountry was messy. Zeke liked that too. He thrust his container in and lifted the full tin up and out. The liquid was a sparkling amber brown. Drops clung to the hair on his forearms. The bittersweet taste of fount-water was heavy in the air. ∿ ∿ ∿ ∿ A week's ration provided all the sustenance and nutrients necessary for survival. A splash of fount-water could heal abrasions or small cuts. Some folks consumed nothing but fount-water and skipped the frills, the restaurants. ∿ ∿ ∿ He liked being underground, in the dark, surrounded by the wealth of the city-state. Just as he was about to submerge the second container, he noticed a message written on the side. The condensation in the fount-water room had revealed a neat row of Eliza's capital handwriting.

YOU ARE MY BLOOD ♥

There was no way to tell when it had been written. ∿ ∿ ∿ ∿ ∿ ∿ With the yoke on his shoulders he walked back out into the bright morning. Ropes of dust snaked through the dry air. ∿ ∿ ∿ Zeke would bring the tins home and Eliza would combine the fount-water with flavors from the grocery, or make tea. If they ever made up. Zeke paused to read the broadsheets on the watchpost nearby. ∿ ∿ Largest was a notice urging girls who didn't want to be paired to join the Auspices in their strange alchemy. Zeke read the news broadsheet instead. There was an apology for the false all-quadrant alert. With uncharacteristic honesty, the broadsheet gave the reason: the string of murdered girls. Yet another body had been found. Citizens were advised to stay inside after dark. And then, hidden at the very edge of the sheet, the most disturbing news of all: There had been a cannon attack. Atlantas had collapsed. ∿

EVIDENCE [L]OST CITY [IN] GEORGIA

ruins provide to hidden [civi]lization

[BURI]ED FINDING

[Historia]ns disagree [over v]eracity of [ar]tifacts

— For years we've [heard o]f cities of gold and [lost] youth on this new [frontier,] whether the legends [are of t]he natives, or were [the] greed of Spain, it [has not] been determined. [Now,] the renowned and [h]istorian Theodore [Bran]shaw has claimed [to have un]earthed ruins in [... be]long to that same [tribe] who submerged [that] city of legend, At[lantis]. Georgians miners, [tun]nel per their usual [... stu]mbled upon a curi[ous ve]ssel unlike any ever [... n]otified the company [who] contacted M[...] [... ma]de the imm[ediate] [... by] steam c[a]r in or[der] [... to see] the evidence, and [offici]ally pronounced it [... of ruined and lost]

Strange Beast Found in Desert and Laid Blame

Ranchers demand recompense for drained livestock. Sheriff says dead coyote cannot be hanged.

TEXAS — The most curious discovery made last Wednesday by the Texian Officer Viktor VanBramble of a corpse, decidedly un-human but large enough to be were its attributes not so befuddling. Dragged into town behind his hound, the body was unveiled from the Officer's burlap sack to the consternation of many an onlooker, gathered there in town square, some with drink still in hand. What followed was a great guessing game. VanBramble himself would give no speculation, stating only the fact of how he had come upon such a creature, not by killing, he said, but only a chance discovery, its decomposed body festering under some dense desert shrubbery. Many townsfolk were quick to decry it as the murderous beast who has been ravaging local livestock, including Mrs. O'Leary's cow from within her own barn. They threw curses down upon the beast as though it could hear them and accept the blame for the drained goats, sheep, and cattle that have been found, blistered-belly-up in the field, robbed of their life blood. The creature indeed had a fearsome appearance, with large fangs and a mangy coat. Some said it was a new and unholy animal, the beast of Revelation, or some species native to Mexico, sent to raid our town. The Sheriff claimed it a sick and deranged coyote, as it was rather gaunt and ill-kept, and though it might be the cause of a killing or two, he could not very well have the beast hanged, and cautioned that our watch should remain ever vigilant against poachers, Indians, and the like.

To The People of Texas

CITIZEN SOLDIERS — I address you on subjects of our common concern: the quiet peace, the vital health and the honor of Texas. Your valor has nobly upheld her fine reputation in the bloody field of battle: but acts of gallantry are not by themselves enough to cement the high character of a perfected city-state. I put these things to you, members and offspring of the Old 300, for the reason that the exigencies of our epoch demand that each rightful incentive to duty is soberly considered by each citizen of our [n]ascent, yet proud, nation. That each of us may look upon our

MORAL PAIR[ING]

A caution to fathe[rs of] high-born daugh[ters]

OPINION — Many a fan[cy is shat]tered — many a heart br[oken,] and many a life is rende[red un]bearable, by the absurd [...] which fathers sometime[s use] in selecting a life-pair f[or their] daughters. Is it all p[ossible] for bliss to be the result [of a] union of two diametric[ally op]posed principles as are [virtue] and vice? Even so, ofte[n it] is considered a better [recom]mendation to a young [man] than moral upstanding [how] frequent is the primar[y ques]tion put forth about th[e] gentleman of, "Is he [rich]? Who is his family?" Su[ppose] he does abound in riche[s, can] it afford a scrap of pro[...] he will become a doting, [at]tentive husband? His co[at] may be fine brown linen, [his] brim hat clean and sha[rp,] he may fare sumptuous [every] evening; but how can vi[rtue be] inferred from such f[acts?] Suppose even he has hun[dreds] floating down every riv[er;] caution a close eye, fo[r it is] quite possible that riche[s may] at some time take wings [and fly] up into the sky, disapp[ear] as a distant spec and n[o more] only. Will you consent [to the] marriage of your daug[hter to a] gentleman who only h[as] ill-gotten and dirty sp[oils of] bloodshed and conquest, [all] inherited even, and not o[f] his own labors. Take hee[d, his] gilded scabbard may [hide a] rusty dull blade. Do [...]

FAM. CANIDAE

GEN. CANIS

8.9.43, 17:00, 90 deg., 10 knots, few clouds

Indian pueblo, estimated 42 miles from Santa Fe

Coyote. (A Spanish word. Perhaps prairie hound for the English?) Gray body with lighter underbelly, black-tipped tail. Long pointed ears and snout. Smaller than I had imagined, my guess is 4 feet long. I found my specimen quite lithe and ragged. I chose not to render his cage. Rodriguez said finding him here was a bad omen, but I can't see how. I have never seen a canid with such slippery grace. His screams, however, are quite wretched. They were answered in the night by his brothers in the wild, unless I imagined it. Their cries at first sounded to me like wailing children stranded in the desert. If my habitat were constantly this unbearably dry, and I was jailed, I might cry out in such a way as well. He must be unbearably thirsty.

◇◇ ⋀⋀ Zeke returned with the fount-water. It was midafternoon and the dust was starting to blow in, whistling around the weather pylons. The sun flashed in and out, catching the silver rooftops. ⋀⋀

⋀⋀ ⋀⋀ ⋀⋀ As he neared the unit, he could hear voices inside. It was Monday, Eliza should be at work. He walked around to the kitchen window and glanced inside. ⋀⋀ Leeya sat cross-legged at the low wooden table, and Eliza was going through the motions of the tea service. She gathered the cups and utensils from the cupboards and put them in the large metal sink. She seemed frustrated. ⋀⋀ ⋀⋀ "Everything is out of place." She pumped the faucet handle vigorously until water began to flow. She washed the dishware in the prescribed order, arranging them carefully in front of her guest. She started to apologize for the lack of fount-water. Zeke headed back for the front door when he heard Eliza say, "It was illegal, but it had to be done." ⋀⋀ ⋀⋀ ⋀⋀ ⋀⋀ He froze, the yoke of fount-water on his shoulders. He crept back to the kitchen window to watch. He felt like one of them, a Recorder. ⋀⋀ "I'm grateful, you know that," Leeya replied. ⋀⋀ ⋀⋀ ⋀⋀ "I just can't believe Daxon caught me," Eliza said. "I mean, I assume that's why I'm fired. I shouldn't have written all those notes. Those drawings." She had lost her job. Why hadn't she called him? "I thought I had an eye for fake records. I thought I was good at falsifying." ⋀⋀ ⋀⋀ "You were. You are. You got me to Texas, didn't you?" ⋀⋀ ⋀⋀ "It's turned out so badly." ⋀⋀ "For me," Leeya said. "Raisin was obsessed with what was happening in the storm country. How could we pair? He just wanted to see the outside world." ⋀⋀ ⋀⋀ "You'll find a pair. You're beautiful. You can practically see the good blood in your cheeks." ⋀⋀ "What about Zeke's cousin?" ⋀⋀ "Bic?" ⋀⋀ "He's single, isn't he? Accomplished. I know you approve of the bloodline." ⋀⋀ "Leeya, that's not a good idea. He's … creepy." ⋀⋀ "Courting is impossible. I should join the Auspices." ⋀⋀ "Don't joke." ⋀⋀ "You can't see me in a robe?" "I get notices from them. All the Gray girls do. I don't have my job anymore, and I still would never join the Auspicium. Auspex is just a nice word for spinster." "How else is a woman supposed to be useful?" Leeya asked. "I don't know if I'm cut out to be a mother. Or a pair. The fellows here are all dumb or blissed out on laudanum." "That sounds familiar. Zeke and I are in such a bad place." Eliza sat down and began to shakily fan her teacup. "I'm afraid he's not going to take the seat. He'll drop out of the lifephase system and disappear. Just like my father did." Leeya was silent. Eliza rarely mentioned her father. "Did you ... want to talk about it?" Eliza's eyes started to blur. "Oh, lady." Leeya got up and came around the table, breaking the ritual. She offered her hand-kerchief, and Eliza used it to quickly wipe her eyes. Zeke thought of his grandfather. He wrote in the dirt at his feet. Those who came before are lost to us now. "He's not your dad. That won't happen. You'll get paired. He just doesn't know what to do with himself." "At least Daxon doesn't know about Zeke's letter. That problem won't be solved by..." One of Zeke's canisters of fount-water slid from the yoke, and hit the ground, ringing like a tower bell. Zeke quickly ducked down and tried to right it. "What was that?" Eliza stopped. She came to the window and looked out. Zeke stayed down. He held his breath. She had told Leeya about the letter. He felt desperate. Fount-water slowly leaked from the loosened lid of the tin. She had given away his secret. "It sounded like someone on the roof," Leeya said. They both listened. Wind wound through the grid. "Paranoia's catching." "There's plenty to worry about inside the walls. I heard there was another murder." "The supposed suicide." "I can't tell if that's better or worse than an animal attack." "It's more lies, is what it is. The case is rife with falsification. A lot of the animal thread references this obscure file number. I tried to look it up, but it's been pulled from the Vault, under the namestamp Daxon." ∧∧ "Figures." ∧∧ "So then, I went back and checked for cross-references and found a couple of mentions of that record number from when the city-states were founded. They refer to the Auspicium." ∧∧ ∧∧ "The Auspices are allowed to have animals in the city-states. They need what's inside them for certain mixtures." ∧∧ "I think that's what makes me maddest about getting fired. Who will work on this thread? I've gone back and compared the records — the murders happen like clockwork. Not exactly animalistic." ∧∧ ∧∧ Zeke felt someone watching him. He glanced toward the watchpost. From just below it, a figure in a wide-brimmed hat was walking toward him. ∧∧ ∧∧

∧∧ It was Henry Bartle. Zeke set down the tins by his front door and quickly walked over. ∧∧ ∧∧ ∧∧ "Zeke, I'm so glad you're home. I've got to talk to you." Bartle stood between Zeke and his front door.

∧∧ ∧∧ **"Where is the letter?"** ∧∧ ∧∧ ∧∧ "I owe you an apology for the other day. I lost control of myself. Seeing you here with … I just — " ∧∧ ∧∧ "I want it back." ∧∧ ∧∧ "It's gone?" ∧∧ ∧∧ **"This fount-water needs to go into the caches or it'll spoil."** Zeke gripped the yoke tightly. ∧∧ ∧∧ ∧∧ "Zeke, if it's gone, then we need to find it. Right away." ∧∧ **"So you deny taking it?"** ∧∧ "I'm in a position to help. I'm a Corrector. Or, as I prefer, Historian. But I've been called a Corrector since we first set up the Vault of Records and carbon'd everything. I've been researching your grandfather. It hasn't been easy, believe me. The size of the Thomas file — " ∧∧ ∧∧ **"You left some of it here."** ∧∧ ∧∧ ∧∧ "Yes, I wanted you to read about one of your ancestors in particular: Zadock Thomas. He lived pre-Collapse, in the mid-1800s. But … I fear … " Bartle lowered his voice. He glanced up at the watchpost. He made the hand signal for *move,* walking toward a dead zone. ∧∧ ∧∧ ∧∧ ∧∧ Zeke followed him. They stood on the edge of the plankway. ∧∧ ∧∧

FOLLOW

"My research turned up things that needed to be corrected," he whispered. His mouth flecked with spittle. "And things that... couldn't be corrected. The Vault is wrong. Those who control it can't be trusted. The legacy requires..." ∧∧ Bartle's whisper was barely audible above the strong wind. Zeke put the yoke down, keeping his fingertips on the cool metal. The Deserters ranted about falsifications in the records. Eliza said it generated huge threads. ∧∧ ∧∧ "Why do you care so much?" Zeke asked. ∧∧ Bartle made the hand signal for *lower your voice.* ∧∧ ∧∧

QUIET

∧∧ ∧∧ "I have... an interest in the Senate seat. I had to leave... my family. Zeke, this letter... without it my research has been like trying to square the circle. It could be the essential — " ∧∧ "Are you working for Daxon?" ∧∧ "Quite the — " ∧∧ "You showed up at a convenient time." ∧∧ "Well, it's true, I do have access to your file. Listen, I know they're after you." ∧∧ ∧∧ ∧∧ ∧∧ ∧∧ ∧∧ ∧∧ ∧∧ Bartle looked about suspiciously. Through the dust, a tram ascended the distant sky. Zeke watched it climb. ∧∧ ∧∧ ∧∧ ∧∧ ∧∧ ∧∧ ∧∧ ∧∧ ∧∧ ∧∧ "Zeke, listen. I care about what happens to you. And what happens to Eliza. My daughter... I'm... I'm Eliza's father." Zeke stayed frozen. He stared at Bartle, trying to see the truth. ∧∧ ∧∧ ∧∧ ∧∧ ∧∧ ∧∧ Bartle began again, nervously. "She doesn't know I'm here. But I've made this bundle ... I've been writing her since... I'm worried she's in danger." Bartle seemed on the verge of crying. He started blinking rapidly to keep the tears from streaming down his face. In the exact same way Eliza did. Zeke softened. He saw that Bartle was upset, that he was telling the truth. ∧∧ ∧∧ "Hey, I ..." Zeke touched his shoulder. "I don't want her to be in danger either." ∧∧ "I know," Bartle said, taking his glasses off and rubbing his eyes with the palm of his hand, "but we all are as long as Daxon's murder case remains open. He's got everyone with a licensed sabre on a list, including you and Bic. That's how the girls were killed. If he doesn't find a culprit soon, he's just going to pick a name off his list. I'm guessing it'll be yours. He disagreed with the Senate about how Texas should be run. He didn't like your grandfather." He lowered his voice further, his breathing labored. "I think I can help, is what I was trying to say." ⌁ Zeke realized this man was a wreck. "Do you want to come inside?" ⌁ ⌁ ⌁ ⌁ "NO! No. You can't tell Eliza I'm here. I'll go to jail. I don't want the Law watching her either." He inched closer. "Has Daxon been at your unit lately?" ⌁ ⌁ ⌁ Zeke met Bartle's eye. ⌁ ⌁ "Zeke, the letter has turned up. The records say there's a copy at the Vault now. Daxon got hold of it." ⌁ "How is that possible?" ⌁ "Maybe he had someone steal it. In any case, an uncarbon'd document supports his case against you." ⌁ "What's in the letter?" ⌁ ⌁

⌁ ⌁ ⌁ ⌁ ⌁ Bartle stopped. He took off his glasses again and wiped the dust from them with his shirtsleeve. He put them back on and blinked up at the ascending tram. It lifted above the duststorm, small and bright as a rising star. ⌁ "Whatever it is, Daxon will use it against you. You need someone at the Vault." ⌁ ⌁ ⌁ "Eliza." Zeke hoisted the yoke back onto his shoulders. The tin containers of fount-water sloshed. ⌁ ⌁ "No ... I'm afraid for her. She's lost her job there. I need to save her. We do." Zeke struggled to balance the containers, which were swinging in the strong wind. ⌁ ⌁ Bartle steadied him. ⌁ "I'd really like to have the letter." ⌁ "You and I both. I'll go searching in the Vault, first thing tomorrow." ⌁ "OK." Zeke entered his unit sideways with the yoke. He spun around and met Bartle's eye before closing the door. It was strange to look at Eliza's father. ⌁ ⌁ ⌁ He set the containers down and peered back through the peephole, locking the door. Bartle was gone. He felt crazy. He couldn't tell Eliza that he had just sent her father to steal something from the Vault. ⌁ ⌁ He had forgotten to tell Bartle not to open the letter if he found it. ⌁

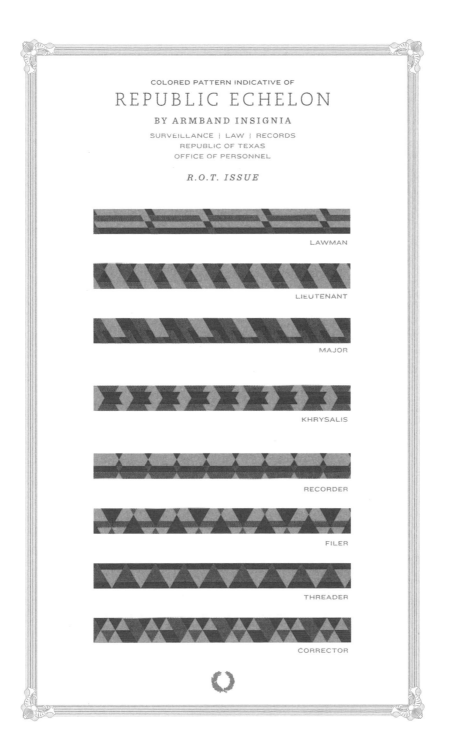

COLORED PATTERN INDICATIVE OF

REPUBLIC ECHELON

BY ARMBAND INSIGNIA

SURVEILLANCE | LAW | RECORDS
REPUBLIC OF TEXAS
OFFICE OF PERSONNEL

R.O.T. ISSUE

LAWMAN

LIEUTENANT

MAJOR

KHRYSALIS

RECORDER

FILER

THREADER

CORRECTOR

➤ Eliza, always in the back of my mind is the idea that the letter I'm composing to you may be the last. This time it seems more certain than ever. Zeke's letter has been turned in. I'm going to the Vault to get it back. This is all to ensure your future.

The Sisters Gray has revealed a disturbing fact. If Elswyth Gray took her sister's child and raised it as though it were her own, the whole bloodline might be in question. She might truly be a Gray child, in the modern sense. Unless Zadock and Elswyth had a natural child of their own, the Senator and his grandson might not be related to Zadock Thomas by blood after all. This could call into question Zeke's right to the Senate seat. You may not be paired with a Khrysalis after all.

If Zadock did not return to Chicago, then there can be no doubt that the child that Elswyth raised was not his blood. This is why it's imperative for me to find the letter in the Vault.

In order to get Zeke to trust me, I revealed to him that I am your father. He was surprised, but agreed to let me track down his letter. I know that this bond will keep him from telling you of my presence. I would not want you to know the danger I now face. When all this is over, Zeke will tell you the truth. I know it. Having looked in his eyes, I can tell he is a good man. I am happy that you have found one to take as your pair.

Since that visit, I have watched over your unit, climbing up into the nearest watchpost when it is unmanned. It often is. Daxon has assigned an unusual number of men to external surveillance patrols. Watchmen walk the edge of the barrier day and night and look out into the wilderness for any approaching danger. I suspect Daxon also has men on the outside. After Atlantas, this should come as no surprise.

The news of Atlantas's collapse is devastating. Many friends lived there. I kept my secret and never moved there. Perhaps

I should have. I cannot tell from the reports how many Queers died and how many are now wandering in the rot. My fellows in Chicago-Land seem to think it a victory for the Queers. What's reported in the broadsheets here does not align with the news I hear over the phonotube. They are saying the desert people, or the Deserters, used a cannon. But where would it have come from? I worry that the government is simply trying to justify building its own arsenal. The thought of an entire city-state disappearing from the map is terrifying. Especially one that housed so many Queers. I fear a resurgence of government-backed bigotry. Especially with the Thomas seat empty.

Atlantas had been a disaster from the start. It was never intended to be a lifephase. But after the first generation went through their phases there were many unpaired adults left. Folks who had refused to pair, or had paired and then split, or women who were too old to bear children, yet had not paired. Procreation is not a perfect machine.

The Senate voted to create a new city-state for older, unpaired singles. The age disparities in Texas grew alarming because many men waited around and continued to court younger and younger women. Simultaneously, legislation was passed banning the active eradication of Queers from all city-states. This led to the Queer Compromise. The Queers would be housed in Atlantas, along with the unpaired singles.

Senator Thomas was deeply against segregation, but decided it was better than the alternative. In protest, many Queers absconded to the rot on their own, rather than get shipped off to Atlantas. It was then that the Law built the steammoats around the city-states. So they could control not only who came in but who left. Now the whole city-state of Atlantas is destroyed.

Maybe it's the Historian in me, but I can only hear echoes of

Atlantas in Zadock's last letter. He wrote from Pecos, the largest of the precolonial pueblos in the region. It was located on the upper branch of the Pecos River, thirty miles east of Santa Fe. Pecos consisted of two pueblos, huge rock-and-mud communal living structures, each four stories high and containing many rooms. The conquistador Francisco Vásquez de Coronado visited this frontier fortress in 1540 when the population was approximately 2,500. Given the population and footprint of our own city-states, I cannot help but compare the two. The image of a city once teeming with culture and life abandoned and left a burned-out husk is chilling.

A captive told Coronado that he could find Quivira to the east, a city of great riches. Coronado was convinced that this was one of the seven cities of gold that he was searching for. To the east he found only small villages and no walled Garden of Eden. His Indian guide confessed that he had lured the Spaniards onto the Kansas plains to die. Then he ran.

Coronado had his hounds hunt the guide down and kill him. The conquistador marched back to Mexico empty-handed.

The legend of the seven cities of gold was widely known throughout Europe at the time, and no doubt was a motivation for conquistadors and explorers. Another was the waters of the Fountain of Youth, a mythical obsession that led Ponce de León to his death, as well as others.

The Navajo called the Pueblo people the Anasazi, the enemy ancestors, and had their own superstitions concerning them as well. Rodriguez is mistaken. Montezuma never lit a fire as far north as Santa Fe. The icon on the door is Quetzalcóatl, the feathered serpent worshipped by the Aztec. Rodriguez's tales are nothing more than ghost stories for an abandoned city.

By the time Santa Fe Trail trade began, the pueblo would

have been largely abandoned. Disease, migration, and conflict with neighboring Apache and Navajo left a population of a few hundred. There was no elixir of life and no city of gold. Rodriguez is correct: The last survivors left the decaying structure in 1838.

I think of Atlantas and its guts sprawled across the southern storm country. The mood of rebellion in this city-state of youth makes it easy to picture a similar fate for us.

The pueblo is a stark reminder that no city is forever, and that the petty hearts of man and the ravages of time will smash all mighty fortresses into dust. Given the size of the population now, there may be no one left to reassemble ours.

I've been on the phonotube with friends back in Chicago-Land. There is fallout from the collapse of Atlantas. It seems as though someone in Chicago-Land is trying to make the Thomas seat disappear and reduce the number of Senators to six. Someone wants a tighter grip on the Senate. Seven is the number of balance. If the seat ceases to exist, Zeke can't claim it and all will be lost. Politics can destroy lives. And families. I will not see you torn from someone else you love.

Given our proximity, I've found it prudent to closely monitor the Law, to make sure that they do not record me. I have a feeling Daxon does not hold to either the letter or the spirit of the law. If he wants to surveil me, he will, and there is little I can do to stop it. Therefore I must keep my head down.

Meanwhile I watch him and his men, seeking patterns. I will find the uncarbon'd letter. It is essential to ensure Zeke's place in the Senate. Or if it doesn't, it is essential to destroy it.

It is a dangerous time. A rebellion is brewing in this nation. Atlantas may touch it off. These murders don't help. Neither would Daxon's killing of an innocent scapegoat. History has often turned on the violent tendencies of a single man.

simply to check on his whereabouts. He hurried home from the telegraph office, a there was more pressing business to attend to at home. He touched the knife concealed in his coat pocket.

Mr. Buell stood at the window, sucking at his small cigar and watching the wind blow the discarded flowers of trees about the wide lawn. When Mr. Gray entered, Mr. Buell hurried back to the typowriter and began to arrange papers in its mouth, for the printing of the museum's next journal. This was the task he had been charged with all week, and it was clear that he had not been at it much this morning. Mr. Gray could think of nothing but dissecting the wretch. His blood rose like a murder of crows.

Mr. Gray leaned over to inspect his handiwork. The type read backward, but he was possessed of a hawk's eye for detail. 'You've got two letters transposed there.' He pointed. 'In the word *beautiful*, the *e* and the *a*.'

'Excellent catch, sir. I hadn't proofed this plate yet, sir.'

'The journal is well overdue.' Mr. Gray's teeth were set.

'So is my paycheck,' Buell said. He wore a rictus of ill humor. Mr. Gray's chest rose, his face steaming. 'See, I've been feeling rather ill lately, and wondered perhaps if I might take some recovery time. This ailment is a detriment to my speed and…'

'Mr. Buell, my daughter is pregnant.'

'Wh… Sir, that can't be.' Mr. Buell pulled out his handkerchief and patted the back of his neck. 'I mean, what happened? Who did this? We must find him and bring him to…'

'Skulduggery! Liar! What would you have me do?'

'I'll do the very thing in your place, the monster must be…'

'Buell, you know very well she doesn't leave the house. There are not other suspects. Louisa is pregnant.'

Mr. Buell paused, frozen for a moment before he leapt up, sending papers spilling all across the floor. He made a mad dash for the door, but Mr. Gray was ready. In a smooth motion, like a kingfisher plucking a fish from rolling waters he was upon Mr. Buell. The younger man found his way blocked by a small, ivory-handled dagger at his throat.

'You listen to me, sir. You…' Mr. Gray's breath was heavy. 'You will not fence your way out of this one, with your curse'd silver tongue. This thing you have done, it will bring great shame on my family's name. I should've sent you on a death's errand long ago. I am your employer, but from this moment on I am your master…' he pressed the knife harder, '…in all things.'

'I'll marry Louisa.' Mr. Buell's jaw worked up and down, searching for the correct thing to say. Mr. Gray gripped his lapel and pulled his stinking jacket tight around his throat, pressing his steel talon into it.

'Not a chance. You'll never see her again.'

'Yea… No, sir,' Mr. Buell managed to cough up.

'You will do exactly as I say, and no differently. If you do not play your part in sparing my girls from the disgrace you have wrought, then I will see to it that your punishment is worse than one a knife can give. Do I make myself clear as crystal water?'

'Yes, sir.' Mr. Buell had gone limp as a doll.

'You will go to Elswyth, and you will ask her for her hand in marriage. As a gentleman would. We will behave as though this child is hers. And you shall never look upon my younger daughter again.' He released Mr. Buell. 'Now be gone from my sight.'

Mr. Buell stumbled backward out of the room, upending the typewriter as he went. Once his footsteps could be heard no more, Mr. Gray grumbled and got down on his knees to pick up the papers scattered across the floor. He shook as he tried to put them back in order, and then he could do it no more. His whole body was overcome by frightful spasms of sobbing.

TRAM TERMINAL

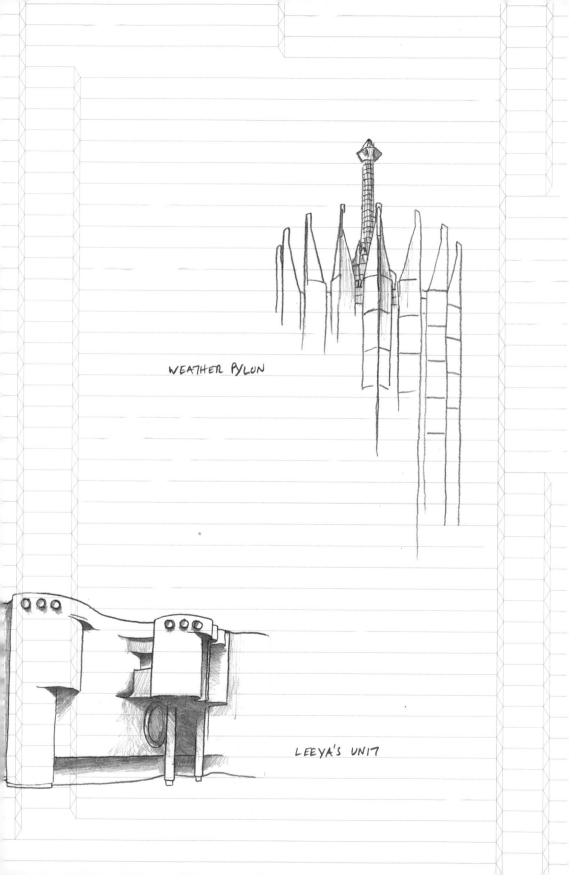

WEATHER PYLON

LEEYA'S UNIT

LEEYA,

I AM WRITING ONCE AGAIN — FEELING LIKE I
AM ON THE BRINK OF LOSING IT ENTIRELY. SHOULD I
DISAPPEAR — I WANT YOU TO KNOW EVERYTHING.

IT'S STILL HARD TO ACCEPT THAT I NO LONGER WORK
AT THE VAULT. LATE LAST NIGHT, I WENT TO RETRIEVE
THE LETTER, AND CLEAN OUT MY THINGS. MY BLOOD ID
OPENED THE MAIN VAULT, BUT MY OFFICE WAS LOCKED.

THE LETTER IS INSIDE — OR AT LEAST IT WAS.
I AM SURE DAXON HAS GONE IN AND SWEPT THE ENTIRE
OFFICE. /////// THE LETTER IS LOST TO ME. ///////

SO IS THE MURDER THREAD. SOMETHING I HAVEN'T
TOLD YOU— ALL THE VICTIMS HAVE BEEN PREGNANT.
IT FEELS LIKE THERE IS NOTHING I CAN DO NOW TO
STOP THE KILLINGS. DAXON IS COVERING SOMETHING UP.
THE LAW IS TRYING TO BLAME SOMEONE CALLED THE
NIGHTMAN, WHO SUPPOSEDLY PROWLS THE PLANKWAYS AT
NIGHT, MOVING ONLY IN THE DEAD ZONES. NO ONE KNOWS
WHERE HE SLEEPS DURING THE DAY. A TALLTALE.

IF I HAD CLEARANCE TO TAKE THE TRAM OUT OF
TEXAS, I'D DO IT RIGHT NOW. I'M PARANOID ABOUT
BECOMING ONE OF DAXON'S TARGETS, NOW THAT I'M ON
THE OUT. WHILE I WAS IN THE VAULT FOR THE LAST
TIME, I GRABBED WHAT I COULD. I FOUND ONE OF THE
LAWMEN'S LOCKERS OPEN, AND STASHED A DUSTBOMB, →
A HANDFUL, ACTUALLY— IN MY SATCHEL, AND MORE
PAPER + PENCILS. JUST IN CASE THEY PROVE EFFECTIVE
WEAPONS AS WELL. I GUESS I NO LONGER HAVE TO
WORRY ABOUT GETTING CAUGHT DRAWING.

I ALSO STOLE THREE HANDWHEELS. LET'S PUT THEM ON
THE ROOF OF YOUR UNIT. THE LAWMEN USE THEM TO SLIDE

FROM POST TO POST ALONG THE SEMAPHORE LINES. IF
THIS MURDERER BREAKS INTO YOUR UNIT, IT WILL BE
YOUR BEST CHANCE FOR ESCAPE.

THE DESPAIR HAS ME NOW. I WAS SO CARELESS
WITH THE LETTER. IT'S ALWAYS BEEN STRESSFUL, BUT
I'VE BEEN SO DEFT AT MANIPULATING DOCUMENTS IN
THE PAST. WE GOT AWAY W/ FALSIFYING YOUR RECORD
EASILY. IT NEVER ACTUALLY OCCURRED TO ME WHAT IT
WOULD BE LIKE IF SOMETHING WENT WRONG.
— NOW EVERYTHING HAS —

I SOMETIMES HAVE THE AWFUL FEELING THAT IT
WAS MY FAULT MY FATHER LEFT. IF I LOSE ZEKE, AND
OUR FUTURE, OUR FAMILY, IT **WILL** BE MY FAULT.

MY BRAIN HAS BEEN WHIRRING ALL AFTERNOON. ZEKE
MAY BE IN EVEN MORE DANGER NOW, BUT HOW CAN I
BRING MYSELF TO TELL HIM WHAT I HAVE DONE?
ESPECIALLY AFTER ALL OF OUR FIGHTING.

YOU'VE GOT TO BE CAREFUL HOW YOU PAIR. IN CASE I
WASN'T CLEAR ENOUGH BEFORE: BIC IS BAD NEWS.
I KNOW HE HAS THE THOMAS BLOOD, BUT YOU DO NOT WANT
THAT MAN AS YOUR PAIR. I'VE BEEN AROUND HIM ENOUGH
TO KNOW HOW BEASTLY HE IS.

I KNOW YOU FEEL LIKE YOU WON'T FIND A PAIR. I'VE
ALWAYS BEEN WITH ZEKE SO YOU MAY THINK I DON'T
UNDERSTAND, BUT I PROMISE I DO. BEFORE I FOUND
HIM, I HAD NO ONE. I WAS UTTERLY ALONE. THOUGH THE
LIFE PHASES MOVE ON W/O US, IT IS ALWAYS BETTER
TO WAIT FOR THE RIGHT ONE. I KNOW THE FATES WILL
DELIVER YOU THE HAPPINESS YOU DESERVE.

LOVE YOU LIKE A SISTER.

ELIZA
✳

SCHEMATIC OF THE

MODEL 21•07

HANDWHEEL

LAW PERSONNEL TRANSPORT TROLLEY
REPUBLIC OF TEXAS INCLINED STRONG
TRANSPORT DEPARTMENT

"THE HOOP/SNAKE"

APPROPRIATE LINES FOR AERIEL ROPESLIDING

HANDWHEEL-READY

SEMAPHORE

VIBRATIONS CAUSED BY PHONOTUBE CONVERSATIONS
CAN OFTEN BE FELT IN THESE LINES, YET THEY ARE
SAFE FOR HANDWHEEL TRANSPORT

PHOSPHOR

SHOULD NOT BE USED IN THE DARK, AS THE FRICTION
THE HANDWHEEL CREATES ALONG THE LINE CAUSES
THE PHOSPHOR CHEMICAL TO GLOW GREEN

WATER

THE FEW LIQUID LINES THAT ARE ABOVE GROUND ARE
MADE OF TIN AND SUITABLE FOR TRANSPORT

STEAM POWER

CHECK BY HAND BEFORE USE: IF THEY ARE HOT, THESE
POWER LINES PRESENT A DANGER TO THE RIDER

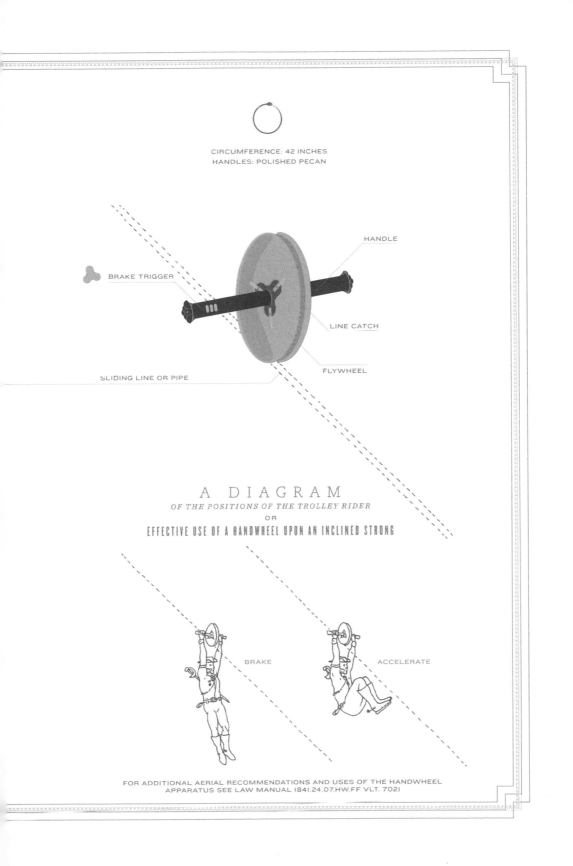

CIRCUMFERENCE: 42 INCHES
HANDLES: POLISHED PECAN

HANDLE

BRAKE TRIGGER

LINE CATCH

SLIDING LINE OR PIPE

FLYWHEEL

A DIAGRAM
OF THE POSITIONS OF THE TROLLEY RIDER
OR
EFFECTIVE USE OF A HANDWHEEL UPON AN INCLINED STRONG

BRAKE

ACCELERATE

FOR ADDITIONAL AERIAL RECOMMENDATIONS AND USES OF THE HANDWHEEL
APPARATUS SEE LAW MANUAL 1841.24.07.HW.FF VLT. 7021

MR. GRAY KEEPS VIGIL O'ER HIS YOUNGEST DAUGHTER.
HE CONSIDERS THE SISTERS' ORDER.
A STRANGE OWL WAKES HIM.

Darkness notwithstanding, Mr. Gray could tell Louisa was fast asleep. The star quilt had been shoved to the floor and she was nearly upside down in the bed. He made to tuck her in properly, covering her with the quilt against the Chicago night. He felt her forehead, which was surprisingly warm.

Though she had fourteen years, she still looked like a child. He had thought she was too young for something like this to happen, and yet it had. He should not have treated her as a child. He should have prepared her for the trials of adult life.

He had determined to keep watch over her tonight. Lest Mr. Buell try something drastic, Mr. Gray would stay stationed in his daughter's room, ivory-handled dagger at the ready. He wished that he could encase Louisa in armor in which she could roll up and hide when the world became a threat.

Louisa would go instead to the Auspicium. It would hide her during her months of pregnancy. From society as well as from the man she fell prey to. She did not have her older sister's wits.

Anne had foreseen it all using his wife's book. What was this gift that allowed them to pull back the veil of time and see what course history might take? He wished sorely for such a skill.

But did Elswyth? He had resisted Aunt Anne's request to recruit his daughters. After his wife died, he needed them by his side. The Auspicium was odd and unholy to him. His late wife had privately called it "the coven." She had little respect for religion. They were strange, her weird Sisters. Mixing tea with blood and crushed bones and other foul ingredients. Holding séances at all hours of the night in their long black robes, incanting charms against the ghosts of all maladies. It was lucky that other churches in the city did not know what transpired behind those walls.

He worried about the situation in Texas. It still seemed more urgent to him than a suitable husband for Elswyth. It was imperative that Irion received his messenger. Even he could easily forecast their grim fate if Mr. Thomas did not complete his task.

If the date the Auspices believed for the end-time proved out, then it would, after all, be best to be behind walls. The fates were mighty and terrifying, and if the Auspices thought that sacrificing goats helped, however unnatural it might seem to him, who was he to say they were wrong? Perhaps Louisa could be held as a ward and not fully indoctrinated.

He sighed and made for the large chair that might be his bed tonight. As he stepped, something snapped underfoot, nearly causing him to lose his balance. He turned and looked at Louisa, who stirred but did not wake. He bent down to retrieve whatever trap had been laid for his old foot.

It was a wooden doll, a tall, skinny man in furry pants. It was handmade but looked particularly crude. He could not remember having purchased it for her. He gathered its broken halves and, noticing that someone had already set flame to the feet, tossed the whole man into the fireplace.

Afterward he sat in the monstrous armchair and arranged the

FAM. HELODERMATIDAE

GEN. HELODERMA

12.9.43, 9:00, 75 deg., 20 knots, no clouds, very low humidity

First morning in Santa Fe

Heela (Spanish). Large lizard of unknown sex. Over a foot long (!) with tail of unusual girth. Covered in black scales, with bands of orange. The largest lizard I've ever had occasion to see. My drawing may seem tumescent, but I've got it right. Found sunning itself in the square of Santa Fe this very morning. I had not been drawing long when a nun came out to wave me away. She was the one who told me the name, and I managed to gather through pantomime and a bit of Spanish that it was a venomous monster feared by locals. She said its very breath was toxic, and though I doubt that, its bright orange markings made me feel there might be truth to her warnings. I pantomimed my own intention to continue to draw it from a safer distance. The nun acquiesced, but stood suspiciously behind me, her arms crossed, until I was finished. I believe it shows improved skill. An unheard-of species!

Dearest Elswyth,

We finally reached Santa Fe last night. There was little moon and the asterisms sparkled clear. The Pleiades herald the change of the seasons. The gaze of cold seven-eyes chilled me to the bone. Gone are the days of the Dog Star and their attendant warmth. In the dark I found it rather difficult to form a clear picture of the town. It is situated in a valley and I first viewed it from the top of a long hill down which the caravan descended. This leads to the city, which has a square and streets like any other. These are lined by an assortment of houses and structures and the occasional cornfield.

After much anticipation, my impressions this morning were rather dour. I suppose I had been expecting some structures of great import and instead found a rather piteous collection of mud hovels.

A large church is situated at the western end of the square and, though we did not enter its outer walls, it looks stately. They rang the great tower bells upon our arrival even at the late hour. An official from the town came out to receive us and Rodriguez conversed with him in Spanish. I understood a little of what was said. McMarrow's Indian host clearly made the official very nervous. It was agreed they would make camp outside the perimeter of the town. McMarrow said that they were not Navaho, only "false savages" and would be no threat. Rodriguez seemed pleased the Major didn't get his way.

It was too late to prepare a hot supper but we did dine on cold meats and champagne. It was a strange and chilly reception. Sitting next to me, Rodriguez whispered to me that Santa Fe didn't care for McMarrow or his Indians. If there were an incident, he said, he would not intervene. This is an unsettling thought, to say the least.

I was then shown to my quarters, under the shadow of "La Iglesia." No doubt the quality of my placement is credit to the friendship of Rodriguez. I take this to be the quarters of nuns. I have a long room with dirt floors, a plank ceiling, and whitewashed side walls. It is startling how unlike a home this foreign structure feels to me. The ground under the open sky has been my bedroom for so many long nights now.

The size and manner of this room is the same as the school I attended as a boy in Chicago. It was situated in Fort Dearborn, in one of the two-story barracks there, no longer used as residences for soldiers. Do you know it? With mud, this room would be identical.

One night there, when I was seven years of age, a great storm erupted, of the sort Chicago has in the springtime. The preceptress thought it safer to hunker down in the barracks for the night, until the storm had passed. Blankets and some candles were fetched, and we were forbidden to return home.

I had never spent a night away from home. Without my father to look over me, I became very afraid of the night. I forget now the incident that caused it, but I must have thrown some sort of howling fit. This led to the usual punishment. I was sat on a chair, nose held against the fireplace. Sitting there with my back to the other children, I espied the key brick was not fit snug in the fireplace. I do not know what drove me to it, but I managed to wiggle it loose. The whole fireplace collapsed into a heap of soot and ash and brick, causing a loud commotion. It was lucky the whole of the wall did not collapse.

The other pupils had to remove the soot from their own jackets as best they could. They were all quite thrilled to have a night away from parents. They played soldiers throughout the night, taking turns on "night watch." I was given further punishment: a quill and a bottle of ink and the tedious task of copying out copperplate lines.

It was a masked kindness, as the preceptress knew penmanship was calming to me. I was still scared, but likely a good deal better off than at the mercies of my rough-and-tumble classmates. I spent the evening sniveling in the corner, listening to the storm and copying out a stereotyped phrase repeated and rhymed...

Many men of many minds,
Many birds of many kinds.
Many men of many minds,
Many birds of many kinds.
Many men of many minds,
Many birds of many kinds.
Many men of many minds,
Many birds of many kinds.
Many men of many minds,
Many birds of many kinds.
Many men of many minds,
Many birds of many kinds.
Many men of many minds,
Many birds of many kinds.
Many men of many minds,
Many birds of many kinds.
Many men of many minds,
Many birds of many kinds.
Many men of many minds,
Many birds of many kinds.
Many men of many minds,
Many birds of many kinds.
Many men of many minds,
Many birds of many kinds.
Many men of many minds,
Many birds of many kinds.
Many men of many minds,
Many birds of many kinds.
Many men of many minds,
Many birds of many kinds.

My teacher's kindness made me think of you, of course, and the kindness I have seen you show children. I indeed loved her, and never wanted to return home from school after that night. How much more will our children long for you, if the fates grant us offspring? I have imagined that in our home together we might have such a room as this. I could use it for drawing and drafting my field notes, and you could have a desk and quill as well, at which to compose your verse. I had been desperately wondering if you'd composed something recently. How cruelly this morning answered my question.

I have become accustomed to sleeping out-of-doors. A night spent under a roof was strange and claustrophobic, and I had troubling dreams. In hope of recovery I determined to stay beneath the sky this morning. As the sun came up, Santa Fe buzzed with anxiety. Word of the Indians had spread, and the townspeople seemed agitated. In spite of this I made to explore the town. The streets were quite active with nuns, women, and children of all ages. The tower bell was clanging ceaselessly and trumpets blared, bright as the morning sun.

I was having a midday meal in the main square with all of our company while the mail was being passed around. Seeing others receive unlooked-for letters with such gladness filled my heart with the hope that I would receive word from you. Men were dancing about or weeping at the thought of loved ones so far away. I began to feel buoyed by the light mood. Some men were kind enough to pass around their telegrams and letters for all to share in. Indeed the mailbag seemed a bottomless well of joy for a short time.

It was as the bag was running dry that I then received the darkest news of this trip. Upon opening your telegram, the stars betrayed me. There is no cure for the foul mood that is now set upon me.

The telegram indeed bore the address of the museum. Your name was there typed out at the bottom and my heart leapt into my throat. But the message itself was short and full of despair...

GREAT SOUTH WEST

TELEGRAPH

CORRESPONDENCE COMPANY

AND CABLE

TELEGRAM........
DAY LETTER.......
NIGHT MESSAGE
NIGHT LETTER....

TELEGRAM

HEAD OFFICE, WESTPORT, MO.

IO SEPT 43   CHICAGO ST.7

To

Date

St. and No.

Place

Store

MR.THOMAS. STOP.
YOU MUST RETURN TO ME BY THE 24th OF OCTOBER. STOP.
OTHERWISE I SHALL BE MARRIED TO MR. BUELL. STOP.

ELSWYTH GRAY.

Above Message was prepaid

4 00/pm.

233

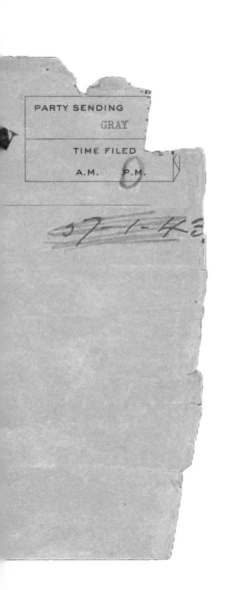

PARTY SENDING

GRAY

TIME FILED

A.M.   P.M.

I have read it a hundred times now and cannot think of what to do. I am not even able to weep as my heart wants to. Instead, I find myself encased in a black despair, unable to think clearly. There is no telegraph office here to answer you. The mailbag came by way of Fort Smith.

The telegram is troublesome in its brevity and I cannot discern your intention. It is difficult to imagine that you want to be wed now. No doubt your father is quite willful. It has occurred to me that he may have been present when the telegram was sent, forcing your hand.

Or perhaps Buell has worked some charm on you. Do you love him? Should I be angry with him? I should have anticipated this attack and never left you to be courted by him alone. I thought my acceptance of this errand would prevent him from dragooning you into a courtship. That he would take advantage of my absence pains me.

The date you have set is impossibly close. At the rate of my travel thus far, I could not deliver the letter and return before this wedding date. Have you devised it so? I had an immediate desire to turn back and travel with the traders who will soon retake the Santa Fe Trail back to Westport. If I were to do this, I could return in time.

But that would mean I'd return with the letter your father gave me still in hand and his errand incomplete. It is difficult to admit, but I know he would not give me your hand in marriage if I return to Chicago a failure, my task unfinished and without any money besides.

I think it better to make haste toward Irion and the endpoint of my journey. Traveling with a smaller mounted party, I can make many more miles in a day. The caravan has provided safety in numbers, but it is slow, and the dangers mostly consist of rain and snakes. Reaching Irion quickly and delivering the letter, I might return to Chicago before the week of All Hallows'. Before you are married.

I resolved to request a special dispatch of men to escort me. Interrupting the Major's usual morning game of cards, I framed my request with the urgency of the letter and your father's business in respect to the war. I made no mention of you. I said the telegram was from Mr. Gray, and when he demanded to see it, I said it had been destroyed. I impressed upon him that I must meet Irion and his men, wherever they may be, as soon as is possible.

McMarrow then flew into a rage, tossing his cards to the floor. He asserted the date I proposed for return was impossible. He excoriated me for dallying along the road, stopping with leisure to look about and draw feeble creatures. He said I had lost true sight of the task at hand and was unfit for the errand, and that the burden now fell to him.

His face was a reddened mask glistening with perspiration. He had drank not a little, yet his words stung true. I offered to go alone and officially relieve him of my errand, as the burden should be mine. He refused outright and ordered me to remain in the company.

I was storming after this encounter. I told Rodriguez of my impossible circumstance. He said that McMarrow was mad—given his violent tendencies, we would be safer without him. He suggested the two of us leave McMarrow behind and ride south. His deputies could easily drive his wagons the remaining seventy-five miles to his estate. On horseback, he and I could arrive there by to-morrow morning.

So I have taken a soldier's ration and a steed, whom I have named Raison d'Etre. This is to reflect that I have but one purpose now—to deliver the letter without fail. Theft is wrong, but what am I to do?

We will travel south along the Camino Real farther down along Nuevo Mexico and come eventually to the disputed border of Mexico and the Republic of Texas. My plan is to look for news of Irion at every stop. Deserting will anger McMarrow, but we can afford no delay.

I think it a good plan, but fear I will need much luck. My heart is heavy at the thought of the telegram and I sorely wish for you. I beg you, wait for me. Reconsider what you are doing. I am coming for you with all the will of my passion. To the front, with all haste!

       May the Speed of Fate Accompany Me, Zadock

MR. BUELL CALLS ON ELSWYTH. THEY GO FOR A WALK

ALONG LAKE MICHIGAN. A PROPOSAL IS

MADE AND ACCEPTED.

Barely rapping on Elswyth's door, Aunt Anne whispered, 'Mr. Buell has come calling.' Elswyth was hardly surprised. She was sitting at her desk when the knock came, thinking on *The City-State*, her mother's book. The last remaining copy was in Aunt Anne's possession. She remembered it only vaguely, a story set in an imagined land where there were proper social roles, the dishes and clothes were very beautiful, and everyone lived in a safe city behind enormous walls. The plot was difficult to follow. It revolved around some imaginary letter—she couldn't bring herself to care what it contained. But the bumbling historian was easily recognizable—her father's foibles were rendered precisely. It made her miss her mother's gentle teasing a great deal.

She thought it might finally be time to share it with Louisa. But how could she read it to her sister, if she couldn't bear to read it herself? The tale could perhaps serve as instruction about the pitfalls of love now that her own book was destroyed. Elswyth would explain that some women give up the married life for a higher calling. She was older and better prepared to take charge of a child, yet they could both be like mothers in administering love. Although this would be difficult, there was nobility in it still. There were many things Louisa was too immature to understand.

Chief among them was Mr. Buell. Elswyth opened her door. 'We don't tolerate such disturbances in the Auspicium,' Aunt Anne said, presenting Mr. Buell's tattered calling card.

'When did you know that Louisa was with child?' Elswyth asked.

'Your sister has the blood, as do you, as will her child. If our ways are to continue we need to pass them on. We can teach your soul to soar to new heights, and its fortress to fend off death's hand. We know well the alchemy of pregnancy.'

'We must all stay here. Father is destitute and can't look after his own affairs. Someone must see to him and the household.' Elswyth snatched the card from Aunt Anne's hand as she might a servant's. She examined it. The card disgusted her. Buell printed it himself on her father's press. She felt as though she could smell the black ink on him already. She longed for the days spent in her sickbed, when she could receive no visitors and had quiet stretches to read her books. It had been a sort of paradise to her. She had even begun to look forward to the bleedings, grisly as they were. They provided an acceptable reason to lay about in bed, light-headed and warm. All callers were optional.

When Elswyth came down the stairs, Mr. Buell was standing inside the door picking through the stand of canes and umbrellas. He was dressed all in black, and had a noxious amount of pomade in his hair. Grease made from the fat of a boar, most likely.

'My dearest Elswyth, you look as lovely as the morn you were born.' He spoke the words as though reciting some tedious script he no longer cared for. 'I thought I might come calling and fetch you for a little walk on the lakefront. I imagine it would suit your disposition. Shall we?'

She didn't reply.

'Even if something isn't the best of all possible situations,' he quickly lowered his voice, 'is there just cause to be unpleasant about it?'

'Very well,' she replied. He was maddening. She wished he would be done with it, so she could return to her room. To be in his presence was unbearable. How would she contain her anger?

They went out the front door and into the wide boulevard. The muddied street had not entirely dried from the day before, and though it was still full of wheel ruts and holes it was busy yet, with businessmen walking about and ladies in full skirts, lifting them above the muddy earth. Small carts were pulled wearily along the ruts. A man in a vest and wide-brimmed hat peddled water in front of the dry goods store for a few cents a barrel. The sun was shining, and Chicago moved forward.

On the far end of the street a team of men were putting down wooden planks. 'Plank streets are ghastly,' Mr. Buell remarked. 'Vehicles press upon them, and all that mud and sewage seeps out. Best to have streets open, so that it can be dealt with. Or at least pave it properly.'

'I rather like them,' Elswyth said. She was aware of a tightness in her chest. 'They keep the dust from blowing about. And I think us lucky to have a finished street. Not all cities have them.'

'That's partly my concern, the way this city is run. If there were some order, then it would not be such a crime-ridden...'

'I prefer it.' Elswyth couldn't simply converse. She kept picturing Mr. Buell with her sister. She had to remind herself that it was for Louisa's benefit that she must endure his company. How would they raise a child together? They continued down to the lake in silence. Elswyth became lost in her own thoughts.

She had never imagined she would be married this way. Her

imagined husband had always been well-off. Her dream of a large house to call her own was now lost. She could never plant her own garden, or decorate the home in a way that suited her. The thoughts of selecting furniture and draperies and a fine set for tea would have to be banished now. She could never make that lovely place to receive her friends and their husbands. She was bound to her father's home.

They sat on a bench overlooking Lake Michigan. Presently, Mr. Buell spoke. 'Shall I tell you of Zed Blackfoot, and the time he scaled the walls of the City of Silver and Gold?'

'No, thank you.' Elswyth's eye lingered on the golden sunset reflected on the lake. 'I don't care for fanciful stories.'

'It's hardly fanciful. I've met the man, and he is every inch of his legend and…'

'I doubt very much you've met him, Mr. Buell, even if he does exist.' She felt her face flush. 'In fact, I've never seen you away from the museum. If you want an adventurer, why don't you look to Mr. Thomas? He is bravely traveling all the way to…'

'He is a fool, Elswyth, patently.' Mr. Buell seemed to match her anger with his own, though he had no right to. 'Don't mistake foolhardiness for bravery. He is now on the border of Texas, a land that three nations war over. How will he survive there? He is on an errand that is beyond him. I consider him lost to us.'

'His letters have been lost to me. How do you know his whereabouts? When you visit the post, are there letters addressed to me?' Her hands began to tremble a little. He was a liar.

'I wouldn't know which letters you speak of. I have seen none. And I deeply resent the accusation.' Mr. Buell's voice seemed to drip with the same putrid grease that coated his hair. 'I know he was your suitor, and now he has gone and left you. We are cousins, if you don't know it, and it pains me greatly to think on the untimely demise of one of my kin.'

'Cousins? Well that puts to rest your boasts of noble blood, doesn't it? I am surprised, then, that you aren't more trustworthy.'

'There are greater magnitudes of difference between us. Still, a tragedy and a shame besides.' Mr. Buell laid his hand over Elswyth's. 'I was contemplating that sad fact when your father came to me…'

'Did he?' She removed her hand and slid farther down the bench, away from him.

'And he told me of the terrible situation your sister is in. I just can't imagine how she got herself into such a predicament.' He was sweaty but eyed her with an unnerving certainty.

'And then a thought occurred to me.' He continued, as though speaking of the weather, or the lake. 'What could be done about these two lovely, yet bloodless, young women, one who has lost her suitor and is getting on for marriage, and one who is too young for marriage yet approaches motherhood? I thought to myself, How can I serve this family and employer that has provided for me so kindly? Then an idea arrived like a bolt of lightning.' He paused that Elswyth might ask what it was.

'I've heard of ideas,' she said. 'Once there was a man who committed suicide simply because he was tired of putting his boots on each morning and pulling them off again in the evening. Seems quite natural to me.' She stared out at the lake.

They would have separate rooms. Perhaps even separate wings of the house. She and Louisa could live in their own wing with the baby and bolt the door at night.

Finally he spoke again. 'Louisa is a rare specimen, with radiant beauty. I would be loath to see it all evaporate. But your father has before looked kindly on my courting of you. And I can see now, the righteous thing to do is that I should ask for your hand in marriage, and thereby solve it all.' He had returned to his script, his voice tired and unwilling. 'What would you ... to that?'

Elswyth remained motionless on the bench.

'I have your father's blessing,' he added.

She still gave no reply. It was such a terrible fate, now that she heard it aloud. She must uphold her family's reputation, otherwise there could be no future for Louisa. That Mr. Buell's reputation would be saved by her actions as well seemed grossly unfair. Especially if he insisted on acting beastly and two-faced about the entire incident. Would he maintain his lies, even when there was no one to mark them?

Despite his shortcomings, Mr. Thomas was honest—an open book. He would have treated her with all due magnification, and worshipped any child they had been given care of. That she knew.

'It really would be best for everyone,' Mr. Buell went on. 'You could have the husband that is overdue you. And we could take charge of Louisa's child, whomever's he may be. In fact, to ensure appearances are convincing, you and I could...'

'I will tell you how it will be.' Elswyth stood up, surprising herself at the sheer volume of her voice. 'You will remain quiet and do as you are told. You will eat and drink when I say so. You will not leave except on my errands. Since you have escaped punishment, I will make your home a cage. And you will never lay a hand on my sister again. Or you shall face my father's wrath. I am in love with Mr. Thomas. Until he returns, you are a prisoner.'

Mr. Buell remained motionless on the bench, stunned by Elswyth's outburst.

She looked over the calm waters. 'I'll see you at the wedding.' She then hiked her skirts and marched herself back to the museum, unescorted.

13.9.43, 3:30, 65 deg., 10 knots, 2/10ths cloud coverage
Desert country near rivers with great mesas on either side

Rodent or weasel perhaps, though I have seen in neither order a
species so large. Striped fur, wicked little claws, and a long serpent
tail. Late last night I woke to find this varmint rooting through
my remaining things. I shouted and kicked dust from where I lay,
but that did not prevent him from gnawing at my sack, looking
at me with what I can only describe as evil eyes, a forked tongue
flickering in and out at a regular interval, quite like a snake.
Eventually I had to get up and beat the ground around him with
my blanket to scare him off. He showed his dirty little teeth and
made nasty faces about it. Our stand off lasted long enough to
make a passable rendering. I name him the Numrat.

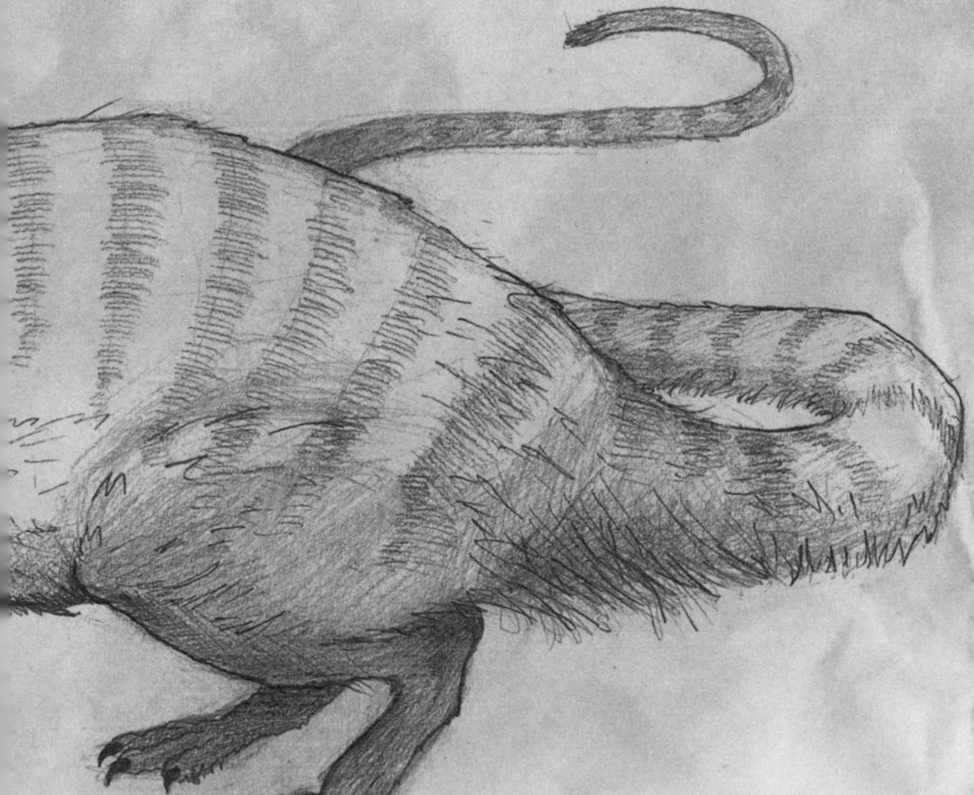

ELSWYTH COMPOSES A SONNET. LOUISA CUTS A HOLE
IN HER QUILT. THE SISTERS GRAY QUARREL.
ELSWYTH SENDS A TELEGRAM.

On a whim, Elswyth composed a sonnet of her own, for Mr. Thomas. Until she'd said it to Mr. Buell, she hadn't realized how in love with him she was. If only she'd followed her heart.

> *When love first called I spurned his advance,*
> *For dabbling in the dew keeps milkmaids fair,*
> *And to the fates above I owed a chance,*
> *Lest season's end bring silver to my hair.*
> *Who should want to wed marriage's false pact?*
> *Not spring, nor butterfly, nor bird, nor I.*
> *For, ever joined are these two by fact:*
> *A ring'd finger and wrinkles 'round the eye.*
> *But now the fates have put thou at remove,*
> *And also ravaged those fields of my youth,*
> *I find myself praying that time shall prove,*
> *Thy courting words realized in blooming truth.*
> *Beauty is but a sparkling of the eye,*
> *Remaining in thine I shan't be passed by.*

She began a letter to him, but could not finish. She placed them both in an envelope and was filled with despair. There was no place to address it to, if she could bring herself to send it. And Mr. Buell certainly couldn't be trusted with the post. She longed to communicate with Mr. Thomas. She must compel him to return. It was the one small hope that remained.

She put the writing materials away, wishing the thoughts that accompanied them would stay put away as well. When she was finished, Elswyth brought her sister's dollhouse up to her room. Louisa was asleep, lolling in the same nightgown she had dressed her in days before. Elswyth resolved that when she woke, she would wrest it from her and launder it in the tub.

Elswyth set the great dollhouse down in the corner of the room and a giant moth fluttered out, startling her. She brushed away the dust and cobwebs, and took some of the dolls out and arranged them about the front door. She glanced at Louisa, prone on the bed. The pitcher of water on the nightstand was empty.

She frowned at the old dollhouse. The dolls were stiff and awkward, as if unsure what to do with themselves. Elswyth knelt down to set them in a more social arrangement. Greeting visitors from a distant land, perhaps before an afternoon tea party. She was setting up the table inside when she heard Louisa stir.

'Mother?' she cried out.

Elswyth stepped to her bedside and pressed a hand on her forehead. It was hot. Perhaps a cold compress was needed more than a new nightgown. 'It's Elsie. I'm here, dear.'

'I want to go to the fair. The petting zoo…'

'You've been to the fair. We can't go now. I've told you. Do you want some water? I'll fetch you some.'

When Elswyth returned, Louisa was sitting up in bed, awake. Elswyth handed her an overfull glass of water, and Louisa managed to spill a good deal on the bedclothes before bringing it to her lips. She drank the entirety in one swallow.

'How are you feeling?' Elswyth fixed the end of Louisa's plait, which had come undone.

'Fine.' Louisa shrank back under the quilt.

'I've brought your dollhouse and your dolls. I couldn't find your favorite though.'

'Maryposa is here.' Her little blonde head appeared.

'Oh, there she... Louisa! Did you cut a hole in that quilt? Mother sewed that, how could you?'

'It's a hole in the cave. Maryposa is staying in the cave.'

Elswyth snatched up the star-patterned quilt to inspect the damage. Louisa had cut holes in seven different sections. It would take a long time to mend. Once the quilt was off, Elswyth noticed her sister's blister-red feet.

'Have you been jumping in the laundry tub?'

'Aunt Anne made me scrub them, and then held them over the fire to dry. She said that makes the baby grow.' Louisa put a hand to her stomach.

'Nonsensical superstition. I suppose she told you to cut these holes in the quilt, that the baby may breathe?'

'They are caves. In the south. We are going away, Mr. Buell and I, on a great adventure, and we're taking Grapes, and we will have our own family in a beautiful home on the prairie in Texas, and I will be away from wretched, smelly Chicago.'

'Louisa, you must grow up. Mr. Buell has no such means. In fact, he's from the same family as Mr. Thomas. Can't you see that everything that monster says is a falsehood?'

Louisa slid her doll back through the mouth of the quilt cave.

Elswyth sighed. 'Louisa, I am going to marry Mr. Buell, and we are going to raise your child. It is the only way to save you ...'

'No.' Louisa sat up. 'No. Mr. Buell is marrying me. I have his child. He promised me.'

'Louisa you are too young to...'

'Mr. Thomas is your suitor, Mr. Buell is mine.'

'Mr. Thomas may never return. And if he does not, though I am loath to, I have to marry Mr. Buell instead. I am old, and my courting time is passed. You mustn't miss yours.'

'No!' Louisa shouted and ran to block the door. Elswyth, being a bit taller, grabbed her by her shoulders and marched her straight back to the bed.

'Why don't you go after Mr. Thomas and disappear yourself?' Louisa began to weep with abandon. When Elswyth tried to soothe her, Louisa wrested free and punched her in the arm with all her might.

The more she tried to restrain Louisa, the more inconsolable her sister became. When Louisa picked up her water glass and shattered it on the floor, Elswyth ran out. She told herself the only thing to do was to leave her to Aunt Anne, who could calm Louisa and clean up the mess. Truly, Elswyth knew that her own composure was on the verge of collapse.

Louisa should recognize her good fortune. She only had to hide away for nine months, then she could continue a normal life and be introduced to society as though none of it had ever happened. It was Elswyth who would be forever ruined.

Elswyth didn't want her sister to see her cry, yet something in her needed to be released. She thought of calling on the doctor and saying she felt ill, just so he would bleed her again. The thought sickened her, but she could think of no other way she might gain some relief. She determined to go, just as soon as she'd visited the post office and mailed Mr. Thomas's letter.

Back in her room, as Elswyth dressed, a new plan arose in her mind. She knew her letters had been compromised by Mr. Buell's meddling, but he had foolishly revealed his theft by naming Mr. Thomas's location. Now that she could guess where he would likely be, a much more reliable way of reaching him there occurred to her—a telegram.

They were costly to send, but all at once she knew that this was the answer to her troubles. Why had she even bothered with a silly sonnet? Leaving her shoes aside, Elswyth tiptoed toward her father's study.

She found him snoring, reclined on his couch. His brow was creased and he muttered to himself, but Elswyth knew his fitful sleep—it would take some commotion to rouse him. Something as soft and quiet as sliding his pocketbook out of his waistcoat would not interrupt his wild dreaming.

She was sad to discover one lone crumpled note inside, but it was the only way. She took it and carefully replaced the pocketbook. Mr. Gray rolled over with a snort.

Elswyth pitied her poor father and all his worldly troubles.

If she were married to Mr. Thomas, he would worship her and Louisa's child besides, she was sure of it. They might raise the child together. Her father would banish Mr. Buell. If the child could have a pretend mother, why not a pretend father as well? Mr. Thomas could save her. It was a last desperate hope.

She flew from the house, scaring up a rat who had been cowering on the doorstep. She scurried toward the telegraph office, through the damp and darkening streets.

She passed a single worker who was fiddling with a new lamppost. The city had just lined the main streets with them, though they gave no light yet. He seemed to be watching her.

Breathless inside, she laid out her father's last lonely note, and immediately requested one telegram to the first station inside the border of the disputed Texan territory: Santa Fe.

The sleepy clerk bent his head, and listened to her dictation for Mr. Zadock Thomas.

You must return to me by the 24th of October.
Otherwise I shall be married to Mr. Buell.

The few simple words were translated into the clacks of the telegraph machine, and then they were sent. An imprint of them remained in Elswyth's mind as she hurried home from the telegraph office. She pulled her shawl close against the cold evening drizzle. She could afford no more than those two sentences. She could hear them ringing through the wires all the way down to that foreign land she could not entirely imagine. If her guesses were correct regarding his whereabouts, then she could trust Mr. Thomas would receive the telegram upon his arrival in Santa Fe, where she had addressed it.

It was but a small shadow of a hope. She missed him so. And she wished sorely to rid herself and her family of Mr. Buell.

Mr. Thomas would make it back in time. He must. He would receive the telegram and turn around straightaway and rush home. He had always been in love with her. He would obey her in this, as in all things. She must simply wait and hope. Her father had never quite approved of Mr. Thomas, but he couldn't argue now. It was the best chance for the future happiness of all of them.

Dearest Elswyth,

There are no postal offices in this dusty country, but I will save up my letters until one can be found. I expect that once I reach Irion's camp, he will have some means for posting letters.

I am near Albuquerque for a brief respite after a long ride with Rodriguez. He has been much happier out from under McMarrow's thumb. D'Etre has proved an excellent steed, and as good a friend as I could hope for among any of the species of the earth.

Rodriguez's family home is just south of Albuquerque in a place called Los Padillas. We were received by Sr. Rodriguez. He was surprised, but welcomed us immediately. The house is being maintained by his unmarried daughter, Doña Abril, Rodriguez's sister. She is a handsome beauty of twenty-one years, with cheeks as red as a turkey's nose. She is so deliberate and perfectly pristine in her manners and I must have seemed rude, for I could not bring myself to meet her gaze.

Rodriguez is a finer gentleman than I had even suspected before, and the comforts of his home and his refinement brought me relief.

The sala fronts the street and, instead of papering, the walls are painted in a singular fashion with sparrows and colorful moths. There are flowerpots and birdcages and a great many hounds. It being late in the season there are no blossoms in the flower beds, but the weather in this part of the west is so mild that the trees continue to bear fruit. I shall have my fill of the Illinois nut, which they call the pecan here.

If the grounds contain the riches of nature, the interior houses treasures crafted by man. Sr. Rodriguez carries the blood of nobility, and upon arriving I felt ashamed of the state I was in, dirty and disheveled. His great walls seemed to lean in with paintings of his ancestors looking down their noses. He has many filing cabinets and bookshelves stacked with fine volumes. You would love it here.

I had intended to leave this evening, the desert being a good deal cooler at night, but Rodriguez would not have it. He said he had thrown open the doors of his home to me and it was required that I at least stay one night. I struggle to tolerate this delay. I am anxious.

Illinois nuts and grapes were both part of the best meal I have had in months. It was served in four courses by Abril along with delightful Mexican dishes of boiled meats, onions, cabbage, and potatoes. We drank aguadiente, a strong brandy the natives make from the root of the agave plant. After a few cups, Sr. Rodriguez asserted that Indians were the finest people of these lands, calling them honorable and just. He said they love each other as many men do not, and that they wisely heed the counsel of their matriarchs. He said his own daughter had spent time with their female shamans to learn their ways. He smoked cigarritas constantly, and offered them to me in a way I found difficult to refuse. They kept going out as I pretended to smoke them.

Sr. Rodriguez then revealed that he knew Irion, much to my surprise. He admired the man and agreed that Texas should not belong to Mexico, despite being a citizen. He has sent money, not only to protect his trade caravans but also to prop up the Texian rebellion and aid Irion's fight. In the end, however, he does not think Texas should join the U.S. either. Instead he called it the crucible for a new society. He said Irion's fight could be ours and described a utopian vision that sounded distant and overwhelming to me. He spoke of superior mechanical technology and a large society working together, focused on its internal affairs rather than on expanding its territory and defending itself against other nations. Sr. Rodriguez asserts that Irion is the man to do it, because he alone among the Texians is able to find peace with the Indians. And he is possessed of a vision.

At the conclusion he called me a fellow rebel. I was so full of food and drink and smoke, I hadn't the head to ask what that meant. I took leave of my hosts and retired to the fine quarters they have provided. I am dead tired, and expect sleep will overtake me quickly tonight.

Yours from a Foreign Land, Zadock

FAM. PHRYNOSOMATIDAE

GEN. PHRYNOSOMA

16.9.43, 11:45, 95 deg., 5 knots, few clouds

Desert country. Outside Rodriguez's estate, Los Padillas

Horned Toad. Reptile. 6 inches. Spiky head and dorsum. Brown with black spots, very much the color of the earth here. A disc-shaped body, with short legs. I found this rather ugly little toad on an anthill outside Rodriguez's stable. He sat atop it, slurping up ants like some dragon feasting on a town of helpless men who had been flushed from their underground hiding-holes. I drew him quickly, as I didn't much like the look of him, and Abril found me doing so. I said he looked like a horned toad, but she named him the Virgin's bull, owing to the larger spines on his head, and to the fact that he wept blood. I could scarcely believe this latter fact, and told her so using the simplest English accompanied by explanatory gestures. Grabbing a long stick, she surprised me by poking at him mercilessly. He hissed and puffed, but she continued, backing him against a rock wall. She said the creature could tell if a girl was pregnant. Finally, completely puffed up and highly agitated, the creature did indeed squirt blood from its eyes in a most terrible way. I have never seen such a horrifying skill, and feel sometimes I understand this alien world not at all.

too ugly to draw...

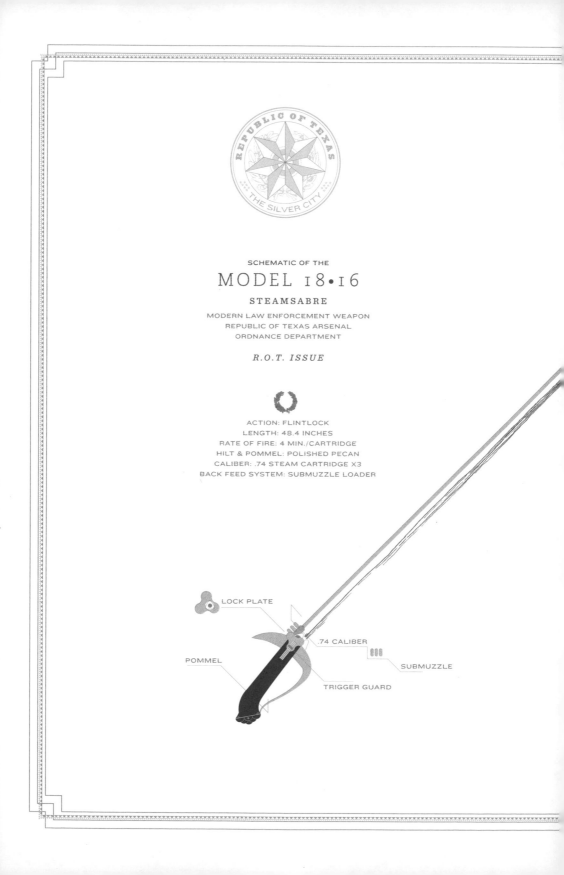

SCHEMATIC OF THE

MODEL 18•16

STEAMSABRE

MODERN LAW ENFORCEMENT WEAPON
REPUBLIC OF TEXAS ARSENAL
ORDNANCE DEPARTMENT

R.O.T. ISSUE

ACTION: FLINTLOCK
LENGTH: 48.4 INCHES
RATE OF FIRE: 4 MIN./CARTRIDGE
HILT & POMMEL: POLISHED PECAN
CALIBER: .74 STEAM CARTRIDGE X3
BACK FEED SYSTEM: SUBMUZZLE LOADER

LOCK PLATE

.74 CALIBER

SUBMUZZLE

POMMEL

TRIGGER GUARD

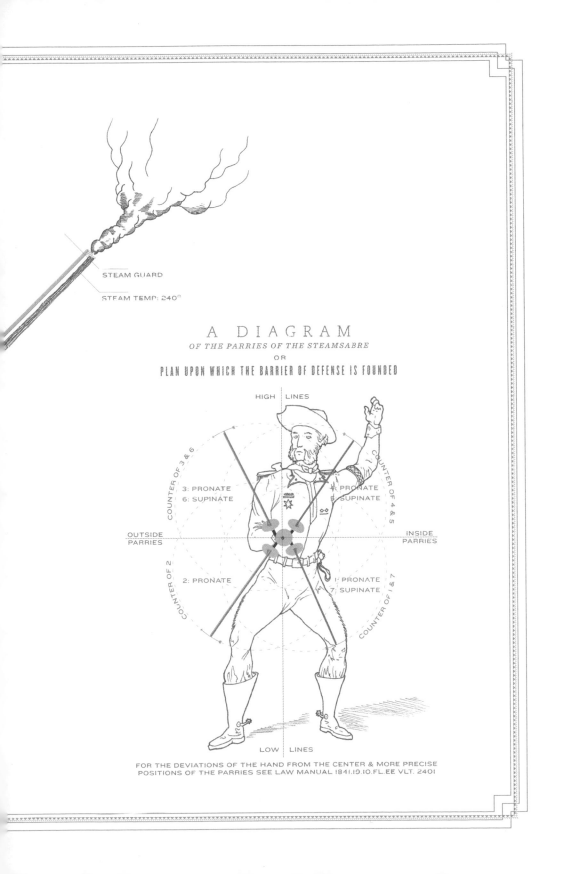

STEAM GUARD

STEAM TEMP: 240°

A DIAGRAM
OF THE PARRIES OF THE STEAMSABRE

OR

PLAN UPON WHICH THE BARRIER OF DEFENSE IS FOUNDED

HIGH | LINES

COUNTER OF 3 & 6

COUNTER OF 4 & 5

3: PRONATE
6: SUPINATE

4: PRONATE
5: SUPINATE

OUTSIDE
PARRIES

INSIDE
PARRIES

COUNTER OF 2

COUNTER OF 1 & 7

2: PRONATE

1: PRONATE
7: SUPINATE

LOW | LINES

FOR THE DEVIATIONS OF THE HAND FROM THE CENTER & MORE PRECISE
POSITIONS OF THE PARRIES SEE LAW MANUAL 1841.19.10.FL.EE VLT. 2401

lunges with a sabre. It was a fighting sabre, no practice weapon. He had decided he should not go about unarmed anymore. These were dangerous times, and the city's police force was paltry.

Mr. Buell slashed over and over into an oak board he had carved out for a target. He practiced all the positions and sequences of every attack he knew, each time more quickly and violently. His flank cut was deadly accurate.

He pretended his target was the body of Mr. Thomas. A stack of his opened letters sat on the floor. He had read them all again, vowing that Elswyth never would. If it weren't for Mr. Thomas, Elswyth wouldn't be trying to control his life. Why should he be made responsible for her selfish heart? He imagined holding it in his hand, a pulsing red pomegranate. Mr. Thomas's return was impossible. He was pale, sickly, and birdbrained besides. Mr. Buell feared he would spend the rest of his days trapped inside walls, married to his cousin's temperamental love.

Mr. Thomas had fallen easily under Aunt Anne's religious spell. He couldn't stand to see them together sipping her wretched teas and speaking of mysteries that could only ever enchant idle minds. Any fool who put stock in the preposterous readings of tea leaves or spiritualist beliefs about the communing of souls had no place in a museum of natural sciences.

He hadn't seen Louisa in many days now. It was his rightful duty to check on the health of his child and its mother. Maybe it would be best to steal them both away in the night. He could save them from being locked in Elswyth's schemes as well.

Though he had previously wanted her for his wife, Elswyth was furious with him now. She would forever pine for the ghost of Mr. Thomas. Mr. Gray, his employer, had lost all confidence in him. Louisa was banished from his presence. And his child would be kept from him. It was all the fault of his bloody cousin.

PLATE 21. THE BLACK-EYED SHUCK

➤Eliza, it seems that Zeke's letter is still elusive. I am desperate to right the wrong that I have done you both. It was reported that the original was turned in to be carbon'd, so I went to look for it in the Vault of Records. It was an easy morning walk: The bats were returning to their roost in the roof of the Vault, so I just followed them to the source of knowledge. Once there, the file number led to a drawer, which referred me to another file in another hall, which then returned me back to the original thread, which had a misfile slip attached... and so on. This has gone on for two days. I have walked up and down the great dusty halls, yanking open flimsy drawers. Sand and bat guano have clogged the gears that allow them to slide out from the cabinets. No one has cleaned. The weaknesses of the Vault and my organization of the Records are being made very clear to me.

Nowhere in these files have I found the missing letter to confirm Zeke's bloodline. Instead they all refer to the Auspices. Their history is shady: They all began as Senators' wives and have some secret hand in running the nation. This makes sense if they hold the key to the fount-water — inside these walls, that substance is life itself. Though they wield this power, their agenda is not clear. They have come out against the watch-posts and force of the Law, Daxon in particular, on numerous occasions. Yet they also shun the Deserters and the chaos they preach. Perhaps they are simply against violence and this is what they teach their young recruits. In any case, I don't know why all these files have been stamped instead of the letter.

What makes my task even more difficult is that I have to keep up the appearance of research at the Vault so that Daxon and his men do not suspect that I'm thumbing through their open threads. At least the research time allows me to investigate some of the oddities in Zadock Thomas's story.

I have found little on Rodriguez's father. It's plausible that he might be Don Mariano Chavez y Rodriguez, the head of an influential and wealthy New Mexican family. Transporting goods over the Santa Fe Trail, down the Camino Real, and to other traders in Chihuahua would have been very lucrative. The trade with New Mexico had reached half a million dollars annually and was growing at a rapid pace.

It would have been an excellent profession in a more civilized time. Before the Civil War, the U.S. was lawless, and much of the west was unsettled and unstructured. Vigilante justice ruled in the territories. Rebellions were inevitable — there was no governing body to keep the peace.

McMarrow led an escort dragoon, sent by the U.S. to protect the overland trade with Mexico. His replacement of standard troops with American Indians was highly unusual, and his abandonment of the traders along the route could have found him charged with treason. Zadock's sole concerns were the animals and Elswyth. He seems only vaguely aware of the political situation around him and what it might mean for an American to be in New Mexico at the time.

I wish he had written more about Sr. Rodriguez's financial relationship with Irion. It makes no sense for a Mexican citizen like Sr. Rodriguez to give support to the Texans. Especially given his daughter's ties to local Navajo tribes. The new Texas government was no friend to the indigenous populations.

But General Irion didn't get along well with his countrymen. He was opposed to Mirabeau Lamar, the third president of Texas. Lamar's separatist policies became unpopular along with his campaign to drive the American Indians out of Texas and the printing of "redbacks," a Texas currency that quickly overinflated and became valueless.

Since the Texan administration he disagreed with had no interest in joining the U.S., Irion took his troops rogue, continuing to fight the war in his own way. He attacked other Texan troops and trade caravans as well as embarking on a mad-conquistador search for cities of gold and fountains of youth. Based on McMarrow's description of him, he is a capable if delusional leader. At times he seems almost as bent and bloodthirsty as Lamar. I worry that these city-states have begun to take on the air of a failed political experiment, echoing this nascent and short-lived Republic of Texas.

Daxon has also broken from his nation and built a cannon. He claims it is for defense, but war machines have been outlawed since the Collapse. I heard him brag openly of throwing someone over the barrier into the rot, proclaiming loudly to his men, "Let the wolves have him." This sort of justice makes me feel less secure. Because of all the dead zones, anyone here could be a killer if they are careful enough to hide their tracks.

I have unhooked my typowriter from the carbon repeater. I can feel Daxon listening to me. I sneak around the Vault now, worried that someone will trace my namestamps. The letter cannot be much farther away. I must find it soon. For you.

I wish you could've known your mother. We had our disagreements, and she knew I was Queer. Perhaps long before I did. She was a lovely person. She had a perfect natural grace. And a special talent for making others feel comfortable and at home. Watching you, I can't help but to see her and that same radiant warmth. I hope that Zeke appreciates this in you.

If Zeke accepts his duty as Khrysalis and takes the Senate seat, then you will move away from this dangerous city-state. I hope when it is all over you will read this thread. Though we can't speak, you would see I tried to help in some small way.

SEVEN FLAGS
O'ER TEXAS

SEVEN FLAGS HAVE FLOWN OVER TEXAS, YET
THE LONE STAR HAS ALWAYS RETAINED ITS
INDEPENDENT, EMBLEMATIC CHARACTER.

SPAIN
1519 — 1685, 1690 — 1821

FRANCE
1685 — 1690

MEXICO
1821 — 1836

REPUBLIC OF TEXAS
1836 — 1845

CONFEDERATE
STATES OF AMERICA
1861 — 1865

UNITED STATES
OF AMERICA
1845 — 1861, 1865 — 2073

TEXAS REPUBLIC OF THE NATIONAL ALLIANCE
2077 — PRESENT

Dearest Elswyth,

In the morning I awoke to a tin tub, in which Abril had already drawn a bath for me. This was a welcome surprise, and it felt vitally refreshing to soak in the cool waters. She had washed my traveling clothes, and I had to wait modestly in the tub for her to return them to me. After I dressed she even clipped my fingernails and toenails, which brought on another spell of bashfulness, but I didn't have the Spanish to graciously refuse such a kind gesture.

Rodriguez seems in no great hurry to leave, which has inflamed my impatience. He has to wait for his caravan of goods to arrive. In the afternoon he took me to the running pens, where we coursed his grayhounds. He has many large and handsome animals, and they are as swift as fowl in flight. He told me his were descended from the original old-world hounds, brought by the conquistadors to hunt rabbits or coyote or, sadly, sometimes Indians.

I reiterated how crucial my errand was. He seemed to think that I would find Irion and help to form the New Society. I insisted my task has no part to play in that grander scheme, but I was anxious to leave.

He said his family had been expelled from Albuquerque, and his father had been forced to relocate his home farther south. Abril had spent much time visiting with the tribe not far from here. Society wouldn't accept this and began to suspect her of using the witchery way. He expressed disdain for his people and praised his sister's learning. Since she is also enamored of the new country, and knows the way, he suggested that I take her with me as a guide.

I refused this as well. Traveling alone with a woman would not only be improper but also dangerous, and I could not bear the thought of exposing Rodriguez's sister to the trials of the hard road. I cannot ask her to wager her life on the gambit I have undertaken.

Rodriguez said that we might leave the decision until morning, when I should depart. He said I might consider the idea more carefully.

He offered to provision me fully and water d'Etre. In the dusk I went outside, pretending to take his words under advisement, though truly I would not entertain them for a moment. I was saying this very thing to d'Etre while brushing him in Rodriguez's stable when the most curious toad caught my eye.

Abril, bringing some feed out for d'Etre, discovered me in the midst of drawing the spiky creature. I showed her my work, though it was a lifeless example of my poor skill. Even so, she taught me what she knew of the horned toad. Presently, I asked after her suitors, and she said she had none, preferring the company of the Indian women who had been teaching her as of late. I had never considered what their religion might be like. She spoke to me of their shamans, great women who guide the tribes in worshipping their ancestors. This idea rather struck me. I scarcely know who mine are. Once away from her father, she seemed to bloom into an outspoken young woman with some command of English. It was not perfect, but she began speaking rapidly of the shamans' rituals and I tried my best to understand.

The Indian women had indeed taught her many things, useful arts for healing. She mentioned the skinwalkers, whom Rodriguez had spoken of at the pueblo. The creatures live outside the tribe and the shamans do much work to keep them at bay. She began to describe something called the Nightway, another sort of magic, a dance that causes the weather to respond to human moods and such. She said it was useful, and that she would perform the spell for me if it helped.

We went into the stable, leaving d'Etre to his meal. We climbed into the hayloft. There she had set up a table, made from an old crate. Upon it were all manner of dried flowers and a single black candle.

She plucked fruit from a cactus pad and ground it into a fine dust. She then used a stiff feather to mix it with water in a clay bowl. She drank from the bowl with both hands and presently reclined, her eyes rolling back in her head. I waited and watched her for the better part of an hour. Moths beat the air around me, the black candle drawing their hawk-size shadows in spirals on the roof above. Some wretched wind had picked up outside and was nipping at us through the cracks in the barn walls. I was unsure of whether to wake Abril from her trance or to return to the house and let her be.

The thought of reporting this circumstance to her father seemed unwise, and just as I resolved to reach out and rouse her from her strange slumber, she bolted upright, eyes white in the gloaming.

She began to speak, with a low and knowing voice, as though we were familiars. She said there was no time to deliver the letter, and I must return to the Gray house without delay. It was then I realized her English had become perfect. Her eyes were very still.

"Anne?" I ventured to ask. I felt as though the threads of a dream were being woven into reality before my very eyes.

"There is a child on the way. An important one."

Once it was said, the telegram and sudden marriage made sense. It is unnerving news, a blow that compounds the injury done to me by the telegram. Is it true, my love? Have you lain with another?

"Was it Buell?" I asked. Though it was plainly Abril in front of me, I knew I was speaking to your Aunt Anne. I could barely contain myself. "My cousin cannot be trusted. I never should have left!"

"Your cousin? This complicates things. Listen closely, Zadock, and do as I say." I could only nod. "The creatures of the air, they know the path through the night. You must follow their flocks. Only the hidden creatures can make your fate now. Burrow into your darkest to-morrow, the Nightway is underneath everything. There is hardly time."

Abril then awoke to herself. I should have hurried! I leapt from the hayloft, badly twisting my ankle. Dark had taken the barn and the lands about. I went outside to breathe some cool night air.

Abril followed me and laid a comforting hand on my back. She was herself again, yet had heard everything. We did not speak for a long while, and I discovered tears on my cheek. Eventually she told me of a spell to curse a pregnant woman, whereby the shaman slits open the belly of a horned toad and puts a human bone inside, that of a child or a twin being especially powerful. She offered to do the magic for me.

I said that of course I wished you no harm, that the pregnant girl was my love and had left me for another man.

Abril said that times of transformation are very dangerous. She said that I should be wary because the stars were watching me, and when they start to change I have to become invisible to them.

She began to enumerate ways to ensure this happened — the dance, eating only fruits, and so forth. She then produced a fine-looking map of the night sky. She said it had been given her by a Texian soldier, and though she could not read it, she was convinced the asterisms it illustrated were alive and would guide me along the Nightway.

I could hardly pay it any attention. I was, and remain, beside myself with anguish. I have been awake all night long.

I could scarcely believe it at first, but as I lay unsleeping on the mat in my sala another thought dawned on me. You sent the telegram because you are pregnant. If I could not be of help, why else would you include a deadline? You have never before been anxious to marry, having waited this long. But now you are with child and must wed before your reputation suffers. Buell is the available partner. But it could just as easily be me. That's why you reached out. You could not, of course, mention an out-of-wedlock pregnancy in a telegram.

The dawn hour is not far off now, and I make ready to leave on my own, unescorted. I feel I must. Haste is now all that matters. I will follow the path of the birds. I cannot wait for Rodriguez or his sister. I must hurry toward home with a haste that may stretch my endurance to the limit. But do not lose hope, my love. I am coming for you. Whatever child is with you shall be ours, I promise it.

With You in This as in All Things, Zadock

BEGIN PHONOTUBE TRANSCRIPT:

R. DEXTRA » I joined up. I'm a conscripted Deserter now. You should too.

Z. THOMAS » That'd be quite a job change for me. Khrysalis to Deserter.

» You don't want that job.

» I don't think Leeya will like that.

» Last time I guess we had a bit of an accident. Me and Leeya.

» What do you mean?

FLAG▸ » She's pregnant. ‹PREGNANCY

» Whoa. Raisin. You're ... that's going to be trouble.

» She told me last week. It's my kid. When they find out, they'll send me straight to ... well, I guess Atlantas is gone.

» Eliza could've got you the papers for emergency marriage. She's fired now. You could try to go to Salt-Lake early.

» I don't want to be in babyland either. That's why I joined the Deserters.

FLAG▸ I'm going to flee the city-state. ‹DESERTER

» That's your parenthood plan?

» You should talk to the conscripter. I did.

FLAG▸ He's called the Nightman. He guides ‹NIGHTMAN people out of the city-state. Over the barrier late at night. Trains "bats" to flee. He lives in the industrial quarter.

» Raisin, you're going to have a baby. I don't like the Republic any more than you do, but ... How will you live?

» It's the only way. Leeya won't take me for a pair, and the last thing I want to do at this age is go to bloody Salt-Lake.

» But you think she'd run off and join a group of armed Deserters with you?

» You're lucky. You already have someone.

» Actually, I also have a small problem.

» There's no way Eliza is pregnant too.

» Hh. No. My grandfather left me this letter. From my great-great-great-great-great-great ... great-grandfather.

» That's a lot of greats. What does it say?

» I don't know. I lost it. It's uncarbon'd.

FLAG▶ » Uncarbon'd. Bad.   ‹UNCARBON'D RECORD

» And they know. There's a deadline out for me. I have seven days to turn it in. Major Daxon has been particularly aggressive. He knows I have it. Or had it, anyway. That's the problem.

» Don't go to jail. Escape. Come to the rot.

» I've thought of giving the seat to Bic.

» Yes! You want to be in charge of this claustrotopia? Enforce these rules?

» I imagine Eliza would be a little uncomfortable as a Deserter.

» I hear they have code names. I'll be Storm-Riler. You can be ... Bird-Boots.

» Ha. Call me when you're sober. Let's   LAUGHTER
meet up. Figure out both these messes.

» Double, double toil and trouble...

END UNIT TRANSCRIPT

◇◇ ⌒ Zeke had to lean on some laudanum. There was a feeling of unbearable pressure inside his skull. He needed the soft release of the drug. He couldn't stop thinking about Bartle and his hunt for the letter in the Vault. He wished he could go with him. Without the letter, he was essentially without a choice. ⌒ ⌒ Eliza was different when she got home from work. Her mood had shifted. She was shaken and tense, but no longer angry. She put her things down and took off her boots, moving slowly. She sat next to him, releasing a long exhale. ⌒ ⌒ ⌒ "Listen, I'm sorry about … our fight." She smiled faintly. ⌒ **"Me too."** Zeke wasn't expecting an apology. ⌒ ⌒ She looked him in the eye. "I lost my job." Her chin began to tremble. Zeke sat up a little. ⌒ **"Why? I mean, why do you think that happened?"** ⌒ "I'm not sure. I took some paper. Daxon has it out for us." ⌒ **"I think Daxon has aims beyond Texas. His speech at the statue ceremony was directed at the Senate."** ⌒ "What will you do?" ⌒ "I can't take the Senate seat. Not without the letter. I feel sure there's something my grandfather wanted me to know. The way it came to me — subtle but deliberate. Besides, they'll arrest me if I can't find it." ⌒ "Well, you can decide once you have it. But I know your grandparents wanted you to take the seat." ⌒ **"Look how much this political stuff has already messed with our lives. Your job."** ⌒ "As long as you still want me." ⌒ "I do. Forever. I am your blood. I just want to get out of here and start our lives — private, simple. I want kids, I know you do too." ⌒ At this, Eliza pulled out a folded transcript and handed it to Zeke. It was his conversation with Raisin from two days ago. Zeke read it. ⌒ "Why didn't you tell me Leeya was pregnant?" Eliza didn't seem mad, just a little hurt. ⌒ "I assumed you knew. I figured she'd tell you even before Raisin." ⌒ "That's strange. But we're supposed to meet tonight. I'm worried that she's been going to the Auspices, talking to them about becoming a recruit. Makes sense,

I suppose, if she's pregnant and unpaired." ∿ "You'd pick Raisin over the Auspices?" ∿ "Maybe they aren't all bad. Someone has to take the Gray girls in. But I don't really know much about the Auspices. I can't imagine Leeya caught up in spells and poisons and all of that. You need to talk to Raisin about this." ∿ "I'll find him. When are you seeing Leeya?" ∿ "I'm meeting her for dinner at seven." ∿ "It's seven now." ∿ Eliza glanced at the clock on the mantel. She turned back to him, her eyes searching. ∿ ∿ "You should go," Zeke said. ∿ ∿ ∿ ∿ ∿ Eliza got up. She took her socks off while hopping into the bedroom. ∿ ∿ ∿ ∿ ∿ Just talking felt better. Zeke knew they would make up now. He picked up Eliza's socks. He squeezed his feet into them. They were too small, coming just over his heels, well short of the ankle. ∿ ∿ ∿ ∿ Eliza returned in different jeans. She held one arm across her freckled chest. She was looking for something. Zeke tucked his feet underneath his body. ∿ "I have something to ask you," Zeke said. Eliza froze. "I won't be mad, but..." Eliza opened her mouth, as if to confess. "You altered Leeya's file?" ∿ ∿ She looked confused. For a moment Zeke thought she was going to lie. "A long time..." Eliza switched to a whisper. "Raisin brought her too young. They both would've been jailed." ∿ "I thought digging in the Vault was dangerous. That's not why you got fired?" ∿ "No, nobody has found that. It was the only way to protect Leeya. I couldn't stand to lose her." ∿ ∿ "You and I waited." Zeke thought about the span of their entire relationship. He thought about how long it had been since Eliza had seen her father. He thought about how long it had taken his grandfather's generation to build the barriers and initiate the lifephases. ∿ We lose all we have done and built and how. ∿ ∿ ∿ Eliza took a deep breath, her ribs stretching her thin frame. "Where did my socks go?" She looked under the table and returned to the other room for her shirt. ∿ ∿ ∿

〰 "I have something else to tell you," Zeke called after her. 〰 〰 "Keep your voice down!" She hurried back in, dressed for the square. "I altered Leeya's file for Raisin too, you know. We were both worried. Tell him to do the right thing." She sat down next to him. "What is it?" He took her hand again and tried to speak calmly. 〰 "Your father is here." 〰 〰 〰 "I'm not sure what you mean." 〰 "I met your father. He's in Texas." 〰 Silence. Eliza looked doubtful. 〰 "And he came to you instead of me?" She grabbed one of her boots and picked at the toe. 〰 "I think he's worried about seeing you." 〰 〰 "How do you know this is my father?" 〰 Zeke paused. He hadn't expected to be questioned. 〰 "I guess I don't. He looks like you. A tiny bit." 〰 "I just don't know why he would tell you this, instead of finding me." 〰 "He … he's looking for my letter. Someone turned it in." 〰 〰 It seemed like it was sinking in now. Eliza put down the boot, next to its pair. She buried her face in her hands. After a moment her shoulders began to convulse in the unmistakable rhythm of sobs. Zeke shifted down the sofa and put his arms around her. 〰 〰 "It's OK. I know how weird this must be. To hear he's alive. You shouldn't see him, though. It's too dangerous." Eliza tried a few words, but nothing really came out. Each time she began to speak, sobs overtook her again. Zeke just held her and waited. He remembered the feeling when his sabre finally cut through the steampipes, and all the power of the city-state leaked out into the night. He felt relief. It lasted until he was made Khrysalis. It wasn't fair that his fate was now decided for him. 〰 "Listen, I'm going to get the letter back. Your father is going to help. We'll get it all sorted out, and then we can get out of here. I'm done with this city-state." 〰 Eliza just nodded. 〰 "I think it might be at the Vault, but I want you to promise me one thing." He lifted her chin to meet her eye. "Don't go looking for it. Or your father. Don't do anything rash." 〰 〰 〰 Eliza didn't answer. 〰

ID RECORD: 42984

CITY-STATE: 3 SILVER•CITY, TX

QUADRANT: NORTHEAST

REPUBLIC OF TEXAS — SILVER CITY

HEIGHT: 5 ft 6in
WEIGHT: 117
HAIR CL: Black
EYE CL: Green
SCARS: None

BLOOD

*ELIZA GRAY

State of Texas

TIFICATION PAPERS

42984

NAME: Eliza Gray
NDER: Female
DAY: 24 21
HASE: Yng Adult
LASS: 7th
TYPE: O positive
ELON: Vault Work

UTHORIZATIONS

THE SILVER CITY-STATE
NATIONAL LIFEPHASE PARTICIPANT

ECHELON

1: Filer
2: Threader
3:
4:
5:
6:
7:

OFFSPRING

NAMESTAMP: E. GRAY R.O.T.

GRAPES IS FOUND.

ELSWYTH RECEIVES HER MOTHER'S BOOK.

AUNT ANNE BREWS A POTENT TEA.

On the uppermost step of the stoop lay Grapes, panting shallowly. Elswyth was leaving the house, to see if any response had been received at the telegraph office, when she found her sister's dog collapsed there. The grayhound was mottled wet and weak with illness.

Without hesitation, Elswyth knelt down and wrapped her shawl around his head. He whined pitifully and she pressed him to her chest. Her first thought was to go and find Louisa upstairs, but then she realized what a shock it would be for her to see her favorite pet in such a state.

She sat with his head on her lap for some time and tried to feed him both biscuits and water. He would eat nothing. He licked his paws, which seemed permanently curled under, perhaps broken. He cried sometimes and fell in and out of sleep. Elswyth was no nurse, and she could not decide whether it was dangerous or vital for the hound to sleep. He certainly could not be bled.

She instead mustered all her strength to lift him into her arms and carry him back behind the house, to Aunt Anne's cottage. As skinny as he was, he was not light.

Her aunt opened the door warily at first but, when she saw the dying hound and the state of her niece, she quickly ushered them in, and Grapes was laid out on the kitchen table.

'Can you save him?' Elswyth pleaded.

Aunt Anne set to work, mumbling under her breath while running her ancient knotted hands over his belly, pressing here and there, trying to feel what was happening inside the dog. Her face was wrinkled in concentration.

When Louisa was little she couldn't properly say the word 'grayhound.' Her attempts sounded rather like 'grapes' and so that became the dog's name.

'There is little hope. I would try to give him our restorative elixir, but the only store is at the Auspicium. It is too late. He has simply wandered too far from home.'

'What good is your alchemy then?' Elswyth pulled at her aunt, who was rubbing the dog's ears, trying to comfort him. 'Get away!' she said. 'Leave him be.' Elswyth stroked his head gently and spoke to him of times they had shared in the past, the bright days of spring coursing on the wide lawn, and of Louisa's great love for him. Aunt Anne stood behind her, watching. It wasn't until she could no longer feel a trace of his breath that Elswyth allowed herself to cry.

It was still in the cottage for some time.

'The soul is like a bird,' Aunt Anne said presently. 'It can travel along the sky, through paths of its own making. It can see through the night everything that is below, and augur some things that are yet ahead. If these paths were known to you, you could have found this dog before his injuries took him.'

Elswyth whimpered softly.

'That is what my Sisters and I teach in the Auspicium. I have just traveled along the Nightway. I have been to see Mr. Thomas.'

Elswyth gave her a look from under furrowed brow. 'Do not tease me with your fairy stories today, I beg of you.'

'He has received your telegram.'

At the shock of this, Elswyth sat up. 'How did you…'

'He will answer it. And return to you. You must wait for him.'

Elswyth dried her cheeks with a small handkerchief. 'You have seen this?'

'More than seen — read. Here it is written.' Aunt Anne pulled the copy of *The City-State* from her bookshelf. 'Your mother knew what would come to pass, and she wrote it all down. Perhaps it is time you revisit the story, so that you might know as well why it is that Mr. Thomas will return.'

'And you told this to him?' She took the book from her aunt.

'He will read it as well. I have ripped out the last four pages, and they are with him, even now. Along with the letter, they wait in the envelope that he bears southward to Texas. When he opens it, he will know what to do. You, too, must read to the end.'

'Why did Father send him away?'

'Elswyth, you must come to the Auspicium. We guide a whole flock of souls. Our walls ring a Garden of Paradise. In the center is a ladder to the sky, a road between life and death.'

'You deal in death, then.' Elswyth's head rose.

'If necessary,' her aunt said. She spoke cautiously. 'The length of life's thread is for the fates to spin, measure, and cut. It is not for us to interfere. However…'

'However?' Elswyth's heart leaped in her throat.

'Lengthening takes a long time. And patient practice. It is the life of a vestal virgin. You must set your soul in accordance with nature. That is what the Auspicium is for. You cannot court men for the rest of your years. Nor ride a steed. You must drink daily of the elixir of life and leave the comforts of society behind.

The lengthening of life is a difficult undertaking. Not so the cutting of the thread.'

'I am afraid.' She smoothed Grapes's fur with her hand.

'Perhaps you should begin with your mother's book.'

'I will read it,' she promised. 'Straightaway.'

'Good. It is also expected that knowledge is shared between Sisters. You have known that Mr. Buell is cousin to Mr. Thomas?'

At the thought of these two men, and the marriage proposal, Elswyth's breath caught in her throat. She nodded.

'It was unforeseen. But no matter now. Though he carries the blood, he is not a suitable replacement. I expect you agree.'

Elswyth nodded again, fortifying herself. She lifted Grapes and slid a large sheet underneath him. She wrapped him tenderly, taking great care in arranging his limbs. When he looked peaceful she said, 'Tell me what the Auspices know of death.'

Rather than answer, Aunt Anne set the kettle to boil and her clawlike hands crept along the high dusty cupboards, taking down jars. Bones, feathers, shifting white sands, a live glowing moth, these all festered inside the glass jars.

'I know a liquid that compels the blood to flee from the veins. I have ingredients enough for a single man's dose. I'd guess you have a man in mind. It is untraceable by doctors, but you must take care not to be discovered administering it.'

Elswyth nodded grimly as her aunt neatly dropped a writhing scorpion into the boiling waters.

'If you use this phial of poison, you become a practitioner of the alchemy. I will consider your life dedicated to our ways, and will expect you to undergo the full initiation, married or not.'

Aunt Anne sealed the phial with a small blackened cork and handed it to Elswyth. Fear rose in her heart.

Dearest Elswyth,

The chilled air this morning necessitates a blanket around my shoulders. The climate has changed. It seems that even in the south winter must pay his annual visit. The dark red spot of Antares is high now and Scorpius has chased Orion's protection from the heavens.

I have seen no birds. I am woeful and alone. I have lost d'Etre. Late last night he was spooked by coyotes. Their terrible cries are like the screams of children. I awoke on the ground and reached for my sabre as they circled closer around us. I feared we would both be eaten. For the first time since leaving the Rodriguez estate, I was glad that I had remained steadfast in my refusal to allow Abril to accompany me.

So afraid was I for my own safety, I could not keep an eye on d'Etre. In a flash, the coyotes were all about us. I stood and shouted and waved my blanket to scare them. They nipped at d'Etre and he startled and pulled his stake from the ground. Before I could grab hold of him, he was lost to the night, running a new race to his certain death.

I swung my sabre wildly and though I did not strike a coyote, the clamor scared them off. I hope they won't catch d'Etre. He is fast.

All morning, I hung close to the road, looking in wider and wider circles for d'Etre. All I discovered was the grave scene of some murdered wagoners. They were so poorly buried that hungry creatures had scratched up their bones. The skeletons lay exposed and rotting in the open sun. I will spare you further description.

Midday, I saw two Mexicans on the road. They had one burro slung heavy with sacks of eggs. I bought two dozen, the little money I have out here being worthless compared to some nourishment. I asked them in the best Spanish I could muster if they had seen my animal and they had not. They had no other news except to say the Indians were attacking on some length of the river. We then parted ways.

Perhaps I should've asked to ride with them back to Albuquerque, where I could procure another mount from Rodriguez, but it seems

I have come far in the wrong direction. The Mexicans said El Paso del Norte is not far from here, and I could make it with a few days' walk. I was surprised, as I thought the mountain pass was south of here.

I have found that somehow Abril slipped the Nightway map in my sack! I sorely wish that I had a map of these lands instead, but this one of the clockwork sky is oddly comforting. It must be from this part of the world. The stars are fixed, but many of the asterisms it illustrates are foreign: desert creatures, on entirely different ellipticals.

I long for d'Etre. My heart is heavy indeed, as he had become my sole companion in these dark days. I cannot stop myself from thoughts of your growing belly and wedding date. If I cannot find another steed within a few days, your deadline will impossible, even with the letter undelivered. Time is about to run out, and I press myself forward and look to the skies for any sight of flying guides.

I must admit despair follows me closely. I wonder if you have not surrendered yourself already. I wonder if it is Buell's child or someone else's, and how you could come to be in such a predicament. I do not care what has transpired, and I take your telegram as a call for help. I am trying to return to you with honor.

Yet some thoughts are dark. Your father suffered me to live in his home, and had perhaps deemed to see an end to that arrangement. He must have known the sort of desert march he was banishing me to.

I follow the only map I have. The stars are now my traveling partners. Above me the teapot, Sagittarius's asterism, dips its fine spout into the spangled waters of the Milky Way, pouring a cool cup of healing tea. What I wouldn't give for the terrestrial equal, with a bit of milk—how I like it best—to revive my weakened limbs.

Besides Spanish daggers this desert teems with snakes and black insects, death always at the heel. The fates have closed all possibilities to me but to walk.

Each Step Is Yours, Zadock

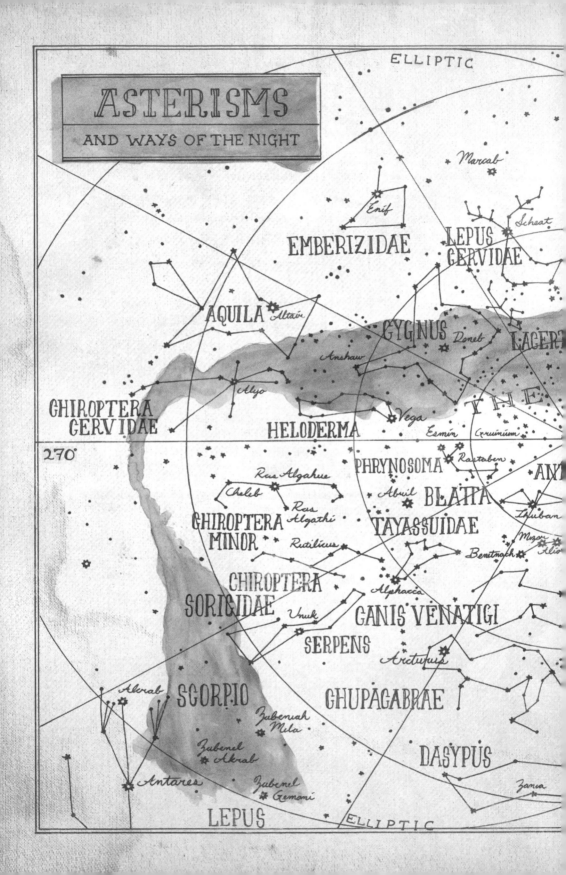

Sleeper

Zibel

LEPIDOPTERUS

Chicago

Rana

Louisa

Joliet

Elgevub

ANTHOCEPHALUS

SATURNIIDAE

ERIDANUS

Elswyth

Mirach

MUSCA

PLIADES

VULPES

LEPIS

Naviaho

Algol

San
Louis

Avreb

GANIS
LANTERNS

Aldedaran

Rigel

Algira

N I G H T W A Y

Bellatrix

Betelgeux

ORION

Capella

BISON
MAJOR

Polaris

PARDALIS

Castor

Manus

GANIS
MAJOR

Dulbe

GRYPTO-
PRYMNUS

Pollox

GANIS
MINOR

Sirius

Mirak

Procyon

"THE LADLE"

BISON MINOR

WANDERING
* STARS *

Graper

STRIGIDAE
PAVO

Axelrod

90°

Zasma

Regulis

⊙ Sun

☿ Mercury

Denebola

☾ Moon

♀ Venus

Alphard

♂ Mars

SEXTANS

♃ Jupiter

♄ Saturn

FAM. SCORPIONES

GEN. CENTRUROIDES

21.9.43, 11:45, 95 deg., 5 knots, few clouds
Desert country, far from water

Scorpion. Large, black. Poisonous, I would wager. Scorpio is now one short month from ascending the throne of the Zodiac, and I see his great pincers come over the horizon every eventide when I attempt to find my way by the stars. He is a water sign. I cannot now make a map, but feel I can at least find my way as long as the stars hold. Thinking to endure what is before me, I must continue to ask myself: *What is a moment in the face of time?*

Orion flies when this ankle-biter rises in the east. His evil seemed almost welcome to me tonight, and I admit I gave thought to extracting his poison and tasting it myself. That now seems preferable to the bitterness I must be content with and the realities I must face, both my current predicament and the hopelessness unfolding in Chicago.

Would that I were a bug, I would hunt down my prey and delight in stinging it or rending it with my claws.

K eeping her composure through the entire evening had been difficult. Elswyth's thoughts kept returning to Grapes. She had stowed the body of Louisa's grayhound in a large wooden trunk in the cellar. She remembered her mother's coffin and the day it had been lowered underground. Now that it had stopped raining, she was faced with the task of burying Grapes in the garden.

That grim undertaking would have to wait until tomorrow. It was an important night for her father—the night of the gala. There were wealthy donors and patrons milling about at a reception in the museum's main hall, though it was not quite finished. She would have to make excuses to society about her sister's illness. Louisa couldn't be introduced that night, as many expected. A good number of the concerned were awkward young men in garish getups. Mr. Buell lurked conspicuously in the back.

Elswyth had spent the evening running from the hall to the kitchen, supervising the incompetent help her father had hired. Nearly as bad were the dancers employed to flit about the gala lifting stuffed birds on sticks, as though they were flying.

Elswyth kept Aunt Anne's phial of poison in her pocket and fingered it nervously. Would it be better to wait till she and Mr. Buell lived together? Her gown felt especially tight about her midsection. She waited until the kitchen was emptied of staff, occupied by duties elsewhere. She uncorked the phial and held it over a cup of tea, but before she could pour it out a thundering applause broke the still air, startling her back into the present.

It was her father's presentation. She had missed it.

She raced into the main hall just in time to witness the dawning disaster. Her father was concluding his speech, accompanied by many fine large lithographs, on his plans for the Museum of Flying. He had just finished demonstrating his careful taxidermy and preservation techniques as well as touching briefly on the subject of the mechanics of flight, and what might be learned from a museum dedicated to all things that flew. The next part of the program was Elswyth's speech, meant to finally sway the hearts of the patrons and secure their much needed support for the year to come.

Her father called her name nervously from the lectern, scanning the crowd. She stood in the back, still wearing her apron, frozen in the shadows. She had spent all hours, day and night, in her room reading *The City-State*. She continually cried, at times for her mother, at times for Louisa or Grapes, and at times for herself. With all that had transpired, she had entirely forgotten to write her keynote address.

The round of polite applause gave way to a low murmur of confusion. A well-liquored voice cut through the crowd, asking why the birds weren't to be kept live.

Her father started to explain why it wasn't prudent to keep live birds inside, and that they must be drained of their blood to preserve them. A great many noses turned up at this fact.

A fluttering of fans was followed by a chorus of similarly impolite voices calling for something with live animals, like a zoological enclosure or even a circus fair.

Mrs. Peabody, one of the most influential guests, with strong family ties to the east and all manner of wealth and prestige, joined in by demanding that the museum produce the kind of entertainments she was used to. She wanted stories of naturalists and explorers going away to far-off lands and coming back with a wealth of new discoveries and tales to tell. In her unconscionably loud voice she said that all the birds in the museum were of the same boring sort that might be seen by anyone.

The murmur of agreement was cut by a yelped insult, from the far back: 'And you live with a witch.' This set off a rumpus. Men cried 'blood-drinker' and ladies shrieked or feigned to faint. Birds on sticks started dropping, as though shot down mid-flight.

Mr. Gray could not manage to quiet the uproar with his mild protestations. Mr. Buell wore an intolerably smug smile in the back row. Elswyth watched her father wave his arms in a weak farewell, as though his speech had gone well and the night was concluded. Her stomach sank. She felt rather like drinking the phial herself. Her father wandered off into the crowd.

She finally found him recumbent on the leather sofa in the taxidermy room. When she first entered, she thought he was asleep. He lay as motionless as the great bison frozen in glass behind him. Approaching, she saw that his eyes were open, and he was staring at the ceiling. He looked distraught.

She sat on the floor next to the sofa and arranged her skirt about her. She waved off the small cloud of dust that rose from the unclean floor. Her father did not move.

Presently, she spoke. 'I am sorry about the speech.'

He lifted his head. 'I am not at my best either, my dear.'

'Louisa wants to marry Mr. Buell.'

'She is but a girl. She does not know what is she wants. Everything has gone wrong. I've failed you both terribly.'

'Father...'

'I've failed my museum as well. There won't be donors enough now. And what visitors will come? Chicago was supposed to be a boomtown. Even if I manage to open it, there will be no one to come. We might've stayed back east. You girls might've been introduced properly. To real society, not this mob.'

'I'm now promised to Mr. Buell or the Auspices. I don't know which. I miss Mr. Thomas.'

'On the other hand, I never could have found my way there. In the east if you don't have a family name or the money already, it is impossible to get anywhere. I'm sorry you girls have Gray blood. It has given you every disadvantage. Chicago was the only place for us, and now it seems it hasn't been enough.'

'I know he has written me letters, though they have been kept from me. He was not handsome or dashing, but he was kind and doted on me.' Elswyth stood and walked over to the worktable, where her father had begun to reassemble the broken moth tray. She pulled a sorrowful specimen up by its pin and held its white gauzy wings to the light.

'This is what I mean about Chicago. There is no one worthy of marriage to you girls.' Mr. Gray sighed. 'Had I known Mr. Buell was a snake waiting in the mud...'

'I needed something to hope for. I've sent a telegram to Mr. Thomas in Santa Fe. He should be there now. I told him to return as quickly as all haste would allow. Before the twenty-fourth, so that I may marry him instead of Mr. Buell.'

'Oh Elswyth.' Her father sat up. 'What have you done?'

'It's a shot in the dark. When Mr. Thomas comes back, I could marry him instead, and we shall raise Louisa's child as our own. If we are hidden away, as planned, it could be that Mr. Thomas gave me the child before he departed on his journey. Though there is some shame in this, our marriage upon his return would rectify it. And Louisa should not be made so upset. Her condition is...'

'Did you implore Mr. Thomas to abandon his errand?'

'Was it not just an excuse to be rid of him?'

'Has your aunt interfered?' Her father was suddenly furious. 'It was all arranged, you and the baby and Buell. Anne should be well satisfied if they are cousins, as Louisa said.'

'This still leaves Louisa her chance at marriage.'

'Elswyth, you don't understand what you have asked. Mr. Thomas is your pet. He will do whatever you say, and if you...'

'Father, I didn't tell him to abandon any errand. I simply gave him a date by which he might return. If I must take a husband, let it be anyone but Mr. Buell. There is a child to be fathered. Think of your progeny. I know I asked for his proposal, but...'

'We must send Mr. Thomas another telegram immediately. We must get word to McMarrow to keep him on course. It is vital that he complete the errand.'

'If he is my pet, as you say, then he has already departed from Santa Fe in haste. There are no telegraph stations west or south of that place—I asked at the telegraph office yesterday. What vital thing does this letter contain, that he can't come home now?'

'The letter isn't all there is to it. He himself simply must reach Irion. Mr. Thomas's life depends on it. As does Irion's. All our lives depend on it.'

'Whatever can you mean, Father? Who is Irion?'

'There's a war. Elswyth... I can't... I can't speak of it. I fear Mr. Thomas will not return. Your mother's Sisters have doomed everything.' Mr. Gray rose from the sofa and clasped his hands together, his brow furrowed. 'Fate is now in General Irion's hands. Mr. Thomas must make it to Texas.'

'Maybe he has already accomplished that. You chose him for the task with the confidence that he could complete it, I might assume?' Her father remained quiet. He wore a hopeless look, his eyes glazed over again, lost in some distant world.

Elswyth could no longer stand it. She grabbed her father's hand and fell to her knees. 'Please, Father, please. If you love me, don't let this happen. You must restore Mr. Thomas. Please let him return.' She implored him, choking back sobs. He lifted her up and embraced her, smoothing back her hair in a way he had not done since she was a child.

'There, there, my dear. Don't fret. This is not your fault.' He grasped her shoulders firmly and bent to catch her downturned eyes. His face was lined with sympathy. 'It was beyond my control, sending him away. I trusted McMarrow to give him the best chance.'

Elswyth stood.

'Even if he makes it to Texas, there is no guarantee the plan will work.' Her father's tone turned despairing. 'Maybe then, your plan should. Whether he turns back or not, I fear the worst. I love you girls above all else. I would do anything required of me, but I no longer know what to hope for. If your lost suitor can travel with the greatest haste, perhaps he can make this wish of yours come true. May the fates save us all.'

Elswyth then embraced him tightly for a long while, squeezing her eyes shut. The room had all but gone dark, and her father watched the last fading light of the Chicago sky disappear from the reflection in the great buffalo's glass eyes.

➤Eliza, I am increasingly desperate in my search for Zeke's letter. I keep coming back to one record. The return of the letter is simply noted and stamped: an uncarbon'd letter, belonging to Z. Thomas, submitted. Maybe it refers to a carbon of the letter after all? Maybe someone opened the envelope?

The rabbit hole that single piece of paper has led me down is incredible. With increasing complexity and skill, someone has covered up any trace of the letter, using labyrinthine references, cross-notes, and misfilings. My desk is a pile of records and files, which just keep multiplying, cyclically, without ever adding up to anything at all.

It is as if someone devised this paper puzzle with the express purpose of showing me, in the most tedious way possible, why my system of knowledge classification and record-keeping is weak and anathema to those who try to find simple facts. The threading system, the carbon repeaters, the cross-files have all failed me in my hour of need.

If I embrace that paranoia, it is clear where this thread is leading. My hand is being held as I am paraded past more records of the Auspices and their strange doings. It seems they don't just recruit but provide shelter for Gray girls and pregnant girls in trouble. They offer an option outside of the lifephase system. They must have solicited you. But I urge you not to follow them. At least until we know what they're after.

I was also surprised to learn that there is an Auspicium located in Texas. Apparently the fount-water requires close monitoring and constant vigilance. The Auspices must be nearby, but I have no idea where in the city-state they live.

If I could sort it out, I could turn this bundle of letters over to you, and perhaps see you just one time, the Law be damned. It is my final wish that we speak, before I am gone forever.

Zadock Thomas also seems on the verge of disappearing. It appears that wandering in the desert made him delirious, and he tried to write in that state. One phrase that's easy enough to pick out is "salt sea" and it didn't take many drawer pulls to find him. He can only be at White Sands, a large gypsum deposit devoid of plant and animal life in southern New Mexico, if this letter can be trusted. White Sands is 240 square miles of sparkling colorless dunes, the remains of a great salt lake and, from the old descriptions, an amazing sight to behold. If he is near there, he's close to El Paso, which means he wandered south from Rodriguez's home, not back north. He is completely turned around.

He also could be hallucinating. Hallucination is caused by exhaustion, psychotropic substances, or a proper psychotic break. Whatever the cause, hallucinations are most common in the evening hours, when the light is low and can play tricks. A desert mirage.

Or it's dehydration. Water was in very short supply, and Zadock may not have been skilled at discovering appropriate sources of clean drinking water. This isn't the only letter where Zadock's mental state must be called seriously into question. It is a distinct possibility that this episode caused permanent psychological damage, if it weren't already present.

Speaking of madness, I asked a Queer friend in Chicago-Land about this Spree character, supposedly outside in the rot. They support him, and he was there at Atlantas. The Queers also warn me he has gone a little mad, living in the rot too long.

Maybe Zadock had a similar condition. Even though his handwriting shows his distress, I'm still inclined to comment on its beauty. This typowriter seems clunky and foreign when compared to the smooth undulating flow of ink on paper.

dead zone

Enough in white   in white   sun, no wander

some metal disc, eclipsing the moon,
moving soft and steady across the
low sky.

endless salt sea, white —
I'm an the edge of
a great disk,   sliding overhead,

I nightway   soul s

O   across time

coming of Vau

blotted out the

& star,   ~~black~~ planet,

    or some men   burning eyes, skin

      in the sun's eye, brought on

by thirst,

    water mirage, white white

        dust

   scorpius ~~rising~~

          dream: sea

at the sky   of s _____

   of sand

esert beakers _____   flying

            ghost

              ghost

               whi

e dead zone

been in her rooms. Elswyth raced back down the stairs. Louisa had been confined to her bedroom, and now she was missing. She thought of the scolding she would give her sister.

She had just read to the end of *The City-State*, save for the last four pages. With the conclusion, she could see a way through. She was desperate to tell Louisa what she had read. There might be an alternative to all the lies about bloodlines and a life in the Auspicium. Elswyth worried that place would transform the spirit of a girl beyond all recognition.

She looked in Aunt Anne's cottage. It was empty save for the putrid smell of rotting herbs. She searched through all the rooms of the house, one by one, and found them all empty. She climbed the long stairs to the ballroom–turned–fencing salle. Mr. Buell, who could reliably be found in some dark corner of the estate, was eerily absent. She lifted her skirts and ventured into the half-constructed rooms, an addition to the house long forestalled, the French roof being the only part near completion.

It wasn't until she stepped out into the front garden that panic overtook her. Aunt Anne's absence could be reasoned out. Mr. Buell and Louisa missing in the same stroke was alarming news.

Why hadn't she used the poison? She ran out into the streets, looking for any sign of Louisa. Had she lost her sister, and the baby, in an afternoon? She patted her pockets for the phial and found it gone. Everything suddenly seemed lost.

The streets bustled about her, filled with workers out for the midday meal. Many were milling about in the park across the boulevard. There was shouting and the ring of hammers on nails. The streets were flooded with vendors and ladies with tiny tip-tilted parasols riding in open barouches, and Elswyth felt it all start to spin about wildly. She darted across the plank street like a spooked antelope. She couldn't catch her bearings or her balance and

➤Eliza, it seems all my investigations are disintegrating. The account contained in *The Sisters Gray* ends abruptly here. The last two sets of printed pages are missing from the book, yet the records indicate that it entered the Vault in perfect condition. The damage is surprising because the book is held together with a strong morocco binding. The missing pages bear the signs of having been forcibly removed.

This is disheartening. It means the question of the Thomas lineage will go unanswered by this book. If Elswyth indeed raised Louisa's child, and never had one of her own with Zadock Thomas, the bloodline is broken. If Zeke is not truly the Khrysalis, then what fate awaits you both?

There is only one place left to look. The letter.

I'm tearing through carbons now, looking for it. The letter could be nothing, of course, just a normal correspondence from Joseph Gray. A solicitation for funds or request for specimens. Perhaps even an overblown opinion about the war for Texas. But my instincts tell me otherwise. If the novel is built on some small foundation of truth, then Gray considered this single letter very important. It must have been more than just a convenient way to dispose of Zadock's interest in his daughter.

Gray died from typhoid fever years later, in 1860, when the country was on the brink of civil war. His wife's six sisters buried him in Chicago, in the graveyard of their family order. The Gray name lived on. A street was named after him, as well as the city's butterfly sanctuary: an impressive greenhouse, and the last remaining vestige of the Museum of Flying.

Zadock left no will, but almost every one of his ancestors did, right through to Senator Zacharyh Thomas. All these wills mention a bundle of letters passed to the next generation. A Khrysalis tradition. That a letter could have survived this long would be a small miracle. Especially since the Great Chicago Fire of 1871 stood in its way. Some thirty-eight years after the city's incorporation, nearly everything in it was destroyed. Journals, letters, and personal documents were all incinerated. Many records that would be useful are lost to time. The fear of this very thing led to the fire ban in our modern city-states.

Zeke's letter, however, must have survived. The loop of paperwork has perhaps pointed to it after all. There are records on Daxon, buried deep in the Vault. Many have been corrected, blacked out, but I can see the fingerprints now. I can find no evidence that the cannon was stolen. The funding records for it have been destroyed. Its existence portends danger to me. I can't help but to think of those Queers who died in Atlantas. Perhaps the Deserters have the right idea.

The thread I am following also connects Daxon to the Auspices. Murder is a convenient way to cast blame on the Auspices, who are trying to recruit troubled girls.

The altered records point to something insidious. Daxon resents the Auspices for taking girls out of the lifephase system. He would prefer to punish them. He dislikes the Auspices' control over the ways and lifeblood of the city-state, and seeks to destroy the Auspicium. But to get rid of them, he'd have to dismantle the Senate as well. Or weaken it enough to bend it to his will. The cannon is his strong right hand.

His interest in Zeke makes much more sense now. To destroy him is to weaken the Senate. You both must steer clear of Daxon at any cost. He wants the letter to delegitimize Zeke. Or frame him as a murderer.

I've scoured the entire Vault on this wild-goose chase. The letter can only be in one place: Daxon's office. The door is locked with his blood ID. I must get inside.

◇◇ ⌃⌃ Zeke found himself waiting once again. He was anxious about Bartle and his mission to find the letter. He was worried about Eliza and the fact that she couldn't see her father. She had gone to find Leeya, to help her. He was supposed to help Raisin and figure out what they both might do. Instead, they found distraction in the company of laudanum. ⌃⌃ ⌃⌃ ⌃⌃ ⌃⌃ It was heartening to be with his friend, even if all Raisin could talk about was government conspiracy. ⌃⌃ ⌃⌃ He ranted for hours about life outside the walls. He said that because the Collapse ruined the earth for living things, the clock had to be turned back. Hunting and gathering had to be rediscovered. Cities had to be rebuilt in harmony with the natural world. Raisin believed that folks in the rot were doing this now, and that the city-state's rare fruit came from their orchards. If only the barriers didn't exist, the folks outside would be ready to merge societies. ⌃⌃ He spoke in reverential terms about "Spree," a leader of Deserters, who had formed the largest safe camp in the rot. The Queers from Atlantas had joined him, and they were arming themselves. Zeke would get heavily invested in Raisin's stories, and start to worry about events outside the walls, until Raisin would continue with some ridiculous detail about time travel or giant animals and Zeke would remember that it was all a fantasy. ⌃⌃ ⌃⌃ Though it was cracked, Zeke enjoined listening. Some moments reminded him of Port-Land, when it seemed to take forever to make it to the next lifephase, and all they did was daydream. It gave him hope. Raisin had a good energy. Until he saw Leeya. ⌃⌃ ⌃⌃ ⌃⌃ She finally invited Raisin over. Apparently, he told her there was life outside the barrier, that they could flee the city-state. Leeya didn't believe the Deserter propaganda. And she certainly didn't think fleeing was a good plan for raising a child. She threw him out. ⌃⌃ ⌃⌃ ⌃⌃ ⌃⌃ Raisin took it hard. Then the despair came on them both. They finished many drams of laudanum. They talked about how they would end up alone or in jail. Zeke was waiting to hear from Bartle. His few sober moments were filled with dread about the impending deadline. ∿ ∿ ∿ ∿ ∿ ∿ ∿ At night they went to the square. Raisin looked at pretty girls but only talked about Leeya. When ladies waved their fans in his direction, he mocked them. Zeke laughed at his rude hand signals. The letter and the deadline retreated from his thoughts. ∿ ∿ ∿ On the way home they laughed even more, stumbling through the freshly washed streets. Raisin told Zeke his theory about how bad Lawmen are stationed out in the rot, part of some army as the first line of defense for the city-states. He said they were harassed and taunted by the Queers who had escaped and wore little more than feathers. The Lawmen were made to wrestle and ride around on dogs in old-timey uniforms. ∿ ∿ ∿ Zeke could hardly catch his breath, he was laughing so hard. He was stopped short by someone else standing on the wooden plankways. Zeke squinted into the dark. Henry Bartle had snuck up on him again. ∿ ∿ ∿ ∿ He made a motion for Zeke to follow him, and the effects of the laudanum lifted from Zeke's head. Zeke in turn made the hand signal for Raisin to *wait*, and Raisin nodded. ∿ ∿ ∿ He followed Bartle, careful to keep twenty paces behind him. Their path snaked through the muddied streets until Bartle abruptly grabbed the toeholds in the side of a lit watchpost and began to climb. ∿ ∿ ∿ Zeke hesitated on the ground. Bartle waved him up. ∿ ∿ Zeke slid his boots into the small metal toeholds at the base of the watchpost. He carefully and purposefully placed one hand after another. Trying not to look down, he stopped as he passed a broadsheet. It gave notice that subversive hand signals were now punishable by imprisonment. Zeke kept climbing, all the way up the giant metal trunk. ∿ ∿ ∿ Bartle grabbed his collar and pulled him up the last few steps. It felt much better to have his feet planted

WAIT

firmly on the phosphor-lit platform at the top. ⌃⌃ ⌃⌃ "Are you drunk?" Bartle asked, then motioned for Zeke to hold his answer. Bartle switched off the large typowriter, the central feature of the watchpost station. There were a few chairs, some binoculars, and Republic-issued blankets. The wind blew stern and steady. Zeke stood on the edge of the platform. He let his natural laud-swaying scare him a bit. It was too dark to see the plankway below. The fall would be long. ⌃⌃ ⌃⌃ ⌃⌃ ⌃⌃ Bartle looked out from the watchpost along the handwheel lines, making sure they were in the center of a dead zone. He took off his glasses, cleaned them on his shirttail, and looked again. He then uncapped every phonotube in the watchpost, listening to each for a moment or two. ⌃⌃ ⌃⌃ ⌃⌃ Before the letter, Zeke hadn't been bothered by the recording. It seemed like they couldn't listen much anyway. He didn't do anything illegal except laudanum, which he hid well. Now he felt differently. He looked at Bartle. He imagined a lifetime of paranoia. He began to write in the dust on the panel. ⌃⌃ Fight or flight or dream: How can I be free? ⌃⌃ ⌃⌃ ⌃⌃ Bartle coughed to get his attention. "I think we're OK to talk. Good job following me up here. You shouldn't be in this state right now." ⌃⌃ ⌃⌃ ⌃⌃ "I'm fine." ⌃⌃ ⌃⌃ ⌃⌃ ⌃⌃ ⌃⌃ ⌃⌃ "I worked hard to clear this watchpost. It's the one place I can guarantee we won't be recorded. Stealth repeaters run underground." ⌃⌃ ⌃⌃ "Have you found the letter?" ⌃⌃ ⌃⌃ "The record was wrong. I've scoured the Vault. I designed it, so believe me when I say I know every latch and drawer. It isn't there." ⌃⌃ ⌃⌃ Zeke sat down. He put his head in his hands. Bartle touched his shoulder. Zeke swayed. ⌃⌃ "What would you do with it if we found it?" Zeke mumbled into his hands. ⌃⌃ ⌃⌃ "I'd open it, of course. See what's inside." Bartle sounded nervous. "And then we'd decide about turning it in." ⌃⌃ "What if my grandfather didn't want it to be opened?" ⌃⌃ "Well, then, he … it sounds as though you have talked to your grandmother."

⋀ ⋀ ⋀ Zeke was silent. ⋀ ⋀ ⋀ "OK, on the level," Bartle said. "I imagine the Senator didn't want to open it. Your family always had secret documents. Your grandfather denied it, of course. He had to. And besides, if it was known that there were documents that the Vault couldn't secure, it would've been an embarrassment." He took his glasses off and fidgeted with the hinge. "I'm sorry for this, Zeke. But we must be sure of your blood. I know it must be hard. I ... I was in your files, looking after Eliza last month. When I saw the missing letter, I reported it." ⋀ ⋀ ⋀ ⋀ Zeke's head swam. He tried to focus on Bartle. His trust wavered. He felt confused. "My grandfather never talked about the letter." ⋀ "Yes, well, we all have secrets." ⋀ ⋀ ⋀ ⋀ "I miss him." ⋀ ⋀ ⋀ ⋀ ⋀ "I am going to make this right. For you, for Eliza. I have found a few of the missing documents on my own. A book here, in the Texas Vault, was my first clue about the importance of what's missing. Zeke, this letter your grandfather left you — there's a reason he didn't turn it in. There's a reason your grandmother didn't choose Bic to be Khrysalis. I want to know that reason." ⋀ ⋀ "So does Daxon, apparently." ⋀ "He could be hiding it very carefully, or ... maybe they don't have it." ⋀ ⋀ "You said they did." ⋀ ⋀ "I put too much trust in the records." ⋀ ⋀ "Daxon's cannon has gone missing. He's apparently losing his mind. They built this big machined — " ⋀ "I know. I mean, about the cannon. I don't think it was ever actually missing." Bartle looked around again, checking every direction. He picked up two of the gray blankets and handed one to Zeke. They huddled under them. ⋀ "Daxon wants to get rid of the Auspicium and dismantle the Senate. Those are his enemies. Not the Deserters. He doesn't even take them seriously. The letter has something he needs, some key to power we can't let him have. I will find it. The safest option may be for you to leave. You and Eliza. Where is she?" ⋀ "She's at Leeya's." ⋀ ⋀ ⋀ "No, she's not.

That was the first place I looked. I've been tracking her for weeks, to make sure we didn't have a run-in. I turn my back for one minute —" "Leeya's alone?" "Yes, she's gone down into the tunnels." "What tunnels?" "There are passages beneath the city-state. The Auspicium is underground. Near the source of the fount-water. It was a surprise to me too. I just read all these files about them." "I thought the Auspices were harmless old women stirring their mixture pots." "They are powerful. And in danger. The last thing we want is Eliza ending up down there as well." "I ... I told her you were here." Bartle was silent for a long moment. Zeke thought he might be blinking back tears again, but it was too dark to see. "She wants to see you." Zeke pulled his blanket tighter around himself. "There's one place I wasn't able to check: Daxon's office," Bartle went on. "It's risky, but that's where we've got to look next. I'll figure out a way to break in." "If you're caught, how will I find the letter? I only have four days left until they can arrest me for it. We'll both end up in jail, and what will happen to Eliza then?" This silenced Bartle again. "If you're going to do something rash, you should at least try to see her first. I think you owe her that much." Bartle put his hand on Zeke's shoulder. "I'm trying to make everything right first. I know she needs to see me. I need to see her too." He motioned for *quiet*, and switched the typowriter back on. He folded the blankets carefully and put them back in place.

QUIET

"You go first, I'll follow after a while," Bartle said. He motioned down the ladder. It felt twice as long on the descent. Zeke's hands were cold, his knuckles bloodless. The wind bit at his ears. Once on the ground he hurried back to the spot where he had left Raisin. His friend was asleep, slumped on the wooden plankways by an industrial building. Zeke shook him awake. "Come on, we have to go back to my unit."

TEXAS REPUBLICAN

DODSON, Public Printers.]   SEPTEMBER 22nd '43   [TERMS—$5 PER ANN., IN AD &c

HEROGRAPHY

BY F.S. ANSHAW

*A Chicago correspondent of
The Republican furnishes this
notice of a new science:*

graphy, or hand writing, will en-
ny person to signal with his hands as
y as he can speak, or any other person
t is not to be confounded with Stenog-
or sign language, as they are differ-
ings in fact. Cherography marries the
ty of speaking with the nuance of the
n word. The necessity of long-hand
g out of letters, even as Stenographers
immense labor, and to the detriment
patch, might be obviated entirely by
graphy. Children can learn Cherog-
with the greatest of ease, in a short
of time. They can acquire the vocabu-
rith more rapidity than adults as they
not yet been visited by practicing upon
e system.

ifficult to give a proper explanation of
graphy in the short space of a column,
will hint at the idea and leave you to
your own conclusions by applying the
ples.

e sounds of the human voice comprise
lphabet of Nature. It contains fewer
ifty distinct elements, as confined by
e. Using this knowledge we might con-
a series of signals to represent sounds
as. We have done so on strict math-
al principles. It is imperative that the
y between the signal and the sound in
instinctively together. The hand re-
n shape simply what the tongue utters
nd as it were in perfect concert.

if one wished to communicate with a
person in a room full of persons, while
lding the benefit of being overheard
who surround them? Cherography will
a deadly blow at the monstrous absur-
f language. Simple signals represent
sounds and ideas. This will rid us of
al barbarities that we have inherited.
the signals are seen by the eye, they
cognized as the thought they express
and rapidly as the corre ...
sounds are heard. Is it not so with the
ers now used for writing and print-
owever, those require of the reader a
nd laborious study of every word or
ation of letters in the language in or-

THE WHITE SAND DESERT OF WEST TEXAS DISCOVERED

Could it be used as new material to construct cities of white?

OR IS IT SIMPLY HAUNTED...

TEXAS — *The following recounts
a great national curiosity, The
White Sands, in the part of
Texas formerly the Mexican
state of Nuevo Mexico.* --
In the Tularosa basin are seen
great dunes of White Sand,
which look like the Arabian
Desert yet are devoid of any
color at all. They run from
the foothills of the nearby low
Rockies out many miles, much
farther than can be seen with
the naked eye. A gradual ascent marks it, which consists
of the very same sands in a
hardened state and sparse desert vegetation upon it.
The surface of the sand re-
tains the day's heat and the
soles of the feet walking upon
it become so heated that it is
necessary to run back and
forth, darting in a ridiculous
manner, as a roadrunner gone
mad. However, not an inch below the surface it is as cool as
a far mountain stream, and as
one moves along, the impression of the feet remain in the
crust of the sand.
The air is then infused with
the strong scent of phosphor,
and when the clouds cover
the sky, the land cannot be
distinguished from the sky,
both blending to form one
solid drapery of white. Indeed,
when it is clouded over, or in
the Eventide, is the best time
to approach the area. In the
dog days of summer the heat
is unfit for men.

kind has been discovered in the
American states, and Texas
has no other white sands. The
mountains surrounding do not
appear to be of volcanic origin,
or an exhausted crater.
Many experiments have been
made to ascertain whether
the sands might be applied to
any useful purpose. Nearby
Mexican villages have employed
moistened white sands to the
adobe walls of their buildings
seemingly to deflect the strong
rays of the high desert sun.
This coating gives the homes
a striking white appearance
when viewed from a distance,
but the desirability of such a
technique remains in question.
The Mexicans also hold the curious legend of Pavla Blanca, a
lovely young woman betrothed
to, and already pregnant by,
the conquistador De Luna, in
the company of Coronado. Am-
bushed by Apaches, she was
struck a blow with fatal effect,
and her body was lost beneath
the ever shifting dunes. It is
said at moonrise her wraith
might be seen, along the tops of
the dunes, mournfully searching for her lost love in a flowing white wedding dress which
bears the appearance of
like wisps of dust, silent across
the shimmering dunes.

LEEYA,

    I DON'T KNOW HOW TO BEGIN. ON ONE HAND, I AM SO HAPPY FOR YOU. I KNOW YOU WILL BE THE BEST MOTHER. YOUR WARMTH AND KINDNESS WILL NEVER ABANDON YOUR CHILD'S LIFE. I JUST CANNOT BELIEVE THAT IT HAS HAPPENED IN THIS WAY. I DO NOT BLAME YOU FOR KEEPING IT FROM ME. WE BOTH KNOW THAT THIS IS NOT WHAT WE HAD ENVISIONED FOR OUR FUTURE. NO TWIN BABIES IN THE TWIN-CITY FOR US NOW. NO WARM DAYS IN THE NATURE REPLICAS OF THAT CITY-STATE, WALKING w/ OUR KIDS AMONG THE TREES.

    IT IS SO DIFFICULT TO IMAGINE SOMETHING OTHER THAN WHAT WE HAVE PLANNED — SOMETHING OTHER THAN WHAT THEY HAVE PLANNED FOR US. YOU ARE IN ENOUGH JEOPARDY, WANDERING OFF THE PATH OF THE LIFEPHASES, BUT THERE ARE OTHER DANGERS YOU NEED TO KNOW ABOUT. LAST NIGHT I VISITED THE MORGUE. THE PREGNANT GIRLS HAVE BEEN PUNCTURED THROUGH THE HEART, AS IF TO DRAIN THEM. IT'S SICK. IT MAKES ME ALL THE MORE DETERMINED TO SOLVE THIS THREAD - WHETHER OR NOT I WORK AT THE VAULT. I WISH I COULD COME SEE YOU - I DESPERATELY WANT TO BUT I CAN'T. THERE IS SOMETHING I MUST DO FIRST. THIS NOTE WILL HAVE TO DO FOR NOW.

    I'VE BEEN KEEPING AN EYE ON ZEKE'S TRANSCRIPTS. I CAN'T STAY AWAY FROM THE VAULT. ZEKE IS NOT DOING A VERY GOOD JOB OF STAYING OUT OF THE DEAD ZONES. HE AND RAISIN HAVE BEEN OUT DRINKING A LOT. RAISIN ONLY TALKS ABOUT THE DESERTERS. IT IS CLEAR HE HAS JOINED THEM. I WISH RAISIN COULD BE A REAL FATHER TO YOUR CHILD. A PRESENT ONE.

IF ONLY HE HAD LEARNED SOMETHING FROM THE
MESS HE MADE BY BRINGING YOU TO TEXAS EARLY.
   THAT ZEKE WOULD EVEN ENTERTAIN THE NOTION
OF FLEEING THE CITY-STATE BREAKS MY HEART.
IT WOULD BREAK HIS GRANDMOTHER'S HEART AS WELL.
      SOMETHING ELSE /////// MY **FATHER** IS HERE,
      HAPPENED ///////   IN TEXAS.

   MY HEART IS PERMANENTLY IN MY THROAT. HE LEFT
ME, HASN'T COMMUNICATED WITH ME MY WHOLE LIFE,
BUT NOW HE'LL TALK TO ZEKE? WHAT COULD I HAVE
POSSIBLY DONE TO HIM BACK THEN? I WAS A CHILD.
   I DON'T THINK I COULD EVEN ASK HIM THAT. I'VE
DECIDED NOT TO LOOK FOR HIM. HE SHOULD COME TO ME,
HE'S THE ONE THAT LEFT. IT PROVES HIS COWARDICE,
THAT HE WOULD COME TO TEXAS AND STILL AVOID ME.
   ON THE WAY TO THE VAULT THIS MORNING, I LOOKED
AT EVERY FACE ON THE PLANKWAYS, SEARCHING FOR
FEATURES I'D RECOGNIZE. IT WAS DUSTY OUT AND I
WAS TEMPTED TO YANK DOWN SOME HAND-KERCHIEFS.
IN EVERY PAIR OF EYES I THOUGHT I SAW MY
FATHER, FOR JUST A MOMENT.
   ZEKE SENT HIM TO SEARCH FOR THE LETTER IN THE
VAULT. NOTHING COULD BE MORE DANGEROUS. WHAT IF
HE'S CAUGHT, ARRESTED, OR THROWN OUT OF THE CITY-
STATE BEFORE HE CONTACTS ME? THE VAULT IS AN
ENDLESS LOOP. TO KEEP THE LAW AWAY FROM ZEKE,
I DOCTORED SOME RECORDS TO MAKE IT APPEAR THE
LETTER HAD BEEN TURNED IN. I CREATED A MAZE OF
·MISFILES AND PAPERWORK. IT WOULD TAKE EVEN THE
MOST SKILLED FILER DAYS TO FIND THAT THE LETTER
IS NOT ACTUALLY THERE

EACH THING I DO SEEMS TO MAKE IT ALL WORSE.
I STILL COULDN'T BRING MYSELF TO TELL ZEKE I
TOOK THE LETTER. I SHOULD HAVE TRUSTED HIM.

I WISH THERE WERE A WAY TO EXPOSE DAXON. IF
I WERE ABLE, THE SENATE COULD ARREST AND TRY
HIM, EVERYONE WOULD DESPISE HIM — THERE WOULD
BE A WAY OUT OF ALL OF THIS — EVERYTHING COULD
BE DIFFERENT. I AM GOING TO DO MY BEST TO MAKE
THIS HAPPEN.

YOUR LIFE IS AT RISK. YOU HAVE TO KEEP YOURSELF
— AND YOUR BABY — OUT OF HARM'S WAY. THERE IS A
MURDERER OUT THERE, ARMED TO THE TEETH. I HAVE A
FEW IMPORTANT THINGS FOR YOU TO KNOW:

✳ IF YOU'RE IN DANGER, THE AUSPICES ARE SAFER
THAN DAXON AT THIS POINT. I KNOW I HAVE BEEN
SKEPTICAL BEFORE BUT THAT IS THE SAFEST PLACE
NOW. JUST DON'T JOIN THEM. THEY RECRUIT GIRLS AT
VULNERABLE TIMES. DO NOT EAT OR DRINK ANYTHING
THEY GIVE YOU — IT WILL CHANGE THE CHEMICAL
COMPOSITION OF YOUR BODY.

✳ ON DAXON'S LIST OF MURDER SCAPEGOATS, I
FOUND MENTION OF A MAN UNDERGROUND, A **NIGHTHAUL**,
(I'D NEVER HEARD THAT TITLE BEFORE). RAISIN
TALKS ABOUT HIM IN THE TRANSCRIPTS. HE SOMEHOW
HAS ACCESS TO THE ROT, OR ANIMALS, HE SEEMS
TO APPEAR ALL OVER THE CITY-STATE AT WILL,
ESPECIALLY IF THERE'S BEEN A MURDER. HE GIVES
ME A CREEPY FEELING. PLEASE BEWARE.

✳ I HAVE STASHED HANDWHEELS ON YOUR ROOF.
IF SOMEONE BREAKS IN, YOU CAN USE THEM TO ESCAPE.
THERE IS A SEMAPHORE LINE LEADING OFF YOUR ROOF.
JUST GO SLOWLY AND WATCH YOUR LANDING:

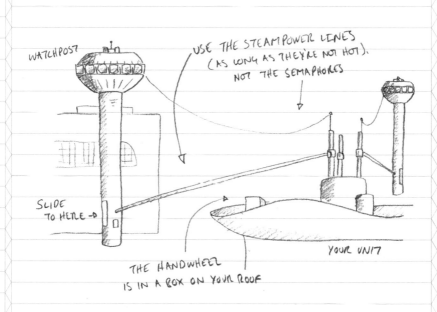

WATCHPOST

USE THE STEAM POWER LINES
(AS LONG AS THEY'RE NOT HOT).
NOT THE SEMAPHORES

SLIDE
TO HERE →

THE HANDWHEEL
IS IN A BOX ON YOUR ROOF

YOUR UNIT

DON'T GO OUT AT NIGHT. IF YOU FIND YOURSELF IN
DANGER, FOLLOW MY INSTRUCTIONS. I DO NOT KNOW WHAT
I WILL DO ONCE MY TASK IS COMPLETE. THIS COULD
BE OUR LAST COMMUNICATION. IT IS IMPOSSIBLE TO
GRASP THAT IDEA — LET ALONE THAT REALITY.

////// THIS WILL ALL BE OVER SOON //////

I LOVE YOU LIKE A SISTER,

ELIZA ✶

Dearest Elswyth,

All is lost. I woke in a white sand desert, sunburnt and without any sense of which way the compass points. I'm not sure of the date, but I do know that I will not return to Chicago by the deadline in your telegram. Though hope is lost, I do not know what else to do but write, so that you might at least know what became of me. The bundle of letters I carry now are my only talisman against utter loneliness.

I have wandered, not knowing my direction nor even my intent. It was a zone of death. Finally the white sands ceased and plants appeared again, and I began to wonder if I had imagined the alien landscape altogether. My sunburnt skin provided evidence to the contrary. It is painful to lie down and nearly impossible to sleep.

I am far from the road, but several times during the nocturnal hours, when my eyes were wide and no sound broke the stillness except the blowing of wind, I imagined I heard wagons in the distance, like the uncanny creaking of ghostly ships. A hunger dream—I imagined it was Irion's supply chain. The cries of the men were punctuated by the cracking of whips, the clatter of hooves and wagon wheels. The sky was lit by a full moon and a host of stars, but I only saw gray silhouettes moving in the night. Animals, riders, whole caravans that flew from my eye when I tried to view them dead-on.

When dawn broke and the crying of the coyotes ceased, I was exhausted. I built a shelter against the sun with my blanket and some straight branches from a desert plant that has no name I know of. During the day and much of the night I vacillated between sleep and waking, trying to rest my cracking mind. The sun is large and vibrates heat without ceasing. There was no shade in the white sand dunes, and the condition of my skin worsens.

Midday there was a severe storm of wind and dust. It blew up suddenly, and the air around me dropped in temperature. It was not accompanied by rain, which would have been welcome, and was very unpleasant indeed. At a distance these duststorms look like violent clouds and indeed carry with them thunder and lightning. I pulled my blanket tightly around me, though it made my red skin scream. Even so, after twenty minutes my person and all my effects besides were covered thoroughly in dust and thorny brush.

I have few eggs left. I greatly desire water, but no pool or river has appeared for many days now. I have one canteen with a ration of only a few days. How relieved my skin would be if I could wash it in cool water. It was with this purpose that I ventured forth as the sun set, and it was then that I made my first true discovery.

I left the flatter land and made toward the mountains in the distance, thinking they might hide streams of runoff or secret pools. It was just as the sun set, a red sliver into the mesa, that I saw it.

At first, I thought it was smoke. There was a single tree out in the desert and I nervously climbed it to afford myself a better view.

Up top, the wind whipping about me, I still could not discern the source of this great black cloud looming on the horizon, the size of which might indicate a wagon train or perhaps a shack completely aflame. It was rising quickly, throwing a dark mass against the sky, interwoven with gold and pink by the setting of the sun.

I worked my way through the brush and the rocks slowly, fearing some marauding creature or Indian attack. The light was failing and, against the clouds gone dark, I began to worry that it was another one of my imagined silhouettes born of an overtired mind. Almost in answer to my thoughts, it shifted and became dark, so full of menace and purpose that it could not be anything I had dreamt.

When finally I crested the hill that blocked its source, I was close enough to see the bats. I couldn't estimate the number, but it must have been hundreds upon thousands. They turned over one another and tumbled through the sky as if they were being twisted up in a tornado of their own making.

Their sound was that of burbling water rushing over smooth stones. I stood still, listening to them throb against the dusk, until the wind, or perhaps the bats themselves, shifted direction quite rapidly and began to stream over my uncovered head. I crouched and looked up, and at once was in their great dark cloud, their wings pushing the air about me. My heart beat against the inside of my chest, as though one of these wild scraps of night sky were also trapped inside me.

I knew it immediately: Here were the flying creatures that Aunt Anne augured. They had come to show me the way home. I followed.

The whole sky was blacked out. If I could have guessed how many passed by in a second, I could have figured the number in the flock, but they moved too erratically for any estimate to feel certain.

Presently their flow shifted to the east, and I crawled forward over the ledge to find myself staring into the gaping maw of a cave. It was a great crack in the face of the earth, black and wide, and the bats boiled forth without ceasing. I wouldn't have guessed one could be so large.

Though it seemed a fearsome thought, what might have been hiding in the darkness of this massive hole, I had to stay. I knew that any room that could house such a great storm of bats must be the entrance to a cavern of immense size. I scraped along on my belly through the sagebrush until I came to the edge of the cavern. Looking down into the dark, I saw that there was no end in sight. The destined feeling of doom it gave me lingers still.

Retreating, I quickly gathered some dead prickly pear and built a small fire just near the edge. The plants were green and about as good for fire as wet tea leaves, but I managed to ignite them. When they were all aflame, I pierced one of the fiery pads with a stalk and flung it down into the hole. I bent carefully over and watched it fall until at last the flame disappeared. A few sparks finally flared against a wall of rock, a hundred yards down if I make my guess.

I kicked the rest of the cactus fire toward the mouth of the cave to light things better. It was a great mess of flames, and it scared the bats, which for a short while stopped their ascent from the hole. When the little flames died, a few brave bats risked the flight out and more followed, and soon they were pouring forth again. Millions, there must have been.

The flames illuminated little, save a ledge but twenty feet down, which seemed reachable and like it was wide enough to stand on. Ignoring any possible misfortune, I descended as a fly on a wall, my breathing heavy against the rock face. I almost crushed the phial of your lifeblood. Once I made the ledge, I crouched down and took off my pack. The stream of bats seemed to be slowing now, and I stared into the stygian dark, deeper and blacker than any night I have known.

Partly because of the daunting task of bringing myself back up and partly because of the wonderment of it, there I sat for a long while. A cool air rose from the darkness and it felt miraculous against my burnt skin, a sorely needed respite from the sun and echoless waves of desert heat. The cool air snapped me back to life, reinvigorating me. I thought on what was down below me in the depths of the cave.

I don't know how much time passed but the Milky Way became bright, again a river of silver birds. At the last fleeting glimpse of Sirius, that far star alone, she seemed to wink at me. This image gave rise to a whole asterism of your visage. I saw your face, your eyes marked by two bright lamps hung in the ether in just the right spots. It seemed a beautiful and haunting farewell. Our entwined fate is a path lost to us now. What am I to do with my feelings for you?

That Dog Star is gone for good, and I found myself looking in a new direction—straight underground. After pulling myself up, I hiked back to the tree I had climbed and hacked off a low branch with my sabre. I used the post, along with my blanket, to improvise a tent, and have made my own little camp not far from the hills that hide the cavern.

Hopelessly Yours, Zadock

◇◇ ⌃⌃ Zeke and Raisin hurried back to Zeke's unit. Bartle was about to risk everything. Zeke needed to find Eliza. She should know her father didn't abandon her. She should know him. Maybe she'd be able to tell if he was crazy. Or convince him of another plan. ⌃⌃

⌃⌃ When Zeke got to their unit, the door stood open. He and Raisin entered cautiously. The place had been ransacked. Furniture was overturned, his things were scattered across the floor. Everything was coated with a layer of dust. ⌃⌃ ⌃⌃ ⌃⌃ Raisin eyed the mess. ⌃⌃ "Whoa." He looked to Zeke for a reaction. Zeke's shoulders were hunched tight. ⌃⌃ ⌃⌃ **"You mind helping me clean this up?"** Zeke picked up some cushions. He bent slowly. ⌃⌃ ⌃⌃ ⌃⌃ ⌃⌃ "Who did this?" Raisin stepped carefully around the unit. He closed the closet doors and pulled down the shades. ⌃⌃ ⌃⌃ ⌃⌃ **"Whoever they were, they did a better job than last time."** ⌃⌃ ⌃⌃ "Someone really wants that letter. What is in that thing anyway?" ⌃⌃ ⌃⌃ Zeke noticed the sabre sitting crooked above the mantel. It looked as though someone had moved it. As he straightened it he saw a tiny smear of blood on the sharp edge. **"I'm afraid they're going to pin those murders on me."** ⌃⌃ "The girls? It's not the Deserters, I can tell you that for sure." ⌃⌃ **"They need to arrest someone soon, and Daxon has an excuse to arrest me. At least until the letter is turned in."** ⌃⌃ ⌃⌃ ⌃⌃ "Was this always empty?" Raisin stood over Zeke's record cabinet. The drawers had been pulled out onto the floor. ⌃⌃ ⌃⌃ ⌃⌃ **"Hh. They were full of my carbon copies."** ⌃⌃ ⌃⌃ "I bet this was the bloody Republic. They do that. They take all your carbons so they can make you into whatever they want to. I've heard about this lots of times." ⌃⌃ ⌃⌃ ⌃⌃ **"Maybe so."** ⌃⌃ "What do you mean, 'maybe'? They want that letter, right? They're trying to scare you. If they wanted to frame you for murder, they would just throw you in a jail cell. This is to shake you up. Make you turn in that letter." ⌃⌃ Zeke picked up a small piece of paper, conspicuously placed on the kitchen counter. 〜〜 〜〜 〜〜 〜〜 〜〜 "What's that?" 〜〜 〜〜 "Note from Eliza." Zeke turned the paper over in his hand. 〜〜 "Where'd she get a pencil? What's it say?" 〜〜 〜〜 〜〜 "Eliza is gone." 〜〜 〜〜 "She left you?" 〜〜 "No." Zeke stopped. "I mean, I don't know. She's not at Leeya's." 〜〜 〜〜 "I thought she was. I'm calling." Raisin picked up the phonotube. 〜〜 〜〜 〜〜 〜〜 "She's not there, Raisin. Neither is Leeya." Raisin held up the hand signal for *silence*. Zeke could hear the echo of the unanswered buzz down the semaphore line. 〜〜 〜〜 〜〜 〜〜 〜〜 〜〜 〜〜

QUIET

"I'm telling you, Raisin. No one is at Leeya's unit. She's gone underground, to join up." 〜〜 〜〜 Raisin stopped. 〜〜 〜〜 〜〜 "No answer." He capped the tube to end the call. "I said I'd take her to join the Deserters." 〜〜 "No. She's joined the Auspices." 〜〜 "We can't let that happen. We've got to go find her. We'll go underground." 〜〜 "You know how to get into the tunnels?" 〜〜 "Sure, that's the first step toward fleeing. This is what I've been trying to tell you, the Deserters know—" 〜〜 "That doesn't answer the question of what happened to Eliza." Zeke looked distraught. He handed Raisin the note. 〜〜 〜〜 〜〜 〜〜 Raisin studied it. "What if Eliza was here when the Republic hit your place?" He opened the door a crack and peered out. 〜〜 "This note could've been written under coercion." 〜〜 〜〜 〜〜 Zeke rifled through all of Eliza's things. He looked for a clue, anything else she'd left behind. 〜〜 〜〜 〜〜 〜〜 〜〜 〜〜 With Eliza gone, his despair came on in full force. He should have trusted her. He shouldn't have planned without her. 〜〜 〜〜 "Because where would she get the paper?" Raisin began to panic. "You're sure this is her handwriting? This is exactly the kind of thing they do all the time. You can't believe what you read. This note is cryptic. Look closely." 〜〜 〜〜 〜〜 〜〜 〜〜 〜〜 〜〜 Zeke grabbed the note out of Raisin's hand. He held it up to his eyes, examining the handwriting. "She's been arrested," he said. 〜〜

ZEKE - I WILL RETURN TO YOU BY
THE 24th OF OCTOBER.
OTHERWISE I WILL NEVER BE YOUR PAIR.

ELIZA

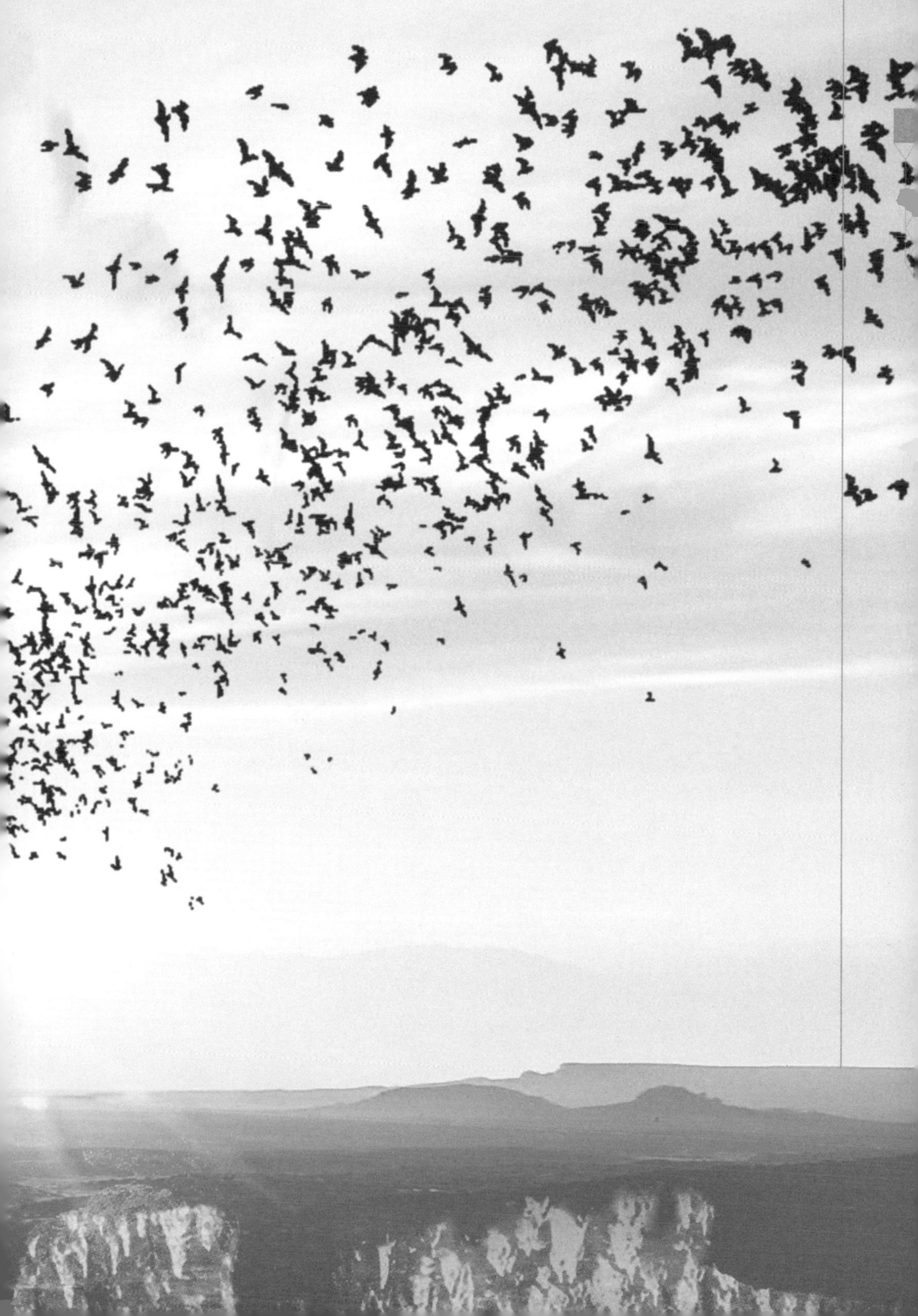

◇◇ ⋀⋀ The phosphor lamps cut the moonless night. Raisin led Zeke through the southwest quadrant. "I want to go to the jail and find Eliza." ⋀⋀ ⋀⋀ ⋀⋀ ⋀⋀ ⋀⋀ "You can't do that. That's exactly why they took her, to flush you out," Raisin said. "We have to figure out another plan. Here, take the edge off." He produced a dram of laudanum from his pocket. ⋀⋀ "Hh." Zeke took the dropper and hurled it as far as he could. It was swallowed in the dark and they heard the glass shatter faintly. ⋀⋀ "Whoa. Calm down. Listen, let's go down in the tunnels. That's where the Nightman lives." ⋀⋀ ⋀⋀ "Eliza isn't with Leeya. Her father said so." ⋀⋀ "If anyone can find Eliza, it's the Nightman. He knows how the Republic operates. The Deserters keep much better tabs on the Lawmen than vice versa." They walked quickly, keeping inside the dead zones. Soon they were deep in the industrial quadrant of the city-state. Raisin stopped near the barrier. ⋀⋀ ⋀⋀ ⋀⋀ He pointed at a small hatch at the base of the steamcarrier garage. He rubbed the dust off with his hand-kerchief. There was a tiny symbol painted on the handle, a wolf with the moon in its mouth, ringed by seven stars. ⋀⋀ ⋀⋀ ⋀⋀ "A wolf eating the moon?" Zeke asked. ⋀⋀ ⋀⋀ "That's the rabbit in the moon." Raisin uncapped a tube embedded in the wall. He whispered into it, "As above, so below." The door clicked and opened in a small puff of dust. ⋀⋀ ⋀⋀ ⋀⋀ Raisin descended the ladder inside the dark hole. Zeke sensed his urgency and followed without hesitation. The door shut behind them. The dark was blinding. ⋀⋀ ⋀⋀ ⋀⋀ The ladder was much longer than the one up to the watchpost. Zeke's shoulders ached. Zeke followed the sound of Raisin's footfalls until they stopped. ⋀⋀ ⋀⋀ "That's the end." His voice echoed in the dark. Zeke stepped off the ladder onto wet gravel. He felt along the walls. They were covered in dripping condensation. He couldn't see Raisin. Zeke's senses sharpened. He had covered every square foot of the city-state on his walks, seen every building from every angle.

My dearest Elswyth,

The angle of the sun on the mountains this morning was cold. I awoke stiff, my makeshift tent no barrier against the cool air that comes with the desert night. Any movement of my body still causes my skin to burn. It is so disagreeable that I lay still for a few hours more, and my idle mind first landed on thoughts of you and the cruel hand the fates have dealt us. I feel as but an echo of my former self. I sorely wish for the pack full of things I long ago decided to bring on this journey, chief among those things the bottle of roborant, which would certainly be a comfort now.

The realization then dawned that Aunt Anne had instructed me to follow the flying creatures, and they had led to the cave. Might this be a path home, my own darkened Nightway? I began to imagine myself once again in its depths and must have drifted back into the embrace of Morpheus, trading one darkness for another.

I was again wakened by a rumbling, the sound of men or beasts, on the far side of the hills. I got up quickly and gathered my things to climb the tree from which I had observed the bats taking flight.

Securing myself in the branches, I heard the creaking of wagons, which filled me with dread and suspicion, so I hung as still as I possibly could. The tree provided cover and vantage point both. It was a party, a few scouts in advance of twenty wagons and perhaps sixty other men. The dust was blinding. At first I hoped for a troop led by Irion, but it was clearly a trading expedition going north from El Paso. There were women among them, and a large number of men — I would guess on account of the freebooters, who will attack any party too small.

I saw them pause at a dip in the hills, and two men disappeared between them with buckets. I thought of calling out to them and seeking a return ride to Chicago. But have I found a shortcut? Presented with the choice I found I lay still until they had finished and moved on again. Texas seems to be fated to me.

THE CITY-STATE

He could have closed his eyes and navigated Texas for the rest of his life, but this was new. He had never been somewhere new. Though he couldn't see anything, he felt the rush of being in a foreign place. He tried to gauge his surroundings. ∿∿ ∿∿ ∿∿ "What's that smell?" ∿∿ ∿∿ ∿∿ "Sulfur," Raisin whispered. "These are the old mines. This whole city-state was built from them. They aren't active anymore — all the raw materials are used up." ∿∿ ∿∿ "Where do we go now?" ∿∿ "We wait. For him." ∿∿ ∿∿ ∿∿ ∿∿ "Who, exactly?" ∿∿ ∿∿ "I don't know his name. They just call him Nightman. He left the Republic and joined the Deserters. His reports are how they know what the Republic is up to. He's famous among the Deserters." ∿∿ ∿∿ ∿∿ ∿∿ ∿∿ "How long do we have to wait?" ∿∿ ∿∿ ∿∿ ∿∿ "Until he comes." ∿∿ ∿∿ ∿∿ ∿∿ "Should we sit down?" ∿∿ ∿∿ The air tasted strange. Zeke thought about how many different places there were on earth. Places he would never go. Somehow this tunnel made them all seem possible. Every plan that his grandfather had ever made had a backup, a fail-safe. Was this tunnel the city-state's fail-safe? Was the letter a fail-safe? ∿∿ ∿∿ ∿∿ "Raisin, I can't believe you never told me about this. How many times have you been down here?" ∿∿ ∿∿ "A few. When I started getting into the Deserter stuff, I was dumb — I tried to ask around about it. They noticed, I got flagged. One day I found a paper note under my door, typed. Directions to this tunnel." ∿∿ ∿∿ ∿∿ ∿∿ They stood still. Time stretched. The dark seemed eternal. Zeke felt alone with his thoughts, like he did lying on the floor mat in the morning after Eliza had left for work. It was hard to imagine doing that now. It was hard to imagine his life before the letter. Everything had seemed so gray, like there was no inherent meaning to his life. ∿∿ ∿∿ ∿∿ ∿∿ ∿∿ He had always thought that being named Khrysalis might change that. It was up to each person to make sense of the world and decide what mattered.

This cave is the thing that matters now. I waited until the men became specks in the forked dust. I then traced their steps, some two miles from the cave. There I discovered a beautiful, bold spring in the midst of a small, thorny grove at the gap between the two ridges. It held perfectly clear limestone water. I stripped off my soiled clothes and took a long cool dip in the waters. It was as though the stream were of roborant or some other restorative elixir, so wonderful did it feel. My skin and gullet were thankful of the soaking.

It was midafternoon by the time I returned to the cave. I removed a few articles from my sack, including the torch and a coil of rope. It was an auspicious time, as the cave mouth faces west. Shafts of sunlight reached down into its opening and lit it sufficiently for me to see through to the floor, a heartening sight. It was also possible to see, from the same vantage, a tunnel off the floor. Leading away to the left, it piqued my curiosity.

It was difficult to get my rope uncoiled, as I had tied the head to the tail to keep it secured in my pack. Once I undid my own knot, I tied the rope around a sharp jutting boulder and pulled with all my weight to secure it. Then, slowly and treacherously, I lowered myself down the side of the cliff wall, passing the ledge I had been perched on the night before.

The rope ran out ten feet from the floor, and I hung for a while, weighing my options. I felt I could drop to the floor safely. It looked smooth and level enough, but reaching the rope again once I had let it go might prove a challenge. Looking around, I could see the entrance of the chasm that I had spotted from above. Its darkness began to throb and beckon me. The dark looked like a liquid night that had been poured slowly into the depths of the cave.

I held still. Time stretched. The dark seemed eternal. I remained motionless as my fate spooled out before me. I could not see the length of it, as my thoughts began to expand and stretch wider and wider.

When folks spoke of the fates, he silently judged them. But now, things had happened. The feeling that had lodged in his chest since he found the letter couldn't be denied. It was beyond his control to decide its meaning. Maybe the fates had decided for him after all, and there was a purpose to his life. He blinked in the pitch-black of the tunnel. Maybe the essential thing to do was to chase that purpose now that it was found. To stop questioning it. Zeke thought about Eliza. He tried not to imagine her kidnapping. She would cooperate, so as not to get hurt. She would evade questions, appear pliant when she was at her toughest. He knew she would be scared. ∧∧ ∧∧ ∧∧ ∧∧ ∧∧ "Raisin?" ∧∧ "Yeah?" ∧∧ "I think I should take my grandfather's Senate seat." ∧∧ ∧∧ ∧∧ ∧∧ A hooting sound echoed through the tunnel. ∧∧ ∧∧ ∧∧ ∧∧ Flickering white pinlights appeared in the distance. ∧∧ "Why would you want to take the seat now?" Raisin asked. ∧∧ "Eliza wants me to. And it might allow — " ∧∧ ∧∧ ∧∧ The pulsing lights were right in front of them. They fell silent. The lights were fireflies. Zeke had only read about them. They bumped around inside a glass jar, which threw little light on the man carrying it. His face was in shadow, hidden under an old cap and a scraggly beard. ∧∧ ∧∧ The man nodded to Raisin. He looked Zeke over with serious eyes. ∧∧ ∧∧ "Hey Nigh...

Hey. Hh, remember me?" Raisin stuttered. "My friend here ... Zeke Thomas. He's got Lawmen hot on his heels. They ransacked his place. We need help." ∧∧ ∧∧ ∧∧ The Nightman motioned them to *follow*. They walked down the tunnel. The dark thrummed around them with heavy breath. Zeke's boots squelched in muck. ∧∧ ∧∧ ∧∧ They walked for a while, following the jar of fireflies. The Nightman seemed to have it balanced on his head. ∧∧ ∧∧ ∧∧ "Does he ever talk?" Zeke whispered to Raisin. ∧∧ ∧∧ ∧∧ ∧∧ "Those who speak do not know, those who know do not speak," the Nightman called back in a darkly melodic voice.

FOLLOW

I heard a voice speak from beyond the cave, beyond the state of Texas, indeed, from beyond time. I began to think on how circumstance had led me to this utterly hidden place and, now that it had, what I might make of it. Whether the fates are truly guiding us or our actions are of our own making, I do not know how any man could say. Even the Greeks, whom I read in grammar school, could not seem to agree on whether our doom is written for us or through some valiant effort, with the grace of the gods, we might escape. We might have an entirely different sort of existence, one that was not drawn for us beforehand. One that we made for ourselves.

Until I lost my chance to be with you, it never seemed to matter much to me, this question of the fates. I suppose I must abide by them, for if they do exist, there is no use thinking about them or struggling against them. And if they do not, then any thought about them at all is a waste of time. They arrived without providence, and I have only my actions and the events of my life.

How shall I thread them together? That is the thought that began to puzzle me down in the black of the cave. What should I make of myself, crouching underground, staring into the unknown? What did it mean that I now found myself here?

Did the fates plan it? Did they have a purpose? Or did I, out of fear that you would never love me, or desperate to somehow prove my worth, design this fate for myself?

Or perhaps it was just a moment, divorced from the purposes of my journey, completely without meaning. Perhaps it was just the cave and I. Nothing had existed before, nothing would exist after. In fact, I felt myself barely there at all—the self I know as Zadock Thomas. I was a new self, which seemed undifferentiated from the cave and the darkness that held me there.

Then a slippage of mud, caused by my own boot, broke the hypnotism of the dark, and I blinked awake. I laughed at myself.

∿ ∿ ∿ ∿ "That's a funny thing to say." Raisin tried a jovial tone. Zeke could tell he was nervous. "So, how's the desertion going? I read about the civilizations out there. And the armies. I'd sign up. If there are plans or whatever. For attack." ∿ ∿ ∿ The Nightman said nothing. Zeke wondered if he knew about the cannon. If it was down in these old mines. ∿ ∿ ∿ ∿ Raisin tried again. "Hey, you haven't seen a couple of girls down here, have you?" ∿ ∿ ∿ ∿ ∿ ∿ ∿ ∿ The Nightman stopped. He took a small ring of keys from a pocket in his sleeve and slipped one into the wall. Zeke hadn't seen a keyhole. A door opened, the exact size of the hatch aboveground. ∿ ∿ ∿ ∿ ∿ ∿ ∿ The Nightman stepped backward into the room. They followed. The inside was no wider than Zeke's bedroom, but it went back a long way. The end couldn't be seen. It was lit from above with glowing plants, the same pale green of phosphor light, calm and steady. ∿ ∿ ∿ ∿ There was a giant silver platter with a half-eaten meal on it—the carcass of some unidentifiable animal, with jutting bones. The walls were lined with stacks of pamphlets, books, and records. It was a mess. Some were tied together with string. Zeke had never seen so much paper. A dusty bed was the only piece of furniture. The Nightman pulled a pile of papers out from under it. He sat cross-legged on the bed. In the light he looked more severe and dirty. He opened his palms. ∿ ∿ ∿ ∿ ∿ "Ask a pointless question, get a pointless answer." ∿ ∿ ∿ Raisin looked at Zeke, and then back at the Nightman. "So, is it true about Spree? Are folks gathering in the rot?" ∿ ∿ ∿ "Bats of a feather..." ∿ "...flock together. Got it." ∿ The Nightman frowned at the interruption. ∿ ∿ ∿ "So what do I do to get to them? What if I want to be a 'bat'? How do I flee?" ∿ "Hold on, Raisin," Zeke whispered. ∿ "Don't worry, I'm taking Leeya." He turned to the Nightman. "So what do I do?" ∿ ∿ The Nightman pulled a sabre from his belt.

Now was a time for action. I could contemplate the fates later. I had to explore the cave while the torch lasted yet. Was there a way out?

There were many boulders fallen in from the mouth. I guessed I could pile enough up to reach the rope should I need to exit the way I had entered. My curiosity had gotten the better of me, and I wanted very badly to see the bats' nest and where the cave led.

Once on the floor, I steadied my torch and made for the tunnel. The blackness around me was dense, and the light did little to cut it. I felt like a tiny bird in the middle of a great night sky. I pressed onward, advancing slowly into the dark with the light held out in front of me as guard. I could see the walls of the tunnel grow around me, and felt as though I were entering the very center of the Earth.

Eventually I reached an immense space that extended several hundred yards. The torch seemed to throw farther here, and I walked quickly. There was a steep drop to the left that I narrowly avoided, taking instead another tunnel that led off to the right, the size of which was unfathomable. I would look for a piece of sky in the roof.

I followed on until I was surrounded by a crop of sharp stalactites. Great pillars of rock jutted up from the floor, sometimes nearly touching the multitude that hung from the ceiling, as though the insides of the Earth were nothing more than a vast churning mouth of animal teeth, frozen in time. Colors rose along the rocks, and the shapes and kinds were arrayed in endless variation, the decorating work of something inhuman. There were colossal white totem poles, and I imagined I'd found the pillared halls of some underground race. The ceilings hung with chandeliers of onyx, the stone wet and dripping in places. There were hanging draperies that looked so delicate that they could be shuttered by my breath but were solid rock to the touch. You would have marveled at the beauty—it was the palatial home I'd imagined for us, carved in stone. The motion of shadows, thick black rivers of ink, kept drawing my eye to the wall.

It was well oiled. Zeke tensed. "You can't run with the hare and hunt with the wolves." The Nightman walked back into his den of paper. "I ... what does that even mean?" Raisin followed him. "That I should go join them? Is this some sort of test?" The Nightman cut the string off a stack of paper. He pulled a file out and flung it into the air. The papers fluttered down around him. He deftly stabbed into them with a snap of his wrist. A pierced pamphlet remained on the end of his sabre. "Even a baby bird can escape the egg," he said, offering it to Raisin. Raisin carefully slid the pamphlet off the sabre. The weapon disappeared as quickly as it had appeared. He unfolded the pamphlet. It contained diagrams annotated with handwritten instructions. It described the steammines that ringed the city-state. Zeke looked over his shoulder, squinting in the dim light. The cover looked like it belonged to a different pamphlet. It read: BATS *of the* REPUBLIC *('43 EDITION).* "This just shows how we get over the barrier, past the steammoat." Once Zeke said the words aloud they felt obvious. "This isn't actually what we need." Zeke was frustrated. "Raisin?" His friend was engrossed in the pamphlet. "OK." Zeke approached the Nightman cautiously. "Here's our situation. My pair, Eliza, has gone missing. I need to get her back. I'm not going anywhere without her." "All birds are gray in the dark." "That's ... She's ... None of this is her fault. I've got a Law deadline. And all I want is to be back at home, with her." The Nightman rummaged through his piles. He lifted a stack that seemed too big for any single fellow to lift. He shuffled things about. His system of organization was a mystery, perhaps even to himself. He reached into his left boot and produced a small pamphlet. "This had better not be something else about escaping civilization. I've heard enough about that."

Had this been created by digging hands? Was some unknown culture concealing itself just behind those rocks? There were pools of ghostly water, so clear that they may as well have not existed. Even though I was loath to break the perfect mirror of the water's taut surface, my thirst had returned. This water was finer than any sullied by the air and soil of the terrestrial sphere, much different than the spring I had found this very morning, and I drank my fill. The water tasted so sweet and pure that I began to doubt even that it was water I was drinking. I splashed it on my ruined skin, which was instantly healed. I filled my flasks with it and must declare that I immediately found my health improved. It was truly the roborant I had been seeking.

The smooth floor gave way to spiky rocks that looked like a plain of stiff grass blades, all straight as though no wind had ever visited them. In the gloom and strangeness of the place, I began to forget completely the desert day above. The air was cool and my lungs felt wet and fresh. The mystery of the world that I had found began to envelop my mind completely, and time seemed a distant concern.

I was shaken from my rapture by a moment that scared me more than any on this journey so far. My torch began to dim, and I realized that I was short on fuel. I hadn't found an exit. The blackness felt as though it were tightening around me. I had not left small markers or some such device by which to guide me back out and up into the day.

As the blackness descended, I hurried back the way that I had just come. My torch did not have much time left. All manner of noises arose, if they hadn't been there all along. The dripping of water, yes, and perhaps the fluttering of bats, but also other noises I couldn't decipher—the rushing of water, the chiming of musical strings, and the very distinct sound of murmuring voices.

I felt out in front of me, afeared that soon touch would be the only sense on which I could rely. Disturbed, I thought I saw doorways and cracks of light that would disappear just as I reached out for them.

MONEY

As Zeke reached out, the Nightman pulled it away. He made the symbol for *money* with his left hand. ∿ Raisin shrugged. "It's probably because you're not a Deserter like me." ∿ ∿ ∿

Zeke ground his teeth. He fished some greenbacks out of his pocket. He handed them to the Nightman, who pointed to Zeke's other pocket. ∿ ∿ ∿ Zeke emptied his other pocket, giving the Nightman all his money. The Nightman handed him the pamphlet. ∿ ∿ ∿ The title read: *STEAMSABRE TECHNIQUES and TRAINING for THE REPUBLIC* ∿ ∿ Raisin took it from Zeke's hand. "Hh, that looks tough." ∿ ∿ Zeke threw up his hands. "**I don't need that. I'm not attacking anyone.**" ∿ ∿ "He who lives by the sword, dies by the sword." The Nightman produced another pamphlet from his right boot. "He who fights and flies away —" ∿ Zeke snatched the pamphlet. It had a picture of the tram on the front. He grabbed Raisin's arm. "**Let's get out of here.**" He pushed the door. It wouldn't open. It was painted on the wall, there was no longer any hinge. ∿

∿ ∿ ∿ The Nightman did a strange side step. He kicked open a waist-high door on the other side of his den. He bowed. ∿ ∿ ∿ Zeke pushed Raisin out of the small opening. He followed. The door disappeared. They stood in the blackness of the mine tunnel. ∿

∿ ∿ "We have to get out of here." Zeke pulled Raisin along. ∿ ∿ ∿ "Easy. According to this pamphlet, it takes two 'bats' to trick the steammines. And once we're in the rot —" ∿ ∿ ∿ "Raisin. I mean we have to get out of this tunnel. I have to find Eliza. I'm not..." Zeke's mouth felt like it was filling with the wet darkness. ∿ ∿ "Blood/Air/Water decides?" ∿ Raisin stopped walking. "Raisin, this is serious." ∿ "I'm serious too. You have to leave the city-state. The Law is after you. You've got no letter." ∿

∿ "Either way, we can't stay down here. Which way is out?" ∿

∿ "Out? I have no idea. It's pitch-black in here." ∿ ∿ ∿ Zeke and Raisin wound down the tunnel, moving slowly in the dark.

Flickers of light played in my peripheral vision, as though some lightning moths had accompanied me down into the cave, flashing distress signals. They were like the strange stars that appear on the insides of my eyelids every time I close my eyes to the sun.

The sourceless voices grew louder. I imagined I heard guttural chants, incanting my doom in the lowest of registers, forecasting my eternal imprisonment in these depths.

Against it all I began to shout in strangled cries meant to calm the noises, but my voice only came back at me, multiplied from every direction, twisted so that it no longer seemed like my own. The echoes and reverberations gave me a fright and I shakily began to run, the floor crumbling beneath me. I was driven mad with a sudden desire to see another light, a natural one that wouldn't disappear in my hand. I slipped over rocks and knocked into stalactites in the panicked dash of an antelope spooked by an unseen predator.

I found my old tunnel and hurried through it, wary of falling in the dark. I imagined I felt a breeze, but it could have been the cold air against the sweat gathering at the nape of my neck. Slipping, I nearly fell into a chasm and sat down hard, barely catching myself on the rocks while still holding above me the dying torch.

This fall knocked some sense into me, and I realized that to hurry too much would mean my death. I tried to slow my labored breathing. I kicked some small rocks into the chasm and heard no echo return. I then dislodged a larger boulder with my foot, again down into the black. It was several heartbeats before it struck something, but even afterward I could hear it rolling down. The chasm extended to a depth many times greater than that which I had climbed down already. I could feel the immensity of it in the pit of my stomach. Presently the sound faded and the cave was quiet again.

Ever aware of my lamp's failing light, I snaked my way back deliberately, but with a good bit more caution. One foot at a time.

Zeke's feet were sore. His head felt muddied. ⌇ "It can't be too far." Raisin looked for the ladder. ⌇ ⌇ ⌇ ⌇ "When I get out, I'm staying in the rot," Raisin said. ⌇ "You have no idea what's out there," Zeke said. They walked for a long time in silence, feeling along the walls. The tunnel branched off and they were forced to chose a direction. It felt like they were going in circles. ⌇ ⌇ ⌇ "Hear that?" They stopped walking to listen closely. A whimpering bleat echoed through the tunnel. "That's someone." Raisin walked quickly. Zeke stumbled behind him. ⌇ ⌇ ⌇ A ring of pale light appeared down the tunnel. As they approached they saw it was not a sliver of daylight but the crack of a doorway shaped like a crescent. Zeke hesitated, but Raisin deftly slid inside and he had no choice but to follow. ⌇ ⌇ ⌇ ⌇ ⌇ ⌇ Zeke immediately felt the presence of others in the room, but his eyes hadn't adjusted to the light. They pressed against the wall, just inside the door. The room was cavernous. An arched roof extended far above them. The air was strange and dense with sulfur. ⌇ The walls were stacked with jars filled with fireflies. They flickered madly, lighting the room erratically. Zeke blinked. ⌇ ⌇ ⌇ ⌇ ⌇ There were rows of wooden benches facing a large silver ring. A small fountain bubbled at the center. It was fount-water, but a deeper color. He could just make out symbols on the silver platform written in mercurial ink. They seemed to shift in the moving light. ⌇ ⌇ ⌇ ⌇ On the benches sat women of various ages. They all wore gray robes and spoke in hushed tones. Their faces and hands were adorned with fine silver ornaments. ⌇ ⌇ ⌇ ⌇ Zeke and Raisin sat down in the back row. The women were all facing toward the central ring, which was hard to see in the dark. ⌇ ⌇ "Where are we?" Zeke whispered. ⌇ "I don't know. I was expecting the Deserters," Raisin said. He picked up a darkened jar and shook it. The giant moth inside quickly flickered to life. It lit Raisin's face with a flutter.

A stray bat, by casting a quick shadow across the ceiling, put me on course. It is to that and the fates that I owe the vision of a blade of sunlight piercing the roof, heralding my return to the surface.

The pile of boulders was not necessary in the end and, abandoning my torch, I could just reach the end of the rope by jumping. It was not easy and many failed attempts bloodied my hands, but I finally got hold of it and pulled myself to the top, warming with relief every length of the rope. It was the way I had entered, but I was free.

Once up top, I lay down on the hot earth and let the sun set behind me. I felt too overwhelmed to move, and indeed lay there until dusk came on. I did not think to look for it, but all at once the great whorl of bats beat to life and covered the sky above my eyes like a blanket, now somehow comforting.

I expected them to trickle out, a few scouts emerging to test the night air, then signal the rest of the troop to move out. But that was not their way. They emerged all at once, as a group, and seemed already agreed upon which direction to fly.

I do not know how they are alerted to the dusk. It is pitch-black in the cave, and remains so cool and steady that I cannot comprehend what sign of waning daylight could compel them to emerge so suddenly and in such great number. Perhaps they are accustomed to the rhythms of the day as birds are to the rhythms of the season, some ancient knowledge carried in their bodies, one that allows them to know when it is time to go. Were I only guided by such a force.

I lay there and watched in growing wonderment at the duration of their emergence, which seemed like it might never end. By the path of the moon, low across the western sky, I estimate it took between two and three hours before the number of bats finally dropped off significantly enough to convince me they were finished. Their number I still can't guess. Undoubtedly they have mastered procreation, and their underground city flourishes with an abundance of life.

THE CITY-STATE

"Where do these things come from?" ∧∧ ∧∧ ∧∧ Leeya appeared beside Raisin, startling him. She sat down on the bench. ∧∧ ∧∧ "Leeya!" Raisin barked, and reached for her. She pulled her hand away. She was wearing a large white robe that made her appear small and girlish. Her long blonde hair was plaited, her eyes fixed with foreboding. ∧∧ "The moth came from the storm country. You put some moonflowers in a jar, and soon you'll have lightning moths. One of the Auspices told me that." ∧∧ "The Auspices?" ∧∧ **"This is the Auspicium,"** Zeke said under his breath. ∧∧ ∧∧ "They all came through the tunnel. Do you want some fruit?" Leeya's voice was off. She produced a dark pomegranate from her sleeve pocket. ∧∧ ∧∧ Raisin took the fruit awkwardly, unsure of what to do. "Leeya, I have a plan." He tried to keep his voice down. "We have to get back up top. Do you know the way?" ∧∧ "The tunnel." ∧∧ "Yes, but which one?" ∧∧ "Spree's. He built it. He dug from the outside and the Nightman dug from the inside. It's two lefts, four rights, one left, down the ladder: You're in the tunnel. And then you're in the storm country." ∧∧ "It goes to the rot? That easy? Why is everyone in here? I mean, what's out there?" ∧∧ "That tunnel is sealed. Not for us to know. For now there's fruit. And fireflies. That is what our child requires." Her voice was strange, without emotion or register. ∧∧ "Let's escape. Right now!" Raisin looked frantically at them both. ∧∧ "It's not for us. No one can go out that way." ∧∧ ∧∧ Zeke finally interjected, **"Leeya, where is Eliza?"** ∧∧ ∧∧ Leeya stood up and left them without answering. An eerie quiet had descended. They nervously watched as Leeya walked down the aisle toward the silver circle in the center of the room. The light thrown from the jars of lightning moths dimmed. Leeya joined six other girls wearing matching white robes. They sat on carved tree stumps in a ring, ankles crossed in the same direction. Seven older women appeared in black robes. The air went out of the room and a deadly quiet took its place.

All is calm now. This was two days hence, and I watched the bats again last night. Each day I have found myself staring down into the cave, long and hard, guessing at its length and the location of the exit, which I could not discover. My imagining of the underworld has consumed my mind and become so preposterous that I have begun to have thoughts of what it would require for humans such as you and I to live in such a place. It makes for a natural shelter, and might easily be guarded from attack or inclement weather. How to get light underground seems to me the principal problem.

My head has been so muddled and sunstruck that it took me this long to realize that I had not yet drawn a single one of the bats. They represented the perfect reason to take up again the mission I had inadvertently abandoned: the documenting of western species.

The bats move rapidly, propelled by repeated flapping of the wings, which seem to move more circularly than those of a bird. They are rather agile in the air, able to turn and change direction according to whim. They do not glide for more than a second and never achieve much velocity. Against a darkening sky, even when seen directly above me, the bat passes like a thought, and if I try to espy the same one twice, it is gone.

This evening, I thought of a strategy to catch one. I stood near to the maw and swung my blanket upward into the cloud that was spilling all around me. It did not take very long to strike a bat from the air and send it tumbling to the desert floor. Though I felt sorry for the attack, I leapt forward and pounced upon the bat with both hands.

At first I gripped her tightly, bracing for the sting of tiny teeth, but presently I loosened my grip as she was curious about the warmth and smell of my hands. She crawled up my sleeve, awkwardly using thumb-like talons on the tips of her wings. The little bat hung on me for a bewitching moment and then took to the sky again, rejoining her family's nightly migration, a communion with the dark.

The ritual had begun. The Auspices approached each girl in turn and washed their feet in small silver bowls. The audience stood. The eldest woman in black took the center. She slid her hood back to reveal a bird's nest of tangled white hair. Her fingers were tipped with metal spikes. With a raspy breath, she began to incant a prayer:

That which maketh the seven stars and Ouroboros, and turneth
the shade of death into dawn, and maketh the day dark with night,
that calleth forth waters, and poureth them out upon the face...

Leeya entered the ring with deliberate steps. She carried a goat. Its feet were bound with bolo-ties. Murmurs coalesced into a lilting chant. Zeke and Raisin stood to see what was happening. The goat's frail bleating could just be heard over the prayer. Zeke had never seen an animal outside of its cage before. It felt dangerous, wrong. ⌒⌒ ⌒⌒ The Auspices all turned away with arcing steps. The eldest woman produced a dagger from her sleeve. Leeya stepped forward with the goat. She lifted the struggling animal over the fountain. There were tears in her eyes. The room was charged. The eldest woman raised the dagger. Her eyes rolled back in her head, and she brought it down quickly to slit the goat's throat. Its lifeblood poured into the gurgling waters. ⌒⌒ Three of the girls in white knelt at the edge of the fountain. They cupped the mixture into their mouths, staining their robes. They drank it as though it were fount-water. Leeya hesitated. Another girl grabbed her hand and led her to the fountain as well. She drank. ⌒⌒ Raisin was transfixed with horror. The chants began again as the whole room went into hysteria. Some of the initiates wept as they drank straight from the fount. Zeke strained to catch a glimpse of the girls' faces underneath their hoods, searching for Eliza. The Auspices began to make their way down the aisles. ⌒⌒ **"We need to get out of here,"** Raisin said. He grabbed Zeke. They slid out of the aisle and hurried toward the back. ⌒⌒

It was then that I realized what I might do until I find my way through the cave. Your father has no bats. The Museum of Flying is entirely birds and bugs. Perhaps he thinks bats are vicious, but there is no blood food out here, if that is supposed to be what sustains them. They must eat the fruits of this desert and insects or other small creatures. Were I able to capture enough specimens and document them properly, they could form the basis for a whole new collection at the museum. Or perhaps the Zoological Garden. Chicago society would surely be fascinated by these wing'd mammals, that are like little pieces broken out of the desert night sky.

Aunt Anne herself led me to the bats. She and her Sisters would support the useful nature of such creatures and their rightful place in a museum of things that have mastered the air. Your father would beg to house my collection. Without it, his museum would be incomplete. Irion's letter would be forgotten.

Would not such success grant me esteem in your eyes? And even if we could not be married, my place at the museum would be secured, and I would be near to you the rest of my days.

My encounter with the bat, along with my defeat at the onset of the darkness, has loosed a new resolve in me. I am now determined, while plumbing the depths of this cave, to discover the home of the bats and the extent of their underground world. You shall come with me, always in my thoughts. I wish badly for some fox fire, or any reliable light to guide me through the black of the cave.

In the morning I shall move my tent and make a proper camp, shielded by the mouth of the cave and hidden from view. Then I should head for the road to the east, to see if I can gain a few more supplies from some small town or passing caravan. I feel this cave is my personal discovery and new calling. I will find a way through. Perhaps this journey was meant all along to lead me to its fateful darkness.

Yours in Great and Cavernous Love, Zadock

RECORD: 1741402

SCRPT DATE: 0021.0010.2143

SUBJECT: ELIZA GRAY & HENRY BARTLE

BEGIN WATCHPOST TRANSCRIPT:

E. GRAY » Dad?

H. BARTLE » Eliza ... I...

» Dad, I can't believe — You're here — I —

» Why are you ... outside ... Vault?

» Are you OK? You — you're covered
    in blood. Your hands —

» ...shouldn't be here ... not safe. Outside of
    dead zones. I ... looked for you. I...

» Here, come sit on the plankway. Catch
    your breath. What happened? Why did —

» I'm sorry ... Eliza, sorry ... for everything.
    I should never ... left you. My daughter...

» Here, put your head here. It's OK. I can't
    believe — you look exactly the same. Why
    didn't you come find me? Zeke said —

» I had to leave. I was forbidden to see you.
    They wanted to destroy our bloodline.
    They made you a Gray. Because I'm Queer.

» Oh — oh Dad, that doesn't matter to me.
    I just thought — Why — Are you hurt?

» No, just ... It's not my blood. Just winded.
    I tried to get Zeke's letter. It's your
    chance ... out. I know it's in Daxon's office.
    I waited for him. He means to ... Hh...

» Calm down. Take a breath. Lean back.

» Yes. OK. You ... you are beautiful. I have
    letters for you. Things you should know...

» Dad, did Daxon do this to you?

» I waited for him. In the corridor with
    a metal filing drawer. As though I was

just ... moving records around. When
Daxon approached his door, I snuck up
behind him. I hit him with all my strength.
With the drawer. Over the head. He ... fell.
He was bleeding from the temple. I wanted
to collect his blood in a phial so that I could
FLAG▸   use it to open his door. His blood ID...   ‹VIOLENCE

» This isn't your blood? Dad, this is crazy.
   You came to Texas to do this?

» It was horrible. His blood was trickling
   from his head into my phial. I heard
   someone coming down the corridor.
   I corked the phial and pocketed it.
   It was Bic. He came around the corner
   and discovered me hunched over Daxon's
   body. He wasn't moving. Bic drew his
   sabre and called out for the guards. I...

» Zeke's cousin. He wants to be Khrysalis.

» More than you think. I ran down the
   corridor. Bic followed me. I escaped by
   sliding into the Vault. I lost him in the
   labyrinth of rows and drawers. I could
   hear him howling. He doesn't know the
   Vault of Records like I do. He's still inside.
   I'm in trouble. They'll sound the alarm if
   Bic doesn't catch me first...

» We need to get away from here. He
   could come out that door any minute.

» I need to go back. I don't have the letter.

» I don't think that Daxon does. I —
FLAG▸   I reported it carbon'd. It never was.   ‹UNCARBON'D

» You —

» Doctored a lot of records. It was a false
report. I lost it when I was fired. It will
take time to see that the letter is missing.

» It took me days.

7 SECONDS DEAD AIR

» I'm sorry. I didn't know you were looking.
But — we can't think about that now. Let's
get you out of range of these watchposts.
A dead zone, somewhere safe.

» You are good at threading documents.
I'm so proud of —

» Daxon is guilty. I wanted everyone
to know that. Or anyone. Especially
someone who is looking at Zeke's file.

» Zeke needs to take the Senate seat.

» I agree. But he can't do that without the
help of the Auspices. This is all in their
hands now. They must keep both Daxon
and the Deserters at bay if they intend to
restore order to the Republic.

» This wasn't the way it was supposed to
be ... When we built the Vault —

» I know. Dad, I wish you had just told me.
I thought you — you didn't care about me.

» I would've been arrested. It seems foolish
to care about that now. I should've known
it'd be inevitable. I wish I had contacted
you. I'm so ... happy to see you. I missed
you so much. Come to Chicago-Land.
Both of you. Would you ever —

» We'll talk about Chicago-Land. But first
we have to get out of here. Our unit
has been destroyed. I'm taking you to
Leeya's. I sent her underground, so she's
not home. No one is watching that unit.
We can lie low, figure out what to do.

» We have to go back. I have Daxon's blood.
The key to his office door. I was so close to
getting the letter. What if it contains —

» He may not even have it! He knows you're
after him now. He'll be angry. Don't put
yourself in danger like that again. Dad,
I — I haven't seen you my whole life.

» It doesn't matter what happens to me now.
As long as you and Zeke —

» He wouldn't want you to do all this.
You'll wait at Leeya's. I'll go find Zeke.
Come on, stand up. Can you breathe?

» I've been writing to you. All these years.
I have this inheritance bundle for you.
How will you ever forgive me? My blood —

» It was hard, has been hard. But I love you.
We have to get you out of Texas. It's not
safe for Queers here. Not after Atlantas.

» It's not safe for you either.

» Zeke will know what to do. It's going to be
OK, come on, let's go. There's someone in
that watchpost.

E.G. INDICATES WATCHPOST TX 277

» We have to get away.

END WATCHPOST TRANSCRIPT

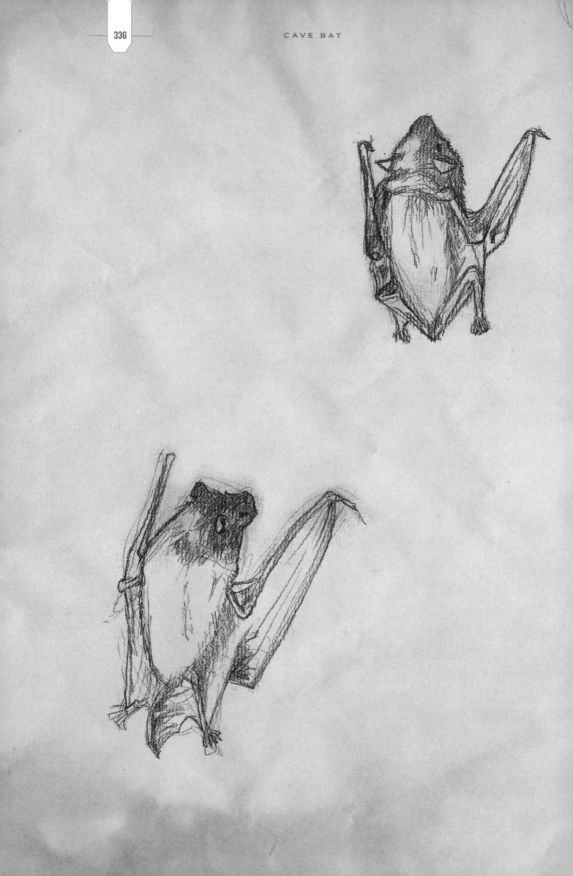

FAM. **TADARIDA**

GEN. **BRASILIENSIS**

26.9.43, 18:15, 70 deg., 20 knots, few clouds

Just outside the desert cave

Cave Bat. Small, brown like surrounding desert. Body is covered with fur and its face is flat and short and indeed more alike to a human than a mouse. Folds of skin about its ears, no doubt for hearing in the cave, and its wings are formed of the same rubbery dark skin. I thought the wings hairless but, rubbing them between my thumb and forefinger, I could feel tiny follicles. Its wings are not so much formed by its arms as its hands, thin bony fingers providing the frame on which the skin is stretched. Imagine having hands so large that by their downward gesture you could be propelled up into the air! Never have hands been so vital to a creature. To hold this one in mine was a thrill unmatched.

Dearest Elswyth,

Going for supplies, I did discover a village, but I am glad to be back from it. The deeper I go into this cave, the closer I am to returning to you. Aunt Anne's vision has renewed my confidence, and I felt buoyed returning to my camp at the mouth of the cavern. During the day, cave swallows take the place of the bats and feed tirelessly upon the buzzing insects, darting in and out of the deep shade below the great mouth, fixed in a knowing grin. There is a way back to you.

I set out three days hence, in the evening, for the provisions required to go farther underground. The stars here are difficult for me to read. The desert heat warps the night air and seems to set them spinning. Instead, I followed the tracks of the road. Twice in the night I heard groups of mounted men, which were easily spotted in their hasty clouds of dust. Being but one man, I was able to conceal myself in the brush. I do not know if they were Indians or soldiers.

There were no caravans, and just as I began to think I would not find a town, one appeared on the ridge of a hill at the break of day, shining like a mirage. Clusters of white buildings caught the sunlight and sparkled brilliantly. At first I thought it was a dream. I was led forward by the songs of swallows, drunk on morning's dew.

As I came into the town, I saw Mexican homes made of the usual mud brick, but coated in rough white sand, giving them an unusual appearance. They first seemed abandoned to me. Connected to the dwelling houses were pigsties, corncribs, and stalls for cattle. A few had cow skulls mounted on the gates. Some children spotted me and, naked as jaybirds, scurried back toward the main part of town. I joined the high road and walked past the houses. Presently men and women appeared along the side of the pathway, their sunken faces unchanging as I passed by. Meat hung from hooks: buffalo or coyote, it was impossible to tell. Dried blood pooled underneath them.

Santa Fe was filthy with life, but this town seemed a city of ghosts.

The few Mexicans here, in dirty clothes and limp rabosas, regarded me with flat black eyes. I tried a nod or raised hand in greeting and received no discernible response. One skeletal man suckled at a small cigarrita, the smoke tracing shapes into the cloudless sky. Bony dogs lay panting against white walls. It was as though the village was in suspended animation, and might start moving again once the sun crested. I felt watched and unwelcome. Only the naked children moved about, scattering just ahead on the periphery of my sight.

I thought I caught a smile on the face of a young girl. I turned in time to see her whip around and skirt back under black fabric hung in the doorway of her hut. My mind was playing tricks, but I was sure for a moment her face was Abril's. I found myself fixed on the doorway, floating into memories of Los Padillas, then, bitterly, Santa Fe.

At the center of the village I discovered a well. I cranked the handle to send the bucket down and back up, and it was returned full of a strange dark water, much to my surprise. I dug through my pack, intending to fill my canteen, and came across your fated telegram. Though your words were harsh, I decided I would conquer that impossible date. Drawing my sabre, I speared the note. Then, reaching out with the weapon, I dipped the telegram into the bucket of water, stirring it so that the ink started to run and the paper dissolve. The water would not consume the document entirely and, frustrated, I swung my sabre and chopped the rope, sending the bucket and the whole cursed thing crashing to the bottom of the well.

A great bell rang and I startled. Still nothing around me moved, despite the alarm. It was then that I began to feel very uneasy and an ominous dread descended on me. I gathered my things and beat a retreat, retracing my path back through the town. Some elder townsfolk, adorned in dark robes, emerged from the deep shadows, and I could feel their eyes burrowing into my back.

As I tried to duck through between two houses, a pair of hands *grabbed me, pulling me into an open doorway. A man spun me around and put his finger to his lips to signal silence. His eyes were full of concern and, understanding his gesture, I obeyed.*

His rooms were cool and dusty, and wholly undecorated. The man sat me in a rough chair. He pointed at me and then drew his finger across his neck, which I understood as a sign of danger. The mood outside gave me no reason to doubt him. He had all the affects of the Indian men I had traveled with, but even lighter skin. He was dressed in the uniform of a Mexican soldier, though I saw he was not. He wore moccasins on his feet and a single feather in his hair. His face seemed trustworthy and serious despite one pink eye, likely from albinism. It contrasted neatly with his darker eye. The Indian was squat, with a close crop of thick black hair. His cap looked to be government-issued and he wore a decorated sabre by his side, one that he couldn't have purchased himself, guessing from how his hovel was appointed.

He brought me a little cheese made of thin milk, pan de maíz, and some nuts. He sat on the floor and watched me eat. I grew restless at being studied, sitting in his chair. I asked if he knew the cave.

The Indian ignored my question. We sat there for a long time, and if I made a motion to leave he barred the way to the door, again making the sign for danger. I became impatient and bored, and began to long for some English conversation or even a book to read.

The idle time, however, allowed a brilliant thought. A book!

It is certainly within my ability to construct a field guide consisting of previously undiscovered species from these lands, especially the bats. My discoveries at the cave could be published and yield a fame wider than a display in Chicago would allow. I should find a publisher and make my fortune independently. I could issue subscriptions for plates, as others have done. Texas is large. I could make many explorations and uncover all the species of bat that make their homes here.

Why should I be a mail courier? Would this other task not suffice to win your father's approval and your hand in marriage? With my heart dedicated to you, I could dedicate my mind to the bats, and you could read my care for you in my work and marvel at what I have seen.

I am set on it now! One day we will return with a full complement of naturalists and equipment to this remote corner of the Earth. I became animated at the idea and began to pace. The Indian only put out his palm, asking me to wait.

Finally, when the sun was at its apex, he opened the wooden door and crept up to the main street, peering left and right. He then fixed a serape over my shoulders. I allowed him to put a brimmed hat upon my head, and he tucked your phial of blood into my shirt folds. I had not even noticed that it had been out on display. Once thusly arranged, the Indian hooked his elbow into mine and led me out into the street.

In the heat of the day, the denizens were gone from the road. The flies buzzed and the skinny dogs lay in the shadows, napping next to the children who had also run themselves ragged. We made our way largely unnoticed. I imagine this was the Indian's design.

A ways outside of town, we sat against a low mud wall with our backs to the village and the sun. The Indian fixed a blanket upon two sticks and weighted the other end to the top of the wall with stones so that it formed a small tent above us. We waited in the shade. I tried to communicate in both English and a very broken sort of Spanish.

Even though the need to be quiet was no longer pressing, the Indian still did not speak. He seemed to prefer silence, and in the end I was able to communicate via gesture. I had come down for food and water. I also needed several coils of rope, some wire, and a kerosene lamp. This lamp and oil was hardest to translate, but the Indian sat patiently until all was clear between us. He then took my canteen, my sack, and the last of my money, and went back toward the village.

I was there against the wall for the rest of the afternoon. I dozed off, woken occasionally by black flies landing on my face. I was much *in need of rest as I hadn't had any since the night before last. I have been sleeping poorly due no doubt to the taxing conditions of this trip. The cave requires a nocturnal sleep pattern.*

When I woke, the sun had just set and the dusk was filled with the cries of coyotes. It occurred to me that the Indian may not ever return. I watched a herd of starved cattle being driven back toward the town. The rancheros were driving them on the far side and the light was low, so they did not see me motionless beneath the blanket.

After they passed, I was startled by a great bat. He landed on the edge of the makeshift tent and hung upside down, facing me. How long he had been there I could not say, but I took his appearance as an omen, and drew him properly to pass the time. He could be the first entry in my field guide to the bats of the Republic of Texas.

Eventually, the Indian did return with all the things I had asked for. I tried to give him the leftover money and he refused, instead taking his spot against the wall next to me. He rested, and then handed me a small card of paper inscribed with Spanish. I translate it roughly as:

The river enters the desert valley lightly because
it flows downward easily. The folks take death lightly because
they are living in the (red?) of life.

I do not know if my translation is true, as I think it is meant as some sort of prayer. It has stayed with me now and all the way back to my camp. As has the Indian. I don't know why. On our way back, we stayed away from the road, for I have begun to know my way and the mountains make for good markers. The moonlight was strong tonight, and I could see about me quite clearly. As dawn approached I was able to spy the returning caravan of bats tracing across the sky. They led us back to the cave that has become the answer to all my worries.

My Love's Purpose Renewed, Zadock

EL RÍO ENTRA EN EL VALLE DEL
DESIERTO LIGERAMENTE PORQUE
CORRE DESCENDENTE FÁCIL.
LA GENTE TOMAN LA MUERTE
LIGERAMENTE PORQUE
VIVEN A LO ROJO VIVO.

FAM. CERVIDAE

GEN. IDIONYCTERIS

29.9.43, 20:15, 70 deg., 30 knots, no clouds, windy

Dry hills with low shrubs and few trees outside Mexican village

Large bat. Gray. Little fur. Outsize tattered ears. Certainly an unknown species. I thought at first he was dead, then realized he couldn't have kept his grip on the tent were this the case. He did seem disturbed in some way. Perhaps very old or sick, or maybe terribly weary from winding his way through a lifetime of labyrinthine dark. I named him the Stag-Ear Bat, for his great ragged ears have the brave character of a buck's antlers.

Task list for Publication of field guide.

"Bats of the Republic"

Explore the entirety of Texas,
  (the underground especially)
  ⁻Document all bat species therein
Complete First Draft
Finalize plate engravings,
  24 total in the initial collection
Mock-up for showing prospective publishers
Sign Publishing contract
Complementary display installation
at Zoological Garden?
  (Rather than Museum of Flying.)
Draft sales pitch for subscribers
Public lecture and Book release
  (Invite Grays)
Book Reviews
Send C.V. to European Inst

Task list for Publication of field guide.

"Bats of the Republic"

Explore the entirety of Texas,
   (the underground especially)
   Document all bat species therein
Complete First draft
Finalize plate engravings,
   24 total in the initial collection
Mock-up for prospective publishers
Sign Publishing contract
Complementary display installation at Zoological Garden?
   (Rather than Museum of Flying)
Draft sales pitch for subscribers
Public lecture and Book release (Invite Grays)
Book Reviews
Send C.V. to European Institutes

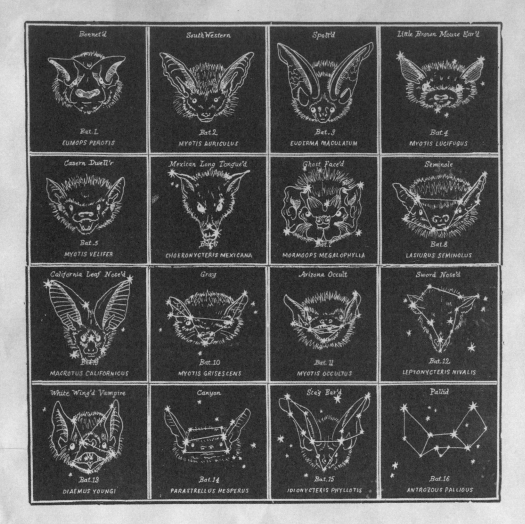

Bonnet'd	SouthWestern	Spott'd	Little Brown Mouse Ear'd
Bat.1	Bat.2	Bat.3	Bat.4
EUMOPS PEROTIS	MYOTIS AURICULUS	EUDERMA MACULATUM	MYOTIS LUCIFUGUS

Cavern Dwell'r	Mexican Long Tongue'd	Ghost Face'd	Seminole
Bat.5	Bat.6	Bat.7	Bat.8
MYOTIS VELIFER	CHOERONYCTERIS MEXICANA	MORMOOPS MEGALOPHYLLA	LASIURUS SEMINOLUS

California Leaf Nose'd	Gray	Arizona Occult	Sword Nose'd
Bat.9	Bat.10	Bat.11	Bat.12
MACROTUS CALIFORNICUS	MYOTIS GRISESCENS	MYOTIS OCCULTUS	LEPTONYCTERIS NIVALIS

White Wing'd Vampire	Canyon	Scag Ear'd	Pallid
Bat.13	Bat.14	Bat.15	Bat.16
DIAEMUS YOUNGI	PARASTRELLUS HESPERUS	IDIONYCTERIS PHYLLOTIS	ANTROZOUS PALLIDUS

BATS *of the* REPUBLIC

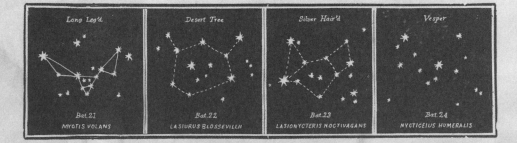

Long Leg'd	Desert Tree	Silver Hair'd	Vesper
Bat.21	Bat.22	Bat.23	Bat.24
MYOTIS VOLANS	LASIURUS BLOSSEVILLII	LASIONYCTERIS NOGTIVAGANS	NYCTICEIUS HUMERALIS

Example cover for

"Bats of the Republic"

Yesterday's quarter moon donated enough light that I was able to ink this concept for the visual part of my field guide to bats.

Each bat should be given a full folio, not unlike the birds of Audubon's book. But this small chart could serve as a quick guide to their facial features, taxonomic names, and distinguishing characteristics.

After a few hours of drawing, I was so awed by the stars that I could not help but include them as well.

FAM. **MYOTIS**

GEN. **VELIFER**

4.10.43, 6:15, 60 deg., 10 knots, no clouds

Near desert cave

Cave bat with moth. Seeing this resourceful young bat devour a moth nearly its size gave me a thought on how bats came to fly. If they are in the habit of making meals of moths, then perhaps by hunting them they grew more and more bold in leaping into the air after them and, by that and observation, learned to fly themselves. A mammal certainly couldn't grow wings for no purpose. I posit they began as shrew-like cave critters and then emerged into the air, miracles of their own invention.

Dearest Elswyth,

I am still stalled at my camp at the mouth of the cave. Though at least I continue to work on my guide. A few days hence I gestured to the cave, and asked the Indian if he could guide me to the exit.

He did not respond. We watched the bats and he seemed unafraid of their swarming emergence. He peered down into the dark mouth of the cave for a long time, and whether his emotions were fearful or contemplative, I cannot say. I prepared myself for the exploration.

I used my sabre to cut the stalks of nearby yucca, and with rope and wire fashioned a rope ladder, using the stalks for steps.

Afterward, the Indian gave me another curious prayer card, fixing his pink and black eyes on mine. I do not know why he carries such a supply, and I was surprised at this one. It was again in Spanish, which I have not heard him speak.

The dark is a vacancy that can be used forever.
I do not know who birthed it. It precedes the desert valley.

After this, I somehow understood that he was willing to go with me into the cavern. We took the kerosene lamp, canteen, and a small sack of provisions. I brought my paper and charcoal, though I couldn't draw much by lamplight, and for the most part I preferred to use the lamp to look for new paths.

We climbed down the ladder into the cave, and it felt a surer means of getting out as well. This time I was prepared — I used a length of twine to trace our path and a series of broken stalagmites to point back toward the entrance. Being lost in the great darkness was not an experience I wished to replicate. Though he remained silent, having the Indian there gave me a measure of comfort in the cave.

At first he moved hesitantly about the rocks, trying his footing like an animal on a cliff. Eventually something in his constitution

LA OSCURIDAD ES UN
VACÍO QUE PUEDE SER USADA
PARA SIEMPRE.
NO SÉ QUIÉN LO CONCIBIÓ.
PRECEDE EL VALLE DEL
DESIERTO.

settled, like mine, and we grew quite accustomed to the underground environment and our place in it. The kerosene lamp served the purpose a good deal better than the lantern I had taken earlier. They cast enough light that we could make regular forward progress.

We spent two days searching the depths, seeing all manner of things you would simply marvel at, my dearest. We crept like desert foxes across precipitous ledges, and tested depths by the soundings of thrown stones. I sat for a while and drew a map and some of the more picturesque formations. Though I feel my skill in rendering an animal alive on the page is now improved, the monuments of this labyrinth are another beast altogether. Seeing what I have outlined in charcoal in the light of day is disappointing and comes in no way close to representing what is in my mind's eye, remembered from the cave.

We hunted for a new way out. Our minor thrills and trials will have to wait for a larger volume, as I plan to set the whole adventure down in great detail as the preface to my guide to bats. My letters to you will help me remember. It is sufficient to say that exaggeration would be impossible with regards to the magnificence beneath this desert.

However, I will recount one particular thrill. During the second day, I was resting in one of the largest cavern rooms and casting the lamp about me when out of the darkness rose the skull of a man. It gave me a start, staring at me in the gloom like a ghoul. I brought the lamp over and saw that it was indeed a whole skeleton intact. It was a surprising thing to behold so deep underground.

Even more unusual was the size of the skeleton, perhaps twice as large as an average man. I began to imagine a prehistoric race of giants, and thought of the Aztecs that Rodriguez spoke of with reverence at the abandoned pueblo. I picked up a femur and it wetly crumbled in my hand. All at once, I understood that the mineral water dripping all around it had softened the bones. For years they had been saturated with lime, and had become swollen and monstrous.

I remember discovering a collection of bones in Aunt Anne's cottage, among her curious objects in glass jars. She said bones are a carriage for the soul. The Nightway will follow the bone map, whether a creature still lives or not. I had hope for my escape.

There were bits of cloth about this skeleton, but not enough to make out what sort of attire the man had perished in. I posited to myself that he might be some lost Indian, unusually brave. But I have discovered no other traces of Indian folk inside the caves, despite some fire pits on the surface. There I can tell they cooked their food using the bats' droppings, which make good fuel for a fire.

The skull had not been under the corrosive drip and remained in perfectly hard condition, though it still seemed quite a bit larger than any human skull I had ever seen. It was a prize worthy of study. Quite used to specimens, I brushed the dust from its face, picked it up, and secured it in my sack. The Indian seemed unhappy at this and gave a panicky kind of snort. It was the only noise he made in the cave throughout the entirety of the two days we were underground, and it resonated through the air with an ominous gravity.

After an unpleasant march across a subterranean field of bat droppings, I realized we had come too far and must turn back. It was disappointing, to say the least. But I could not risk running out of fuel again. We made our way back to the entrance following the twine into the dead heat of day. The light, I must admit, was jarring to my senses. We again built up our little tent and slept exhausted until eventide. I dreamt of you. The fluttering roar of the great bat cloud awoke me.

Though my goal is finding a way through, I am becoming accustomed to this cave. It is cool inside, night or day. That pleasant refuge from the desert heat makes it an ideal place to conduct my study of the creatures who have lived here for countless generations. I hope that Aunt Anne's prophecy holds true, and they will teach me the way home. Already I have spotted two more species of bat, as those depths serve as perfect shelter from the harsh desert sun. The discovery and documentation of all these new creatures, to say nothing of their entirely magnificent habitat, will surely bring great accolades. The book will only be the start of it. I shall have to have my own display, perhaps a hall dedicated to me in the museum. Your father cannot but embrace such a discovery, and I will be able to spend my days with you in the great comfort of success.

I will now send the Indian back to the town for more fuel and supplies. The search for the cavern's hidden exit will continue. The Indian doesn't know the way through, but his companionship serves for safety. We have done some hunting in the surrounding desert, and he is very good at catching rabbits. Though it would disgust Chicago society, I must admit some pride in my dinner tonight. I stuck three desert mice on a stick and cooked them without butter, salt, or anything else. Even this hardly gives me pause now.

Our sleeping habits have also changed to suit our environment. It is best to sleep during the day, and we are both up through the night. As the moon rose tonight, the Indian handed me another curious card.

You must be without desire in order to observe
the dark and even darker.

I do not know how his words seem to find my inner thoughts, but this particular card made me feel as though I have missed something essential in the caverns. I plan to stay on this very spot until my way is found. Perhaps I'll send the Indian on with Irion's letter. I will draw and capture as many bat species as I can in the meantime. There are many passageways that my lantern could not find the end of. One leads home. By the end of this journey, I shall have a field guide singular in its subject and of a quality to rival any. It will be dedicated to you.

Yours Beneath a Starry Sky, Zadock

DEBE SER SIN DESEO
PARA OBSERVAR
LA OSCURIDAD Y
LO MÁS OSCURO.

FAM. **VESPERTILIONIDAE**

GEN. **EUGNORISMA**

8.10.43, 11:15, 85 deg., no wind, no clouds

Desert country, daytime

Another new species: the Autumnal Mottled Moth-Bat. Diminutive with large mottled white-and-black wings, delicate and beautiful. This bat hides its unusual hindwings under the cryptic forewings when resting. Antenna-like ears, attracted to the light of day. Diet consists of pollen and honeysuckle. The species overwinters as an egg. You would adore him, surely.

Bat flight

Bird flight

100 ft

20 ft

300 ft

Nest of Bats

Rabbit hole

Pit

apox 1 mile from mouth

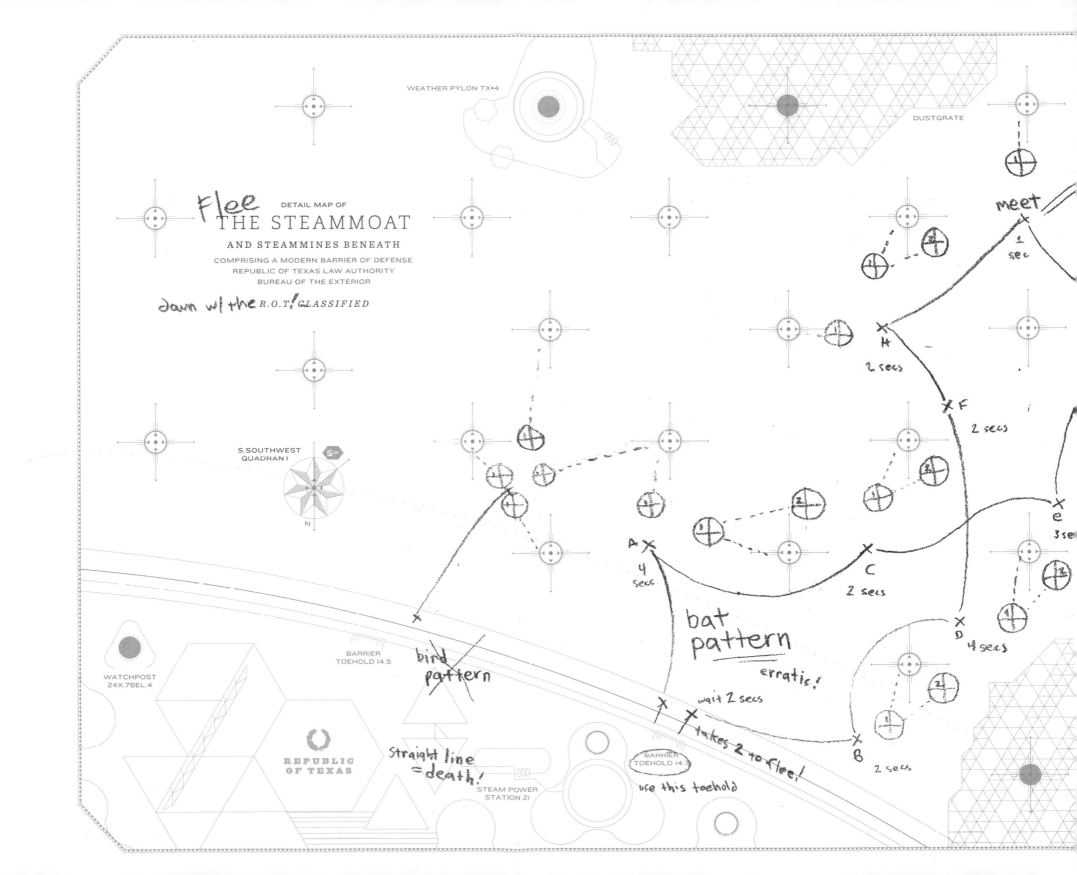

WEATHER PYLON TX•4

DUSTGRATE

Flee
DETAIL MAP OF
THE STEAMMOAT
AND STEAMMINES BENEATH

COMPRISING A MODERN BARRIER OF DEFENSE
REPUBLIC OF TEXAS LAW AUTHORITY
BUREAU OF THE EXTERIOR

down w/ the R.O.T.! CLASSIFIED

meet
1 sec

S.SOUTHWEST
QUADRANT

Sw

2 secs

H

F
2 secs

N

A
4 secs

C
2 secs

e
3 se

bat
pattern
erratic!

BARRIER
TOEHOLD 14.5

bird
pattern

D
4 secs

WATCHPOST
24X.76EL.4

wait 2 secs

straight line
=death!

takes 2 to flee!

REPUBLIC
OF TEXAS

BARRIER
TOEHOLD 14.7

B
2 secs

use this toehold

STEAM POWER
STATION 21

Cavern Map

Night way

xas room

Bat hand

Wing

Escape

right hand tunnel unexplored

1 mile

entrance

night way

N
W   E
S

texas room

bat's nest

rabbits

pit

Bird's Eye view

exit

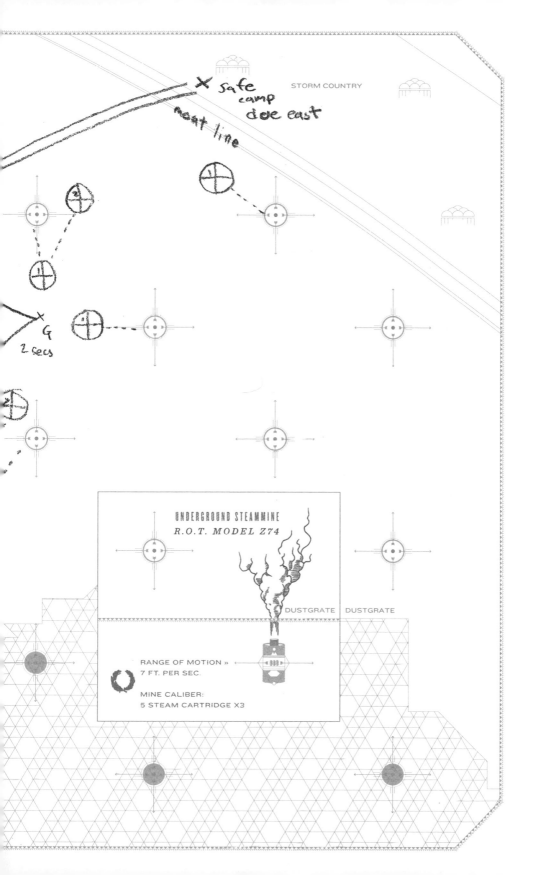

STORM COUNTRY

X safe
camp
doe east

moat line

G
2 secs

UNDERGROUND STEAMMINE
R.O.T. MODEL Z74

DUSTGRATE   DUSTGRATE

RANGE OF MOTION »
7 FT. PER SEC.

MINE CALIBER:
5 STEAM CARTRIDGE X3

Zeke and Raisin ran for a long time. They found the ladder and crawled out of the hatch door. The watchposts loomed above them, ominous shadows shifting along the platforms. "It'll take two of us to flee, according to this." Raisin studied the pamphlet's instructions for crossing the steammoat. Zeke brushed dust off the hatch door. The symbol of the wolf with the moon in its mouth was gone. Had they come out of another exit? A silhouette slid into the light of the watchpost. It was Eliza. Zeke's chest flooded with relief. She quickly made the hand signal for *escape*. Shrieking Law whistles filled the air. She ran. They ran after her. "Where are we going?" Raisin shouted in the blur of confusion. "Hurry up," Eliza shouted over her shoulder. She ducked down a narrow street with old plankways. It was not well lit by the phosphor lamps. She stopped running and began to move quickly along the sides of the units, sticking to the shadows. "It's an all-quadrant alert. Recorders in all the watchposts, no dead zones. I'm guessing it's for you," she spoke quietly. "The Auspices wouldn't let you out through their tunnel, would they?" "How do you know about — " Raisin started to ask. "Wait." As they emerged from the narrow street, Eliza held the hand signal up to Raisin and pulled Zeke into the half-light, just out of earshot. Her eyes were bright, and she studied Zeke's face carefully. He felt so thankful to see her, that it didn't even seem to matter that he was up top, in the open. She looked beautiful, the gentle glow of phosphor light soft on her skin. "Zeke, I have something to tell you." Worry lines formed at the edges of her eyes. "I took the letter." Zeke held his breath. "I was worried and I wanted to make sure you'd be safe. It was a mistake. I lost it, and made a false trail through the Vault. I don't know where it is now." **"Your note — "** Zeke began. "After I delivered Leeya to the Auspicium, I went back to

ESCAPE

the Vault. I wanted to find the letter. I found my father instead. " ∧∧ ∧∧ ∧∧ Zeke took her hands and held them. Strands of hair bisected her face in the sharp wind, a strand sticking to her softened lips. ∧∧ ∧∧ ∧∧ "You didn't know what was involved in that letter. Neither did I. You will always be my blood." ∧∧ ∧∧ Almost before he was done speaking Eliza had grabbed his torso tightly and squeezed with all her strength. And then they were kissing, desperately, passionately. It felt as though they hadn't had this kind of kiss in years. Grateful and sad and wild. It contained all the thankfulness of being reunited and the fear of what was to come. Zeke wrapped his arms around her. ∧∧ ∧∧ ∧∧ ∧∧ They were spotlighted. Law flashers, from the nearest watchpost. ∧∧ "Run!" Raisin loped toward them, panicked. ∧∧ ∧∧ Eliza pulled something from her pocket and slammed it to the ground. In a blink they were enveloped in a cloud of chalky white dust. The light scattered, and Zeke couldn't see anything. ∧∧ ∧∧ He felt Eliza grab his hand and pull him away. Moments later they were running down another side street. ∧∧ ∧∧ ∧∧ ∧∧ ∧∧ "What was that?" Raisin coughed. ∧∧ "Dustbomb," Eliza said. ∧∧ Raisin gave Zeke a look of astonishment as they scurried down the streets. Eliza made a sharp right turn, and they stopped to crouch in the doorway of the fountry. ∧∧ It was closed at night, and the archway provided just enough cover to keep them out of the light. The smell of the fount-water was strong. Raisin was winded. ∧∧ "We have to" — his words came slowly — "rescue Leeya" — in bursts of steam — "Auspices ... murder — " ∧∧ Eliza interrupted him. "She's safe with them. They shelter girls who are pregnant. She won't really join. She's just hiding out." ∧∧ ∧∧ ∧∧ "Could have..." Raisin's breathing was still labored, "...fooled me." ∧∧ ∧∧ "With the murderer still on the loose, she shouldn't be up top. There's a man in the tunnels called the Nightman..." ∧∧ ∧∧ "It's not him!" Raisin's shout caused another coughing fit. ∧∧ ∧∧

"Keep your voice down," Eliza hissed. ∧∧ ∧∧ ∧∧ ∧∧ Zeke finally interjected. "The Nightman is with the Deserters. He's strange, but he's not the murderer. He was trying to help us escape the city-state…" ∧∧ ∧∧ Raisin nodded vigorously, holding up the pamphlet. "…in a way." ∧∧ ∧∧ ∧∧ "Too dangerous. And open conflict would be bad for everyone. My father" — Eliza began to blink rapidly — "attacked Daxon. He was trying to find the letter. He's Queer, they banned him from talking to me. But … our meeting was recorded. They're after him. And I haven't seen him for so long." She looked at Zeke as though she might cry. ∧∧ ∧∧ A carrier slid by slowly. They froze. Its flashing lights briefly illuminated the doorway of the fountry, but it didn't stop. ∧∧ ∧∧ ∧∧ "We need to get off the plankways," Zeke said. ∧∧ ∧∧ "Let's go to Leeya's unit. That's where my father is." Eliza stepped out into the light. ∧∧ ∧∧ "Now." ∧∧ ∧∧ They followed her through a labyrinth of small winding streets. She seemed to know where to go to avoid the watchposts. They were in the singles' quadrant, the southeast. Raisin struggled to keep up. ∧∧ ∧∧ ∧∧ They turned a corner and she pulled them into Leeya's unit. The shades were drawn. A trickle of light from outside illuminated the room. Dark shapes slowly formed into furniture. ∧∧ ∧∧ ∧∧ Raisin was winded again. He looked upset about all the running. "How did you know about that hatch?" ∧∧ "Investigating the animal rumor. The Recorders have a high incidence of spotting them in that quadrant," Eliza said. ∧∧ ∧∧ "That can't be real," Zeke said. ∧∧ ∧∧ "According to the thread, a loose animal is an official suspect in the case. All the murders coincide with animal sightings. A little too neatly. The Major likes to claim there's a connection, but…" ∧∧ "…records can easily be falsified." Henry Bartle stepped into the room. "Thank the fates you all made it." He embraced his daughter and put a warm hand on Zeke's shoulder. "We're on the verge." ∧∧ ∧∧ "This is the man who tried to rob your place?" Raisin sneered. ∿ ∿ ∿ "That's my father, Raisin." Eliza seemed almost shy to say it aloud. Raisin closed his mouth. ∿ ∿ "Zeke, I want you to understand what's at stake, and I fear time is short." Bartle blinked. He didn't have his glasses. ∿ ∿ "I don't quite know how to put this ..." ∿ "You're being framed," Eliza said. "I went through everything. There's plenty against you in the records." ∿ Her eyes held his gaze. Now that they were next to each other, he could see — they were exactly like her father's. ∿ ∿ "Eliza picked up Daxon's trail through the records," Bartle said. "I was trying to break into his office at the Vault, to get the letter. And I got caught." ∿ ∿ Eliza's spine straightened. Zeke could tell that the thought made her nervous. ∿ "Bic was there. He caught me as I was collecting Daxon's blood and confronted me. I managed to get away, but they're hunting me. Daxon means to keep you from the Senate. He's trying to pin the murders on you." ∿ ∿ "Figures," Raisin said. "We're getting out of this city-state anyway, before the Republic locks us up." ∿ ∿ "How are you going to do that?" Bartle gave Raisin a considered look. ∿ "We're going to go over the barrier. We have a pamphlet, I mean, a plan." ∿ "Zeke, is this true?" ∿ ∿ Raisin spoke for him. "We're going to a Deserter hideout. We know someone on the outside. Spree, he's a —" ∿ "He's a little mad," Bartle said. "But I wouldn't say that's the worst plan. There's not much choice. Spree might know what to do about that letter. Better him than the Republic, certainly. We can't leave it behind, Zeke. I still think the letter is in Daxon's office. The only way to get in is with a drop of his blood. I have a phial full, but they're after me now. We hardly have any time left. Bic can't be trusted. He's in with Daxon somehow." ∿ "I want out." ∿ "Let's all just flee," Raisin said. "Why won't anyone listen to me?" ∿ ∿ ∿ ∿ ∿ ∿ ∿ "There's a whole city full of folks here. Zeke is their steward. That's what a Khrysalis is."

Bartle fumbled in his pocket. ⌁ "This is not a government I want to be a part of." ⌁ "None of us have a choice," Eliza said. ⌁ Raisin crossed his arms. ⌁ "The best way to save yourself, and my daughter, is to find that letter," Bartle said. "Daxon must be exposed. Zeke, I have something for you." He wheeled out a records cabinet. It was locked with steel clockwork. He keyed in a code. A drawer slid open. He produced an old leather-bound volume tied with string. It was the bundle of Zadock Thomas's letters, with Bartle's notes attached. ⌁ "It may be of use, if you can keep it secret and manage to read it all," Bartle said. "The records in the Vault have been altered. The Republic trades in lies. They are hiding something out in the storm country, something big. Everything in this file is an original." ⌁ "You can tell because in the carbons they took out the bats," Eliza said. ⌁ "The bats?" Zeke asked. ⌁ "You'll get to that part." She smiled. He wanted to kiss her again. ⌁ He slipped the bundle of papers into his sack. ⌁ "Zadock was a great — " Bartle's words were cut short by shrill steam whistles. Bright white light poured through the windows, flooding the room. Law flashers from outside. An amplifying tube sounded above the whistles. ⌁

"HENRY BARTLE, EXIT THE UNIT IMMEDIATELY BY ORDER
OF THE REPUBLIC OF TEXAS. YOU STAND ACCUSED OF
OBSTRUCTION OF BLOODLINES AND THE LAW."

⌁ "Run!" Bartle shouted. "Stay on the inside!" ⌁ He pushed them toward the back of the house. Eliza hesitated. Bartle pulled a phial of blood from his pocket. He lowered his voice to a desperate whisper. ⌁ "I've left a carbon for you in our secret file in the Vault." He handed the phial to her. "Follow the plan. Go!" he shouted, slamming the door after them. ⌁ Eliza scrambled through the back hall, phial in hand. Her eyes darted. Zeke and Raisin followed. ⌁ They climbed a wooden ladder in back. It led to the rooftop. The watchposts were manned with Lawmen. They shouted and pointed at the door. Many more encircled the front of the house. Steamsabres hissed to life. ⋀ ⋀ "I stole these from the Vault. In case something happened." Eliza opened a wooden box on the roof. She gave Zeke a handwheel. Two ornate handles formed the axis of a wide steel wheel. Zeke gripped it tightly. ⋀ Eliza pulled out two more and handed one to Raisin. Zeke looked at her. He felt his love for her swell. She had always been sharp, but he had never seen her act with such purpose. She fixed her handwheel on top of a steam-power line. ⋀ "The line's not powered," she said. It ran down to a watchpost a hundred yards from the unit. "It's not hot. Come on." ⋀ She pulled Raisin's hands to the handlebars and pushed him off the roof. He whizzed down the makeshift zip line. ⋀ **"What about your dad?"** Zeke asked. He gripped his own handwheel and balanced it on the steam pipe. ⋀ "He's got another way out. Go!" Eliza pushed him. She followed close behind. ⋀ ⋀ Zeke sliced through the night air. His eyes stung. He pulled his knees up to his chest and grasped the handles tightly. They flew dangerously fast down the line. Raisin was out in front. He kicked his legs, trying to slow down. ⋀ Raisin shouted. Zeke looked up to see a watchpost rush toward him. He let go, and fell. He hit the ground hard, bruising his heels. ⋀ "Dad!" Eliza shouted behind him. He turned to see her drop. The plankways were far below. Eliza hit them rolling. She was unharmed. She jumped up and looked back to Zeke. He felt her indecision empty his chest cavity. He opened his mouth, but it was too late. ⋀ Eliza ran back toward the pool of light, where a figure lay facedown on the ground. Bartle was being bolo-tied by Daxon, whose head was wrapped in a bandage. They were surrounded by Lawmen and typing Recorders. ⋀ Raisin lifted Zeke to his feet. Zeke tried to pull away, to follow Eliza. ⋀ "You can't save anybody if you're in jail," Raisin shouted. ⋀ He yanked Zeke's arm. ⋀ They ran in the opposite direction of the Law flashers. ⋀◇

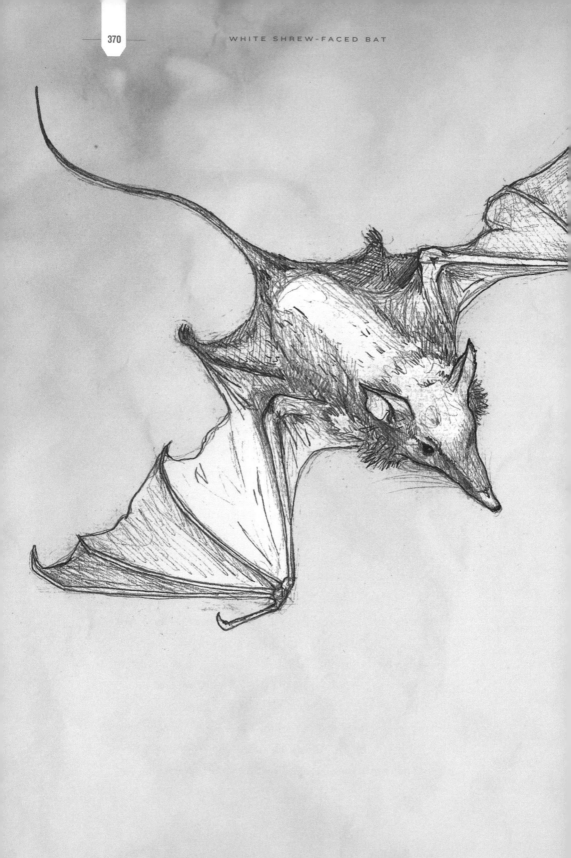

FAM. **SORICIDAE**

GEN. **LEPTONYCTERIS**

12.10.43, 9:15, 70 deg., 15 knots, few clouds

Mountainous desert region covered with small spiny grass and occasional prickly pear

Shrew Bat. Average size, grayish-white coat. Elongated face and tail. Hearty digging talons on the tips of wings. After observing cave bats for so long, I hoped again for another species I might document, and today my wish was answered. I believe I have found yet another bat that, if indeed unseen by any before me, will take its rightful place in the great Southwest Hall of the Museum of Flying. I imagine him a close cousin to the cave bats I now know so well. With a shrew-like face, all in white, he is a curiosity indeed. I am giving chase in the hope of finding his mates or nest. Why is this type so rare? Has his colony suffered a collapse, or are they carefully hidden from me? Perhaps this species can dig underground, like a shrew. Have their burrowing holes been added to over so many generations that the cave is a great hall of their making?

Dearest Elswyth,

I'm afraid my trip home has been stalled by some very unfortunate circumstances. I write with a heavy hand today, and a sore one, the reason for which will presently be clear. I do not mean to scare you, but prepare yourself—this letter may be unpleasant.

I napped in the last haunted hours of night. Before sunrise, the bats began to return in fits and spurts to their roosts on the roof of the cave. The Indian had gone to town for more supplies. The dawn is a time of great activity for the bats, and by the early light I continued my documentation, though I was alone.

The bats entered the cave in their looping patterns, gathering in bunches on the ceiling. The well-fed hung fat, like overripe grapes, nestling against one another, adjusting to the cool air of the cave. I was sketching these little clusters, the very picture of warmth and tenderness, perfect for a plate in the published version of my field guide, when something strange to the cave caught my eye: a white bat. I thought I might be seeing things, it was so small and quick.

I immediately followed it into the cave. The white bat flew past its bedded-down compatriots on the roof, a comet streak against a churning field of black. It had pink-tipped ears and a head and snout like a shrew. I am convinced it is some undiscovered species. This white bat was a trophy specimen heretofore unmatched even in my imagination. Every time it stopped, I would add a little to my sketch.

In my haste and craning to follow the bat in the little light available, I forgot the treachery of the cave floor and the crevices that crisscross it. This was my first mistake—inviting injury. It felt as though some bony hand reached up from the earth and pulled my foot into a narrow rut, snapping my ankle neatly as a twig.

My cry echoed for a long time and there was no longer any white bat, only sparks of pain flying around my vision. A broken ankle from hiking the Missouri plain or back home lunging for a touch while fencing would have been a nuisance. However, deep in the black of the cave, I knew immediately my life was in great peril.

I crawled back much of the way I had previously walked, a dirty and painful business. But if I hadn't been on my belly, I wouldn't have espied the small jag of light beckoning me. I'd like to recount that I bravely discovered a new exit to the cave, but in truth it was the only available and necessary one for a hobbled man. It was a tight crevice, but I managed to slide through, happy to return to the open night air.

Though it was a new way out, up on the surface I could easily see our tent. I had traveled no distance at all. However, my disappointment did not last, because what came next was truly terrifying.

Dawn had not yet broken. Light began to gather around the edges of the cacti and blister out into the sky. I heard the screams of a child and I thought for a moment that they were my own, some injury stored in my mind in the form of a terrible noise. I now wish the cry was of my own delirious imagining, but it was not.

A dark shape in the distance was slowly growing larger and blotting out the lightening horizon. It was loping toward me. Before I could take a breath, a beast was on me with fangs and fur and claws. Kicking with my one good leg and spinning wildly in the dust, I struck out with my broken foot, keeping my face covered with my arms for fear of being mauled. I have never been fearful of hounds, but the attack was mounted with such speed and ferocity, I began to think I would know what it was to be eaten alive by a growling living thing.

My loud cries must have hastened him on, but they would have been of no use had the Indian not been making for our camp already. I heard his warlike shout and there was a blast, like an egg full of gunpowder had been thrown to the ground, and the air was full of smoke. The Indian emerged, beating the beast back with a long pole of stripped yucca stalk. He continued an exhaustive attack with his improvised sword until the beast ran off, whimpering in the gray light.

It is to the Indian that I undoubtedly owe my ability to recount this story. I have lost much blood this disastrous day. I barely recall the Indian wrapping me in a saddle blanket and carrying me to the Mexican village. When I opened my eyes, I expected to see him by my side.

Instead, I was met with a surprise—Abril Rodriguez, attendant at my bedside. My pain immediately lessened. Our language barrier remained but it hardly mattered, so familiar she was to me. I was so relieved to see her all the way out in this forsaken place. My surprise still hasn't left me. She is far-winged indeed.

We asked questions crosswise for some time. I asked for Aunt Anne, but she didn't understand. I gathered that she had followed me here on her brother's orders. To my great astonishment she knew of the cave. She kept pointing to my injuries and asking rapid questions.

It took me a long time to puzzle out that "coyote" was the given name of the Indian (Abril called him Nocturno Coyote de Siete Colas) and not what had attacked me. She is a friend of the Indian and, not wanting to reveal herself, she hired him to look after me. I want to take umbrage at this, but after the results of my adventuring it is clear she was dead right to do so. I thanked her for the star map.

The creature that attacked me she named the chupacabra. I know cabra means goat, and told her how unlike this thing was to a goat.

I got overexcited, and she laid me back down in the bed to calm me. She made sure I was as comfortable as possible by applying to my wounds a salve made of a crushed plant whose English name she did not know. Her magic is potent. I thought if the cave would not serve, she could perhaps show me the way by which souls and birds travel, that my soul might come to meet yours, even as I lie infirm here.

Abril said that the Nightway is not easy, and to learn it would take me a long time indeed. My health would have to improve first, if I were to become a practitioner. She set to brew a tea from the peyote plant, which I first heard about from McMarrow's Indian scouts. They use it for religious visions of the soul, though it also lessens pain. Sleep must have taken me then, because when I looked over again Abril was gone. I'm left in the hovel of the village healer, an old wizened woman with black hair and a rabosa to match. With her shriveled hand she has spooned me bitter tea this past hour. My soul has had no vision, instead I feel bilious. But the tea helps with the pain. I am sitting now and able to write. Do not fret, I will safely recover here.

There were some other disturbing details I've discerned from fragments of Abril's Spanish. Apparently I am not the first victim of such an attack. She seems to describe many more in the village who have suffered similar wounds. I continued to repeat: coyote grande. Though it was unlike to the cagey fellow I drew near the pueblo. Perhaps the beast was a rabid or agitated specimen. The hair on a cat's back stands that it may present a more intimidating silhouette, so this could've been the strategy of some rankled or diseased coyote.

I tried to pantomime this hair-raising theory to Abril before she left. As I worked at my story, she pointed to a small table across the room, which holds the skull of what looks to be a peccary.

I remembered the skull I had discovered and realized my large sack was missing. Most of my other effects were, thanks to the Indian, under my sickbed. Including my bundle of letters for you.

The old woman began to speak about digging up graves. It seems someone has been disinterring the bodies of the dead and removing their hearts, though whether that is a crime or some service to the dead I was unable to clarify. This put the literal thought in my head of "an old wives' tale," though this tale is horrific no matter the teller.

The bites on my body are not severe; it is still my ankle that pains me the most. I felt I must relay these events to you, however gruesome. How will I ever return now? I must rest. It is small comfort to know that no nightmare could compare to this day's ordeal.

Your Soldier Survived, Zadock

BEGIN WATCHPOST TRANSCRIPT:

Z. THOMAS » I don't know if I should even go inside. What if they're waiting for me in there?

R. DEXTRA » We're definitely being recorded. Look.

R.D. INDICATES WATCHPOST TX 724

» Doesn't matter. They can type all they want. The Lawmen are all at Bartle's.

» Do you think they'll throw him over?

» Daxon had him in bolo-ties. I don't know what happened to Eliza.

FLAG▸ » This is getting bad. We should go get Leeya and flee right now. Tonight. ‹FLEE RISK

» I can't flee, Raisin.

» You have to. They have that letter. And Eliza. If they find you, they'll lock you up for murder. Think about it.

» Daxon will kill Eliza.

» He won't. She's valuable. She knows things he doesn't. But he's not going to let her go. She and her dad are going to stay locked up. At least until this city-state is overthrown. Even if the tunnels are blocked, the Deserters are still bringing the war. They've got the cannon. The Nightman told me. It was used against Atlantas, but they captured it on its way back to Texas. We'll all be free of this mad claustrotopia soon.

» And be out in the rot? Eliza has been abandoned too many times in her life. She ... I can't leave her here alone.

» You saw what just happened to Bartle. You can't get past Daxon.

» Unless I have something he wants. I should've never let the letter out of my sight. He's scared of it.

» Daxon has this whole place on lockdown. As long as the barriers are up and the Senate is clueless, he is going to do whatever he wants in this city-state.

» Bartle failed to prove how crooked Daxon is, but I can get it pasted on every broadsheet in the city-states. He deserves to have his authority stripped.

» Eliza took the phial of his blood, the key.

» I'll have to break the door down then.

» How are you even going to get in the Vault to begin with?

10 SECONDS SILENCE

» Eliza has extra uniforms. In our unit.

» I'm not running straight into the hands of the Law. They're trying to set you up. This is mad.

» No madder than going over the barrier.

» Fine. Then I'll find someone else to flee with. It'll be way easier than infiltrating the Vault, which is swarming with Lawmen. Without a key, even.

» Fine. Good luck in the rot.

» Good luck being a Republic prisoner.

SUBJECTS PART

END WATCHPOST TRANSCRIPT

Dearest Elswyth,

I have just wakened from the most fiendish dream. I took an extra measure of the peyote tea, to aid my sleep. My delirium is overtaking me and my head is hot while my legs shake with cold.

In the old woman's hovel I saw myself in a mirror, but there are no mirrors in this place. A man as real as any stepped into the dusty light. By his dress and stern demeanor I knew at once the apparition was McMarrow. Not knowing I was in a dream I tried to sit up, despite the pain.

"From where did you come?" I asked, my countenance disturbed. He adjusted his uniform, and this he said unto me:

"The body and the soul are separate, and though the body lies still the soul may journey far. This is not your deathbed, Zadock Thomas. You must rise. Your beloved is in grave danger. She is not lost to you. Fulfill your promise. Follow

Dearest Elswyth,

I have just awakened from the most fiendish dream. I took an extra measure of Abril's peyote tea, to aid my sleep. My delirium is overtaking me and my head is hot while my legs shake with cold.

In the old woman's hovel I saw myself in a mirror, but there are no mirrors in this place. A man as real as any stepped into the dusty light. By his dress and stern demeanor I knew at once the apparition was Irion. Not knowing I was in a dream I tried to sit up, despite the pain.

"From where did you come?" I asked, my countenance disturbed. He adjusted his uniform, and this he said unto me:

"Though a body lies still the soul may journey far. Rally your own soul. This is not your deathbed, Zadock Thomas. You must rise. Returning home will do no good. You must complete your errand to win your life and love. Follow the fates, which even the gods fear."

He spoke with such a grave timbre that I was moved to the core. Recovering myself, I reached under the bed to fish from my pack your father's letter, thinking here and now was the moment to deliver my burden unto him, but when I looked up he was gone and my bedroom had turned silver, the walls sparkling with a light like that of my bejeweled cave. Where Irion had stood there was now the distended and grotesque cavern skeleton, his frozen teeth leering at me, reaching for my ankle. I pulled the blanket over my head and woke up alone again in the old woman's hovel. In the dark, my stomach churning, I faced the skull of the peccary, the puppet of my fever dream.

Might a man of uniform be a soul walker like Aunt Anne or Abril? I have no other explanation for this visitation. I know not the hour, but await anxiously the break of day. Abril has not returned. I long for her to come back, not only for the sake of my wounds but so I can tell her of this visitation from the Nightway. I wait sleeplessly, the old woman's snores marking the minutes of this witching hour.

May I Only Ever Dream of You, Zadock

FAM. TAYASSUIDAE
GEN. PECARI

16.10.43, 3:45

Old woman's hovel

Peccary Skull. I cannot sleep, so I draw. These bristly black skunk pigs are only seen in this desert region. They are small and easily take fright at humans. Abril calls them Javelina. Though he is long perished, this is the only one I've seen close up.

It is October now.
How much longer will I live?

This hovel stinks of death in a way the cave never did.

Dearest Elswyth,

I am torn in two. Should I return to you now? Should I deliver your father's letter? I suppose both are impossible, as I am forced to lie here until my recovery is complete. I dreamt again of you, in peyote slumber. We were in the cave. All was dark and we were without physical bodies. Now that my life hangs by a thread, all I long for is you. You are all that has ever mattered. The realization that it was our souls that were meeting dawned just as I was awakened. Am I learning the Nightway? Did you, too, dream of us together?

As soon as I opened my eyes, Abril began speaking rapidly. I tried to tell her of Irion's visit and his message about delivering the letter before returning home. She would not be interrupted and her voice began to take the character of hysteria.

I understood that my pack, containing the human skull, had been discovered by the cave. What I could not figure was why she kept pointing very deliberately to the phial of your blood around my neck.

"Otra hija," she said. "Muerte en desierto. No sangre." She touched the phial on my chest and I began to understand. A girl was drained of blood. I carried the evidence around my neck. My wounds told a story of struggle and death. My bag contained a skull.

"Vamonos." Abril attempted to pull my arm toward the door. I refused, explaining the condition of my ankle, and how I had been plagued with fever dreams that could strike at any moment. I could hardly sit up, let alone walk. She continued to prod in a most determined fashion, pulling the serape over my head.

I refused to move, as I am in no state for travel. If murder charges were to be brought against me, any civilized court would allow my recovery before bringing me to trial. I am no monster. Violence between men is abhorrent to me, doubly so toward innocents.

The more I tried to explain all this to Abril, the more exasperated she became. She foresaw great violence overtaking the village.

Then an idea flashed across her face like a shooting star. She pulled my sketchbook from my sack and repeated "chupacabra" until I understood. I hastily gave form to the shapes I had seen in the dark the night of my injury. Though my hand was shaky, I managed a vision of the true perpetrator of these attacks. It was a brilliant idea: I could not be the scapegoat when this vile creature was on the prowl.

Chupacabra, I labeled it, and Abril carried out her plan. "El vampiro," she said, and took it along with a few of my other drawings to show the court, or village elders, those men who had come for me when I had sliced the bucket from the village well. If they have the charge of maintaining order, it should serve them to take me at my word. I sent my letter of introduction and calling card from the museum, that they might see I was a man of learning and of Naturalism, here to document this territory. I had fallen prey to the same beast that plagues their village. I was not the murderer but rather a victim.

Abril has just departed to deliver the message. I feel sure that she can tell my story in a sympathetic way. I told her to say that the creature tried to drink my blood, to liken him to whatever has attacked the girls of this village. It had hairy hands, not unlike to a monkey's, which it used ferociously. She has seen my wounds, which strengthen my case.

The phial of your blood, on the other hand, does not. Abril was much perturbed to see it. I am now left on my own to destroy this evidence. It pains me, as it is the one token I have borne all this way, a small piece that holds your heart close to mine. If I had my way I would die with it around my neck. But if I am to clear my name and claim my health, then I must rid myself of it.

Was it the phial that allowed you to visit my dreams last night? I cannot bear to destroy it in another way, so I will drink it now and hope that it gives me the strength of my love.

I Beg the Forgiveness of All, Zadock

◇◇ ⌃⌃ Raisin walked away. Zeke walked in the opposite direction, pulling his brimhat low, and kept to the walls. He didn't want to be seen. ⌃⌃ ⌃⌃ ⌃⌃ As he wove his way back to the northeast quadrant, he began to think about home and everything he and Eliza had shared before it was all turned upside down. He hadn't embraced the quiet of his life, or the peacefulness of simply waiting. He had wished for adventures, like those in the histories. Or those in the stories that his grandfather would tell of the Collapse and the birth of the city-states. There seemed to be no possible way to take the Senate seat now. ⌃⌃ ⌃⌃ ⌃⌃ ⌃⌃ ⌃⌃ ⌃⌃ ⌃⌃ Zeke had to decide what to do. He wasn't about to turn himself in. But Raisin had a point: Walking into the Vault and trying to enter Daxon's office would very likely have the same result. Yet the letter was there. ⌃⌃

⌃⌃ He needed to think. He walked down a narrow alleyway. The walls of various units jutted out from every angle, boxing him in. There were crawl spaces to air ducts and swinging hatch doors that revealed impossible configurations of steampipes and phonotubes. Many were coated with dust, clockworks choked up, screws loose after hasty construction. This alleyway was his favorite dead zone. It was completely shielded from the surrounding watchposts. He sat, glad to be alone. He used his finger to write in the dust. ⌃⌃ Hope diminishes in proportion to choice. ⌃⌃ ⌃⌃ ⌃⌃ ⌃⌃ ⌃⌃ ⌃⌃ ⌃⌃ Laudanum would have helped. Zeke had not slept. His feet ached. His thoughts spun in circles. He could not remember the last time he'd had a cup of fount-water. His health must be failing. ⌃⌃ ⌃⌃

⌃⌃ He remembered all the nights Eliza had been ill. More from anxiety than any physical ailment. She would dream of her father and wake up in a sweat. He would hold her as she trembled or cried herself back to sleep. She never remembered much in the morning, but he carried every night with him. The only way to get Eliza out was to go to jail himself. They couldn't both be free. ⌃⌃ ⌃⌃ ⌃⌃

〜〜 He would get the uniform. 〜〜 〜〜 〜〜 〜〜 〜〜 〜〜 〜〜 〜〜

〜〜 There were no Lawmen guarding his unit, a bit surprising. He walked around to the front and slid open the door. The shades were pulled. Dark piles lined the floor. There was no one in the livingroom.

〜〜 〜〜 He heard a scratching in the bedroom. He tread quietly. Someone was there. Keeping along the walls, he slowly peeked into the bedroom. Something strange and dark was moving about on the floor. An animal. 〜〜 〜〜 〜〜 〜〜 〜〜 A choking yelp involuntarily escaped from Zeke's throat and he jumped back out of the doorway. It couldn't be an animal, it must be a person, hunched over. He heard more scrambling, and looked back in just in time to see the shape clamor out the bedroom window, tearing the shade down behind it.

〜〜 〜〜 〜〜 He ran to the sill and looked out over the plankways. There was nothing to be seen, neither man nor animal. He sat down on the floor mat, his heart flapping in his chest. It was too dark to know what he had seen. 〜〜 〜〜 He wanted to turn on the lights but didn't want to attract attention to his unit. The watchposts were certainly keeping an eye on it. 〜〜 〜〜 〜〜 He fumbled his way to the closet and fished out one of Eliza's brown Vault uniforms. He slipped off his clothes and tugged on the brown uniform. It was definitely too small, but he managed to squeeze into it. 〜〜 〜〜 〜〜

〜〜 〜〜 As Zeke began to button it up he heard something, the same sort of scratching, this time at the front door. He thought of the sabre on the mantel. He rushed back into the livingroom to arm himself. 〜〜 〜〜 The front door was open and the flickering phosphor light framed a dark silhouette. Fear flashed through Zeke's chest. For a moment it seemed like the animal had gone around and beat him to the front door, ready to pounce. But it was Bic, out of breath. He was holding the sabre. 〜〜 〜〜 〜〜 〜〜 〜〜 〜〜

〜〜 〜〜 〜〜 〜〜 〜〜 〜〜 "Bic. What are you doing...Did you see something outside?" 〜〜 "This place is a mess." Bic kicked his way into the room. "I know you're running from the Law. I'm here to turn you in." 〰 〰 〰 〰 〰 **"Why would you do that?"** 〰 〰 〰 "For credit, I guess. Either way, Daxon will find you and arrest you. There's no way out of the city-state." 〰 〰 **"I wasn't trying to leave."** 〰 〰 〰 〰 〰 "I know you've been in the tunnels." 〰 〰 〰 Zeke studied Bic. His cousin knew more than he had been letting on. 〰 〰 "The tunnel out is sealed. The Auspex recruits have all met…untimely ends. The Auspices are scared. As they should be. They've sealed up the tunnel so nothing can harm their precious flock. But the time has come for all of them. They thought they could save themselves by stealing Daxon's cannon and hiding it underground. But he'll find it. They've been holding sway over the Law for too long. Lording over us all with their fount-water." 〰 〰 **"Daxon has been manipulating you. He means to eliminate the Senate. Not just me."** 〰 〰 〰 "You're not the only one with the blood to claim that seat. And now you never will. The fact that you're wearing a Vault uniform means you're up to something. That's not your rank." Zeke looked down at the tightly stretched brown uniform. "Or your size." 〰 〰 〰 **"I'd like my sabre back."** Zeke's voice was calm. Bic shot him a false grin. 〰 〰 〰 〰 "You're a disgrace to this family. You're headed for jail. And you never should have been named Khrysalis in the first place. You couldn't take care of the letter —" 〰 **"How do you —"** 〰 Bic raised his voice, not allowing Zeke to interrupt his tirade. 〰 〰 "You don't even know how to take care of this sabre. The bloodline can't be entrusted to you. I am the Khrysalis now." 〰 Bic's eyes burned with hatred. Zeke considered his cousin. His pride was more wounded than Zeke had thought. He was cornered, dangerous. A thought occurred to Zeke, like lightning shooting down a weather pylon. 〰 "OK," Zeke said, "you're **Khrysalis, then. I cede to you."** 〰 Bic looked suspicious. It was not the reaction he'd expected. He had been ready for a fight. "You do?" "Sure," Zeke said. "I was never much cut out for it. I don't like politics, I don't like crowds. You'd be a much better leader than I would." "That's what I've always said." "Gram is the only one with the authority to declare you Khrysalis though." "She barely knows who she is," Bic said. "Even so, that's the law. I guess we'll have to talk to her." His grandparents had fought Correctors and Lawmen and those who were corrupt in the government their entire lives. Senator Thomas's time in power had been rife with controversy and political maneuvering on the part of his enemies. In the end, his grandparents lost many skirmishes. But they won some important ones too. The barriers were erected, all records were taken from the citizens and duplicated, and the lifephases were implemented. Atlantas had been a difficult battle. But his grandfather hung on till the end. The Senator knew how to fight. And if he could keep his enemies from destroying him completely, then his wife would have the right to name a Khrysalis. "Let's call her right now." "OK," Zeke replied. "You'll tell her you cede to me?" "Call her." Bic picked up the phonotube. He started to dial, then paused. "I know the number," Zeke offered. Bic reset the phonotube, and Zeke slowly recited the numbers while his cousin punched them in. The phonotube clicked. The echo of a whistle rang down the semaphore line. Zeke imagined his grandmother shuffling through her house, past the old dusty portraits and doilied end tables. He hoped she was relatively alert today. She was slow to answer the phone. "Hello, this is Annlyne." Bic wasted no time launching into his story. "Gram, Zeke is in trouble with the Law. His place has been ransacked.

His pair and her father have been arrested. Zeke probably will be too, any minute now. He's disgraced the bloodline, lost Gramp's letter, and can't be trusted with his sabre any longer. I am here to pick up the pieces. I think you have always known that I should be Khrysalis, and now that Zeke has agreed, the only formality left is for you to —" ∿ "Someone wants that letter?" ∿ Zeke chimed in, shouting toward the phonotube. "The Law. They want to frame me. They took Henry Bartle," Zeke said. ∿ He picked a lamp up off the floor of his unit and set it back on its table. ∿ "I'm going to try to get it back, Gram." ∿ "No time. You have to get out of there now. Leave Eliza, leave the letter. Flee the city." Zeke's grandmother's speech was quick and lucid. "Any way you can." ∿ ∿ ∿ He had never heard her voice sound this way. Bic turned away slightly, his head tipped back, his mouth hanging open in shock. Zeke pulled the phonotube out of his loose grip. ∿ ∿ ∿ "I was going to flee with a friend, but he's gone. Won't I … I'll die in the rot alone." ∿ "You'll be fine. I lived in the storm country for years." ∿ ∿ Zeke joined Bic in surprise. "You did? Wh—" ∿ "But I was speaking of the tram, dear. I'll hold your clearance open. Can you do that?" ∿ ∿ "Yes." Zeke felt electrified. His grandmother seemed to understand everything immediately. ∿ ∿ ∿ "You come to Chicago-Land right away. You've got clearance. Do you understand?" ∿ ∿ ∿ ∿ "I'm not sure if I can get —" ∿ "Zeke, you are in danger. The daily tram leaves soon. Bic?" ∿ ∿ ∿ Bic nodded, forgetting she couldn't see him. ∿ ∿ ∿ ∿ "He's here," Zeke said, pressing the phonotube back into Bic's hand. ∿ ∿ ∿ ∿ ∿ "Bic, I want you to find Eliza. You tell Major Daxon that I immediately order the release of her and her father both, and I'll have the Senate come down on him if he fails to comply. She is to receive special escort to the Auspicium. Do you understand?" ∿ ∿ ∿ ∿ ∿ ∿ ∿ Bic just nodded again. ∿ ∿ ∿ "Bic, dear, I'm serious. Do you understand what you must do?" "Yes, yes, sorry. I'll go." Bic didn't know how to disobey her. "But what about who gets to be Khrysalis?" "There is no time for that now. Go…this instant!" Her voice almost cracked under the strain. That seemed to wake Bic up. He bounded out the door, sabre still in hand. "Zeke, dear, are you still there?" Zeke picked the phonotube back up. "Listen, I'll have the Senate call Major Daxon as well. Then he'll know the National Alliance is listening in on him. When you get here we'll start assembling our case. Your grandfather would be sorry to miss this one." **"Eliza should go to the Auspices?"** "Those are my Sisters, Zeke. They will protect her. The government and the Auspices have always been the two hands that have steered this broken civilization. That is the best place for her. If she is to be your wife, she'll need to start learning their ways. When I joined the Auspices I had to undergo years of mental and physical training. We were the first drinkers of the fount-water, a highly concentrated form that aids conditioning. It is difficult to learn how to drink. My Sisters are masters of alchemy, subtle narcotics, and bloodlines. After the Collapse, when so many starved, they learned to control their inner alchemy and the functions of their organs. It can be a painful process, but I also gained mastery of my metabolism. None can poison me, and I can extend my mortal years far beyond those of most folks. But that may not do us any good now, if Daxon can't be stopped. He never should have been appointed, and we can't let him keep control any longer." **"But why…how did you—"** "Dear, I know you have questions, but I really must hang up and call some Senators right away." Zeke's skin tingled. "It's going to be OK, dear. But I need you to look alive. That tram is leaving in twenty-four minutes. You need to get out."

Elswyth—I fear the plan has not worked. Abril has just returned. No language was needed to communicate the fact that the elders did not believe me. They seek to cast stones of blame at a suitable murderer.

Perhaps they are right. What if the thing that attacked me in the night was not a bloodthirsty chupacabra but rather a man in wolf's clothing? Were those horrible hairy hands I saw simply a hallucination in the low light? A creature that size could not subsist on blood. A bat is the largest species to drink blood. All the other blood-drinkers are bleeding leeches, vampire moths, flying or crawling insects, all with their attendant violent societies and little internal horrors.

Abril has just opened the window for me to see. There is a mob of villagers, brown robes curling in the violent wind. They carry torches. They are coming for me. Now. Would that I were invisible...

I will keep writing until the end. I hope this bundle of letters finds you. They all bear the address of your father's museum. If there are enough plates, publish my book after my death. The proceeds may be the only way I could help you now. Everything I have undertaken was done for you...

Rifle shots. I would not have guessed this town had firearms. Out the window—the mob has been met by an army, mounted on steeds. The Mexicans? Abril is latching the door...The shots are deafening...

Under the bed now...horror...a soldier struck the butt of his rifle against the door. I hid here, trying to pull Abril to safety. She insisted on confronting him, said that she had a charm. He broke in...Abril had no time. I couldn't even call out. In an instant he had sliced her throat and spilt her lifeblood on the floor. In front of me is only a crumbled black rabosa with a hand reaching out, curled in death like Aunt Anne's...

I am still hiding, like a coward. I know him. It is the man with the bared teeth. McMarrow's old troop. If only the Major is with them, I might be spared. Oh fates, what are you...

Rifle shots. I would not have
guessed this town had firearms.
Out the window — the mob has
been met by an army, mounted on
greyhounds. The Mexicans?

Abril is latching the door...

The shots are deafening...

Under the bed now. horror...

a soldier struck the butt of his rifle
against the door. I hide under the
bed, trying to pull Abril in safely.
She insisted on confronting him, said
that she had a charm. ~~He~~ broke in

Abril had no time I couldn't
even call out. In an instant he had
sliced her throat and spilt her life
blood on the floor, before me

I am still hiding, like a coward

I know him.
It is the man w/ the bared teeth

McMurrow's old troop. If only
he is with them   I might be spared

Oh Flater, what were you —

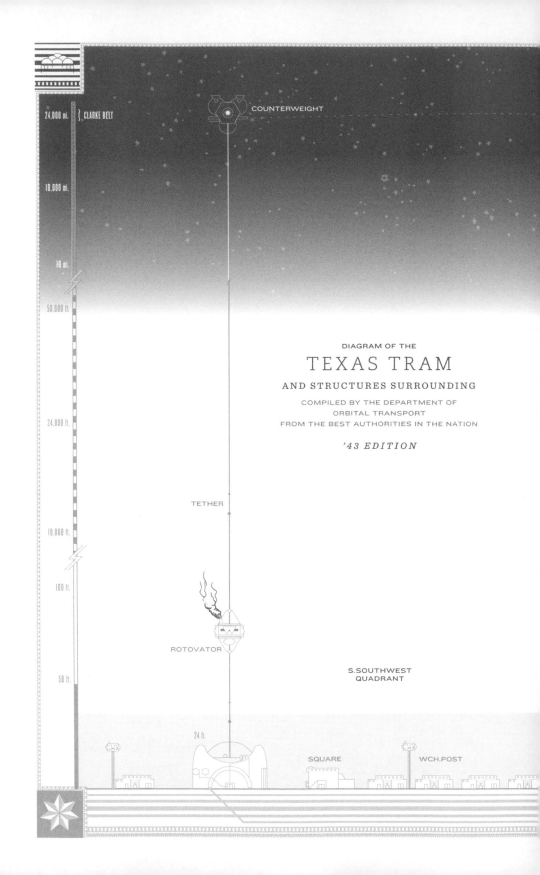

24,000 mi. } CLARKE BELT

10,000 mi.

10 mi.

50,000 ft.

24,000 ft.

10,000 ft.

100 ft.

50 ft.

COUNTERWEIGHT

DIAGRAM OF THE

TEXAS TRAM

AND STRUCTURES SURROUNDING

COMPILED BY THE DEPARTMENT OF
ORBITAL TRANSPORT
FROM THE BEST AUTHORITIES IN THE NATION

'43 EDITION

TETHER

ROTOVATOR

S.SOUTHWEST
QUADRANT

24 ft.

SQUARE

WCH.POST

GEOSYNCHRONOUS ORBIT

STATITE CAR   SOLAR SAILS

24 hr. ROUND-TRIP

WEATHER
PYLON

48 ft.

BARRIER   STEAMMOAT   STORM COUNTRY

◇◇ ∿ Zeke hurried down the plankways, trying to remain hidden. He pulled his jacket around his shoulders. The morning light was beginning to color things in. The wind squeaked anxiously through the gaps between units. ∿ ∿ ∿ The phosphor lamps were dimming. Something else was pulling a lot of steam power. Zeke walked toward the city-center. ∿ ∿ ∿ His grandmother had concocted a plan quickly. Sometimes she was cloudy, but she was never wrong. His mind still reeled at the thought of her as an Auspex, so familiar with the strange ways of those women. ∿ ∿ The tram to Chicago-Land made him anxious on the best of days. He thought about the court case they might assemble. He hadn't done anything against the law. A minor vandalism. A deadline for one uncarbon'd document. His grandmother must know good Defenders. He could get his record corrected once and for all. ∿

∿ ∿ ∿ ∿ The main watchpost at city-center slipped into view. Its silver time and date clockwork read 06:10, OCTOBER 22. Zeke stopped. Two days till the deadline. He had lost track. The letter was due soon. ∿ He walked faster. The plankways creaked in time with his heartbeat. His grandmother was serious about the danger he was in. He couldn't puzzle it out on his own, so he would return to Chicago-Land. His grandmother must know what the letter contained. ∿ ∿ ∿ Zeke entered the tram terminal. He crossed to the ticket bays under the time board. Seven city-states, six trams:

♄	CITY-LAKE OF LEAD (CHICAGO-LAND)	06:24
☉	CITY-STATE OF THE SUN (MONTANA-LAND)	07:12
☿	CITY-PORT OF MERCURY (PORT-LAND)	08:48
♀	CITY-STATE OF COPPER (TWIN-CITY)	14:20
♂	CITY-STATE OF IRON (ATLANTAS)	- -: - -
♃	CITY-LAKE OF TIN (SALT-LAKE)	16:42

A girl lifted the window of the ticket bay. "Can I help you?" Zeke fumbled in his jacket for tram fare. "Next tram in ten." She smiled politely. ⌇ The Nightman had taken all his greenbacks. "Can you...put it on the account of Annlyne Thomas? She'd be my clearance referent." ⌇ "Just a sec." Zeke held his breath. Daxon could have a block on his travel. Her nimble fingers found his file quickly. She punched a card. A carbon repeater whirred behind her. "Got it. Here's a ticket. Gate 7." There was no block. But that repeater might tip off the Vault that he was trying to leave the city-state. ⌇ ⌇ Zeke walked toward the docking gates. He slipped the ticket into his pocket. ⌇ "Hey." There it was. Caught. Zeke turned around. "Gate 7 is that way," the ticket girl said. He exhaled. He wandered over to the broadsheet postings, but couldn't make sense of the news. He hadn't slept in days. He needed to sit. ⌇ He picked a long white bench. It gave him a clear view of the open ceiling. He would see the tram come in. No one was in the terminal. The sun was scaling the eastern edge. Hazy light caught the carbon fibers of the tram tether, lighting it brilliantly. ⌇ Zeke folded his jacket under his head. He lay down on the bench. It felt good to rest. It had been a long time since he was still. He found his finger tracing out words. ⌇ Once I was as still as I was meant to be. ⌇ His eye followed the tether up. It disappeared high up. The cable winked in the sun. Each time he sat up, it looked like the steam rotovator might be getting closer. ⌇ ⌇ Zeke liked ascending and descending on the tether. The silver rotovator was spacious. He would look out the thick windows. Chicago-Land was the biggest city-state. Floating above it, he could see the lake, the clustered units, the dull and beaten barrier. ⌇ Zeke didn't like passing from one city-state to another. The statite car scared him. The inside was cold and white. It was uncomfortable being shut in with other passengers, barely able to move. Though he dreaded traveling by tram, now he was anxious to board and be whisked away from Texas as quickly as possible. ⌒ On tram flights the statite car hovered on solar sails in geosynchronous orbit. The Earth rotated below, blackness above. The only good thing about the ride would be the stars. Zeke could always see so many, arranged in fascinating new constellations. The steam thrusters would scream, then fall silent. Ten minutes stretched long, but that's all it took to traverse the continent. ⌒ If everything worked. He was scared of tram malfunctions. ⌒ Zeke felt himself drifting to sleep on the bench. He only wished that Eliza was with him. That they would descend into Chicago-Land together. They'd be well-received at his grandmother's home, comfortable and warm. ⌒ A commotion woke him. Shouting from the terminal entrance. Zeke sat up and looked over the back of his bench. ⌒ "That's him!" The ticket girl pointed at him. ⌒ ⌒ A mob of Law uniforms stormed into the terminal. Major Daxon was leading them, bandage still wrapped around his head. Bic must have reported his plan to the Law. The Lawmen ran toward him, unholstering their steamsabres. ⌒ Zeke took off, leaving his jacket on the bench. He skidded across the polished wood floor. Daxon shouted at him to stop. ⌒ The public entrances to the terminal were covered by Lawmen. Zeke made for the emergency doors to the tram platform. He slid them open. The scream of an alarm whistle sounded. Safety-suited workers waved their arms in confusion. Zeke still wore a Republic uniform. He ran across the platform. He could have been steam-cooked but the rotovator wouldn't land with workers on the platform. ⌒ Zeke ran toward the wall that ringed the terminal. His feet were sore. Each step shot pain up through his ankles. He glanced behind him. The tram workers had triggered the emergency locks. Angry Lawmen stood at the glass doors, pounding. Daxon shouted at the workers. ⌒ Zeke reached the edge of the platform field. He scrambled over the short white wall, exhausted, and started running again. ⌒

ATCHPOST OF THE WEST

EXAS REPUBLICAN

OSON, PUBLIC PRINTERS.] OCTOBER 22nd '43 [TERMS—$5 PER ANN., IN AD ANC

The Evensong Ritual

BY ABNER KUYKENDALL
Special to The Republican

At the close of a mid-summer's day but a month ago, I had the high honor of entering the new church of Texas.

I was guided by a Nighthual, a grave man, who led me to the secret entrance of the underground church. I was irresistibly led along the tracks of animals to the temple of the living waters. I asked my guide why there should be only the tracks of animals leading to the sacred place, and did they not keep them there, and he revealed nothing. He wore the appropriate uniform but his face and manner were that of the silent Indian. He revealed that the auguring of birds had led them to this place, and that one must be careful to differentiate between the classes of birds whose direction across the sky foretold things and the classes of bird, such as owls, ravens, waterfowl, and nightjars, through which the fates spoke in song.

We entered the underground chamber at the hour of Vespers, as the last of the day's light slid below the horizon. The priestesses knelt at the altar, which overflowed with water. There were not but two or four persons in witness besides those who officiated at the altar, and they were cloaked besides. Other requisites of the church — the organ or choir or cross — were nowhere to be seen. Above the altar a window of flickering light reached to a height of twenty-some feet, though the source of the light was a mystery as we had seemingly descended far below the earth. The window was grated with iron, wrought in beautiful shapes, and before it a long white drapery hung, thin and listless.

The priestesses now began the service and their voices were scarcely heard, so cavernous was the chamber. Presently, the other female voices swelled forth in equalled harmony, an evening Hymn to the darkness. I started — never before had I heard such chanting.

Presently my guide rose to the altar and shocked me by taking the central place. Clouds of dust rose about him, and I first thought I saw his shadow shift into the shapes of other creatures. While they chanted their fateful numbers and struck chords of silver it seemed he turned from man to animal. I realized I must have been mistaken and the Nighthual was simply placing various animals upon the altar to be blessed by the priestesses before slaughter.

As I gazed at the white curtain I saw light bending behind it, and became satisfied

BAT GUANO: THE NEW BLACK GOLD

Natural Fertilizer and Gunpowder Found in Bracken

C.G Fordtran & Co. have a new lucrative business in our land of Texas — the mining of bat droppings from

Dearest Elswyth,

I am alive. I fear my last letter was alarming. You should receive all of these at once, if I ever find a post. It was a close scrape, but this brief note will serve as proof of my life. I am on the march, albeit doing no marching of my own.

The attacker was indeed the man with the bared teeth, and all of McMarrow's disgraced company besides. They are wearing Republic of Texas army uniforms, the initials R.O.T. embroidered on the sleeves with the patterns denoting rank. I pointed at these and the man with the bared teeth simply said "We turned" through his missing lip.

The militia attacked the village that I was in last night. They had spied the mob from an encampment along the mountains, and rode down quickly to disperse them with their rifled muskets. They shouted and cursed while raiding the town, setting fire to the buildings using the villagers' own torches.

The Texian men are armed to the teeth. Even their sabres are like machines. My own sabre is no longer by my side. It was lost in the fracas at the village, a bitter thought I must accept, for it seems the fates have conspired to render me defenseless.

The militia have terrific guns. They were loaded with grapeshot, usually reserved for hunting quail. The death spray of that ammunition made a carnage of the villagers, and many were injured horribly.

Abril had no such luck. I cannot compel the scene of her death to leave my mind's eye. Its horror replays again and again, even whilst I am asleep. I feel her soul's absence. What will I ever tell Rodriguez?

I feel deep despair at these events though I am saved by them.

The man with the bared teeth, along with another soldier, carry me on a gurney through this uneven stony terrain. This is due to my ankle, which still will not tolerate walking. It is a small mercy that I find myself as deadweight rather than simply dead.

I do not like to talk to Abril's murderer, but he sees fit to talk to me. Without his lower lip, he has no b's or p's. It is difficult to look at him, much less listen to him. He had heard a white man was living out by the old cave. The mention of it set my spirits tumbling. Perhaps the cave is a known place after all, and I'm not its pioneering colonist.

They learned I was bedded down in the village, and decided I had been taken prisoner by the Mexicans, so they set about rescuing me.

I asked if they were under the command of General Irion, and might they take me to him. He gave a choking laugh at this, though I'm not sure why. He said that Irion could be found, spittle on his lips. I did not like the way he said it, so I did not press my inquiry further.

The territory changes by the hour, the desert slowly giving way to rugged hills with just enough topsoil to hold small mesquite brush and knotted live oaks. The men do not talk much, but when they do, it is clear their missions are of their own devising—arranged chiefly for personal pleasure or gain. I doubt that they are indeed of the Republic of Texas army but rather wear those skins to carry out their freebooting. When no one was looking, I sewed Irion's letter into a pocket inside my shirt, using a bit of thread from the gurney.

I asked where we might be marching to, and the man with the bared teeth halted the whole troop. They all turned to look at me, on the gurney, on the ground. "S'pose you'd like to tell us where to go?" He drooled. "We'll take you home to your rotten cave, or you can come with us. Might find what you're looking for." The men all laughed at this. He then assigned another soldier to carry his end of the gurney and resumed his place at the head of his band of highwaymen.

I have no choice, of course. I am hobbled. But if Irion is nearby perhaps there is some small hope left. If I do nothing else before I die, I might complete the errand I set out to do and aid your father in his urgent communication to his friend. Irion must be near, it is as though I feel him waiting there, along the Nightway.

                 Broken but Yours Alive, Zadock

FAM. STRIGIDAE

GEN. PAVO

20.10.43, 23:15, 80 deg., 20 knots, 3/10ths cloud coverage, humidity

Low rolling hill country. More plentiful shrubbery. Some small trees

Plumed Owlette. One foot tall, excluding tail feathers. Mottled gray with bright purple plumes and wing tips. Tonight, just outside camp, I heard the most unusual birdsong, a cry much like the hoot of an owl but in a higher register, a falsetto sounding a lonesome and solitary note over and over again. In the low brush I found its source, a new bird of prey. She is similar to, if a little smaller than, other owlettes I had observed burrowing into cacti near Santa Fe, save one major difference: her resplendent plumage. I could not miss on first glance the large wispy feathers trailing from her ears in two graceful crescents, an iridescent royal purple which caught the moonlight quite sorrowfully. I cannot figure their purpose in a seemingly nocturnal bird. How could such markings attract a mate in the dead of night? I felt sad for this desert nightingale, alone in the dark with only her own beauty.

Zeke awoke to Eliza's voice. She was singing softly. He had the sense of being in a dream. But he found himself in a bed, awake. He didn't know where he was. He sat up. The air was dank, the smell familiar. The room came into focus. He was underground. The Nightman wasn't there. ⌇ ⌇ Eliza sat upright in a chair next to him. She studied him, concerned. ⌇ ⌇ "I feel zonked," Zeke said. ⌇ It took a minute to register that seeing Eliza in the tunnels was surprising. He reached out for her hand, grasping it hard. She wasn't in jail. He wished he could hold on to the moment. The two of them alone in the dim light. Seeing the emotion in his face, Eliza gently crawled into bed next to him, careful not to disturb his sore body. ⌇ ⌇ ⌇ "I'm glad you're safe," they said, almost at the exact same time. The coincidence prompted a smile. ⌇ Safe, holding hands. Heard, inside a voice. ⌇ The morning started to return in fragments. Zeke had run from the tram back to the industrial quadrant. He'd found the hatch with the wolf and moon. He'd felt his way along the tunnel until he heard Raisin's voice in the dark, and knocked on the door of the Nightman's room. ⌇ ⌇ ⌇ ⌇ Raisin had been surprised to see him. The Nightman was not. Raisin's anger had dissipated, and it was as though their earlier argument hadn't happened. Once Zeke calmed down, he'd told part of his story. Raisin was excitable. He showed Zeke more of the Nightman's pamphlets. He thought one proved the weather pylons harnessed the energy from lightning to activate the city-state's secret time machines. He tried to convince Zeke to flee with him, according to the directions on the pamphlet. ⌇ ⌇ ⌇ ⌇ Apparently he had gone to see Leeya in the Auspicium again, and she had refused to be his pair in fleeing. He had been waiting for another pair. Lots of folks were going underground now, joining the Deserters. Raisin hadn't mentioned that Eliza was also in the tunnels. ⌇ ⌇ "What time is it?" ⌇ "It's 7:42.

You've been out for twelve hours. Or more." ∧∧ ∧∧ "The deadline."
∧∧ ∧∧ Zeke tried to move. It felt like his body was still asleep. ∧∧
"It's tomorrow. Your father said he left a secret file for you."
Eliza made the hand signal for *calm*. ∧∧ "I can't get anywhere
near the Vault right now. The city-state is still on high alert.
I don't think the deadline matters much anymore. This is
bigger than the letter." ∧∧ "We've got to get out." Zeke slowly

CALM

undid his blanket cocoon. Eliza stood up. Seeing her now made
him realize how much he had missed her. The time without her
had seemed so long. He sat up, his body stiff. ∧∧ ∧∧ "Bic freed
you? You received an escort down here?" ∧∧ ∧∧ "What are you
talking about?" ∧∧ ∧∧ "He was supposed to. How did you get
out of jail?" ∧∧ "I was never in jail. I ran back to try to save my
father, but it was too late. I didn't let myself get caught. But my
father is...they arrested him." Eliza's blinking betrayed her fear.
"I came to ask the Auspices to help free him. They're the only
ones who have the power." ∧∧ "And will they?" ∧∧ ∧∧ "I'm not
sure. The Auspices are holding council. We should go there. But
I didn't want to leave you. Raisin is in the Auspicium right now, in
case something happens." ∧∧ ∧∧ "Why the council?" Eliza filled
a tin cup with fount-water from a flask. She handed it to Zeke. ∧∧
"They're being accused of opening their tunnels and letting animals
into the city-state. It was Bic who issued the charge. But I smell
Daxon behind it. I think he's trying to link them to the murders and
turn the city-state against them, flush them up from underground.
It's a witch hunt. The Lawmen dragged in a strange animal. They're
offering it as proof, though everyone down here knows the tunnel
out remains sealed." ∧∧ "The Nightman?" ∧∧ "Useless. Just
speaks in these riddles." ∧∧ ∧∧ "No, I mean, where is he?" ∧∧
∧∧ "Gone. Maybe in the rot. I don't think he can be trusted, even if
he's not the murderer. The Auspices seemed to have some kind of

control over him, but I think he's a loose cannon. Raisin got him to agree to let you stay in this room, though. To recover." ∿ ∿ Zeke sighed and sat up. ∿ ∿ "The Deserters claim to control a cannon now," Eliza continued. "They've issued a 'Come & Take It' challenge to the Republic." ∿ ∿ Zeke put on his boots. ∿ Eliza took a deep breath. ∿ "Zeke, if this all somehow goes wrong, I want you to know that I would follow you into the rot. We could be married and build a cabin, and have a family. I don't care where I am as long as I'm with you." She smoothed his hair back in a way that he had almost forgotten about. Her touch was soft. The pinpricks on her fingers seemed mostly healed. He just stared into her eyes. He didn't want the moment to end. ∿ ∿ "We should go." She picked up his hand and, ducking, led him through the Nightman's door. Soon the light from the doorway faded and they were in the deep black of the tunnel. In the lightless void, with the strange underground air back in his lungs, Zeke felt some hope for the future return. ∿ Eliza moved around confidently in the dark. Zeke tried to quicken his step, but the toe of his boot caught on something and he stumbled. He dropped to one knee and let go of Eliza's hand to catch himself. ∿ When he reached up again, he couldn't find her hand. ∿ ∿ "Eliza?" he called out, afraid. ∿ ∿ "I'm right here." He scrabbled for her in the dark. ∿ ∿ "I can't find your hand." ∿ ∿ "Reach out, I'm right here." She sounded like she was standing right next to him, but spanning his arms out and reaching all around him, he only felt the shift of cool air. ∿ ∿ "I've lost you." ∿ ∿ ∿ "You haven't. I'm still here. Why don't you just follow my voice?" ∿ ∿ "OK." ∿ Eliza said, "This way," and Zeke could tell she was a few feet in front of him. He moved in the direction of her voice. She began to sing, the same soft song that had woken him. He followed the haunting melody down the long black road underground, still reaching out uselessly into the dark. ∿ ∿ ◇

◇◇ ⌇⌇ Zeke and Eliza finally saw the sliver of light that led to the Auspices' chamber. They could hear the Sisters talking, no longer the incanting drone of ritual but sharper, political tones. As they approached the door, they felt a presence. Sliding out from the dark, like an eclipse, the Nightman appeared. He was stationed at the entrance in full Republic uniform. He slid the door open. ⌇⌇ "You're ... with the Auspices?" Zeke's voice cracked. ⌇⌇ ⌇⌇ "Those who keep a coyote need no bite." The Nightman grinned widely, stepping aside. ⌇⌇ ⌇⌇ Compared to the darkness of the tunnel, it was bright in the wide chamber of the Auspicium. The lightning moths were jumpier than before, their signaling more urgent. The benches were empty save for a few figures in gray robes. All the initiates in white robes were gone. ⌇⌇ Long flickering shadows led to the Seven Sisters, who were now positioned around the middle of the silver circle. At first Zeke thought they had grown impossibly tall, but he quickly realized they were standing on the tree stumps. ⌇⌇ In Zeke's peripheral vision he saw a slinking animal shadow, not unlike the one in his apartment. It made his hair stand on end, but when he turned to look, there was nothing. ⌇⌇ ⌇⌇ ⌇⌇ Zeke walked down the aisle. Something sticky seeped out from under the benches. Zeke lifted his boot. The sole was covered in blood. ⌇⌇ ⌇⌇ The Nightman was now at the center of the Auspices' silver ring, speaking loudly. Zeke couldn't see how he'd made it from the door to that pedestal so quickly. He was already in mid-sentence. ⌇⌇ Zeke and Eliza sat down in a row near the back. She had taken a gray robe off a hook near the entrance and pulled its hood up over her hair. Zeke felt exposed. They slid in next to someone, and it wasn't until they were almost touching that he saw it was Raisin, sitting stock-still in the dim light. ⌇⌇ "Glad you're awake," Raisin whispered. Zeke, sitting between Raisin and Eliza, lowered his voice, so as not to disturb the proceedings, and spoke to them both:

THE CITY-STATE

ZEKE THOMAS: My grandmother ordered me to flee. I tried to take the tram out but Daxon got there first. She made it absolutely clear that I need to get out of here and make it to Chicago-Land as soon as possible. I'm not exactly sure of her reasons.

RAISIN DEXTRA

» She's given up on Texas.

ELIZA GRAY

» *She's giving you Texas.*

ZEKE THOMAS: I have two ears, but I can only hear one thing at a time. If you're both whispering, I can't understand anyone.

» Who cares?

» Listen, she knows everything is about to fall apart. This city-state is doomed. She wants you to get out so you'll be safe. The Republic of Texas is on the brink. This trouble has been brewing all year. You can feel it in the air.

» *Just listen to me.*

» *You're supposed to take your spot in the Senate now. The time for waiting is over. She wants you in Chicago-Land so you can be confirmed, so someone can manage what's happening in Texas. You have to save this place.*

ZEKE THOMAS: I don't know what to do.

» Flee with me. We have to get out now. Trying to understand that steammoat pamphlet has convinced me that using this tunnel is the only way out.

» *Stay in the tunnel with me. It's sealed. It's the safest place until the Senate can send other troops. No one can come in or out of the tunnel.*

ZEKE THOMAS: The Auspices are going to open the tunnel?

» Yes.

» Spree is coming back in. He's going to bring all the folks in the storm country into the

» *No.*

» *They would never compromise the order of the city-state. They are an integral part of*

THE ECHOED RESPONSE IS TRIANGULATED BETWEEN TWO SPECIALIZED EARS.

RAISIN DEXTRA

ELIZA GRAY

city-state through the tunnel. They're going to tear down the barriers from the inside. They say there are more Deserters than Lawmen now. The Republic of Texas is weak. They've lost their cannon. We have to flee. We can meet up with the Deserters before they come through the tunnel. We'll tear the barrier down, like they did in Atlantas.

» The Nightman has been getting a steady stream of visitors lately. There's going to be a ton of folks in Spree's army. It takes two bats to flee, though, and so far everyone has come with a partner. That's why I'm still down here. I need you.

its functioning. The last thing they want is to see civilization destroyed. They are the secret keepers of the fount that sustains us all with life-giving alchemy. Why would they opt for death and chaos?

» *They are also the only ones who could manage to get my father out alive. I had to take this robe and pledge myself in order to get them to agree, but I think it'll be OK. I've heard rumors that the Seven Sisters themselves are married, mostly to Senators or Majors. That's why they keep their faces hidden. They function aboveground as well. To be a sister, I need you. To live.*

›››››› ZEKE THOMAS: **That's nice to know. But what about Leeya?** ‹‹‹‹‹

» I asked her. She said no. I think Eliza told her not to, honestly. But that's OK. Once the walls come down, she'll see. And then we'll be in the free open country. I just need to get out there. I was waiting for you. So far, no one else trusts me enough to flee with me. You put your life on the line when

» *She'll be fine down here. Safest place for her. And for her baby. She got initiated too, prepared for the inner alchemy. They teach the recruits how to make their souls walk. And how to make fount-water. It doesn't simply bubble up from nowhere. Fossil blood requires very special treatment.*

EVEN IN COMPLETE DARKNESS THEY ARE ABLE TO IDENTIFY OTHER ANIMALS.

RAISIN DEXTRA

ELIZA GRAY

you do that. I don't know if I trust any of them, either. Folks down here are suspicious of me. That uniform you're wearing won't help you flee.

It is their duty to keep the fount pure. To learn the power of inner alchemy is an honor. It was silly of Leeya to think about fleeing with Raisin.

>>>>>>>> ZEKE THOMAS: **Even with the Nightman's pamphlet?** <<<<<<<<

» With getting us to the barrier anyway. I think you'll agree that the pamphlet is nearly impossible to understand. I think I get it. But I'm still not sure we could pull off a move like that. And on the first try?

» Did Eliza just say my name? Is she talking about me?

» Zeke if you want to save her, the best thing to do is to get out now. This city-state is about to be at war. No matter what. Don't you see that?

» Tell me you want to leave.

» Yes. That Raisin believes in that pamphlet is absurd. No one really flees like that. That's how they weed out unwanted recruits. Folks they don't want to be Deserters, or folks they want the Law to capture. A trick that amuses the Nightman. The tunnel is the only true way in or out. All the "bats" end up dead. The Nightman is the Sisters' familiar. His bloodline has served them for centuries. He maintains the exclusivity of their tunnels. The way out.

>>> ZEKE THOMAS: **I need to get to Chicago-Land. And the tram is** <<<< **not an option. I have to cross the rot.**

» We'll just go through the tunnel. The Nightman will convince these witches to open it. He's got a phonotube out to Spree, so he'll know

» That's impossible. The Senate will send someone for you. This is the best place to stay. The Auspices are closely aligned with the Senate,

BATS USE THE EXTRA-SENSORY ABILITY OF ECHOLOCATION TO FIND THEIR WAY.

RAISIN DEXTRA

ELIZA GRAY

we're on our way. In fact he'll probably send an escort. Like I said, they've got a ton of scouts. An army, really.

» They've captured Daxon's cannon. It's a really advanced weapon, and I know the Major is hopping mad about it. That's what this war is all about. And taking back the land. The Earth should belong to everyone. What right do they have to keep us in here?

» The Nightman is basically in charge of the Auspices. They're under the protection of the Deserters and will do whatever he tells them to.

whatever Daxon would have people believe. The Republic has to be complicit. They need the Auspices for the fount-water. The Auspices control the supply. In some ways they are the true rulers of the city-states, because they sustain them and give the folks life. The law doesn't apply down here. The Auspices pass in and out of the city-states freely. Just like the bats. Their souls can walk in the night. Black against black, unseen. They're hugely influential with the Deserters too.

»»»»» ZEKE THOMAS: **Then what are they arguing about up there?** «««««

» The Nightman is ordering the Auspices to unseal the tunnel. That way the Deserter army can be let in and other folks can be let out. The flow between the inside and outside world will begin.

» *The Auspices are telling the Nightman that they won't open the tunnel. He'll have to tell the Deserters. As much as that idea would serve their ends, the Auspices will never do it. It's too dangerous.*

»»»»»»»»»»» ZEKE THOMAS: **So what's our next move?** ««««««««««««

» Get ready. As soon as those tunnels are open, we take off. You to Chicago-Land, me to war.

» *Wait. Your grandmother knows best. She'll send help. No one wants Texas to fall apart.*

⌃⌃ ⌃⌃ Zeke's whispering conversation with Raisin and Eliza was interrupted by what was happening in the central ring. Voices had become sharp and the conflict was escalating. Many of the black-robed Auspices had their arms raised ominously above their heads. ⌃⌃ Zeke could hear the Nightman talking pointedly. His voice was different. It was serious now, real. "It is decided then. The tunnel will be unsealed. Though the Deserters may occupy the city-state, none will be harmed. They will maintain security forces until the Law in Texas can be replaced by the Senate. We can trust Spree. His cannon is capable of holding the Republic's forces at bay." ⌃⌃ ⌃⌃

⌃⌃ ⌃⌃ "No!" Eliza shouted, standing. "My father... You're starting a war!" The Nightman's speech stopped. He and the Auspices turned to look at her. Everything became very still. Zeke pressed his back against the bench and tried not to breathe. ⌃⌃ ⌃⌃ ⌃⌃ In the quiet of the room, the faint sounds of an alarm could be heard from above their heads. ⌃⌃ ⌃⌃ ⌃⌃ "Someone sounded the alert," an Auspex said. Her voice was a creeping whisper. ⌃⌃ ⌃⌃ "Our intentions were known." ⌃⌃ ⌃⌃ ⌃⌃ ⌃⌃ "Betrayed from within. A dirty numrat," another said. ⌃⌃ ⌃⌃ "Those three," the eldest sister said. She pointed at Eliza, and the Nightman began to advance toward them. Zeke scrambled to his feet. The Nightman had the grim look of a predatory animal in his eye. Eliza stood and pulled a dustbomb from underneath her robe. ⌃⌃ ⌃⌃ ⌃⌃ Covering her face with one hand, she slammed the bomb into the ground. It exploded magnificently. The dust unfurled in billowing gray clouds and quickly filled the small space. The weak light from the moth-filled jars was blotted out. ⌃⌃ ⌃⌃ ⌃⌃ Chaos enveloped the room, scrambling mixed with the shouts of panicked Auspices in the dark. Zeke felt someone grab him by the hand and pull him toward the door. He followed, stumbling and coughing violently, keeping his eyes closed tightly against the dust. ⌃⌃ ⌃⌃ ⌃⌃ ⌃⌃ ⌃⌃ ⌃⌃ ⌃⌃

⌁ Then they were in the sharp air of the tunnel, the noise of the Auspices' chamber fading behind them. Zeke tried to call out to whoever was pulling him roughly along but could not find his voice. ⌁ ⌁ ⌁ ⌁ ⌁ Eventually, they stopped. His hand was guided to the ladder. He gripped it tightly, a certain thing in the blinding black. ⌁ ⌁ ⌁ ⌁ ⌁ ⌁ ⌁ "Eliza?" Zeke finally managed to cough out. ⌁ ⌁ ⌁ "It's Raisin. Go. This is the ladder." ⌁ ⌁ "I'm not leaving without —" ⌁ "Zeke, you don't have a choice. Eliza threw that dustbomb to give you a chance and to block the tunnel. She's crazy. Who knows if they'll be able to open it or if the Deserters can get in now. But time is running out. The barrier is our best chance. Eliza was trying to save you. Go!" ⌁ ⌁ ⌁ ⌁ ⌁ Zeke started to climb. His boot slipped off a rung, and he nearly fell. He felt Raisin reach up and grab his leg, to steady him. His friend urged him on. ⌁ ⌁ Raisin's voice grew fainter. Zeke opened the hatch door. Alert whistles screamed in response. Up top, the chaos was worse. ⌁ ⌁ ⌁ ⌁ ⌁ "All-quadrant alert," Raisin shouted, "head for the barrier!" ⌁ ⌁ ⌁ ⌁ ⌁ ⌁ They ran straight down the middle of the plankways. Folks were running all over, clutching piles of papers to their chests or trying to haul jugs of fount-water to safety. Everyone looked panicked. Zeke couldn't tell if they were scared of the Law or of what might be coming over the barrier. Conflicting orders echoed from the tops of the watchposts. ⌁ ⌁ Zeke paused to look around and try to make sense of what was happening. It seemed unreal, like a staged event. There wasn't any immediate danger, but folks were screaming as though they were being attacked. Law flashers colored everything, and folks all around them were being put in bolo-ties. ⌁ ⌁ ⌁ ⌁ ⌁ "Don't watch," Raisin shouted. Ducking behind a large steam-power generator they were confronted with a set of toeholds leading up the sheer face of the barrier. ⌁ ⌁

FAM. **CUCULIDAE**

GEN. **GEOCOCCYX**

22.10.43, 18:15, 80 deg., 5 knots, no cloud coverage

Texas Hill Country

Road-runner, I'll put down, because that's what one of the Texians called him. Brown, gray, and black feathers. Elongated beak. He has the appearance of a cuckoo of sorts, though his legs are distinctive and his body is much larger, almost the size of a gosling. Rather than three front toes and one behind, each foot has two toes in the front and two in the back. This leaves tracks of little Xs in the dust, and it is impossible to tell whether they are coming or going. I wish that I could walk at all, let alone so quickly. Barren desert has given way to limestone hills, crumbling and ancient, decorated with low trees and small dry shrubbery, which the bird darts around rather than flying over. I wonder if he is deserving of a place in the Museum of Flying, if he cannot himself fly. They are curious and nimble, and blend in well with their surroundings. This running bird makes me think only of escape. How I miss my own two feet.

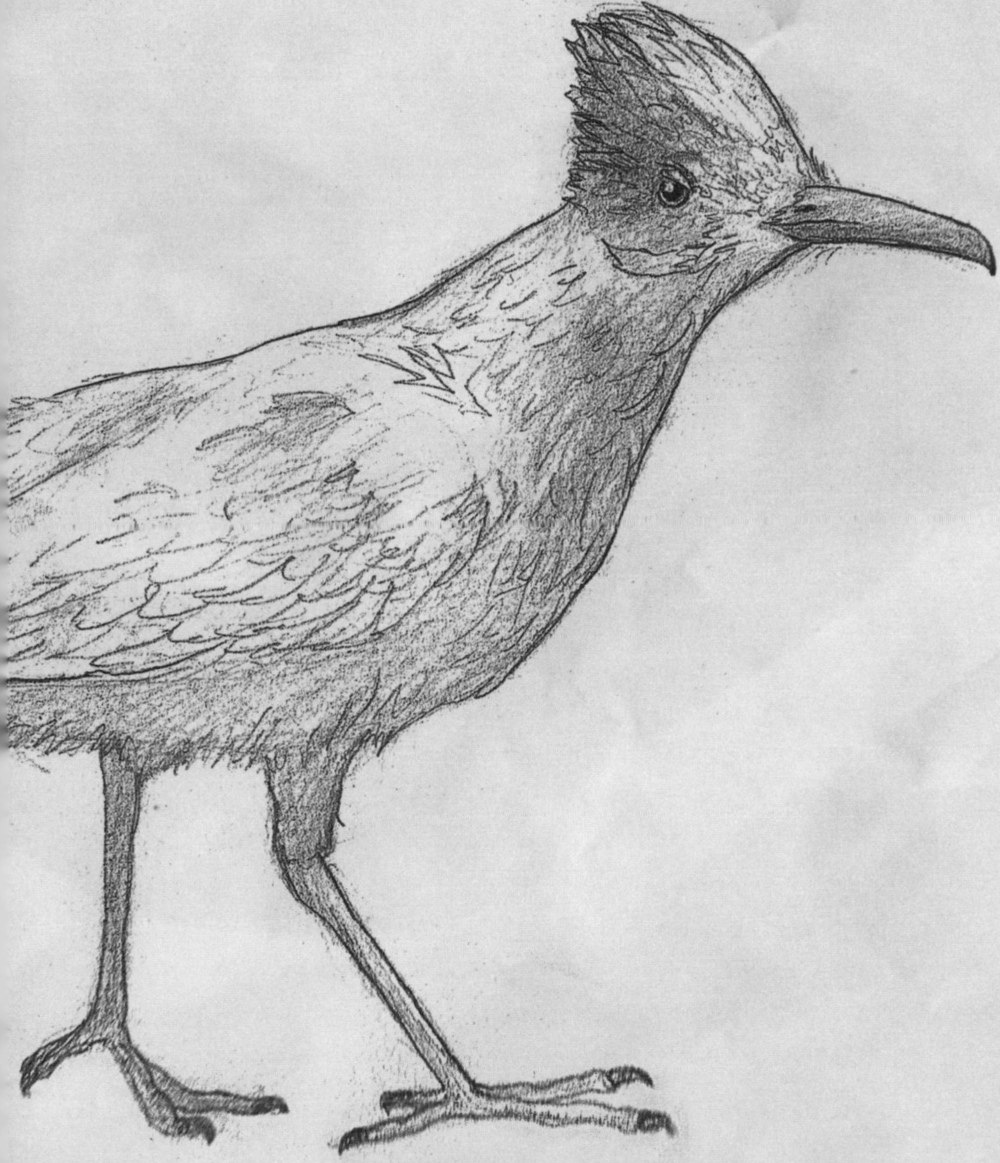

◇◇ ∿ Zeke and Raisin crouched on the ledge of the barrier. The weather pylons rose like teeth in a churning storm they could barely contain. The wind was hard and fast up on the ledge. They had pulled their hand-kerchiefs up over their noses and mouths, but the sand still stung their eyes. ∿ ∿ ∿ It hadn't been easy to get on top. Zeke had climbed a barrier once when he was a kid living in Salt-Lake. He'd gotten in trouble. He'd known better than to go over the edge into the moat, better than to leave home. ∿ ∿ ∿ Texas was too dry for a moat. They had built steammines instead. They were said to be a fail-safe security, but the outside was still closely watched. Loopholes lined the base of the barrier, facing outward into storm country. Each hole was just wide enough to aim a scorpio out. These catapults launched bolo-catches farther and faster than any man could. Lawmen manned each loophole. They patrolled the ledge. They were supposed to be ready to catch anyone who tried to flee the city-state. In truth they were equally occupied with who or what might attack the city-state from the outside. ∿ ∿ ∿ ∿

∿ ∿ Zeke and Raisin had found an unpatrolled ledge in a dead zone. The industrial quadrant was abandoned. The Lawmen were all out making arrests. Raisin had spotted the toeholds and they'd climbed up quietly, hoping that no one would notice given the chaos. The all-quadrant whistle sounded steadily in the distance. ∿ ∿ "This is the only way to save Leeya. And Eliza." Raisin had been quiet since they emerged from the hatch. "We have to find Spree. He's going to open this barrier." ∿ "It's a long walk to Chicago-Land," Zeke said. ∿ ∿ ∿ ∿ ∿ ∿ They looked out at the steammoat field. The grate was covered in dust and tumbleweeds, lit by the glow of the city-state. He could see the clockwork steam-mines moving beneath it. Beyond the weather pylons was a jagged fence. Hung on it was a flag with a drawing of a cannon and the phrase COME & TAKE IT. A Deserter taunt. Beyond the fence was the storm country. The rot. ∿∿ ∿∿ Zeke and Raisin hurriedly read the pamphlet again, trying to memorize the moves. They did Blood/Water/Air for who would go first. Raisin lost. Zeke would be the second mover. ∿∿ ∿∿ Zeke tried to internalize all the instructions. He needed to move with precision. In the pamphlet, it didn't look too far to the fence. Raisin tried to memorize his standing places and how long he should remain in each to trick the mines moving beneath the grate. They would each have to know where the other was, how long to wait, and when to run. ∿∿ ∿∿ ∿∿ ∿∿ The wind became sharp, laced with the smell of sulfur. Zeke looked out at the low horizon. He thought he'd see a curvature in its shape, but it was flat. He could hear birds falling to the ground, steamed out of the air by the weather pylons. ∿∿ ∿∿ ∿∿ "Why kill the birds and let bats fly over?" Raisin mumbled under his hand-kerchief. He was stalling. ∿∿ ∿∿ ∿∿ **"I guess that's just how the pylons were built. We need the bats in the Vault to protect everything."** Zeke wondered if they should go over the plan again. ∿∿ ∿∿ ∿∿ "Maybe they couldn't keep bats out anyway, and the Vault is just the excuse." ∿∿ ∿∿ "Hh." Zeke took a deep breath. **"You feel ready?"** ∿∿ ∿∿ ∿∿ ∿∿ ∿∿ ∿∿ "I guess. So on the count of three, we both rappel down our ropes, and then I make the first break, right? And you know your movement pattern, right?" ∿∿ ∿∿ ∿∿ **"I hope those steammines move slowly."** ∿∿ ∿∿ "Lots of Deserters have made it out this way. I mean, supposedly. I don't know how many didn't. This wind is intense." ∿∿ ∿∿ ∿∿ ∿∿ ∿∿ ∿∿ **"OK. I'm ready."** ∿∿ "One, two, three: shoot." ∿∿ They rappelled down the face of the barrier. Zeke's throat tightened. Gravity pulled them down sharply. Zeke let go of his rope too early and landed on his tailbone. ∿∿ Raisin's landing was smoother. He took off across the field. The steammines started tracking his movement immediately, the clockwork clicking to life. Hissing geysers of steam shot up through the grate behind his heels.

He swooped from side to side. Then he stopped dead in the planned holding place, the first of seven. The mines reconfigured and started to lurch toward him beneath the grate. The steam whistles from within the city-state sounded an escape alert. ∿∿ ∿∿ It was Zeke's turn to run, while the mines were drawn to Raisin's spot. He leapt up and zigzagged across the dusty grate. The steammines were fast. He felt disoriented outside the walls that had surrounded him for so long. He could not stop moving until he was in his designated spot or the mines would cook him. He dove to reach his holding place. ∿∿ ∿∿ ∿∿ Lawmen began to dot the ledge. They shouted wildly. The covers of the loopholes slid open. They loaded the scorpios with bolo-catches, meant to tie Deserters' ankles and bring them to the ground. ∿∿ ∿∿ The first run was the longest. It had gone well. Raisin ran as soon as Zeke made his spot. He hopped forward, taunting the steammine that tracked his path. ∿∿ Zeke counted the seconds. Raisin would be to his next spot by now. He sprang up. A bolo-catch whizzed by, grazing his calf. The scorpios were firing. He ducked and dodged and finally made his next spot, diving again. He sat up to watch Raisin's next run. ∿∿ Raisin left his standing spot. He tore at full speed across the grate. It was too soon. He wasn't swerving enough. Zeke heard a bolo-catch eject and scream through the air. ∿∿ Zeke shouted. Raisin slowed. The bolo-catch caught his back foot and circled around his legs like a whip. Raisin fell face-first on the grate, a cloud of dust rising and filling his lungs. ∿∿ "Keep moving. Move!" Zeke half stood. He looked back and forth from the barrier to his friend. A cheer rose from the Lawmen. Raisin's legs were tangled. He coughed and flinched wildly in the dust. He rolled onto his back, trying to reach his feet and undo the chafing web of the bolo-catch. ∿∿ Jets of steam shot up around him. Raisin yelped as he tried to roll away from their scalding blasts. It was too much for Zeke. Even though he knew the mines could track straight movement, he ran out onto the open grate, directly for Raisin. ⌃⌃ Zeke had almost reached him when he felt the sting of his own fate. He didn't have time to react to the whiz of the bolo-catch before it snaked around his ankles. The ground rushed toward him. He stretched out his hands and fell forward, skinning his palms on the grate. He was ten feet from Raisin, ankles tied. ⌃⌃ As Zeke crawled toward him on his belly, he felt blood drip down his ankles. He pulled with his elbows against the grate. ⌃⌃ "It's over," Raisin yelled. Steam shot up around them in volcanic blasts. The mines closed in. ⌃⌃ Zeke reached Raisin and yanked his friend's boots off. He ripped at the rope of the bolo-catch. Raisin wriggled his feet free. ⌃⌃ ⌃⌃ "You shouldn't have stopped," Raisin said. He leapt to his feet. His bare feet were free. He bent down to untie Zeke's. ⌃⌃ "Don't! Look!" Zeke pointed into the grate. A steammine was directly below Raisin. He leapt out of the way just in time. Zeke's feet disappeared in a jet of scalding steam. ⌃⌃ Zeke choked on a scream. Pain shot up his legs. He looked at his feet through watering eyes. His melting boots dripped into the grate. His toes were exposed, marbled skin and blood. The loopholes slid open at the base of the barrier. Lawmen came streaming out with weapons drawn. ⌃⌃ "Run," Zeke shouted at Raisin. ⌃⌃ "But you—" ⌃⌃ "Run!" Zeke coughed. Steam and dust mixed in his lungs. ⌃⌃ ⌃⌃ "They won't kill me. Find the safe camp. Go tell Spree. Run! Now!" ⌃⌃ ⌃⌃ Raisin looked up at the advancing Lawmen and back down at Zeke. Then he ran. They fired after him. Bolo-catches zinged above Zeke, but Raisin had a good start. He made the fence beyond the pylons. He leapt it deftly and disappeared into the clouds of the storm country. ⌃⌃ The Lawmen surrounded Zeke. Steamsabres pointed at his neck. They jerked him up by his armpits, ignoring his mangled feet. He gasped in pain. They dragged him back to the loopholes, back to the angry Law whistles, back to the city-state. ⌃◇

Dearest Elswyth,

The militia made camp in the night. I could see lightning flashing its forked tongue in the distance and hear the coarse notes of thunder that followed. I prepared for a drenching, but it did not come.

The encampment is made up of white tents, like a semicircle of dirty teeth set in the dark soil. I am exhausted and on edge at once.

All the men talk of is war. General Irion is believed to be camped nearby. They are afraid of some machined cannon he captured. Supposedly it is a new contraption, an artillery that integrates gear work and is powered by a steam engine. Possessed of devastating power and unlike to any other weapon, or so the story goes.

They say Irion means to use the cannon to blast through the walls of a great fortress, one of the lost citadels that the Spanish have always looked for and never found. Another exaggeration.

How will I escape my circumstance? Sometimes I feel as if these letters to you are the last way I'll be able to visit Chicago ever again. I only have seven leaves of paper left. I have to think carefully about where I want them to transport me. I need to be away from here.

There was a fine day last spring, I wonder if you remember it? We were sitting on the stoop of your Aunt Em's farmhouse. I had accepted a rare invitation from your father to attend something that included his family. I had a high spirit about me that could not be trampled.

The reason for my presence at the farmhouse was supposed to have been some modest sample-collecting in the fields. It wasn't long after I arrived that I gleaned this task would fall away, and the true mission joined — one of being with family.

The land yielded up a pleasant grove of trees, flowering bushes ringed the yard, and there was a fine breeze blowing all the time.

There was food, a large farmhouse spread. The air was filled with laughter and talking. Your aunts were dressed gaily and wore ribbons in their hair. Presently your father became embroiled in a discussion of market forces with a colleague, and I found myself alone on the back stoop with you. Do you know how I have treasured this moment?

You had been given charge of the small children there, including a pair of distant nephews. They were maybe two years and four? The boys had taken a keen interest in a goose pond not far from the porch. You called out that they mustn't get their shoes and stockings wet. They immediately stripped off all their clothing, an act that made you roll with laughter at their overeager obedience.

The boys chased the geese around the pond, shouting out names for them and trying to catch them. They were yard geese and so had clipped wings but still were just a bit too quick to grab, and good thing too. Had the boys managed to get hold of one, they most certainly would have been bitten.

But they never did tire of it and you laughed again and again, brushing my knee each time. Between breaths, you turned to me and told me that you loved children dearly. I have often wondered if there was a hint in the sentiment. It fills my heart to think it so.

With joy, I raced out into the yard after the boys and snatched up a goose with my bare hands. It honked a shrill alarm while the boys petted and poked it, but the show was all for you.

How far I have come from that place. This land feels like the end of the earth. I am banished to my tent. The men are arrayed around the campfire, raising clamor. They are as drunk as boiled owls.

I can't help but overhear their preposterous conversations. They do seek Irion, but for nefarious reason. The man with the bared teeth continues to repeat the legend of the seven cities of silver and gold, handed down from the Spaniards who died trying to find those places. Legend had it that one city was close to this territory. The stories tell of a fountain of youth, and how it arrested the age of all the inhabitants within. Such tales have led many men to their deaths.

He says that Irion has made it his work to scour the fields of west

Texas until he finds this lost city. The militia is waiting to see if Irion indeed discovers a city, so that if he does they might plunder it. They are presently arguing about how he will do it, and if he means to dig underneath it, as he did in the Battle of the Secret Tunnel.

As I said, they are drunk, and daft besides. For example:

Today they caught an armadillo and tied it to a post. I had a thrill at finally seeing one of these elusive creatures, but you would have been sorry for the state it was in. They had its tail knotted with twine, and it was alternately pulling at its tether to get free and curling into an armored ball and biting at its own tail in despair.

They seem to be laughing at the poor little pig now. It is no way to treat a creature of this earth. I remember when I first arrived at the Museum of Flying and undertook to learn the skills of the naturalist.

I had purchased an old goose from the market with the intention of practicing the taxidermy of waterfowl. The preparation of study skins was still new to me. I followed the instructions set out for me by your father, and when I was finished I held the bird in my hands and turned it over and over. The perfect white down, the gently faded spots, even the long elegant feet all struck me as sacred in that moment. The rows of perfectly neat feathers, made by no hand.

I became overwhelmed with regret at killing such a fine specimen. Death for a useless exercise, made only to please your father. I began to weep, quite beyond my control. The strength of the design, the sheer physicality of the bird, juxtaposed with the frailty of the life within that container. The small hot breath with which the fates have imbued every living creature, the animating force. Those children at the farmhouse. Your father's displeasure. More than my heart can bear.

Rrr! I cannot concentrate. Outside the clatter of ugly embittered voices is unceasing. And the wicked laughter growing ever louder. I can no longer stand for this. I will lay this pen down and return shortly.

Not the results I'd hoped for. I'm furious. I badly need rest.

Just now, I got up from my tent and interrupted their circle around the fire. Though my foot fares a bit better, it is still an irritant to rise and walk. I made a polite case for peace and quiet, and they jeered. It was then I saw what wretched game they were playing at.

They were casting stones at the poor armadillo, still tied to its post. The soldiers laughed as the rocks bounced off its hide. With each stone they yelled, "Remember Fredonia! Remember Bexar! Remember Goliad! Remember Atlanta! Remember the Alamo! Remember San Jacinto!" They were playacting as though its armor were the walls of a city and the stones were fired from the slings of the soldiers. One declared that he carried a torch to burn the city down, and began casting bits of burning wood at the little armored pig.

Finally one man rose and, shouldering his rifled musket, said, "Your defenses are useless against Irion's great machined cannon." His shot was so loud even the most inebriated of his compatriots jumped. It found the heart of the defenseless armadillo, and all the men rose up in riotous laughter. The creature's lifeblood pooled in the dust.

I took great offense at this needless slaughter. When I protested, the man with the bared teeth stated that it was a lucky thing not all their prisoners were tied up and tortured so. I decried that I was not a prisoner. Flustered, I asserted that Irion was to be held in the highest esteem. In folly, I said that I was seeking him for my own purposes.

Half of the man's face sneered. He said that we would all go to join his cause. One of his lieutenants added, "By stealing all his gold," and the pack again erupted in yelping laughter.

I marched back here, to my tent. I do not care to waste the few leaves of paper I have left on this bile, but I am livid. They have just posted a guard outside my tent. Apparently I truly am a prisoner.

All things must move or die. What would the fates have me do?

Yours on the Brink, Zadock

FAM. **DASYPODINAE**

GEN. **DASYPUS**

24.10.43, 2:15, 70 deg., 10 knots, 6/10ths cloud coverage

Hill Country

Armored Pig (Armadillo). About 18 inches, small with plated bands across its back. Almost like a turtle crossed with a hare. Its primary defense must be to jump, because the specimen I observed danced at the end of its tether desperately. Eventually, so threatened, it tried to curl into a ball. It pained me to see it in such a tortured state, unable to flee for safety or turn inward for solace. I suppose it is better for the creature to be out of its misery. May this drawing extend its life in some small way.

RECORD: 1740411

SCRPT DATE: 0010.0010.2143

SUBJECT: BIC THOMAS &

BEGIN UNIT TRANSCRIPT:

B. THOMAS » Don't be scared. I'm a friend.

————— » How did you get in?

» I'm with the Law. I'm here to protect you. I would never hurt a beautiful girl.

» Are you from the Auspicium? Am I accepted? I want to —

» I don't work for the witches, but you should be glad of that. They'll only make you sacrifice goats and drink their blood. Let's not mix your blood with theirs.

» My blood?

» You might have the chance to mix it with a Senator's instead. I could offer you a life you never dreamed of. Come with me —

» I won't be an Auspex recruit? And become one ... of the hidden ones?

» Well, in a manner of speaking. There is —————————————————

» ————————————————— ——————— I got for the Vault —————

» ————————————

» ————————————————

» ————

» ————————————————————

» ————————————————————

B.THOMAS
B. THOMAS/ID.42784
0010.0010.2143

:ACCESS
:DATE
429 P.

» ▇▇▇▇▇▇▇▇▇▇▇▇▇▇▇▇▇▇▇
▇▇▇▇▇▇▇▇▇▇▇▇

» ▇▇▇▇▇▇▇▇▇▇▇▇▇▇▇▇▇▇
▇▇▇▇▇▇▇▇▇▇▇▇▇▇▇▇
▇▇▇▇▇▇▇▇

» ▇▇▇▇▇▇▇▇▇▇▇▇▇▇▇▇▇ght.
▇▇▇▇▇▇▇▇▇▇▇▇▇▇▇▇▇

» ▇▇▇▇▇▇▇▇▇▇▇▇▇▇▇▇▇▇or
▇▇▇▇▇▇▇▇▇▇▇▇▇▇▇hought
▇▇▇▇▇ supposed ▇▇▇▇▇▇▇n
▇▇▇▇▇▇▇▇▇▇▇▇▇▇▇▇▇
▇▇▇▇▇▇▇▇▇▇▇▇▇▇▇▇▇
▇▇▇▇▇▇▇▇▇▇▇▇▇

» R▇▇▇▇▇▇▇▇▇
» I ▇▇▇▇▇▇▇▇▇▇▇▇▇▇
f▇▇▇▇.

▇▇▇▇▇▇▇▇

I   » ▇▇▇▇▇▇▇▇   <▇▇▇R

» ▇▇▇▇▇▇▇

END UNIT TRANSCRIPT

LEEYA,

IT'S ALL COMING APART NOW. I DON'T KNOW THAT YOU'LL EVEN BE BACK TO FIND THIS LETTER OR IF THIS CITY-STATE WILL STILL EXIST. THE OPENING OF THE TUNNEL WILL BE LIKE A FLOODGATE, AND THE ROT WILL RUSH INSIDE AND EVERYTHING WILL CRUMBLE. THERE ARE NOT ENOUGH LAWMEN HERE TO DEFEND TEXAS FROM AN ATTACK.

I NEVER THOUGHT THE AUSPICES WOULD OPEN THE TUNNEL... I DETONATED A DUST BOMB UNDERGROUND. IT WON'T STOP THEM FOR LONG, BUT IT WAS ENOUGH TO KEEP ZEKE IN THE CITY-STATE. IF HE'S GONE, THERE IS NO ONE WHO CAN SET THINGS RIGHT.

I AM DESPERATE TO FIND HIM, ENOUGH TO GO BACK TO THE VAULT. IT WAS A CALCULATED RISK, THANKFULLY DAXON WASN'T THERE. I CHECKED ALL THE WATCHPOST RECORDER FILES FROM THE PAST FEW HOURS. NO ONE HAS SPOTTED ZEKE OR RAISIN.

MY FATHER OBTAINED A PHIAL OF DAXON'S BLOOD BEFORE HE WAS TAKEN AWAY. I USED IT TO OPEN DAXON'S OFFICE. I SEARCHED THROUGH EVERY PIECE OF PAPER, TERRIFIED THE WHOLE TIME I'D GET CAUGHT.

//////// ZEKE'S LETTER IS **NOT** THERE. ////////

BUT MY FATHER'S SEALED FILE WAS. AS WELL AS A STACK OF BLACKED-OUT RECORDS - A THREAD ON BIC.

I DON'T KNOW WHY I HADN'T SEEN IT BEFORE. THE VIOLENCE IN BIC'S EYES. THE WAY HE LOOKED AT GIRLS, THE WAY HE WANTED TO POSSESS THEM.

THE SCARIER THING IS KNOWING THAT DAXON IS BEHIND HIM. HE PROMISED BIC THE SENATE SEAT ONCE ZEKE WAS OUT OF THE WAY. THEN HE USED BIC'S

PROCLIVITY FOR SEXUAL VIOLENCE TO HIS OWN ENDS.
HE POINTED BIC IN THE DIRECTION OF THE AUSPICES'
RECRUITS. HE WANTS TO HURT THEM.

   HE <u>ENGINEERED</u> THE MURDERS, ENCOURAGED THEM.
HE WILL SMOKE OUT THE AUSPICES. HE MEANS TO
OVERTHROW THE SENATE AND TAKE POWER. HE LIED TO
BIC ABOUT THE SENATE SEAT. HE MEANS TO DESTROY
THEM ALL. THE LETTER MAY NOT MATTER AFTER ALL,
IF THE THOMAS BLOODLINE IS ERADICATED.

   HIDE UNDERGROUND OR KEEP TO THE DEAD ZONES.
BIC IS A MONSTER. I FEAR HE MAY COME LOOKING FOR YOU.

   I REALIZE NOW IT WAS NEVER THE NIGHTMAN. HE
MOVES IN SHADOWS, BUT ONLY TO SERVE THE AUSPICES.
HE HAS BEEN AT THE SCENE OF EVERY MURDER, ON
THE SAME TRAIL I AM. HE DOESN'T WANT THE GIRLS
DEAD, HE HAS BEEN WORKING TO PREVENT IT.

   IF ANYONE KNEW I WAS STILL HERE, I WOULD BE
ARRESTED LIKE MY FATHER, BUT I <u>WON'T</u> ABANDON
HIM. THE LAW SEPARATED US ONCE, I WON'T LET IT
HAPPEN AGAIN. I'M SITTING HERE STARING AT HIS
SEALED FILE. I FEEL UNABLE TO OPEN IT. NOW I
KNOW HOW ZEKE FELT ABOUT HIS GRANDFATHER'S LETTER.

   ~ ARE SOME THINGS BETTER LEFT ALONE? ~
MAYBE IT DOESN'T EVEN MATTER NOW... I HAD TO
WRITE ALL THIS DOWN SO SOMEONE WOULD KNOW. I BEG
THE STARS THAT IT WILL BE YOU, BUT SOMEONE NEEDS
TO SEE THIS TO KNOW WHAT DAXON HAS DONE.

   THIS NOTE IS MY LAST BYE FOREVER. I DO NOT
KNOW WHAT WILL BE THE END OF ALL OF THIS.

   I LOVE YOU LIKE A SISTER, FOREVER,

    ELIZA ✳

◇◇ ⌄⌄ The Lawmen threw Zeke in a jail cell, his wrists locked in bolo-ties. They closed the glass door and sealed it with a pressurized steam valve. ⌄⌄ ⌄⌄ A single phosphor lamp droned above him in the cell. His feet were seared. The bolo-catch was still around his ankles. There was nowhere to sit. Standing was excruciating. He fell over and lay where he fell. ⌄⌄ ⌄⌄ He was beyond despair. Even if the barriers came down, there was no way out of this cell. He needed to get to Chicago-Land. His grandmother's plan to secret him away and activate his authority had failed. And he hadn't been able to sneak out into storm country on his own. Raisin was out there, dead or waiting. Zeke would never know. ⌄⌄ ⌄⌄ He felt tired. He didn't care what happened now. He waited for Daxon. It didn't matter anymore. He wanted to see Eliza again, just once. To know that she would be OK. Maybe he could bargain for her, give up the Senate seat. His feet pulsed with pain. ⌄⌄ ⌄⌄ The door hissed. Daxon was there. He swayed over Zeke. He had a large gash on his forehead. ⌄⌄ "Get these bolo-ties off." The Lawmen snapped to. They picked Zeke up and pushed him out of the cell. They carried him down the jail corridors. Other prisoners pleaded or prophesied as they walked by, tapping madly on the glass. ⌄⌄ "Put him in interrogation?" one of the Lawmen asked. ⌄⌄ "No, my office." ⌄⌄ They forced Zeke into a metal chair. He winced. It took all his remaining strength to keep his feet from touching the floor. The Major sat across from him. The office was a mess, like it had been ransacked. Zeke looked around Daxon's office, searching for where he might've hidden the letter. His eye landed on a hatch in the floor, poorly covered by a rug. He wondered where it led. Someone closed the door behind them. Zeke strained to turn around. It was Bic. ⌄⌄ ⌄⌄ "Hello, cuz." His face was all smug victory. ⌄⌄ "You're not easy to catch. But that's what the steammines are for." Daxon's face stretched into a grimace. ⌄⌄ "I would have thrown you over myself, if you hadn't done the job for me. Side of the barrier you belong on, ask me." ∿ The Major sat down. He pulled a laudanum phial out of his desk drawer. He added three drams to his glass and took a long draw, showily smacking his lips. ∿ ∿ "Hardly matters now. The letter seemed a threat, but if we've got you, and all the crimes you've committed, we're watertight." He looked up at Zeke, his eyes tired, searching. Zeke returned a blank stare. ∿ "The Senate issued a decree yesterday that you were to assume your seat," Bic began. ∿ "I'm not so sure you even have this letter, anymore," Daxon interjected. "But you won't have the Senate seat either. The broadsheets will be informed that we've finally caught our murderer, here in Texas." ∿ "You'll be murderers as well." Zeke motioned to his feet. A small shadow of dark blood had formed underneath them. ∿ ∿ Daxon whistled. "That injury won't play well in court." ∿ "Release me to the hospital unit. To Chicago-Land." ∿ "Hh. We've got records of you entering and exiting those tunnels." ∿ "The same ones that the animal came from. On the nights of the murders." Bic grinned. ∿ ∿ "You might be careful with that particular fabrication," Zeke said. "Could come back to bite you." ∿ ∿ "This thread is all tied up. The Auspices are implicated. If they hadn't opened their illegal tunnel for you, you could have never caused all that trouble." Daxon took another long swig of his drink. ∿ "Sealed up now. And the Auspicium will be dissolved. There's no reason this city-state can't make its own fount-water." ∿ Bic fingered the handle of his sabre. "And then, of course, you tried to flee." ∿ "Clear admission of guilt." ∿ "Not to mention a crime itself. Treason of the highest order." ∿ "You're about to have a lot of treason on your hands." ∿ "My cannon is extremely dangerous. Your friends in the desert have no idea how to use it. They are putting everyone's life at risk." His face was swelling with anger. "Do you know the survival rate at Atlantas? We'll lose a generation. We'll 'come and take it' all right.

I'll hobble your Deserters and have them crawling on their bellies like the snakes they are." ⌃⌃ Zeke stared at the floor. ⌃⌃ ⌃⌃ "This city-state is mine. I won't have it subverted from below. Or from above. There is a new Khrysalis for the Thomas seat." He stood, putting a hand on Bic's shoulder. His eyes were unfocused. "And things will be different in the Senate too." ⌃⌃ Bic stiffened. "If you'll excuse me, cousin, I have preparations to make. Seems the burden of our bloodline has fallen upon me." He walked briskly out of the room, jaw set. Through the open door of his office, Daxon called to the Lawmen. ⌃⌃ ⌃⌃ "Put him in one of the big cells. Bandage his feet. Make sure he lives." ⌃⌃ They grabbed his arms and led him up another corridor, pushing him inside a cell. They pulled a valve and the door sealed. The cell walls were solid glass. Zeke sat down on the single bench. ⌃⌃ There was a cell next to his. He could see a man inside, through the glass. He blinked hard. It was Henry Bartle. His nose looked broken. ⌃⌃ Zeke opened his mouth. Bartle raised a hand. ⌃⌃ "Jail Recorders." He indicated a man in the corridor sitting at a raised desk with a typowriter. ⌃⌃ Zeke nodded slowly. Bartle waited until the Recorder glanced down to type, and then flashed a quick series of hand signals to Zeke. ⌃⌃ ⌃⌃

Zeke nodded and rested his back against the wall. Four o'clock? There wasn't a clock in sight. It seemed impossible that he was here. Retreating into his mind didn't seem like much of a possibility. How would he bide his time? He stared at the floor, the white wall, through the glass. There was enough condensation to write: ⌃⌃ Fate is time's meaning, measured by the mind. ⌃⌃ **"You want to hear a story?"** Zeke addressed Bartle, but looked straight ahead.

He could see Bartle nod out of the corner of his eye. "I've just been sitting here, and the fair came to mind. Do you remember it? They'd bring a petting zoo inside the city-state for kids." Bartle nodded. Zeke could hear the Recorder clacking frantically on his typowriter. He didn't mind. "There was this one game they had. I think it was supposed to teach us about the mines. How the city-state was built from the hollowed ground beneath it. How we got metals and fount-water and all that." Bartle shook his head. "No? You never took Eliza? The game was a wall of little cavities, hollowed out like mines. They were jagged inside, and just big enough for a kid's arm to fit through. Part of the thrill was bravery, I guess, to reach into some dark hole like that. You had to go in up to the shoulder for your hand to come out the other side. And if you did it, there was a fair worker standing behind the wall who would put a prize in your hand." Zeke looked over at Bartle. He raised an inquisitive eyebrow. "A fair prize. Nothing special. But they made it seem like if you picked the right cavity, you'd hit pay dirt. I think the only two prizes they actually had were hard candy and these little carved birds, painted white. The thing is, I didn't really want either. There were better prizes at the fair. But I spent all the greenbacks my mother gave me playing this one game over and over. I was hooked on the mystery of it, I guess. I ended up with one pocket full of birds and one full of rock candy. I left crying and begging my mother for more tries at the game." Bartle shrugged, like that should have been expected. "I knew there was someone behind there with only two kinds of prizes. I'm not sure why it made me so upset." Zeke lifted his tender feet onto the bench and lay down. "I know what I want now. I'll take care of Eliza." The clack of the Recorder's typowriter ceased and the jail was silent. Finally Bartle spoke. "I wish you had opened the letter."

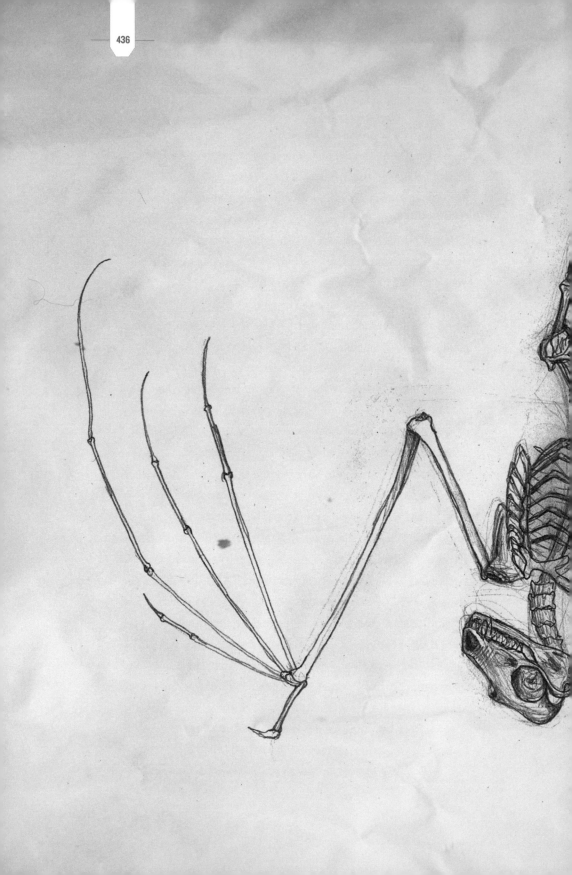

_Eliza, this note is a backup. I'm working on arrangements
for us to flee, but in case something happens to me
before then, I leave you these instructions. I hope
that you never have to read them.

Saturday mornings at 4am you will find the door
to the steam distributor unlocked. It is a regular
maintenance phase, and usually in a dead zone. If I
am captured, only cutting the steam power to the entire
city-state will release the jail-cell doors.'

This is a last resort.

I've found Daxon's namestamps on a dizzying
collection of documents. In the brief time I was
inside I could not parse them all out: telegrams,
handwrittenmx notes, a grayhound training-manual. One
thing was clear: he traffics in falsified documents.
Beyond the thread of murders,many concern what
is happening outside the barriers: new cities and
folks who have organized civilizations and armies
in the years since the Collapse. The Queers were right.
I fear Texas will become another Atlantas. These
barriers wonitt hold. We need an escape plan.

Though reality seems to be shifting underneath us,
there is one thing I must make clear. I leave you
these last instructions to underscore the importance
of the missing letter. I hope my plans do not fail us
even if I am arrested by the time you read this.
Tell Zeke all of this. Whatever happens, the letter
must still be recovered at all costs. It cannot be
allowed to fall into Daxon's hands.

These final letters see Zadock fall apart completely.
He has lost his mind. His decisions have become rash,

his actions unconsidered, and his purpose all but lost.

There is evidence of insanity in these late letters.

Zadock becomes more liberal with the attributes he gifts his fantastical animals. More troubling is that after he loses his way in the southwestern desert he seems to believe in these mutated creatures. He invents amalgamations such as ''the Plumed Owlette!'' and an anomoly like an albino bat gives birth to a whole new species. To manufacture false animals to win publication and fame is one thing, to record observations of them as though they are real is quite another.

I also distrust his other descriptions. Take Irion's weaponry. The steam power used in his day was mostly on boats. It wasn't widely applied, and certainly not used for weaponry until after the Collapse of 2043.

I feel convinced that much of what Zadock's letters contain after Santa Fe is pure fabrication. The question then becomes "Why?" Was it purposeful invention, meant to supply him with creatures he could use to impress the patrons of the Museum of Flying? Or to self-mythologize-- create a biographical legend where there was none? To become a hero in Elswyth's eyes? The truth stalks from just beyond the edge of the dark.

Zadock Thomas didn't write much else in his life, only about flora and fauna in small pamphlets relating to the museum. An illustrated volume on bats was eventually published and remains the only official work to bear his name. It is in the Vault somewhere. As he planned, it is titled ''bats of the Republic.''

The details of the journey's end are lost. There is no verification of the bloodline. The unopened letter is never made mention of again.

Maybe I'm suffering from delusions, just like Zadock.
His instability of the mind could have been caused by
any number of factors: a foreign climate harsh with
strange air, lack of proper diet and nutrition, a
sustained injury and its attendant pain, or substances
like Abril's peyote, a known hallucinogen.

This sealed file contains the last letter Zadock ever
wrote. After reading all his others, I expect you've
come to the same conclusions I have. Do not break the
seal unless you already know what you will read.

It contains something else. It may be the letter.
But I can't be sure. It's a faded impression on the

back of a page, like an old-fashioned carbon. There's
no way to know who Gray was writing to, or if it's the
one. Records must be read carefully: though firsthand sources are the best, they too can be deeply
flawed, and when there is no corroboration, the careful
Threader always considers them suspect. All should be
cross-checked, compared, verified. Always hold the
thought that some larger power or higher mind could be
manipulating everything.

Daxon's grip is tightening. His plans stretch far
beyond the Texas barrier. I'm worried about what will
happen to you. I hope you are safe. If Zeke is locked
up, they will surely bring you in as well. Seek to
escape, or if not: find a hiding place.

My fate in that regard is sealed. I was recorded
w/ you. And then I took Daxon's blood. I have shown
my hand. They are coming for me. If no one finds that
letter soon, I'll be thrown in a cell.

I am sorry I have ruined your bloodline, amd left
you alone and nameless all these years. I know now
that being with you is more import nt thn any of that,
I know it from getting the chance to be with you again.

How I wish I had known what to do all those years
ago. With you, with our family. All that's left now
is my small hope for your future with Zeke.

I hope the p th the fates have set out for you is
easy to realize. Mine never was. Like anx impossible
trick, the patterns always seemed just beyond my
grasp. The mind cannot solve the puzzle of the mind.
But I suppose that which is most important in the
world cannot be organized or classified. Meaning

multiplies and confounds. It seems our hearts breed
feelings, and we cannot fully capture them, subject
them to our taxonomy, or examine them under the glass
of a display ccase. They float up restlessly into the
air on wings we cannot understand, and flap away
beyond the mortal grasp.

All along the universe swells, swallowing its own
tail, a great sighing spiral, repeating itself.

We should all be with those we choose.

Our secret s are ours to

FILE #: I7.40942
REC DATE: 20*I0*43
FILE DATE: 24*I0*43

A: № 24

NOTICE:

CONVICT AS FALSIFIER

CARBON: THIRD/secret

VCTR: S*E.R.O.T.

HALL: 24

ROW: 1711

SHLF: 2

DRWR: 22-D

FLDR: 7

THE SILVER CITY·STATE
THE NATIONAL VAULT OF RECORDS

Here is the file. It is all I have to give.
DON'T OPEN unless it's the end.

believe where she found herself. It all seemed like a story to her. A story, yet one that was inevitable, as though things could be no other way. Elswyth plotted it while she braided Louisa's hair.

Mr. Thomas's return was triumphant. But their wedding had to wait until she could nurse him back to health. The fine beauty of that summer day. How the geese flew in an arrow above their heads when the wedding bell was rung, pointing a way toward the future. Mr. Buell had been tried and banished from the city. It was astonishing how little Elswyth thought of him, out there on his own. She wondered if the wilderness were preferable to poison.

Mr. Thomas was hard at work on his field guide, and Mr. Gray had dedicated a hall at the Museum of Flying as 'Thomas's Tunnel of Bats.' Dark and strange, it had become immensely popular with all the new Chicagoans looking for a thrill, leading to a steady source of revenue for her father. And a resplendent wedding.

Louisa had calling cards from seven suitors for that day, all fine young men, desperate to escort her to her sister's wedding. Well, six calling cards filled with longing and one filled with mirth. Aunt Anne had made a card from the Auspicium, asking one last time for Louisa's pledge. All were amused by its cleverness.

Aunt Anne truly did not require any more new recruits—the Auspicium was growing in membership and strength.

But not growing nearly as finely as John William. He was a beautiful boy. Quiet, bright, and curious. Elswyth loved him above all else. He asked her to read *The City-State* to him every day. He never tired of the chase or the hiss of the steam weapons.

Once the last four pages had been restored, Aunt Anne saw that the book found a publisher and illustrator both. More importantly, the prophecy was fulfilled.

At least, if things were as Elswyth imagined them.

If only true life were a story like this one...

The night is a tunnel, she thought, *a hole into tomorrow...*
—*Bene Gesserit witch Jessica in Frank Herbert's* Dune

The outcome in any work of fiction is arbitrary.
—*Peter Chung*

Who are you, anyway?
—*Favorite saying of my grandson, probably*

OLD THREE HUNDRED

SCHEDULE 24 — Inhabitants of the *Republic* of *Texas*

In the County of *Thomas* on the first day of *October*, in the year *2015*

Ledger of all Commissioned Officers, Warrant Officers, Sympathizers, Deserters, Threaders, Filers, Trumpeters or Drummers, Correctors, and Rank and File, who were brave enough to first venture into these lands, not having been enumerated elsewhere.

Dwelling House, in the order of visitation.	Name in Full.	Special & Heartfelt Thanks.	Master Instructor in the Writing Arts.	Occupation of Reader or Supporter.	Historical Personage, life pillaged.	Note.	National Alliance Institution.
♡	Anderson, Ragnar	✔		X	X	I LOVE YOU. BLOOD	
14	Anshaw, Carol		X				
4	Audubon, John James				X		
31	Axelrod, Sam			X		L.Y.L.A.S. /S.C.A.R. 4EVA	
22	Ball, Jesse		X		X	FOR THE GOOD ELEPHANT	
27	Beachy, Kyle	✔	X	X			
45	Bloom, Rob		X			FOR SEEING	
26	Bouer, Chris			X		FOR THE MAD ANIMALS	
13	Burgue, Allison			X			
37	Case, Mairead		X	X			
12	Cross, Mary		X				
7	Desaulniers, Janet		X			FOR CONSTELLATIONS	
48	deWitt, Patrick			X			
28	Dodson, Seth			X		BLOOD	
43	Dodson, John Thomas			X		BLOOD	
38	Doniphan, Alexander William			X			
19	Durica, Paul			X		FOR HISTORICAL ACCURACY	
16	Farrell, Stephen		X			FOR DESIGN	
41	Francis, Will			X			
34	Genovese, Maria			X			
5	Gibson, George Rutledge				X		
15	Goulish, Matthew		X				

THANK
ACKNOWLEDGMENTS
YOU

102

Assessor. *Zachary Thomas*

Acknowledgments, Hearty Thanks, and Deep Debts of Gratitude are owed to the following persons.
Strict care will be taken that no information is disclosed with regard to individual persons.

Dwelling House, in the order of visitation.	Name in Full.	Special & Heartfelt Thanks.	Master instructor in the Writing Arts.	Occupation of Reader or Supporter.	Historical Personage, life pillaged.	Note.	National Alliance Institution.
32	Gray, Amelia			X			
44	Hoffmann, Markus			X			
46	Hughes, Andy			X			
42	Karr, Stephanie			X		BLOOD	
2	Karr, John Ross				X	FOR YOU. BLOOD	
3	Karr, Joyce VanGundy				X	MISS YOU BOTH BLOOD	
18	Kinsella, Tim			X			
17	Macnamara, Peggy		X				
47	Madrigal, Rita			X			
6	Magoffin, Susan Shelby				X		
40	Marks, PJ	✓	X	X		FOR EVERYTHING!	
29	Markel, Ryan		X	X			
10	McManus, James		X	X			
25	Messinger, Jonathan			X			
8	Newberry, Julia				X		
39	Niffenegger, Audrey			X			
20	Norborg, Heather			X		FOR RESEARCH	
9	Pike, Zebulon				X		
11	Ridell, Jill		X				
21	Somervell, Alexander				X		
30	Somerville, Patrick			X		FOR THE END	
45	Spence, Marya			X			

(24)

Number of Drafts 7

Number of Bats 2.4 Million

#24

Assessor. *Zachary Thomas*

COMPANY

Acknowledgments, Hearty Thanks, and Deep Debts of Gratitude are owed to the following persons.
Strict care will be taken that no information is disclosed with regard to individual persons.

Dwelling House, in the order of visitation.	Name in Full.	Special & Heartfelt Thanks.	Master Instructor in the Writing Arts.	Occupation of Reader or Supporter.	Historical Personage, life pillaged.	Note.	National Alliance Institution.
36	Stealey, Scott			X			
35	VanBramer, Viktor		X	X		BLOOD	
23	Villanueva, Maria		X	X		PARA EL ESPAÑOL	
33	Weist, Bruce			X			
1	White, Jim				X	ᵐᵐ	
(1)	Bat Conservation International					FOR THE BATS	X
2	Columbia College Chicago Faculty Grant						X
4/17	The Field Museum of Chicago						X
(31)	SCAR (Scottsdale Conference and Retreat)						X
(7)	School of the Art Institute of Chicago Merit Scholarship						X

Z. THOMAS

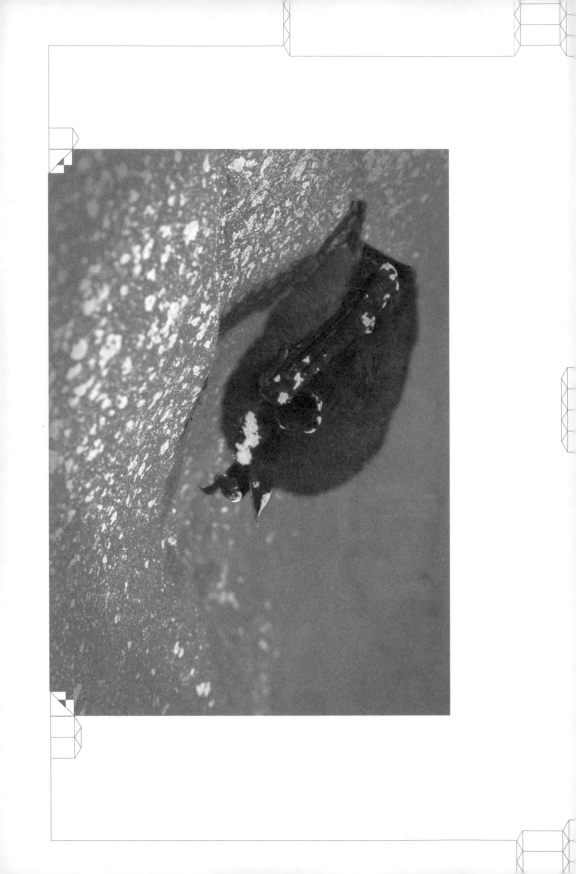

∧∧ ∧∧ W H I T E - N O S E   S Y N D R O M E is a relentless new disease that has devastated the North American bat population in recent years. White fungus appears on the faces and wings of hibernating bats, causing them to wake up in the middle of winter when food sources are scarce. The mortality rate at the caverns where the disease is discovered often approaches 100 percent. More than six million bats have died since 2006. This ecological disaster is the most precipitous decline of wildlife in a century, and has wide-ranging implications for the environment, farming, and biodiversity. A portion of the proceeds from this book will go to help fight White Nose Syndrome. To find out how you can help, please contact Bat Conservation International, Austin, Texas.

BatCon.org

ᴧᴧ ᴧᴧ ᴢ A C H A R Y T H O M A S comes from a long line of
overthinkers. He is a fifth-generation Texan, born deep in the
heart and raised in the desert southwest. During his young-
adult lifephase he ran with a rebel group of writers in Chicago
under the banner of *featherproof* books. Recently, he and his
pair transferred to the city-state of Helsinki, where he fences
and teaches in between dreams.

ZachDodson.com

Fig. **13** DIAEMUS YOUNGI

Fig. **14** PARASTRELLUS HESPERUS

Fig. **15** IDIONYCTERIS PHYLLOTIS

Fig. **16** ANTROZOUS PALLIDUS

Fig. **17** TADARIDA BRASILIENSIS

Fig. **18** CORYNORHINUS TOWNSENDII

Fig. **19** MYOTIS MELANORHINUS

Fig. **20** LASIURUS CINEREUS

Fig. **21** MYOTIS VOLANS

Fig. **22** LASIURUS BLOSSEVILLII

Fig. **23** LASIONYCTERIS NOCTIVAGANS

Fig. **24** NYCTERIS HUMERALIS

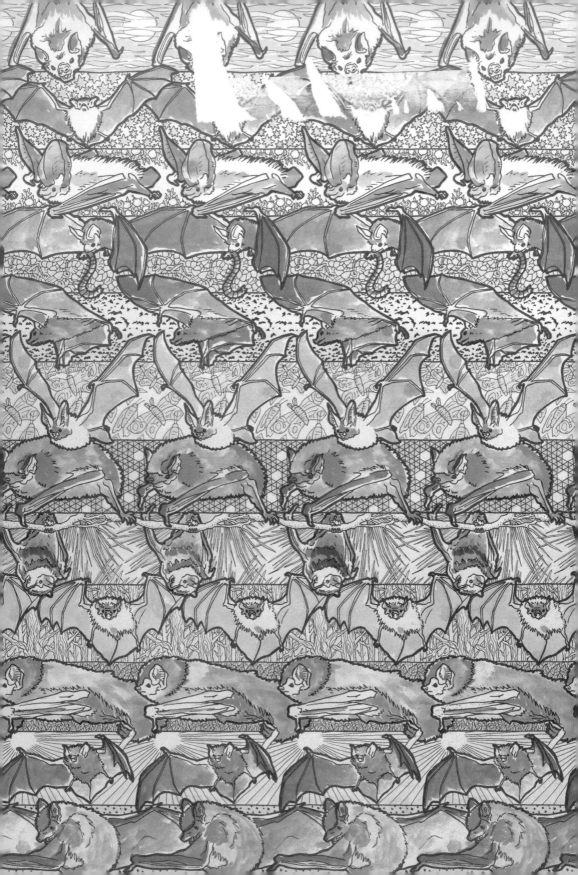